A Time For Us

Josephine Cox

HEADLINE

First published in 1996 by
HEADLINE BOOK PUBLISHING

First published in paperback in 1997
by HEADLINE BOOK PUBLISHING

10

ISBN 0 7472 4956 3

Typeset by Avon Dataset Ltd, Bidford-on-Avon, Warks

Printed and bound in Great Britain by
Clays Ltd, St Ives plc

HEADLINE BOOK PUBLISHING
A division of Hodder Headline PLC
338 Euston Road
London NW1 3BH

For my sister's boys, Michael and Stephen.

Stephen, I know how well you are coping and I know your mother would have been proud of you, as we all are.

Michael, I'm sorry things have not been easy for you. I know how very hard it is and I want you to remember what your mother told you both. You know she loved you, no matter what. She always believed, in this life you can only do your best.

I know that's what you're doing.

God bless, and be good.

CONTENTS

CONTENTS

PART ONE

1985

Love and Friendship

Chapter One

'Give us a kiss!' One brown eye gave a cheeky wink.

'Shame on you, Mike Nolan.' In spite of the laughter bubbling inside her, Sally managed to keep a straight face. 'And me a married woman, too!'

'The man doesn't deserve you.'

'I'm glad you think so.'

'Don't you sometimes fancy a change?'

'Wouldn't tell you if I did.'

'Go on, Sally, be a devil,' he pleaded. 'One kiss, that's all.' He winked again, making her smile. 'What he doesn't know won't hurt him.'

She feigned indignation. 'Do I look like the kind of woman who would cheat on her husband?'

The mischievous brown eyes looked her up and down. 'Hmm.' He rubbed his chin, and smiled at her. 'Perhaps not. But all I need is a quick cuddle behind the vegetables.' He glanced towards the shop doorway. There was no one about. He grew bolder. 'And if you're feeling extra generous, I wouldn't say no to a bit *more* than a cuddle.' Grinning like a naughty boy, he raised one eyebrow quizzically. 'If you know what I mean?'

Flattening her hands against his chest, she pushed him away. 'You randy old bugger!' Pleasure lightened her pretty blue eyes fleetingly. 'I know what you mean all right. And the answer is still no!'

Groaning like a man in pain, he grabbed her by the waist. 'You're driving me mad!' he cried. 'I'VE GOT TO HAVE YOU!'

'Have you any idea what you look like?' She could hardly contain her laughter. 'Cabbage stains on your overall, and the smell of carrots in your hair. What woman could fancy you?'

'Jesus, Mary and Joseph . . . you're a wicked woman.' With great difficulty he tried to drag her round the back of the counter. 'Five minutes on the floor should do it,' he promised, going red in the face as he tried to lift her off her feet.

'Put me down, you daft devil!' she laughed. 'The time's long gone when you could sweep me off my feet.'

Keeping his arms round her, he demanded in a hurt little voice, 'Mrs Nolan, are you insinuating that I'm past it?'

Now it was her turn to eye him up and down. 'Well, you must admit you aren't as slim as you used to be,' she answered kindly.

'Neither are you.' He squeezed his arms tight round her waist. 'But I'm not complaining.'

'And you'd better not!' She touched her finger against the end of his nose, her voice falling tenderly as she told him, 'We might as well face it, my love, we'll never be eighteen again. We're both a bit thicker round the waist . . . a bit dafter as the years go by.' She ran her finger over his mouth. 'But I still love you, Mike Nolan. More than ever.'

It was a moment before he could speak. In that

moment he looked into her wistful blue eyes and his heart was full. 'You're as lovely as the day you walked down the aisle,' he murmured.

'And you're still the most handsome man I've ever met,' she told him. 'Just as cheeky . . . just as much fun.' Giggling like a schoolgirl, she reminded him, 'Just now, though, when you were pretending to be my lover, anyone might have walked in and heard the conversation. *Strangers* even!' She blushed a fierce shade of red. 'God knows what they would have thought.'

'Strangers?' He feigned astonishment. 'This is a family greengrocer's, known to all and sundry from one end of Blackburn to the other. The only "strange" person who might have caught us acting the fool is old Polly Entwhistle.' Making a face that was uncannily like that of the old troublemaker, he even sounded like her. 'I'll have a pound o' them there apples . . . nice and soft so me teeth won't come out. Oh, an' mek sure there are no worm-holes in 'em. Oh, yes, and I've brought back the bananas you sold me last week. They've gone all yellow, so I want me money back, an' no argument!'

Sally couldn't help but laugh. 'Serve you right if she did walk in and give you a piece of her mind,' she warned, glancing furtively towards the door.

'Do you love me?'

'I must do, or I wouldn't put up with you.'

Content now that he had made her say that, he let his mind roam back over the past twenty-five years: their courting; their doubts when they found she was pregnant; the rushed marriage, and the wonderful, happy years that had followed.

5

Sally had been eighteen when they met. He was twenty. Two years later they were hastily married, and everyone warned the marriage wouldn't last.

Their love for each other had proved everyone wrong, thank God. Seven months after they walked down the aisle, they were blessed with a precious daughter whom they named Lucy. The years following had been more wonderful than he could ever have imagined. He and Sally were in their forties now, and as much in love as ever. Not a day passed when he didn't pray there might be many more wonderful times to come.

In the twenty-two years since she had been born, Mike's daughter Lucy had become his pride and joy.

His wife though, was his very life.

Now, with such love inside him that it hurt, he held her small, pretty face between his hands. Gazing with unashamed adoration into her bright blue eyes, he whispered, 'What in God's name would I ever do without you, eh?'

'Oh, you'd be all right,' she teased. 'You're a good-looking fella . . . you've got your own shop, and you can still make a woman's heart beat faster in bed.' She smiled affectionately. 'If I wasn't around to keep you on a leash, the girls would come running from every direction. You wouldn't be short of company, I can promise you that.'

He visibly shivered. 'Don't talk like that, sweetheart,' he pleaded. 'If I didn't have you, I wouldn't even want to live.' Only the good Lord knew, he loved this woman with every fibre of his being. The very thought of losing her was terrifying.

She had never doubted his love. She didn't doubt

it now. 'None of us lives for ever,' she reminded him.

Choosing to ignore her remark, he asked boldly, 'Do I get that kiss, or don't I?'

She didn't reply. Instead she wrapped her arms round his neck and stood on tiptoe to reach him.

Lucy Nolan and her friend Debbie turned into Penny Street.

The two of them were laughing and chattering, enjoying each other's company and sharing little snippets of gossip in the way of young women. 'I'll be glad to put my feet up,' Debbie sighed. 'I don't mind re-potting plants, in fact I quite like it, but in the middle of July, it's sheer bloody murder in the greenhouses.' She held out her hand and glared at her fingernails. 'Look at that!' she moaned. 'It'll take me a week to get the dirt out.'

Lucy shook her head. 'It's your own fault,' she said with a warm smile. 'I heard Old Ted tell you time and again to put on your gloves.' She wasn't being hard on her friend. She loved her dearly, but Debbie had a habit of getting herself into all kinds of trouble, and then, in a comical way, putting the blame on someone else.

Debbie Lately lived up to her name because, no matter how early Lucy phoned to get her out of bed in the mornings, or how hard she tried to make her change her habits, her friend was always late. Late for work; late for appointments; late when she and Lucy went out on a Saturday night; and late to catch every bus, train and taxi. Last year, when the two of them went to Spain on holiday, Debbie kept the plane waiting for ten minutes; she'd gone to the loo and couldn't find her way back to the departure lounge. If it hadn't been for Lucy setting out to find her, they might never have got to Spain at all. Then there was the time when she spent half an hour chatting up a man waiting at her till while the queue grew and grew, until a fight broke out among the customers. The upshot of that was Debbie being threatened with the sack, and half the customers abandoning their purchases and marching out.

She had a habit of chatting up the men, and they took to her like rain to a gutter. And it wasn't as though she was a stunning beauty or a sparkling wit – far from it. Short and plump, with thin, mouse-coloured hair, she was quite ordinary. Her jokes were awful, and she always opened her mouth where wiser folk knew when to keep quiet.

Lucy and Debbie had gone through school together. They'd endured puberty, courted boys, shared secrets, loved and lost, laughed and cried, and always found consolation in each other. On leaving school six years ago, they had found work in the same garden nurseries. Here they had grown from girls to women, and their friendship had flourished and strengthened. These two shared a special bond, a fierce protective instinct towards each other. A unique and wonderful friendship that others could only envy.

Debbie Lately was generous and truthful, honest and childlike. And though she was no beauty, she had a warm, caring soul and the prettiest, brightest blue eyes; they sparkled when she was happy, and darkened when she was sad. Mischievous one minute, reflective the next, they didn't miss one single thing.

She was perceptive and outspoken, often to a fault,

and when it came to her lifelong friend Lucy, would tear the throat out of anyone for hurting her.

She realised now that Lucy was unusually quiet. 'What's wrong?'

Lucy swung round to face her. 'What makes you think anything's wrong?'

'Because you've hardly said two words.'

Lucy shrugged her shoulders. 'Just thinking.'

'About what?' Debbie was a persistent little soul.

'Nothing in particular.'

Debbie opened her mouth to say something, then changed her mind. 'Okay. Suit yourself,' she replied flippantly.

They continued to stroll along Penny Street as though they had all the time in the world, with Debbie whistling aloud and Lucy deep in thought. Presently, Lucy's soft, troubled voice was heard. 'Debbie?'

'What?' This time she showed only a determined disinterest.

Lucy slowed her pace, her mind racing. She didn't want to worry Debbie. On the other hand, she needed to talk about something she had witnessed earlier.

Debbie kept up the sham for a while longer, then when Lucy fell silent again, could bear it no longer. 'LUCY! Will you tell me what's wrong, or do I have to drag it out of you?'

'It's something and nothing. I'll tell you later.' She should have known better. Now Debbie would never let it be, she thought.

And she was right.

Catching hold of Lucy's sleeve, Debbie drew her to a halt, her voice more gentle as she urged, 'There *is* something wrong, isn't there?' Thoughts of young

9

men, and sex, and the awful consequences, fired her vivid imagination. 'My God, you're pregnant!'

Lucy laughed. 'Don't be so daft!'

Debbie gave a sigh of relief. 'Honest to God?'

'Yes . . . honest to God.' Lucy began to walk on. 'And I'll thank you to remember it was you, not me, who went into a field with a strange bloke, and didn't come out for nearly an hour!' She gave Debbie a wry little smile before going on at a faster pace towards home.

Debbie ran to keep up with her. 'Alfie Burrows is *not* a strange bloke.'

Lucy laughed. 'That's a matter of opinion.' In fact the young man in question was the local watchmaker who took great delight in explaining the workings of every clock and watch he encountered. He was red-headed and painfully shy, absent-minded, dressed as if clothes had gone out of fashion, and when teased would blush like the fires of Hell. Needless to say, that was reason enough for Debbie to tease him endlessly and without mercy. But he loved her all the same. Once he'd even asked her to marry him. Debbie teased him over that too. She said she might consider it if he gave up watchmaking and took her on a world cruise. He'd never asked her again.

Now Debbie laughed out loud, a raw raucous sound that sent a stray dog scurrying for shelter. 'You're right,' she giggled. 'He *is* a weird little bugger. But all the good men seem to have disappeared, so you grab what you can when it's handed you on a plate.'

Shocked, Lucy stopped and stared. 'So you *did* do it?'

' 'Course we did! Why do you think I let him take

10

me into the field?' She made a grimace. 'Trouble is, he got a bit too excited and pushed me right into a bloody cow-pat. Before I could roll away he was on top of me. My knickers were round my ankles and he was on the job before you could say Jack Robinson.' She flinched at the memory. 'To tell you the truth, I didn't enjoy it all that much. I mean, you wouldn't, would you? Not when your bare arse is squelching on a cow-pat?'

Lucy didn't know whether to laugh or cry. But she did recall: 'I wondered what that horrible smell was. Even the bus conductor gave you a funny look.'

'Hmm! That's nothing to what I got from my dad when I arrived home.'

'Angry, was he?'

'He smelled the cowshit right away. Then he wanted to know where I'd been to get it all over my skirt. Then he interrogated me about the bloke I'd been with. When I told him who it was, he fell about laughing and said for a minute there he was worried, but now that he knew I'd been keeping company with Alfie Burrows, he didn't imagine I'd get into trouble because Alfie didn't have the know-how or the "tackle" to *get* a girl into trouble.'

Lucy was curious. 'And has he?'

Debbie gave a knowing little smile. 'Little does my dad know,' she confided. 'I wonder what he'd say if I told him Alfie Burrows has the biggest cock I've ever seen. What's more, he knows how to use it.'

Lucy burst out laughing. 'What am I going to do with you, eh?'

Debbie gave her a sideways glance. 'So, what's worrying you then?'

Having been sidetracked by the conversation about Alfie and the cow-pat, Lucy had almost forgotten the initial conversation. 'What do you mean?'

'You were about to tell me what was worrying you.'

'Was I?'

'You know bloody well you were.' Debbie frowned. 'If you're not pregnant, what is it?' Her face fell. 'Aw, Lucy... it's Jack, isn't it? He's thrown you over, hasn't he?'

'No, he hasn't. What I was going to tell you has nothing to do with Jack, or with me being pregnant, and it has nothing to do with you either, so will you stop jumping to conclusions?'

'All right then. What is it?'

Lucy knew how panic-stricken Debbie could get over the slightest little thing, and began to wish she had never said anything.

While Lucy took a moment to think, Debbie looked consideringly at her friend, admiring the long slim limbs and the attractive easy way she walked; the clear creamy skin and that pretty, straight nose above full lips and a small square chin. Her wide mouth was quick to smile, and the striking dove-grey eyes expressed her every mood.

Lucy was unusually lovely. Her thick, dark hair worn with a fringe reached down to her shoulders, and she had a certain quiet grace that endeared her to everyone she met. She could be painfully shy, yet loved people and had a natural winning way with them.

She was not only lovely to look at, she was lovely to know. Fiercely protective of those she loved, she had a kind, giving nature, and a way of winning a person over before they even suspected it. She also had a shrewd, canny business sense, so much so that in the past year, Old Ted at the nurseries had shifted more and more responsibilities on to her able young shoulders.

It was Old Ted Lucy meant to talk about. 'I'm worried about him,' she confided. 'I was taking a tray of seedlings to the potting shed and found him there, leaning against the wall, gasping and wheezing . . . fighting for breath.' He had given her a real fright.

Debbie was alarmed. 'Was he having a heart attack?'

'No, but he was in a bad way. I asked him to go and lie down and said I'd send for the doctor, but he wouldn't hear of it.'

'Is he dying?' Well meaning though she was, Debbie was not the most discreet person on God's earth. 'If he dies, we'll lose our jobs, won't we? I mean . . . that no-good son of his will sell the place and we'll be out on our ear.'

Lucy gave her a withering look. 'He's not dying. The poor old thing's just worn out. He works like a dog from morning to night, and won't take a rest unless he's made to. He won't even eat unless I nag him, and he still insists on doing all the heavy work himself.'

Debbie looked worried. 'But what if something *did* happen to him? Oh, I know he's a grand old thing, and I'd be really sorry if he was to die, but . . . well, the only thing I'm good at is making plants grow. I'd have a terrible time finding another job. Besides, I like working for Old Ted. It's his awful son I'm worried about. That bugger's all right, with his big farm and his fancy house. He's in the south and we're in the north. What does he care, eh? He never even comes to see his own father. And if he doesn't care about Ted, why should he care about the likes of us, eh?' She went on and on, worrying herself sick, just as Lucy had feared she would. 'He'll sell the place from under us, that's what he'll do.'

Lucy wasn't listening. She was too concerned about the old fellow. 'Ted will have to take things easier,' she mused. 'He'll be sixty-seven next week ... too old to be running that place. In the time we've been there, the workload has doubled.' She looked at Debbie with alarm. 'Do you know how much we took last week?'

'No.' Debbie had no interest in figures.

Lucy enlightened her. 'We took a thousand pounds on plants, and two hundred pounds on fertiliser. You don't earn that much money without blood, sweat and tears.'

'It's all your fault.'

Lucy was puzzled. 'What is?'

'The amount of money we take. You're right, the workload *has* doubled, but only because you've made the whole place more successful.' She playfully punched Lucy in the arm. 'You're making the old bugger a fortune. It's time he made you a partner.'

Lucy smiled at that. 'The nurseries are his life,' she said. 'But he would never take on a partner. What! Have someone else's name alongside his above the gate?' She could understand the old fellow feeling the way he did. 'Haven't you noticed how he polishes that sign ... like it was the most precious thing in the world?'

She always felt a certain amount of pride when watching him. For Old Ted it was a daily labour of love. Every morning, he would carry the ladder and bucket down to the big gates, where he would climb the ladder and polish the sign until it shone.

Debbie stopped to stretch out her arms. 'Have I seen him?' she echoed. 'HAVE ... I ... SEEN ... HIM!' She rolled her eyes to Heaven. 'Honest to God, Lucy, I sometimes wonder if the old bugger's been wound up. Regular as clockwork, he gets out the ladder and bucket, fills the bucket with clean water, ambles down to the gate and spends half an hour polishing that bloody sign!' Making extravagant gestures with her arms, she said loudly: ' "EDWARD BECKENDALE ... EXPERIENCED NURSERYMAN." I should think they can see it all the way from Blackpool.'

Lucy smiled at her antics. 'He's a lovely old soul, though,' she said. 'Since his wife died and his son left home all those years ago, the nurseries are all he's got left. He's worked hard and deserves to be proud.' In fact he deserved more. He deserved to be happy, but there was a quiet, private kind of sadness about Edward Beckendale. 'The only time he seems really content is when he's tending to his plants,' she commented wistfully.

'Oh, he's all right. He's got more than most.'

'Material things, maybe. But he's got no family ... no one to share things with.' For Lucy that was the saddest thing of all.

Debbie made a face. 'He can have my dad any day of the week.'

'You don't mean that.'

15

'You don't know my dad! All you see is the way he smiles at you when you call round. You don't hear the foul temper and the endless questions.' She mimicked him perfectly, even to the hang-dog look: ' "Where have you been 'til this time, our Debbie . . . ? What have you been up to, eh . . . ? Are you behaving yourself . . . ? Keeping out of trouble, are you? Get yerself pregnant and you're out that bloody door so fast your feet won't touch the ground! DO YOU HEAR ME, OUR DEBBIE? D'you hear what I'm saying?" '

Lucy had to laugh. 'It's your poor dad I feel sorry for,' she teased. 'What's he done to deserve you, that's what I want to know?'

'Get away! He's a bloody monster! I wouldn't mind, but I'm twenty-two . . . same age as you, for God's sake. And your dad doesn't treat *you* like you're a two-year-old.'

'That's because I'm more sensible than you.'

'Cheeky sod!'

'Oh, stop moaning. Think about Ted. He's got nobody to nag him. Nobody to love. Nobody to talk to when he feels down.' He was such a lonely old soul, but he wouldn't let anyone near. 'I can't help wishing his son would contact him.'

'Oh, he will!' Debbie was convinced. 'The minute George Beckendale knows there are pickings to be had, you won't see his arse for dust. He'll be strutting round Ted's property before the old sod's cold in the ground.'

'You could be right. But there's nothing we can do about that. All we can do is to look after Old Ted, and make sure he isn't overdoing things.'

Debbie's fears returned. 'You don't think we'll lose

our jobs, do you, Lucy?' she asked woefully. 'I'm really worried now.'

'I knew you would be,' she sighed. 'That's why I wasn't going to say anything. But it needs the two of us to watch out for him. I can't always be in the right place at the right time.'

'Have you said anything to that young girl . . . what's her name?'

'Sophie?'

'Posh bloody name! No wonder I can never remember it.'

'No, I haven't said anything, and I won't. She's only fifteen, just out of school. There's no sense in worrying her.'

'You've worried *me* though.'

'That's nothing new. *You'd* worry even if you won the pools.'

'Ah! But I could do my worrying lying on the deck of my own yacht as we cruised the seven seas.' Debbie gave a wicked grin. 'I'd be surrounded by hunky men, and waited on by jealous females.'

'Oh? And where would I fit in?' Lucy was used to her friend's dreaming.

'You'd be down in the galley washing the dishes, of course.'

'Of course!'

They were quiet for a minute, dreaming and wishing, wondering what the future held, and just enjoying each other's company. These two were more like sisters than friends . . . closer even than that, because there was no rivalry, no envy, and nothing they would not share. 'I've never met anyone who's won the pools,' Lucy remarked.

'Neither have I.' Debbie had her own views on the matter. 'I reckon it's all a fiddle. I reckon nobody's *ever* won the pools.' She became serious for a minute. 'I bet I know what you would do if you won.'

'Go on?' Lucy had realised long ago that there were times when Debbie knew her better than she knew herself.

'You'd offer to buy out Old Ted, and make those nurseries the biggest in Lancashire. You'd keep the old bugger on for as long as he lived, give him a generous wage-rise and let him stay in his scruffy old bungalow 'til his toes turned up.' She grinned like a naughty schoolgirl. 'Well? Am I right?'

'You're a witch.' Lucy threaded her arm through Debbie's, her voice soft and sincere as she told her, 'I know Ted's bawled you out a few times but he doesn't mean anything by it. He's a lonely old man, Debs. Don't be too hard on him.'

Debbie admitted, 'I suppose it is my fault. I do seem to get on the wrong side of him, don't I?'

Lucy just smiled. They both knew the truth. Already that season Debbie had suffocated a whole batch of tomatoes when she forgot to open the greenhouse vents on the hottest day of the year. Both Lucy and Old Ted were rushed off their feet looking after customers, and so hadn't noticed 'til too late.

The week before that, she had been trusted to set the sprinklers over the petunia seedlings. She forgot that, too, and by the time Ted arrived on the scene, they were wilted beyond redemption.

Recalling all this, and more, Debbie had to confess, 'I expect you're right. If the old bugger's given me a rollicking, I've always deserved it. Anybody else would have sacked me for the daft things I've done . . . especially after what happened this afternoon.'

Lucy gave her a reproving glance. 'Least said about that the better,' she declared.

'All the same, it was a stupid thing to do.'

'So will you help me to keep an eye on him?' Lucy couldn't hide her relief.

'Okay. I'm still worried, though . . . about my job, I mean.'

Lucy looked at her friend's stricken face, and her heart went out to her. 'Tell you what,' she said, 'I'll make you a promise. If for any reason we do lose our jobs, I'll set up on my own and you'll have a job for life, if you want it. What do you say to that?'

'I say that'll do me fine . . . until I find a bloke who's willing to take me on and look after me.' The smile returned to her homely face.

'Alfie Burrows would do that tomorrow,' Lucy laughed.

Debbie thought about that, and her answer surprised even herself. 'If I can't find anybody else willing, I just might have to settle for him,' she remarked casually.

Suddenly, as if the idea of being married to Alfie had given her a fright, she changed the subject. 'If we're going out on the town, we'd best get a move on.' She quickened her steps, but even then her short little legs couldn't keep up with Lucy's. 'Besides, I want to catch your dad before he shuts shop. I promised my mam I'd stop off to get her a pound of grapes. The cat from next door raided our fruit bowl last night and ate the bloody lot . . . grapes, apples, pips and everything!' she groaned. 'I wouldn't mind, but the thieving bugger had the cheek to mess on the doormat before he sneaked out of the window.' Giggling at the memory, she explained, 'You should have seen our dad's face when he trod in it bare-foot . . . all squashed in between his toes it were. Cor! I've never seen him so hopping mad. Me and our mam made it worse by falling about laughing in the doorway.'

The two of them were still chuckling when they passed Widow Leadbeater's house. As always the old dear was sitting on a chair by the door. 'Beautiful day, ain't it, loves?' she said, brushing away a persistent fly. 'Makes me wish I were sixteen again.' She was nearing ninety, but her small round face and prim little figure made her appear much younger.

Lucy exchanged greetings with other neighbours as she wended her way to her parents' shop. There was young Bernard Brindle, a snotty-nosed kid with dark hair and big brown eyes; he was sitting on his front doorstep with his nose stuck in a comic as usual. 'Good, is it?' Lucy asked, but he was too engrossed to answer.

His brother Richard was two years younger. Seated on the step next to Bernard, he was looking fed up. 'It's *my* comic,' he moaned. 'He pinched it off me. When our dad gets home, I'm gonna tell him.' He had blond curly hair and a freckled face. He also had a ready smile. 'Hey, Lucy! D'yer want to see me new pigeon?'

'I can't, sweetheart,' she answered kindly, 'I'm late already. But I'd like to see it tomorrow if that's all right?'

'Okay,' he said, starting a fight with Bernard by

20

way of a distraction. Soon they were screeching and giggling, and the comic was torn to shreds in the tussle.

'Little buggers!' Debbie said. 'They want their arses kicked.'

Lucy didn't agree. 'Oh, they're all right,' she told her. 'It's just high spirits. They'll be the best of friends the minute our backs are turned.' She'd seen it all before, and the boys never came to any harm. The Brindles were a large, happy family. Down this busy lively street, there were many such. They all knew Lucy Nolan. Most had known her from birth, and all had a soft spot for her.

Debbie was aware of the affection between neighbours in Penny Street. 'Do you think there'll ever come a time when you leave here?' she asked.

Lucy didn't answer right away. But when she did, there was such conviction in her voice that Debbie was subdued. 'One day,' she said quietly, nodding her head, 'one day when I'm ready to make my way in the world, I expect I'll have to pay the price.'

With a little shock, Lucy realised that leaving Penny Street would be the hardest thing she had ever done. Yet in some instinctive, inexplicable way she had always known she was not meant to spend the rest of her life here.

In a minute they were outside the shop. Both of them saw the intimate little scene through the window, but it was Debbie who commented, 'Cor! Look at them two!' She giggled. 'Kissing and cuddling like a pair o' lovers.'

It was true. Blissfully oblivious of any onlookers, Mike and Sally were locked in each other's arms.

'They love each other,' Lucy declared proudly, 'what's wrong with that?' She continued to gaze at her parents, her young heart filled with devotion.

'Nothing!' Debbie whispered. 'Only sometimes you wonder about older people, don't you?'

Lucy turned, grey eyes puzzled. 'What do you mean?'

For the briefest of moments, Debbie looked embarrassed. 'Well . . . you know . . .' She shrugged her shoulders and wished the earth would swallow her up. 'Making love and all that. Older people. I've often wondered how old you have to be before you stop.'

Lucy smiled. 'No wonder you forget to water the plants,' she said. 'If that's the sort of thing that fills your head when you're supposed to be working.'

'Got to think about *something*, or I'd go stark raving mad.'

'That's funny.'

'What is?'

'Well, I thought you were mad already!'

'Bitch!'

'I know.'

They giggled, and Debbie persisted, 'When *do* older people stop doing it?'

'When they stop loving each other, I expect.'

'Not them two, though, eh?' She drew Lucy's attention back to her parents. 'They look as though they're still crazy in love.'

Lucy smiled, a quiet, knowing little smile. 'They are,' she murmured. 'When Jack and I have been married for as long as they have, I hope we're as happy as Mam and Dad.'

'So you are gonna marry him then?'

'If he asks me.'

'You lucky bugger! I wish I could get a man like Jack Hanson. Matter o' fact, if you decide you don't want him, I'll always take him off your hands.'

'No chance.'

Debbie sighed. 'I didn't think there would be.'

Suddenly the shop door was flung open. It was Lucy's dad. 'What are you two hanging about for?' he demanded light-heartedly. 'Waiting for a bus, are you?'

'Hello, Mr Nolan.' Debbie smiled. 'No, we're not waiting for a bus. We're waiting for you to stop kissing and canoodling.' Nudging Lucy, she remarked in a serious voice, 'These older folk. Isn't it terrible the example they set?'

'Terrible,' she agreed. 'There ought to be a law against it.'

Lucy's mam called out from inside the shop, 'You two! Stop embarrassing my husband.' Before the last word was spoken, she appeared at the doorway. ' "Kissing and canoodling" wasn't invented just for the young,' she said. 'Me and this handsome fella's been married long enough to do what we like, whenever the fancy takes us.' Giving Mike a peck on the cheek, she asked, 'Isn't that right, love?'

He didn't answer, but his lingering glance told them all how much he adored her. 'Are you coming in, love?' he asked Debbie, stepping back for Lucy to pass.

'Just to buy some grapes for Mam, but I'm not stopping,' she said. 'Me and Lucy are off out tonight, and I've to get ready.' Calling after Lucy she reminded her, 'Pick you up at eight-thirty then?'

Lucy knew her friend of old. 'No,' she answered wisely. 'Eight o'clock on the dot, and I'll pick *you* up. That way I won't be sitting here twiddling my thumbs.'

'Whatever you say.'

'And be ready when I get there, or I'll go without you!'

Debbie gave a smug little grin. 'You always say that, but so far you never have. Thanks, Mr Nolan,' she said, taking the paper bag of grapes he'd weighed out for her, and fumbling in her purse for change.

Lucy sighed. What do you do with someone like Debbie? she thought. 'There's always a first time,' she warned. 'So you'd best be ready.'

'By the time you get to my house, I'll be waiting, don't you worry. All dolled up and ready to go.'

With that impossible promise ringing in their ears, Debbie went on her way, merrily whistling, swinging her handbag, and every now and then doing a little tap-dance on the pavement.

'Just look at her!' Lucy laughed. 'You'd never believe that less than an hour ago she demolished Old Ted's shed to a pile of wood.'

'You're having me on!' Mike gasped. 'How in God's name did she do that?'

In between bursts of laughter, Lucy explained. 'For weeks, she's been begging Ted to let her have a go on the tractor. Today he finally gave in, and she promptly crashed it straight through his shed. As if that wasn't enough, she ran over two hundred bulbs he was drying out, and mangled twelve window boxes he'd just finished for the Royal Hotel. Thankfully no one was hurt, but Ted nearly had a fit.'

Mike was bemused. 'Crashed right through the shed, eh?' he groaned, scratching his head. 'I can't believe it.'

'Oh, I can!' Sally chuckled. 'I'm never surprised by *anything* that young woman does.' She had a soft spot for Debbie, but was always careful not to let her loose in the shop for too long.

There was the sound of an approaching motorbike, at first just a low, persistent drone. As the sound increased, Mike became apprehensive. 'It's that young lunatic again!' he declared, stepping to the edge of the pavement.

The drone became a roar and suddenly the bike was speeding up the street towards them, a huge, powerful thing, driven by a youth in jeans and sweater.

Faster and faster he came, skidding on the cobbles as the machine swerved and danced from side to side. The roar was deafening. As it sped past, Mike ran after it, shaking his fist and yelling at the top of his voice: 'I'll have you, you bugger! One of these days there'll be a kiddie playing in the street, and you won't have a cat in Hell's chance of stopping. But I'll have you! So help me God, I will!'

'He can't hear you.' Sally drew him back. 'We've reported him to the police. Let them deal with it,' she urged. 'If we knew who he was, we could go and see his parents.'

'Bloody maniac!' Mike was shaking with temper. 'He wants a swift kick up the arse.'

The neighbours agreed. They watched the bike speed away and all were of the same opinion. 'Mad as hatters, the lot of 'em,' grumbled old man Cotton as he limped indoors. Meg Leatherhead's baby had been woken by the noise and was screaming like a banshee. As for Lucy, she was more concerned for her dad, who seemed unusually agitated. 'I'll call in and see the police again tomorrow morning,' she promised. 'I want to make sure they're taking it seriously.'

Still bristling with anger, Mike took his women inside. 'You two go on,' he told them, 'I'll see to everything here.'

While they went to make a start on the dinner, he crossed to the shop window and stared out. 'Young lout,' he grunted. 'No respect for other folk.'

Calmer now, he went about his familiar routine. He locked the outer door then emptied the till and cashed up. After that, he did his rounds of the display trays, taking out any bruised and yellowing fruit. Then he cleaned out the trays and restocked them from the back store-room. He made a note of what he would need to replenish his overall stock, and that done, satisfied himself that all was secure before taking himself and his money-bag into the living quarters. 'Something smells good,' he remarked, closing the door behind him. 'I'm that hungry I could eat a scabby rabbit.'

Sally looked up from laying the table. 'It's your favourite,' she said. 'Pork and home-made apple sauce, with roast potatoes and baby carrots.'

He sniffed the air and blew it out again with a sigh. 'Now you know why I married you.' He winked. 'You always were the best cook in Lancashire.'

'Thanks for nothing,' she laughed, pretending to be shocked.

He came over and kissed her soundly on the mouth. 'And because you were the prettiest little lass I'd ever seen,' he said tenderly.

She pushed him away. 'Go on, you daft old bugger.' But the look in her eyes was as warm as his own. 'Go and get washed,' she murmured, 'while I dish up.'

'Aye, all right,' he answered, looking round the room. 'Where's our Lucy?'

'Upstairs, washing her hair. She's only this minute gone up. I told her she needn't help with the dinner, but you know what she's like.'

'Yes, thoughtful. She knows you've been on your feet all day.'

'So has she. Besides, she's arranged to meet Debs at eight o'clock. She'll be seeing Jack, I expect, and wanting to look her best.'

'So?'

Sally tutted. 'Just like a man,' she said. 'You don't know the first thing, do you, eh?'

'What now?' It was true. Women were a mystery to him.

Pointing to the mantelpiece clock, she explained, 'It's already ten minutes to seven . . . that gives her just over an hour to eat her dinner, get herself ready, and over to Debs's house by eight. You know what'll happen, don't you?' Without waiting for an answer she went on, exasperated, 'She'll wolf her dinner down and get indigestion, or else pick at it and go off hungry.'

Lucy's voice sailed ahead of her into the room. 'Stop worrying,' she said, 'I'm ready for my dinner. I've already washed my hair, so all I've got to do is my face. There's time enough.' She looked at her dad. 'Go on,' she said with a grin, 'get yourself washed and back here, or she'll be starting on *you* next.'

'She already has,' he replied. Putting his hand across his face as though fending off an impending blow, he turned to Sally. 'All right! All right! Don't hit me!' he pleaded. 'I'm going now!'

Cowering, he backed out of the room, leaving the two of them chuckling. 'Honest to God!' Sally laughed. 'The older he gets, the dafter he gets.'

The contentment in her mam's pretty blue eyes gave Lucy a safe, happy feeling which became a surge of love. 'I'm lucky to have parents like you,' she murmured. 'Especially when Debs has such a hard time of it at home.'

When, ten minutes later, the three of them were seated round the table enjoying their meal, the subject of Debs was raised again. 'So she's not happy at home?' Sally asked. 'Debs, I mean. I didn't think things were all that bad between her and her parents.'

'She doesn't say a lot.' Absent-mindedly jabbing a potato, Lucy confided, 'It's what she *doesn't* say that worries me.'

'Why's that?' Putting down his knife and fork, Mike took a swig of his tea. 'The lass always seems happy enough to me.'

Hesitating for a moment, and wondering whether she had a right to say anything, Lucy decided she had to confide in someone. And who more trustworthy than her own parents? 'That's just it. She's always laughing and larking about . . . saying how her dad does this and that . . . how he watches the clock when

28

she's out, and how concerned he is when she's late.'

Mike shook his head. 'There's nothing wrong with that,' he said, 'I'm no different.'

'Yes, you are,' Lucy affirmed. 'It's not just that he gets angry if she's late, he puts her through an inquisition.' She found it hard to explain. 'He laughs at her . . . makes fun of her. And . . .' She paused, finding it hard to explain her instincts.

'What is it, lass?' Mike urged. 'What's on your mind?'

Unsure, Lucy looked up at her mam, who all this time had been quietly listening. 'It's all right, Lucy,' Sally told her. 'If you've got something on your mind, it's best said.'

Encouraged and relieved, she confided, 'I know she makes light of everything, and I know she's a scatterbrain, but she never talks about her family the way I talk about you. When she talks about her dad, there's something wrong . . . the look on her face.' Lucy shook her head, trying to make the words convey what was on her mind. 'She gets all nervous and excited . . . like she's really frightened.'

There! It was out, and now she felt better. It was true what they said: a trouble shared was a trouble halved.

Sally's gentle voice broke into her thoughts. 'What are you saying, love?'

'I'm not sure,' she answered truthfully, 'it's just that . . . I don't know.' She had her suspicions, but that's all they were. 'She hardly ever talks about her mam. And when she talks about her dad . . .' she paused again, '. . . there's just *something* . . . I can't put my finger on it.'

Mike popped a carrot into his mouth and chewed for a while before telling her kindly, 'You've known her a long time, lass, and there's never been anything wrong in that family that we know of.'

Sally agreed. 'That's right, love.'

Mike looked from one to the other. 'Shall I tell you what I think?'

They both smiled. 'You'll tell us anyway,' Sally teased.

'I think Debbie is a lovely, friendly little thing, but we can none of us pretend that she's a saint. I expect her dad has been driven to distraction over the years, and now, when she's that much older and away into the wide world, he's having to put his foot down a bit harder. Being the person she is, Debbie is probably rebelling.' Leaning back in his chair, he sighed like a wise old man. 'It's not easy, you know, being a dad. And, to tell you the truth, if Debbie had been *my* daughter, I reckon I'd have gone off my head long before now.'

Sally wanted to know, 'Lucy, have you any real reason for thinking Debbie is afraid of her dad?'

'No.' None that she could explain. None that you could see with the eye; except for the bruises she often came to work with, and which she laughed off as her own fault for being 'accident prone'.

Sally sounded relieved. 'It's only natural for Debbie to feel angry and upset when her dad moans about her staying out late.' She smiled at her own memories. In fact she and Lucy's grandfather had had many a set-to about what time of night she should be in. 'Besides, knowing Debbie, she probably doesn't take too kindly to being bawled out.'

Lucy thought about that. 'You might be right,' she said, wondering if maybe that was the case after all. 'In fact, she still hasn't forgiven Old Ted for bawling her out today.'

'There you go then,' Mike said, popping another carrot into his mouth. 'And if that didn't warrant a "bawling out", then I don't know what would.' He took another swig of his tea. 'She's a nice enough lass,' he concluded, 'but it's her poor dad I feel sorry for.' Wiping his mouth on a napkin, he asked, 'Is Old Ted sending him a bill for the damage Debbie did?'

'I don't think so. It *was* an accident.'

'Hmm! He's got every right.'

Sally intervened. 'Edward Beckendale isn't like that.'

'All the same, you can see why Debbie's dad has his hands full, can't you, eh? No wonder he loses his temper. I expect he'll be glad when she's married.' He chuckled. 'It'll have to be to somebody who doesn't mind his house being demolished, because she'll never change, not now. The poor little bugger's been a disaster area ever since we've known her.'

'That's a bit harsh, isn't it?' Sally was smiling, though, because he was telling the truth. Even as a child, Debbie Lately was always getting into one scrape or another. Now she was a woman, nothing had changed.

Full to bursting, Mike pushed away his plate. 'That were a lovely meal,' he told Sally.

'Enough for you to help me wash up?'

Lucy was on her feet and clearing the table before her dad could reply. 'I'll wash up,' she offered. 'You two must be worn out.'

'You'll do no such thing, my girl!' Mike told her. 'And I'll have you know, me and your mam have got more energy than half the young 'uns these days.' With a cheeky little grin on his homely face, he clambered out of the chair. 'Are you seeing Jack tonight?'

Lucy blushed deep scarlet. 'I'm hoping to.'

'Right then!' Draping an arm round her shoulders, he led her to the door. 'Make yourself beautiful and give him our regards.'

Lucy was filled with pleasure. 'You like Jack, don't you?'

Sally was collecting the crockery. 'We *both* like Jack,' she confirmed. 'He's a fine young man.'

Leaning towards Lucy, her dad whispered, 'I'd be tickled pink to see my lovely daughter wed to a man like Jack Hanson. A man who would cherish you the same way I've cherished your mam all these years.'

She kissed him on the cheek. 'You're an old romantic.'

'Hey! Not so much of the "old", if you don't mind. But you are thinking of getting wed, aren't you?' Mike persisted. 'You and Jack were made for each other.'

'Oh, so now you're trying to marry me off, eh?'

He was mortified. 'You know better than that.'

She hugged him. 'Didn't mean it,' she said. 'As a matter of fact, Jack hasn't asked me to marry him, so I can hardly say yes, can I?'

'It's only a matter of time. Anyone can see there's no other girl for him.'

'Maybe. But there's no hurry for either of us,' she said. 'Jack has things he wants to do before he settles down. And so do I.'

'Fair enough. But don't leave it too late, sweetheart.' He turned to look at Sally. 'When you've found someone special, don't let anything take them away.'

'I'll try not to.'

Lucy saw how her parents gazed at each other, and not for the first time, wished with all her heart that she and Jack might find the same deep love and happiness that these two had been blessed with.

It was just as well that Lucy could not see into the future.

Chapter Two

Debbie ran from the house, tears smudging her mascara and her hands shaking so badly she could hardly light her cigarette. 'Bastard!' she kept muttering. 'Hateful bastard!'

Behind her, the house was quiet. It always was. *Afterwards.*

At the bottom of the street, she sat on the high wall, her tear-filled eyes looking for Lucy, hoping she would not arrive early. Praying Lucy would not see the truth in her friend's ravaged face. 'Oh, Lucy, I wish I could tell you,' she muttered, drawing deep and long on the cigarette. 'But I can't. I *daren't!*' She laughed, a hollow, pathetic little sound. 'You're all I've got, Lucy Nolan,' she whispered. 'And if you knew what was going on . . .' Her voice thickened. 'You'd turn the bloody place upside down!'

She thought of Lucy, and it calmed her. 'You're a real pal, sweetheart, and over the years you've got me out of many a scrape. But I wouldn't get you involved in this. What! You might look quiet and demure, but underneath you're a raging bloody inferno. And I know, 'cause I've seen it. When that fat lady were thrashing her young 'un, and you stepped in to put a stop to it – twice round the

35

gasworks she were, and her with an arse as big as a tank and a voice like a sergeant-major!'

She threw back her head and laughed out loud. 'But you soon had her on the run. And what about that big dog when it were tearing into Old Ted? You soon pinned it to the ground with a broom-handle.' Rolling her eyes to Heaven, she drew nervously on her cigarette. 'Jesus! I don't know who were more frightened, me or the bleedin' dog!'

'Debbie.' It was her mother, a small woman with dark hair and a white pinched face. 'Come back into the house, love.'

Staring at the ground, Debbie shook her head. 'It won't happen again.'

Debbie was unmoved. 'I've heard *that* before.'

'Your dad's gone to the pub with his mate. You and me . . . we can have a little talk, if you like?'

'Don't want to.'

'Please.' Her mother sat on the wall beside her. 'Your mascara's all run. Come back and wash your face. You don't want Lucy to see you like this, do you?'

'Why?' She turned to stare into dark, pleading eyes. 'Frightened the truth might come out?' The dark eyes were lowered. 'Oh, don't worry, Mam. Nobody will find out from me. I'd be too ashamed.'

'No more than me,' her mother murmured. 'But I want you to come back now, please. I'll make us a cup of tea, eh?'

Debbie's tears started to fall again. 'Oh, Mam!' she whispered, eyes filled with pain. 'Why can't things be like they used to be?'

Her mother touched her hand reassuringly. 'I

know, love, I know.' Debbie's pain was echoed in her own tragic eyes. 'Will you come back? Just for a little while?'

Relenting, Debbie slid off the wall. 'I'm only coming back to wash my face,' she said, 'and because I don't want Lucy to know. Lucy's not like me, Mam. She won't let things go, and she'd not rest until she got to the bottom of it.'

Her mother nodded her head. 'That's how a real friend should be,' she said.

They walked along the street, together yet miles apart. Each bearing the scars of what went on behind closed doors. Each tortured by the same shameful secret.

Noreen looked at her daughter and was filled with an odd sort of pride. 'You look lovely,' she told her. 'That colour really suits you.' Debbie was wearing a cerise pink dress which flattered her figure and made her look taller. 'Your father's right, though,' she remarked casually. 'The skirt *is* a bit short.'

'I'm not a kid, Mam. I'm twenty-two years old. It's time I was given a bit of freedom to wear what I want, and go where I want.' Irritated, she hurried in front. On reaching the terraced house, she ran straight up the stairs, washed her face, renewed her make-up and was about to depart when her mother called her from the kitchen. 'Your tea's out, love. I've put extra milk in to cool it.' She appeared at the kitchen door. 'Your dad won't be back for a while yet so we've time to talk . . . if you want to?'

'I'm not sure,' Debbie replied thoughtfully. 'Lucy's bound to be here any minute.' Torn two ways, she pretended to check the contents of her handbag.

Aware of her mother's anxious face, she looked up. 'Oh, Mam!' she groaned. 'What's the use of talking? We've talked before . . . time and again. It never changes anything.'

'It's just as bad for me. You know that, don't you?' There were tears in her eyes, and her bottom lip started to tremble.

Debbie's heart melted. 'Oh, our mam!' she murmured, taking the little woman in her arms. 'What are we going to do, eh?'

They held each other for a while before Lucy's familiar voice reached them. 'Hello! It's me.'

'Just coming!' Debbie called.

'I'll come to the door,' her mam told her. 'Maybe we'll get a chance to talk when you get home, eh?'

Debbie nodded. 'We'll see.'

Lucy gave Noreen a big warm smile. 'You look worn out,' she said. 'Debbie been giving you a hard time, has she?'

Noreen returned the smile. 'As ever,' she replied. When the two young women set off down the street, she called after them, 'See you later, our Debbie. Have a good time, you two.'

'That colour really suits you, Debs.' Lucy glanced at the pretty pink dress with its straight skirt and neckline. 'You should wear it more often.'

Debbie's quick smile betrayed nothing of the violence that had erupted in her house only a short time ago. Instead, she looked bright and bushy-tailed, and appreciative of Lucy's flattering remarks. 'You don't look so bad yourself, kiddo,' she said with a grin. Lucy was wearing a short-sleeved blue blouse over a long, white skirt; her small waist was clasped in a white leather belt, and her dark hair shone like a raven's wing. 'But then, you could wear a sack and still look gorgeous.'

'So long as Jack thinks I look nice, that's all right.'

The bus to town was already pulling in. 'Quick!' Debbie yelled, running down the street. 'If we miss this one we'll have to wait half an hour for the next.'

The conductor winked at them as they got on. 'Don't want to keep the boyfriends waiting, eh?'

Puffing and panting, they fell into their seats. 'Two returns to the market square,' Debbie said, handing him a pound. 'And mind you give me the right change. Last time you did me out of ten pence.'

He counted the change into her hand with unusual deliberation. 'Right?'

'Right!' Making a face as he walked away, she dropped the change into her purse. 'Thieving bugger!' she muttered. 'He must make a fortune by the end of the week.'

'You can't be certain it was him who short-changed you,' Lucy reminded her. 'It could have been anybody. You might even have lost it when you dropped your purse outside the flicks.'

Settling into her seat, Debbie conceded, 'You're right.' She glanced at the conductor who was standing by the outer door, looking thoroughly miserable. 'I'll apologise when we get off,' she promised.

Lucy's soft grey eyes surreptitiously regarded her. For the briefest moment there had been something about Deb's downcast face that revealed a troubled mind. She had to ask, 'Are you all right, Debs?'

There was only a smile visible now. 'Yes. Why?'

'I don't know. You seem preoccupied, that's all.'

It was more than that, and it worried Lucy.

'I'm fine,' Debbie lied. 'Just wondering what you'll say tonight, when Jack asks you to marry him.' She chuckled, keeping her deeper feelings well hidden. In fact she was thinking of her mam and dad, of how it used to be, and wondering whether things would ever come right in that house.

Lucy sensed that she'd been lied to, but there was nothing she could do. If Debs didn't feel able to confide in her, then she would just have to be patient. Meanwhile, she would go along with her. 'What makes you feel Jack will ask me to marry him tonight?'

Debbie looked at the slim and pretty figure, the rich dark hair and those wonderful grey eyes. 'He'd have to be crazy not to!'

Embarrassed, and eager to change the subject, Lucy asked, 'And what about Alfie?'

'What about him?'

'Do you think he'll be there tonight?'

'If he is, he'd better stay away from me.'

'You don't really mean that?'

'Oh, he's all right, I suppose, but he's too serious.' Debbie's blue eyes twinkled. 'And anyway, I haven't sowed enough wild oats to settle down just yet.'

'You're wicked.'

Debbie wasn't listening. Instead she was leaning forward to whisper in Lucy's ear: 'How many times have you done it with Jack?'

Hiding her embarrassment with a flippant reply, Lucy said, 'Oh, at least a hundred.'

'Liar!'

Feigning astonishment, she demanded, 'What makes you think that?'

'Because you've only known him six months. If you'd done it a hundred times you'd be walking on your sodding knees by now.'

'And you'd know, would you?'

'I should, because I do it twice a night and three times on a Sunday.' At the look on Lucy's face she roared with laughter. 'Truth is . . . I've only done it once in the past six months, and that was when Alfie Burrows caught me unawares. I wouldn't mind, but I didn't even like it! It were like riding a runaway camel upside down!'

While they chuckled, a fat old woman prodded Debbie in the back with her handbag. 'Stop talking dirty,' she warned, 'or I'll have you thrown off.'

Stifling her giggles, Debbie remained silent for the rest of the journey. When the fat woman passed down the aisle to disembark, she gave Debbie and Lucy a scathing glance. 'Disgusting pair! And the conductor a Methodist preacher too.'

Debbie stared at Lucy with a startled expression. 'Methodist preacher, eh? Who would have thought it?'

Shamefaced, Lucy followed her friend down the aisle. 'I hope he wasn't too offended,' she whispered.

As she waited for Debbie to step down to the street, Lucy was visibly startled when the conductor approached her. 'Was that true?' he asked in a soft, preacher-like voice.

'Beg your pardon?' Thoroughly ashamed, she was wishing she'd got off first instead of Debbie.

'What you said . . . about having done it a hundred times in six months? Was that the truth?'

Lucy stared at him aghast, at his wide shocked

41

eyes and red excited face, and the suggestive way he was pressing himself against her. 'Why, you dirty old bugger!' she cried. 'No! It wasn't true! In fact, it was more like *two* hundred times!' Leaving him wide-mouthed with shock, she jumped off the bus and almost broke her ankle when her heel caught in some grating.

'I thought you were right behind me,' Debbie complained. 'What the Hell kept you? I've been walking along here talking to myself. Anybody would think I were off me bleedin' head.'

Clutching her ankle, Lucy told her about the conductor.

From the platform of his bus, the red-faced fellow stared after them with shocked eyes. 'Go to church and confess your sins!' he shouted.

But they couldn't hear him. The two of them had gone round the corner. The sound of Debbie's laughter echoed down the street. 'TWO HUNDRED TIMES!' she roared. 'If he'll believe that, he'll believe anything!'

And, hobbling though she was, Lucy had to laugh. They were still laughing when they arrived at the door of The Palais.

The place was buzzing. Outside there were groups of young people, laughing and talking and occasionally nuzzling up to each other. 'Too bleedin' hot for that.' Debbie sounded jealous. 'Let's get inside.'

It was packed. Soft romantic music played, while on the dance floor couples were wound round each other, eyes adoring as they gazed into each other's faces. Debbie was jealous. 'Must be the mating season,' she sniffed.

Lucy pointed towards the bar. 'There's Alfie,' she said with a little grin. 'Waiting for you, I expect.'

'God Almighty!' Hiding behind a smooching couple, Debbie groaned, 'If he claps eyes on me, I'm off.'

'Don't be daft. He's harmless enough.'

'*You* have him then!'

As soon as Alfie saw them his face lit up like a beacon. Smiling broadly, he made a beeline across the room. Lucy felt sorry for him. 'What harm can it do to let him have a dance?'

'A lot. Dancing with a deadbeat like Alfie won't do my reputation any good.'

'What reputation?'

'Spiteful cow!'

'Go on. Say yes,' urged Lucy as Alfie neared them. 'Look at the smile on his little face.'

'Like I said . . . *you* dance with him.'

'I'm spoken for.'

'Coward.'

Alfie looked unusually trendy in a pair of brown cords and a denim shirt. His brown eyes lit up when they lighted on Debbie. 'I've been looking for you. Will you dance with me?'

She shrugged. 'So you can trample all over my new shoes, like last time?' She didn't forgive easily.

Blushing fiercely, he ran his hand through his shock of red hair. 'I'm really sorry about that, Debs,' he stammered. 'But I've been taking lessons. I'm a better dancer now.'

'Hmm!' Debbie looked him up and down. 'Come into money, have you?'

'What d'you mean?'

She tugged at his shirt. 'This is new, ain't it?'

'Yeah.'

'And these?' She touched his trousers with the tip of her toe. 'I ain't seen these before neither.'

His face broke into a smile. 'I bought them for tonight,' he explained. 'Only last time you told me to come back when I weren't so scruffy.' He gave her a shy smile. 'What d'you think?'

'I think you should have bought some that fitted better. These trousers hang on your arse like they were made for a bloody elephant.'

The smile vanished. 'I spent nearly a week's wages on these trousers.'

'You were done!'

Lucy detected a note of real cruelty in Debbie's tone. Not for the first time she suspected Debbie and her father had had another set-to. All the same, it wasn't fair to take it out on Alfie.

Addressing the stricken lad, she told him, 'If it's any consolation, *I* think you look great.'

'Thanks, Lucy,' he said. 'That's nice of you.' But it was clear he felt no better.

As he turned to go, Lucy drew Debbie to one side. 'That was really hurtful,' she scolded. 'Now get after him and apologise.'

'Or?' There was that spiteful tone again.

'Or I'll knock your bloody head off your shoulders!' She was astonished by her own anger, and the way she had so easily fallen into Debbie's way of talking.

Debbie giggled. 'Hark at you!' she declared with amusement. 'And people think *I'm* common.'

'Well, you could have been a bit more friendly. The poor devil's got himself all smart and probably been here for hours . . . just waiting for a glimpse of you.'

Debbie preened herself. 'Quite right too,' she teased. 'Keep 'em waiting, that's my motto.' Swinging away, she told Lucy, 'Jack's got his beady eye on you. You'd better go and say hello.'

'Will you apologise to Alfie?'

'I'd rather walk naked through the town centre.'

The music changed to a faster tempo. 'He says he's been taking lessons,' Lucy persisted. 'This would be a good time to try him out.'

Debbie sighed. 'Oh, all right. But if he jumps on my feet, I'll break his bleedin' neck!'

Lucy watched as Debbie went reluctantly across the room and spoke to Alfie. As she led him on to the dance floor, his face was a picture of delight.

No one really expected him to start dancing like a professional, so when he did, both Lucy and Debbie were amazed. It was like watching an ugly duckling turn into a swan.

First Debbie was shocked, then self-conscious, then immensely proud. When most couples stopped to witness Alfie's new talents, she threw herself whole-heartedly into the rhythm, as usual wanting to be the centre of attention.

Smiling to herself, Lucy wended her way through the crowd, down to the front of the room, where she waited by the foot of the stage, her grey eyes searching out the young man playing saxophone in the band. He saw her, gave a wink, then began playing her favourite song, 'I'm Not in Love' by 10cc.

'Jeez! He can make that saxophone talk!' The bouncer was a mountainous, red-necked fellow in his forties, an ex-boxer who only had to cough for the ruffians to be out of the door. But now, as he gazed up at Jack, he was like a little boy, seeing magic happen right before his eyes.

Suddenly the dancing had stopped and everyone was gathering round the stage, all looking up, mesmerised by the beautiful and powerful rendering of a very emotional ballad.

Lucy was thrilled. It had been Jack's playing that had first attracted her to him, last Christmas when she and Debbie had come to The Palais, the first time that he had been booked to play. Before that he played only occasionally with the band, working as he did managing a local hotel and saving every penny he made for the day when he would have his own business.

On that Christmas Eve, the crowd had gone mad for him. Consequently, the owner of The Palais offered Jack a long-term contract. Since then he had played every weekend, and the place was always packed to bursting.

Jack made a handsome sight. With his long, lean legs, strong build and thick dark hair, he sent the women wild. Now, as he played, wrapping himself round the saxophone as though embracing a lover, his eyes were closed, his whole being enveloped in the haunting tune.

Suddenly, his eyes were open, dark green eyes filled with emotion, gazing down at Lucy with a suggestion of love, a promise of things to come. Adoring her from the very beginning, he had eyes for no one else.

She couldn't tear her gaze away. Jack was easily the most handsome man in the room. He was a good man, hard-working and ruthlessly ambitious, yet with a kind, compassionate nature and an easy honest manner that put people at their ease.

Lucy loved him with all her heart.

Later, when the band took over and he came to her, she let herself be guided round the floor, her head against his broad shoulder, moving with him to the soft music and wishing the evening would never end. 'Love you,' he murmured in her ear, and she tingled all over.

All too soon it was time to leave.

Debbie stumbled across the room, her face bright pink and her lipstick smudged. 'Me and Alfie are going for shish and fips,' she announced, giggling like a schoolgirl after too many Babychams. 'Want some?'

Worried, Lucy suggested she and Debbie should go straight home, but her friend wouldn't hear of it. 'I'll take care of her,' Alfie promised. And Lucy knew he would.

'No more drink, though,' she told him.

'Don't worry.' He winked as they left. 'I'm in charge now.'

Jack and Lucy were the last to leave. The hotel he managed was only a short walk away. With his arm round her, Lucy felt secure against the world. 'You played wonderfully tonight,' she said, snuggling up to him as they strolled towards the hotel.

'That's because you were there,' he murmured. In the light from the street-lamps, his dark green eyes were smiling. 'You bring out the magic in my soul.'

She laughed softly. 'Are all musicians like you?'

Squeezing her until she squealed, he demanded, 'Explain yourself, woman.'

'I mean . . . romantic.'

'*All* men are romantic when they're in love,' he said. 'Even your dad.'

Surprised, she insisted, 'What's Dad got to do with it?'

He hugged her tightly to him. 'I've never seen a man so much in love as your dad.' He kissed the top of her head. 'But I know how he feels.'

A warm feeling spread through her. 'Mam and Dad have always had something special.'

Jack held her tighter. 'Like you and me, eh?'

In that unique moment she was both embarrassed and proud. Embarrassed by the overwhelming feelings that coursed through her, and proud because, out of all the women who would have given anything to be walked home by Jack Hanson, he had chosen *her*.

'Penny for them?'

Flustered by his nearness, she blurted out, 'What about Alfie Burrows?'

'What about him?'

'You said all men in love are romantic. So would you say *he* was romantic?'

He smiled down at her. Voice low and sincere, he said, 'Yes. I'd say Alfie was romantic . . . probably more than most.'

Drawing to a halt, she looked up at him. 'Why do you say that?'

'Because he may be a little man, but he has a big heart.'

She thought about that for a minute. 'You're right,' she agreed, 'Alfie hasn't got a lot going for him outwardly, but he has the loveliest nature, and says the prettiest things to Debbie.' She smiled. 'He'd give her the world, but she's always making fun of him, and sometimes she can be really cruel. Deep down, though, I think she likes him.'

'Well,' he mused, with a twinkle in his eye, 'you might well be right. After all, they've gone for shish and fips together.'

While she was laughing, he swept her into his arms. 'Did I tell you you look ravishing?'

'Yes.'

'And did I say how much I love you?'

'You did.'

'And have I asked you to marry me?'

She felt the blush creep up her neck. 'No,' she whispered, heart beating like a butterfly's wings. 'You never asked me that.'

'Hmm!' His dark eyes were like the deepest ocean, melting into hers, flooding her with emotion.

To Lucy, it was as though the whole world stood still. Suddenly she was pressed close against him, her face brushing his and his mouth touching her neck. Then he was kissing her madly, passionately, as if there was no tomorrow.

When a couple walked by, sniggering and staring at them, they broke away from each other. 'Harlot!' Jack managed to keep a straight face. 'You'll get me locked up.'

As they continued their journey, Lucy thought she would never feel more happy than she was right now. With Jack's strong arm round her shoulders, and the feel of his body against hers, she felt so safe. She felt warm, content, and oh so very much in love.

As they came into the foyer of the Royal Hotel,

his words flashed through her mind. 'Did I ask you to marry me?' he'd said.

And, no, he had not asked her that. Not before tonight. And not quite tonight either.

A wave of disappointment dampened her happiness. Maybe he would *never* ask her!

As they came through the door, they were greeted by the receptionist. 'Good evening, Mr Hanson.'

Margaret Bridgeman had one of those 'glued-on' smiles that said, 'I'm here to serve, and nothing is too much trouble.' A tall, attractive spinster of forty years, she had short, brown, expertly styled hair and sharp, quizzical eyes that missed not a thing.

The invaluable Miss Bridgeman never failed to turn up for her duties smartly dressed in a pale silk blouse and dark straight skirt, sensible shoes and expensive tights, and was always discreetly bedecked in gold: gold earrings, gold rings, and on her bony wrist the daintiest, prettiest watch, with numbers so tiny she had to screw up her small brown eyes in order to tell the time.

She was frighteningly efficient, charming but aloof; content with her life, and fiercely dedicated to her work. Within five minutes of interviewing her, Jack had decided she presented the right image for this hotel. Housed in an impressive Victorian building, the Royal had catered for all kinds of clients in its long and occasionally less than illustrious career.

When Jack was taken on as manager, this once-grand hotel had been rundown and sadly ignored by the increasing numbers of businessmen who visited Blackburn thanks to new local industries.

The more discerning visitors often preferred to stay out of town in the country hotels.

Jack changed all that.

With great difficulty, he persuaded the owner to invest more money in the hotel. He did so only reluctantly, but had never regretted it.

Under Jack's guidance, every room was refurbished and upgraded. Most of the old, tired staff members were dismissed with glowing references and generous pay-offs; new younger staff with a modern outlook and outgoing personality were sought. During the course of a week's intensive interviewing, Jack was able to take on the kind of people he knew would proudly enhance the hotel's brand new image, the two most important people being, in his opinion, the master chef and the receptionist, in that order.

With his new staff and a refurbished hotel, Jack then masterminded an aggressive and extremely successful advertising campaign. Clients began to pour in, and now, just two years after his arrival, his hard work and determination seemed to have paid off.

The Royal Hotel was now rated 'one of the best in Lancashire'.

Lucy had seen it all happen, and was deeply impressed with Jack's unswerving dedication and natural flair for business.

She took a moment to glance round the foyer: at the cream-painted fluted columns, the plush red carpet, and the many attractive paintings hanging on the walls. The highly polished round table was dressed with a wonderful colourful display of fresh flowers, and there was a huge bouquet of dried lavender standing before the marble fireplace. All in all, the entrance exuded an exclusive ambience that brought people back again and again.

At this late hour, isolated groups sat round the coffee tables, enjoying a nightcap and discussing the day's events. Mostly they were businessmen, but there were others ... young couples on a weekend away together, and older couples spending a second honeymoon on a special weekend package that Jack had devised. Many couples had revived a flagging relationship on such a trip.

Seeing her attention drawn by the old couple who sat holding hands, he whispered in her ear, 'Jack's special ... Friday to Sunday for half-price, and a bottle of house wine at dinner.'

'I think it's a lovely idea,' she murmured. 'Normally they might not be able to afford a weekend away, especially in a hotel like this.'

There was an air of grandeur about the refurbished hotel, but more importantly there was also a warm, comfortable atmosphere. 'You've done well, Jack,' she remarked. 'I remember this place when it was crumbling on the outside and drunks slept in the doorway.'

'Shh!' When the main doors opened and a group of smart-suited businessmen headed for the desk, he discreetly steered her away. 'Don't want you frightening the guests,' he chuckled.

Feeling mischievous and fired by the two Martinis she had drunk at The Palais, Lucy played along. Raising her voice, she said sternly, 'I'm sorry, Mr Hanson. I can understand why you don't want the guests to know about the fire in the kitchen, but I draw the line at your creeping into my bed any hour of the day and night.'

Pressing his hand to her mouth, he laughed softly. 'You little devil!' Not quite certain whether the guests had heard, and being reluctant to find out, he propelled her to the lift at great speed.

Once inside, she peered out at the faces turned in their direction. 'Sorry,' she apologised. 'It was just a joke.'

'Somehow I don't think they believe you,' Jack whispered.

Certainly the men looked envious, and one woman in particular gazed at Jack with the hungry smile of a barracuda. 'Watch that one,' Lucy laughed as the lift doors closed. 'She looks like she might have sharp teeth.' But she could understand why any woman would look at him in that way. Jack was all man.

Upstairs in his comfortable top-floor apartment, Lucy made tea while he kissed her neck and threatened to strangle her. She couldn't apologise enough. 'I don't know what got into me,' she said.

He laughed. 'You're a little witch!'

Swinging round, she handed him the tray. 'Take this to the table, my good man, and be quick about it!'

Bowing in a servile manner, he took the tray and placed it on the coffee table. Then he sat on the settee and opened his arms to her. 'Would ma'am like a cuddle?'

Willingly, she went to him. 'Ma'am would very much like a cuddle,' she answered, falling into his arms, her heart soaring with happiness when he brought his mouth down on hers. The kiss seemed never-ending. It warmed her blood and touched her soul, and when it was over, they gazed at each other and their love was a bond that drew them even closer.

For a while neither wanted to end the moment. They lay in each other's arms, content just to be there, with Lucy wondering whether he would pop the question now, and Jack wondering when the time would be right.

He rolled her to him and they kissed again. There was a need in her and he sensed it. The time was right. 'I've changed my mind,' he whispered softly against her lips.

Her lovely grey eyes frowned. 'What?'

Tenderly, he bit her lips with the edge of his teeth. 'I said, I've changed my mind.'

Heart sinking, she pulled away. 'Changed your mind about what?' This was the moment she had always dreaded, the one when he would say he no longer wanted to see her.

He was quiet for a minute, keeping her waiting, his dark eyes smiling. 'The tea,' he said at last. 'I've changed my mind about the tea.' Keeping a straight face, he pointed to the tray on the table. 'Anyway, it's gone cold.'

She was incredulous, but deeply relieved. 'You devil!' Hammering against his chest with her fists, she laughed out loud. 'I thought you were going to say you'd changed your mind about *me* . . . that you didn't want to see me any more.' The relief was overwhelming, but deep inside there was the smallest niggle of anger. She loved him so much. Too much.

'Would you care?' There was something about his voice that made everything all right. 'If I didn't want to see you again,' he insisted softly, 'would you care?'

She nodded. No words could say how she would feel if she should never see him again.

Touching the tip of her chin, he raised her face to his. 'If I didn't see you,' he whispered, 'there would be no point in anything.' This time when he kissed her, she clung to him, kissing him back with a ferocity that took them both by surprise. Then, just as suddenly as she had gone to him, she thrust him away. 'Sometimes I wonder if there is any future for us.' The strength of her own feelings was overpowering.

His slow smile was both wonderful and irritating. Shaking his head, he told her, 'Lucy Nolan, you should be ashamed.'

For no apparent reason, anger spiralled up in her. 'Ashamed? Why?'

His face grew serious, voice harsh as he reprimanded, 'For bringing me cold tea, of course.'

Laughing and fighting, the two of them rolled on to the carpet, Lucy filled with delight and loving him more than ever, and Jack adoring her like no other woman he had ever met, convinced beyond doubt that this was the moment.

Lifting her bodily, he laid her on the settee. 'Thirsty?'

She smiled. 'Just a bit.' Gazing into his dark green eyes, Lucy believed she knew his every mood, his every thought.

She was wrong.

When he walked to the phone she sat up, straightening her skirt, her gaze following his every move. There was something about him tonight. Something that made her a little nervous. 'Don't you want to make love?' The moment the words were out of her mouth she regretted them. Now he really would think she was cheap.

His smile made her easy. 'I've only got to look at you, Lucy, sweetheart,' he sighed, 'and I always want to make love.'

She looked away, embarrassed and unsure. His voice filtered into her thoughts, crisp and authoritative. 'That's right,' he was saying. 'Straight away.'

Replacing the handset, he sat beside her and they talked of other things: of her parents and their thriving greengrocer's; of Debbie and her madcap ways. They discussed Alfie and the fact that he might be good for Debbie, if only she would give him a chance.

Finally the conversation came round to Lucy. 'I'm proud of you,' he said. 'Debbie's told me how much faith the old man has in you, and I know you've turned his business round.' He kissed her tenderly, arm around her shoulders. 'If Old Ted had any sense he'd make you a partner.'

Lucy chuckled. 'What? Paint someone else's name on the sign next to his?' Her face filled with horror. 'Never!'

They would have talked more, about her and maybe then about Jack, but the bell to his apartment rang and he jumped up to answer it.

It was the waiter. 'Your order, Mr Hanson,' he said, pushing the trolley into the room.

Jack followed him to the door. A few soft words were exchanged before the waiter departed. Lucy had sensed the reason. 'You told him off, didn't you?'

'Why should I do that?' Returning to the trolley, he prepared to take off the cloth.

'Because he was so long in bringing it.'

'Ah! So *you* noticed too?'

'Well, all right, yes.'

'And if you'd been a guest, you might have complained?'

'Maybe.' She also had a head for business and was well aware of the annoyance slack service could cause a customer. All the same, she couldn't help feeling just a little sorry for the waiter. He looked so young.

Jack knew she was concerned, so put her mind at ease. 'Don't worry, sweetheart,' he urged. 'It was just a gentle reminder that service is a priority in this hotel. The waiter is young. He's also new here. Like all of us he has to learn. Now that he knows, I don't expect it will happen again.' He winked. 'I promise not to have his head at dawn. Happy now?'

Her quick, warm smile told him what he wanted to know.

In a minute he had whipped the cloth off the trolley. In another minute he raised the bottle of champagne. 'Celebration!' he said, hoping the moment really was right.

The small explosion of the cork made them laugh. 'Champagne!' Lucy was thrilled. 'What are we celebrating?' Walking across the room, she wrapped her arms round his waist.

'You and me,' he answered, kissing her upturned face.

Filling two glasses, he handed one to her, then, leaning forward, looked at her with such emotion she felt his love like a presence. 'Will you marry me,

57

sweetheart?' he whispered, voice trembling.

Lucy's answer came from her heart. 'Oh, yes.' Her smile echoed the joy inside her. 'I'll marry you.'

After sealing the promise with a kiss, they linked arms and sipped champagne.

Then, tenderly, he swept her into his arms. As he took her to the bedroom, Lucy made no protest. She looked into his face, at the strong square chin and the shock of dark hair half covering his eyes as he gazed down on her, and her heart was full.

This was her man.

In all of her life she would want no other.

Soon they were naked, lying on his bed warm against the cloud-like quilt, bodies merging into one, she beneath and he on top, kissing, touching. He was sending her crazy. The soft, moist tip of his tongue toyed with her nipple, teasing and tempting, until it stood erect and proud as his own member.

Running the flat of her hands up and down his spine, she could feel the tautness of his muscles. Now he was kissing her neck, making her groan with pleasure. With a series of gentle, determined thrusts he entered her. It was as if her soul was being invaded. Like a bird set free, she felt herself elated . . . filled with such joy, such fierce soaring emotion, it was almost too much to bear.

His hard, strong arms caressed her buttocks, body moving backwards and forwards, taking her with him, drawing her upwards. Until, all too soon, the passion was spent.

Exhausted, they clung together. Still in love, still wanting each other, but in a different way now. 'I love you,' he murmured against her mouth, and her joy was complete.

Every woman fears that once a man has made love to her, the love itself will be gone. A woman always knows. And Lucy knew now . . . that Jack's love was as strong as ever.

She and Jack had something very, very special. Something that transcended ordinary sex. Theirs was a warm and precious gift that would carry them through their youth, into old age and beyond.

Alfie was frantic. 'No, Debbie!' Squashed against the wall, he glanced towards the entrance to the alley. 'What if somebody sees us?'

'Don't be so bloody daft!' Debbie screeched with laughter. 'Nobody ever comes down here, and if they do, we'll charge 'em a pound a peep.' Chuckling and moaning, she tried desperately to get his trousers down. 'Gawd Almighty, Alfie, have you got the buggers stitched up or what?'

A shadow crossed the mouth of the alley, sending him into a panic. 'Quick! Somebody's coming, gerroff! GERROFF!'

The shadow passed and Alfie visibly relaxed. 'This isn't the place to do it,' he chided. 'It's not right.'

'Miserable sod.'

Like any man he was tempted. But not here. Not like this. 'You're drunk,' he told her. 'I'm taking you home. What's more, you can walk. The fresh air will do us both good.' In fact, right at that minute, he wouldn't have minded a cold shower.

Drunk and disorderly, Debbie protested all the way. She fought with him, swore at him, called him some names that wouldn't even be heard at a rugby club supper, and there were times when he wondered what he saw in her. But he loved her. And love was a powerful thing.

Debbie's mam was waiting for her. 'You little fool,' she said, looking anxious. 'Your father's out looking for you. Get inside before he sees you on the street like this.' Taking hold of Debbie, she rushed her indoors. 'It's all right,' she told Alfie as he stepped forward. 'I'll see to her. You'd best go before her father gets back.'

Debbie winked at him. 'Go on, yer bugger!' she said. 'An' don't ring me . . . I'll ring you!' She laughed until she was out of breath, then in hushed tones told her mam, 'I'm sorry but me and Alfie, we've had a good time, we have.' She was still laughing when her mother closed the door.

Alfie was halfway down the street when he heard the ring of boots against the pavement behind him. When he turned, he saw the big man striding towards the Latelys' house.

His grim, determined thumping on the front door echoed down the street.

For one worrying moment, Alfie wondered whether he should go back and explain that Debbie had come to no harm, and that he was just as much responsible.

He even turned and went a short way back along the street.

But then he smiled to himself as he recalled her parting words: 'Don't ring me . . . I'll ring you!'

He laughed at that. 'She wouldn't thank you to interfere, Alfie boy,' he decided, then he went smartly on his way, convinced that by the time he got round the block she would be in bed, fast asleep and dreaming up more ways to torment him.

In fact, by the time he got round the block, he was far enough away not to hear the pleading and crying as Debbie paid the price for her disobedience.

Far from dreaming when she went to bed, she lay awake for many hours, made sober by the beating she'd received. And wondering how long it must all go on.

Chapter Three

Lucy was horrified. 'What in God's name happened?'

'I've already told you, I got drunk and fell over.' Guilt and shame flooded Debbie, and she couldn't look Lucy in the eye. 'Oh, stop nagging.' She grinned, but the pain in her jaw was excruciating. 'You're worse than a bloody parent. Where've you been? What have you been up to?' Shifting on the settee, she tried to make herself more comfortable, but every bone in her body ached. 'No more questions, Lucy,' she pleaded. 'I've already paid for my sins.'

Something about Debbie's evasive manner left Lucy uneasy. She had her own terrible suspicions, but this wasn't the right time or place to voice them. She wasn't even sure she had a right to voice them.

There were so many questions Lucy wanted to ask. Instead she simply said, 'What about Alfie?'

Surprised, Debbie looked up. 'What about him?'

'Well . . . where was he when you were so drunk you fell over?' She reached out to brush a lock of hair from Debbie's forehead. 'And why did he let you get so drunk in the first place?'

She felt astonished that Alfie could have let Debbie get into such a state. In the back of her mind, though, she had already decided it was really nothing to do with him, and nothing to do with Debbie's 'falling over' either. But that was what her friend wanted her to think, and so for the moment she went along with it. 'Wait 'til I see him! I'll have a thing or two to say, I can promise you that.'

Debbie's gaze fell. 'It wasn't Alfie's fault,' she muttered. 'He did his best to stop me from getting drunk, but you know what I'm like. He even walked me home.' She chuckled. 'I was so drunk, I tried to seduce him in the alley, but he wouldn't have it.'

'That's because he really cares for you, Debs.'

'Maybe.' She gave a full-throated laugh. 'But if his bloody trousers weren't glued on, we'd have had a right randy session.'

Lucy chuckled too. 'I bet you frightened the life out of the poor little bugger.'

'Alfie's all right. Too decent for me, though.'

'Oh?' Lucy was puzzled. 'If he's so decent, how come he let you hurt yourself like this?' She stared at Debbie's bruised face and the pathetic way she sat huddled on the settee, as though every movement was agony. 'Knowing how Alfie feels about you, I would have thought he'd have his arm round you all the way home.'

Debbie did some quick thinking. 'It was after he left,' she said. 'I was waving him off and fell down the bloody steps. He didn't even know.' Rolling her eyes, she cleverly changed the subject. 'And now I expect I've lost me bleedin' job, ain't I?'

Knowing she had deliberately changed the subject, Lucy didn't press the issue any further. 'What makes you think you've lost your job?'

'Ain't that what you're here to tell me? Old Ted's

had enough of me ... causing accidents ... coming in late ... and now calling in sick. He's sacked me, and I don't blame the old sod.'

Lucy quickly put her mind at rest. 'Your job's safe,' she promised. She didn't say she had had to plead with Ted to keep Debbie on. 'He understands you can't help being ill.'

Debbie took offence. 'I'm not ill. I've never been ill in my life.'

Lucy shook her head. There was no winning, she thought. 'All right then ... bruised and battered.'

Debbie stiffened, her eyes wide with fright as she demanded, 'What d'yer mean ... "bruised and battered"?' For one awful minute she feared her friend had guessed.

Lucy knew then. She saw it in Debbie's face. For one brief moment she was tempted to voice her suspicions but her instincts told her that Debbie was not ready to confide. 'I didn't mean anything by it,' she explained. 'It's just an expression.'

Visibly relaxing, Debbie said, 'Mind you, I do look a mess ... covered in bruises and aching all over ... like I've been in the ring with Muhammad Ali.' A deep, long sigh seemed to raise her from her seat. 'I'm sorry, kid,' she moaned, 'I'm nothing but trouble to you.'

Lucy took hold of her hand. 'You're my best friend,' she said affectionately. 'And anyway, haven't we always looked out for one another, you and me?'

'I don't deserve you.'

She looked so sorry for herself that Lucy had to smile. 'I know,' she said, grey eyes twinkling.

Just as Lucy hoped, it did the trick. 'Why, you

snotty-nosed cow!' Playfully hitting out, Debbie roared with laughter. 'I'm worth ten of you any time.'

'If you say so.'

Opening her arms, Debbie coaxed, 'Give us a cuddle.'

The hug made her squeal. 'That's enough,' she moaned. 'I didn't ask you to break my bleedin' ribs!'

Debbie's mother came in then. Placing a tray of tea and biscuits on the coffee table, she looked at her daughter, then at Lucy, and the shame on her face was pitiful. 'You can see why I had to ring in and say she was sick?' she explained anxiously. 'She hasn't lost her job, has she?'

For the second time Lucy reassured, 'No, Mrs Lately, Debbie's job is safe.'

Relief flooded the other woman's face. 'Thank God for that!' She sighed. 'Her father would go mad if she lost her job.' Quickly she added, 'Mind you, it would have been her own fault. Did she tell you how she got drunk and fell over?'

In a brighter voice, Debbie interrupted. 'Stop worrying, Mam. Lucy already knows I fell down the steps, and Old Ted's not going to sack me, so everything's all right.'

Noreen smiled, but no smile in the world could hide the haggard, frightened look on her face. 'I'll leave you to it then,' she said, turning away. 'I expect you've got a lot to chat about.'

'Go on then,' Debbie urged when her mother closed the sitting-room door, 'I want to know all about it . . . you and Jack. What happened? Did he propose? And did you say yes? When's the wedding? And, don't forget, I expect to be chief bridesmaid.'

Lucy's shy, proud face told the tale.

'Oh! Wow!' Laughing and screeching, she grabbed Lucy and kissed her. 'He asked you, didn't he?' she yelled. 'Mam! Lucy and Jack are engaged. What d'yer think to that?'

Noreen appeared at the door. 'I think that's wonderful,' she told Lucy. 'Congratulations. I only wish our Debbie could settle down.' That said, she returned to her kitchen where she busied herself preparing dinner. 'The man of the house will be home soon,' she muttered. 'Better get a move on.'

Debbie wanted the whole story. 'So have you set a date?'

Lucy's heart fell. 'It's not that easy.'

'Why not?'

'Jack and I had a long talk, and we've decided to wait at least a year before setting the date. You see, he wants his own hotel, and reckons he'll have it within a couple of years.' In her heart she knew he was right. 'He says his own hotel will be the best wedding present we could have.'

'Two years, eh? Can you wait that long?'

Lucy was certain. 'We talked and talked, and I know he's right, Debs. Anyway, two years isn't all that long. Meantime we can keep saving.' She had been astonished at the amount of money Jack had already saved. 'He showed me his bank balance,' she confided. 'Do you know, he's already got fifteen thousand pounds saved?'

Debbie's eyes stuck out like hatpins. 'That's a bloody fortune! Where did he get it?'

'From his wages . . . overtime . . . playing in the band . . . tips. He saved every penny he could, and

67

now he says it won't be too long before he sets his sights on his own business.'

'He'll need more than that, won't he?'

Lucy had said the very same. But: 'Jack's got a good business head. When he sees what he wants, I'm sure he'll find a way to get it.'

'Then you'll get married, and I'll be chief bridesmaid?'

'Of course.' The thought of walking down the aisle to Jack was just wonderful.

'And can I pick my own dress . . . and colour?'

'Don't see why not.' It was a small thing to ask.

Debbie stared at the ceiling, her face glowing with pleasure. 'A wedding! With me as chief bridesmaid.' Levelling her cheeky gaze at Lucy, she told her, 'I'm sorry, kid, but they'll all be looking at me and not you. I mean . . . I'll be so beautiful, they won't be able to tear their eyes away.'

'I'll have to put up with that.'

Though she was delighted to see Debbie in a lighter mood, Lucy knew she would have to be cruel to be kind. 'Don't lie there feeling sorry for yourself,' she suggested firmly. 'You'd be better off at work, so get yourself up and about. Go and see the doctor . . . ask him to give you a proper check up, and get some witch hazel for those bruises.'

'All right, bossy boots.'

'See, you're feeling better already.'

'That's because you're here. Will you come and see me tomorrow night?'

'Do you really need to ask?' Neither Hell nor high water would keep her from Debbie at a time like this.

'Yer a good mate.'

Lucy's smile spread slowly over her face, her grey
eyes soft with affection as she hugged her friend.
'I'm off now, but I'll call in straight from work
tomorrow. Okay?'

'Okay.'

On the way out, Lucy called cheerio to Noreen.

Rushing from the kitchen, the little woman gave
her a wave. 'Mind how you go,' she advised. 'The
roads are so busy at this time of night.'

Lucy drove away carefully. She hated driving and
only occasionally used the car. She wondered about
Debbie and her parents, and what exactly went on
behind closed doors.

'I know there's something very wrong,' she murmured, easing her dad's car on to the main road.
'But if you don't confide in me, Debbie, there's
nothing I can do.' She winced. 'Even then I'm not
sure whether I could make a difference. But I can
promise to be there when you need me. And if you've
got me and your mother, then that's three against
one.'

Her own mother was waiting at the shop doorway.
'Where've you been? Why didn't you phone and say
you might be late?'

Lucy remained on the doorstep. 'What's the panic?'
Judging by the worried expression on her mother's
face, Lucy realised there was something wrong.

'Better come inside.' Sally turned, and Lucy followed her into the sitting room. 'It's Old Ted,' her
mother revealed. 'He's been taken to hospital.' Seeing
how shocked and anxious Lucy was, she swiftly
allayed her fears. 'He gave the sister our number . . .

wants you to go and see him. According to the sister, he had a bad fall, banged his head against the wall as he went down. But there's nothing broken and there seems to be no real damage. All the same, they're keeping him in, just in case.'

Lucy swung away. 'I'll have to go to him,' she said. 'He must be frantic. He's always had a terrible fear of hospitals.'

'I knew you'd want to go straight away,' her mam said. Handing Lucy a brown paper bag, she told her, 'I made you a cheese sandwich. Make sure you eat it, now. I'll have a nice ham salad ready for you when you get back.'

Appearing from the upper reaches of the house, Mike came down dressed in an old blue overall and covered in dust. 'Stop fussing, woman,' he told his wife. Wrapping his arm round her shoulders, he gave her a squeeze. 'I don't think Lucy will starve for the want of one meal.'

Sally pushed him away. 'Get out of here, you,' she said, brushing her shoulder. 'You're covered in dust.'

'Only because I've been putting them shelves up you've been nagging me about.' He winked at her. 'Anyway, there was a time when you wouldn't have worried about a speck of dust.'

'That was before I had a new carpet. Now get out of here.' Sheepishly he went, winking at Lucy on the way. 'Tea in ten minutes,' Sally called. 'And take that boiler suit off before you come.'

Addressing Lucy, she said, 'Drive carefully, love.'

Lucy promised she would, and quickly departed.

At the hospital Ted was causing a riot. 'I don't want

no dinner!' His angry voice reverberated down the ward. 'An' I'll not have them young things washing me every two minutes neither. So piss off, the lot of yer!'

The young nurse gave him a ticking off. 'Eat your dinner and behave. You should be ashamed, using language like that.'

He glared at her. 'Aye? An' *you* should be ashamed, undressing an old man and peeping at his private parts.'

As she came towards Lucy, the girl shook her head and grinned. 'They're all the same,' she said. 'I wouldn't mind, but they've got nothing worth peeping at!'

Ted was delighted to see Lucy, his old face crinkling into a smile. 'I knew you'd come,' he said, struggling to sit up straight. 'You've never let me down yet, bless yer 'eart.'

After giving him a little kiss on the forehead, Lucy helped make him more comfortable. In a hospital nightshirt, and lying against the stark white sheets, he looked so frail. Without the cap he always wore round the grounds of his nursery, his pink scalp was easily seen through the thin silver hair. 'I heard you shouting as I came in,' she said with amusement. 'What was that all about, eh?'

'Them buggers!' For one minute he actually looked ashamed. 'Morning, noon and night, they'll not leave me alone.'

'They only want to help.'

'Aye, well, I'd rather they didn't.'

'The sister told Mam you should be home soon.'

'Sooner than that if I have my way. Now sit yourself

down, there's a good 'un. You're making me neck ache looking up at yer.'

Drawing up a chair, she did as instructed. 'What happened, Ted? Mam says you fell over. What in God's name were you doing?'

'A bit of this and that,' he said evasively. 'You'll see when you go in tomorrow.'

Frustrated, she shook her head. 'You shouldn't be climbing in the first place. Why didn't you leave whatever it was until I could do it?'

'Because you do too much already.'

'That's what you pay me for, isn't it?' She soothed him with her lovely smile. 'Look, Ted, while you're in here, you're not to worry. I'll take care of everything until you get back.'

'That's what I want to talk to you about.'

'Oh?' Something about his serious expression alarmed her. 'Are you thinking of getting someone else in, is that it?' She wanted him to believe it wouldn't matter, but it did.

It mattered a lot. If Ted got someone else in over her head, she would hate it; though she would never question his judgement, and neither would she make things difficult. And even if she felt slighted, she could never leave because, in the time she had been there, Lucy had come to love the nurseries almost as much as Old Ted did.

Looking very worried, he confided, 'That no-good son of mine has written me a letter.' Closing his eyes, he leaned back against the pillows and, for a moment, seemed reluctant or else too weak to go on.

Lucy waited patiently.

Presently he opened his eyes and looked directly

at her. 'After all these years, he's coming to see me.'

Lucy saw how moved he seemed, and how his kind old eyes filled with tears. Mistaking it for fatherly emotion, she exclaimed, 'Oh, Ted, that's really wonderful.'

'Wonderful be buggered!' he snarled. 'He's not coming here to see his old father. He's coming to see what he can take for himself . . . coming to measure the land for development and me for a bloody coffin. *That's* why he's coming, and for no other reason.'

Lucy was horrified. 'But it's *yours*, Ted. Surely he can't take it away from you?'

The old face twitched angrily, growing redder and more agitated. 'He might be my own flesh and blood, but I'm ashamed to say he's a bad lot. If he thought for one minute he could get his greedy mitts on my land, he'd move Heaven and Hell. I'm telling you, lass, he'd do it in a minute, even if it meant having me put away.'

'Put away?' Lucy shook her head in disbelief. 'No son would ever do that.'

'No decent son, maybe. But George doesn't know how to be decent, and he never will.'

Seeing how agitated he was getting, Lucy said hopefully, 'You could be wrong, Ted. He might have changed. Maybe he really does want to see you. Maybe he regrets staying away all this time.' All the same, she wasn't convinced. No son would have stayed away this long unless he had little or no feeling for his father.

Ted corrected her. 'No, lass. It's *you* who's wrong. George Beckendale has never been any good, and a leopard doesn't easily change his spots.' The hard, angry look on his face betrayed his innermost thoughts. 'No. He's on his way to take what he sees as rightfully his.'

His fists clenched and unclenched as he told Lucy in a stiff, hostile voice, 'But he'll not get it! I've had that parcel of land for nigh on forty years. When I bought it from the council, it were just a sorry little allotment, neglected and unwanted. But I took it on and brought it back to life.' A glow of pride lit his face. 'Two years later I bought the adjoining land, and the bungalow with it. Since then I've worked my fingers to the bone. I've sweated blood and tears over that land, and I swear, as God's my judge, I mean to die on it!'

Lucy had never seen him like this. Though Ted had a burly physique and was still physically able to work the long hours he did, he was undeniably old and past his best. But now, in that moment when he was fired with hatred and burning with a fierce, almost arrogant pride, she glimpsed something of the man inside; the young, strong, passionate man he must have been in his youth. And she was overwhelmed.

'He can't take it from you,' she declared, with equal determination. 'I won't let him!'

When he reached out, wrapping his gnarled old hand over her fingers and saying in a trembling voice, 'Bless you, lass. I only wish to God I'd had a son even *half* as decent as you are,' she was lost for words.

Hot, burning tears rose in her eyes. She blinked them back. 'I still think you're wrong, Ted,' she admitted. 'How can he take what isn't his?'

He laughed softly, then in a low, harsh voice, told

her, 'You don't know what he's like. If it meant having me committed to a mental home as senile, or put in an old folk's place because I supposedly couldn't take care of myself, he wouldn't even blink an eye. After that it would be all too easy to take what isn't his.'

He leaned forward as though imparting a secret. 'He *pays* people, d'you see? People of importance . . . any man or woman who can help him get what he's set his heart on.'

'What are you saying, Ted?'

'I'm saying he has his fingers in a lot of pies. He's an opportunist. He farms. He builds. In fact, he does anything and everything that can rake in the money . . . legal or otherwise.'

'I see.' She still didn't understand what he was getting at, but was beginning to realise just how powerful and ruthless a man George Beckendale might be.

Old Ted went on, 'It's common knowledge that the whole of this area is prime development land. That makes my little piece of Heaven worth a small fortune. I'm not interested in the money, I'm happy enough to go on as I am until they put me under the land I love so much. But George? Well now, he's a very different kettle of fish. No doubt he's got wind of the fact that his father's land is ripe for development, and now he's on his way to stake his claim.'

'What can I do?' Lucy asked tenderly. 'Tell me what I can do?' If she was a man she might handle it in a different way. She might even resort to violence, challenging George Beckendale face to face. But she was a woman. And a woman had to live by her own wits and ability.

But she would do whatever she could to help Ted in his dilemma, and, after what she had just heard, she felt ready for anything.

However, she was *not* ready for what Ted had in mind. 'I want you to buy the nurseries from me . . . lock, stock and barrel.'

Lucy was speechless. She could only stare at him, and wonder.

Falling back against the pillows, he chortled, 'I haven't gone off me rocker, if that's what you're thinking.'

'I wasn't thinking that,' she assured him, although she wasn't quite certain what she *did* think. 'I just don't know if I heard right. Did you just ask me to buy the nurseries from you?'

'I did, lass . . . lock, stock and barrel.' While she was still reeling with amazement, he went on hurriedly, 'I've been thinking about it ever since I got his letter saying he meant to visit. Selling the land to you is the only way I can keep it out of his grubby hands. O' course, there'll have to be certain conditions. First of all, I would want to stay on in the bungalow for the rest of my life. And secondly, I'll work on the land, just like I've always worked on it . . . only this time you'll be the boss and I'll be the employee. What d'yer say?'

'I say you must have banged your head a bit harder than the doctor realised. First of all, you could never bring yourself to sell Beckendale Nurseries . . . not in a million years. And even if you could, and even if I was desperate to buy, I could never afford it.'

'There's ways and means.'

'Come on, Ted. You said yourself it's worth a fortune as building land. So if you really think selling is the only way to stop your son from getting his hands on it, why not sell to a property developer? That way you could either buy more land nearby, or retire in style.'

'Do you really want me to sell the land to someone who'll put a housing estate on it?'

'You know I don't.'

'Then I'll have to sell it to you.'

'Talk sense, Ted.'

He gazed at her, seeing only goodness. When his old eyes met her honest grey ones, he knew he was doing the right thing. 'If I had to trust one person in the whole wide world,' he said fondly, 'it would have to be you.'

'Thank you for that, Ted,' she began. 'But—'

'No "buts".' When she was about to speak again, he pressed his finger to his lips. 'Shh now, and listen. I've got it all worked out. If I were selling, and you were able to buy the land, would you want it? Answer me truthfully now.'

Lucy couldn't deny it. 'If you were absolutely determined to sell, and I had the means to buy it . . . there's nothing I would love more.'

'Good! Then it's settled.'

Lucy smiled patiently. When Old Ted got a bee in his bonnet, he was easily carried away. 'Not so quick,' she cautioned. 'First of all, I don't have the means to buy Beckendale Nurseries, and secondly, I have every intention of talking you out of selling. There has to be another way.'

'There is.'

Immensely relieved, she grabbed him by the hand. 'There! I knew it.' Curious, though, she asked, 'What other way?'

'Just now, you wanted to know what you could do, and it's this.' He took a deep breath. 'You and I could become partners. I'll keep only forty per cent, so you'll have a controlling interest. That way George can't touch me or the land . . . without going through you first.' He stopped her again. 'No, just hear me out, lass.' In a quiet, serious voice, he continued, 'There'll be no question of money changing hands between us. I'll still have my home, and will still work on the land just as before. You'll receive a wage, and we'll work together like we always have.'

He paused for breath and it was more than she dared to interrupt him. 'It'll cost you nothing to come in as senior partner.' She moved to protest, but he put up his hand. 'I asked you to hear me out!' When Lucy closed her mouth, he went on, 'I want nothing for the partnership except this. After we've each taken a wage, to be agreed on, all profits will be ploughed back into the business. That way, we both benefit. Beckendale Nurseries will grow and prosper, and if I know you, will soon be worth ten times more than they are now. And, God willing, we shall all be safe from outsiders.'

His old face was wreathed in smiles. 'You've always said you could treble the turnover if I let you loose. Well, now I'm giving you a free hand, so go to it, lass. Show the world what you're made of.'

Lucy was dumbfounded.

Such was the generosity of his gesture, it was a

full minute before she could talk, and when she did it was to thank him from the bottom of her heart. 'I won't let you down,' she promised. 'I'll make Beckendale Nurseries known from one end of Lancashire to the other.'

'I know you will, lass.' His old heart was at peace now. In Lucy he saw his salvation.

'You're giving me a marvellous opportunity,' she told him. 'I don't know how I'll ever be able to thank you.'

Grabbing her hand, he pressed it to his mouth and kissed it like the gentleman he was. 'It'll be thanks enough knowing you're there, and George Beckendale is being kept out.' He smiled at her happily. 'Now get yerself off home.'

Getting out of the chair, she put her arms round his neck and held him for a while. 'You and me together . . . we'll show the world, eh?'

'And play that devious son of mine at his own game, eh?' He chuckled with merriment. 'It does my old heart good to think we've outwitted him.'

They were closer than at any time since she had known him. 'You're not to worry about anything,' she said. 'Not George, not property developers, not anything.' A hardness crept into her voice. 'There is just one condition, though.'

Stepping back, she gave him a severe look. 'You wouldn't let me argue with you, so you're not to argue with me or the deal's off. All right?'

'What's the condition, you bugger?'

'That as soon as Beckendale Nurseries are in full flow and earning enough so I can pay for the partnership, we'll have someone in to make a valuation.

79

When that's done, I mean to pay back every penny I owe you.'

He considered it. 'All right,' he wisely agreed. 'But we'll have the nurseries valued *now*, and set a figure for your share of the partnership. It has to be done *before* you build Beckendale Nurseries up, as your share is bound to be more valuable then. That way you won't be paying twice over for your hard work. Moreover, the money will *not* be paid over until such a time as I ask for it.'

The deal was sealed with a handshake and a cuddle. 'You've made an old man very, very happy,' he said, and she told him he couldn't be any happier than she was at that minute.

When, a short time later, Lucy walked down the steps to the street, she felt as if she was walking on air. 'You've been given a chance in a million, Lucy gal,' she told herself. 'Now do as Ted said . . . go to it, lass! Show the world what you're made of!'

Her parents were thrilled. 'My God! That's bloody marvellous!' her dad said. Her mam told him not to use such language, but was so excited at the news herself that she rushed off to make tea and forgot to put any in the pot. 'We can't celebrate on hot water, Mam,' Lucy laughed, and ran out to buy a bottle of wine from the off-licence.

The three of them drank to Ted's good health, and Lucy decided the best way she could repay him was to make him a very rich man.

The next day she told Debbie.

'I'm not surprised.' Her friend was thrilled. 'Nobody deserves it more.'

Lucy was full of plans. Breathless with excitement, she bounced a few ideas off Debbie. 'No good asking me,' she laughed. 'You know how bloody useless I am.'

They talked all the same, with Lucy outlining her plans for the future and Debbie listening intently. 'Keep me on, gal,' she said testily, 'an' I'll try not to ruin it all for you.'

'You couldn't ruin it,' Lucy told her. 'And just to be certain, I might make you up to supervisor. That way you'll have more responsibility.'

'You'll be taking a risk if you do that,' Debbie warned. 'You've seen what a mess I can make of things.'

'I've also seen what a good job you can do when your mind's on it.' Old Ted had given Lucy a chance, and now she wanted to do the same for Debbie. 'It won't hurt to give it a try,' she encouraged.

Debbie began to think it might not be a bad idea after all. Besides, it might take her mind off the awful situation at home. 'Will I get a pay-rise?'

'If you earn it.'

'You can count on me, gal.'

'I'm already counting on you.' Lucy believed that giving Debbie more responsibility would make her more responsible in turn. Knowing Debbie's past record, there was no doubt it was a risk, but if Ted was in agreement, it was a risk she was prepared to take.

Seeming to read Lucy's thoughts, Debbie said quietly, 'Ted still hasn't forgiven me for killing his beloved plants. He'll never agree to me having more responsibility.'

'Hmm.' Lucy had a horrible feeling she might be right. 'I'll talk to him,' she promised. 'But if the business is to prosper, I'll need to run a tight ship. There'll be nothing for nothing at Beckendale Nurseries. We'll all have to pull our weight.'

'Don't worry.' Debbie was unusually serious. 'I know what you're saying, and you have my word . . . if you give me a chance to be part of it all, you won't be sorry.'

Lucy looked at her for a moment. 'You and I have known each other too long,' she murmured presently, 'and now I can't do without you.' She would always keep a special corner in her heart for Debbie. There were all kinds of love. There was a parent's love, and a man's love. There was the kind of love you reserved for old friends like Ted, and a certain affection that came from knowing people in your street. And then there was another love . . . for sisters and brothers, blood and kin, ending only when life itself is ended.

Lucy had neither sister nor brother, but she had Debbie. A great reservoir of love had drawn them together and kept them together, and, God willing, it would hold them fast until the end of their days.

'Penny for 'em, gal?' Though she knew Lucy as well as anyone, Debbie could never be quite sure what she might be thinking.

Lucy's soft, lazy smile made her smile too. 'Don't be nosy,' she chided. 'If I wanted you to know what I was thinking, I would have told you.'

'Oh, I see!' A sly little grin spread over her homely features. 'Thinking of the boyfriend, eh?'

'No.'

'Well then, you must be wondering how much of a pay-rise to give yer old friend?'

'I might be.'

Debbie laughed out loud. 'I knew it! You're doubling me wages, eh?'

Now it was Lucy's turn to laugh. 'Double nothing!' she exclaimed. 'I'll be trying to build the business up, not finish it off altogether.'

'You won't be doubling your own wages then?'

'That's the last thing I'll be doing.'

'Good job yer ain't like me, gal. I'd be living it up and letting everybody else do the hard work.'

Lucy didn't believe that for one minute. 'No, you wouldn't,' she said. 'If you were given the chance, you'd be as proud as I am, and just as determined to make a success of it.'

Debbie didn't answer. Instead she astonished Lucy by covering her face with her hands and softly crying. At once, Lucy had her in her arms. It was on the tip of her tongue to ask what was wrong, but some deeper instinct made her remain silent. And, as Debbie cried on her shoulder, Lucy was even more convinced that her heartache stemmed from trouble at home.

After a minute, when Debbie raised her tear-stained face, Lucy prayed she would confide in her. But she was disappointed. 'I'm a silly cow, ain't I?' Rubbing away the tears with the back of her hand, she sniffled and blew her nose noisily.

'What upset you?' Lucy asked gently.

'*You* upset me.'

'Me?' Lucy was mortified. 'I wouldn't do that for the world.'

Debbie sniffled again, her big tear-filled eyes

looking up at Lucy with gratitude. 'You don't know how precious you are to me, gal,' she murmured. 'You've been given this wonderful opportunity to take Beckendale Nurseries on to greater things, and you want me to share in it . . . *me!* Somebody who's caused more damage than a herd of elephants round the bloody place. Anybody else would be glad to see the back of me, but not you.' She sniffed again. 'Tell me the truth, gal. You know I'll likely be a burden, so why don't yer get rid of me, eh?'

Lucy appeared to be thinking hard, when in fact she was trying not to laugh. 'Well, it's like this,' she began in a sombre voice.

'Go on! Don't worry about hurting my feelings. I want the truth.'

Still serious, Lucy went on, 'When I'm up to my neck in bills and paperwork . . . when the fertiliser bags split open, and the deliveries are late, and I've got a splitting headache and don't know which way to turn . . . when I'm wondering whether I've made the biggest mistake of my life in taking up Old Ted's offer . . .' She shook her head and sighed.

Debbie got the picture. 'I know,' she finished. 'Then you'll wish you'd never kept me on?'

'I'll thank the good Lord I kept you on, you daft thing!' Lucy laughed. 'Because when the world's caving in on me, and I'm getting crusty and miserable, you'll be in the middle of it all . . . making me laugh, making me cry, brewing the tea and cheering me up with your dirty jokes.'

'You bugger!' Debbie shrieked. 'You had me worried for a minute.'

* * *

Lucy wanted to tell Jack her good news face to face.

She made no mention of it when he phoned her during the day, but could hardly contain herself when she arrived at the hotel for their dinner date. 'I've found us a quiet spot,' he said, leading her across the dining room to a table in the bay window. 'There's something I want to tell you.'

The moment they sat down he saw the gleam in her eye. 'It looks like I'm not the only one who's got news,' he said. 'Come on. What are you keeping from me?'

Unable to keep the secret any longer, she told him what Ted had done for her. She outlined his reasons for doing it, and showed her disgust for the son who, until now, had displayed little or no interest in his father. 'Ted is convinced his son wants to get his hands on the land,' she confided. 'Making me a senior partner is his way of making sure it stays safe.'

Jack was delighted at the news. 'Ted Beckendale is nobody's fool,' he assured her. 'He knows what he's doing, and couldn't have made a wiser decision.' Calling the waiter, he ordered champagne. 'This deserves a proper toast,' he said, smiling. 'I'm thrilled for you, sweetheart, but not surprised. It was only a matter of time before Ted realised your true value.'

But behind his ready smile lay a certain uneasiness. He had not told her his own news yet, and knew it would be an ordeal for them both.

They toasted Lucy's partnership with Old Ted, and Jack said he'd always known she would make good one day. 'Ted might be worried about his son, but he sees something very special in you,' he said. 'He knows he can trust you, and that you're a good businesswoman. He would never have taken you for a partner otherwise.'

'All the same, Jack, it's a golden opportunity, and I mean to make it work.'

'Oh, you will.' He had no doubt that she would make a great success of it.

After one glass of champagne and a beautifully prepared but practically untouched dinner, they made their way up to his apartment.

When they were snuggled up together on the settee, she suddenly remembered. 'Oh, Jack! I've been so full of my own news, I forgot to ask about yours.'

In the candlelight her smile was beautiful, her voice trembling as she asked, 'We can get married earlier, is that it?'

His gaze fell. 'No, sweetheart, it isn't that.'

'What then?' When he hesitated, her heart fell like a lead weight inside her. 'You don't want to get married after all? Is that what you're trying to tell me, Jack?'

Her voice was flat and low, but in her mind she was shouting, pleading: 'Don't say it, Jack. Please don't say it.'

He raised his gaze, quietly regarding her with those wonderful ocean-green eyes that sparkled with a mixture of sadness and pleasure. 'Not marry you?' he asked in amazement. 'How could I not want to marry you?' His warm, loving gaze enveloped her. 'Everything I do is done with you in mind.'

Relief flowed through her. 'But there is something wrong! Is it bad news? Please, Jack . . . tell me.'

He shook his head, and her heart was easier. 'No, it's not bad news,' he assured her. 'Although I suppose you could look at it that way.'

Before she could question his remark he went on, 'I've been asked to take on another hotel. It's much bigger, with far more potential than this one. It's in a prime position with two acres of land. There are also numerous outbuildings, with planning consent to turn them all into self-contained units.' Still concerned about having to reveal the news, he held her hand tightly. 'This could be the big one, Lucy,' he confided. 'Something tells me it might even bring us nearer to owning our own hotel.' That would give him all that he had worked for.

As his news unfolded, Lucy grew more and more excited. She threw her arms round him. 'Oh, Jack! That's marvellous!'

'Lucy. . . I . . .' He was so afraid he might lose her.

His downcast expression alarmed her. 'What? Jack, what haven't you told me?' She knew there was something, and for some inexplicable reason, she felt it would come between them.

'The hotel isn't local.' He saw her face fall, and gave her no time to comment. 'It's been closed for over a year, but I know it could be a real money spinner. It's on the sea-front. All it needs is a bit of imagination and a big heart.'

'Jack?' Anxiously, Lucy interrupted him. 'You said the hotel wasn't local?'

Desperate to convince her, he pretended not to have heard. 'I've been offered a free hand to do as I like,' he went on hurriedly. 'And twice as much money as I get now. Do you realise what that means? I can save like I've never saved before, and we can get married all the sooner.'

'Jack!' Tenderly, she placed her finger on his lips, her troubled grey eyes looking into his. 'Where is it . . . this hotel?'

He sighed, then took hold of her and kissed her, using the moment to find the right words. 'It isn't on the other side of the world, if that's what worries you.'

'But?'

'It's on the Isle of Wight,' he said. 'Ryde . . . right on the front.'

'The Isle of Wight?' It was far enough away for Lucy to be disappointed. 'It means we might not see each other for weeks . . . even months on end.'

'Come with me then.'

She stared at him in disbelief. 'And do what?'

'Help me turn a dilapidated old building into the best hotel on the island.'

For one delirious moment she was tempted. 'There's nothing I would love to do more . . .' she murmured.

'But you can't leave Ted to the mercy of his son, is that it?'

'Something like that.'

His smile told her everything was all right. 'It wouldn't be because you have something to prove, would it?' he teased.

'It might be,' she answered. 'But, more importantly, I've already given my word to Ted, and I'd hate to let him down.'

'You're a loyal friend,' he said. 'That's one of the reasons why I love you.'

Gathering her into his arms, he led her to the bed. 'I want to give you the world,' he murmured. 'You know that, don't you?'

She would have answered, but his mouth covered hers and then there was no need for words.

Not when she could speak with her heart.

Chapter Four

The following week both Ted and Debbie were back at work, fit and healthy as ever. By the end of the first day, Debbie had accidentally split open two bags of peat. Old Ted threatened to sack her on the spot, but Lucy talked him round. 'She's doing ever so well,' she coaxed. 'Give her a bit more time and she'll be fine.'

'All right,' he conceded, 'I suppose she's getting better by the day. But if she runs into me one more time with that bloody wheelbarrow, I'll have her guts for garters!'

Peace was soon restored and Lucy returned to her own demanding tasks. 'You'll be the death of me yet,' she told Debbie. But she wasn't listening. She had her eye on a tall dark-haired young man who had come to buy a cherry tree for his old mother.

Unfortunately, just as Debbie rushed to serve him, his pretty wife appeared from behind some shrubs. In a minute they were shamelessly canoodling. 'What can I do for you?' she asked, stepping between them. Parting them gave her a certain sadistic satisfaction.

Lucy watched from the office window. 'You little sod!' she laughed. 'If you can't have him, nobody can, is that it?'

But she couldn't stand by the window for long. There were so many jobs still to be done, and what with having the weekend off to go with Jack to the Isle of Wight, she had to make certain everything was in order. Ted hated doing the office work. 'What can't be done before you go, can be done when you get back,' he'd told her airily, so she had her work cut out with last-minute necessities.

She didn't even have time to enjoy a cup of tea. And as if that wasn't bad enough, Ted's ginger cat crept into the office and devoured her packed lunch while she was helping dig out the foundations for the new greenhouse.

Undaunted, she cadged a cheese sandwich off Debbie and ate while she worked.

It was Friday, the end of one of the busiest weeks they had ever known. Lucy felt guilty at having the weekend off because that was when the majority of customers turned up to collect their plants and produce. On this occasion, though, her business instincts had to be suppressed because this was the weekend when she and Jack would leave for other shores, and only she would come home.

'You're a bloody slave-driver!' Debbie complained as she wheeled a barrowload of manure past the office. 'I shouldn't be doing this, not now I'm charge hand.' She wrinkled her nose at the pungent odour emanating from the barrow. 'Carting shit ain't my style.'

'Hey!' Infuriated, Ted wagged a finger at her. 'That's enough bad language, my girl!'

'Sorry.' She gave him a sheepish grin. 'I forgot myself.'

Hearing raised voices, Lucy rushed out of the office where she was writing up the stock notes. 'What's wrong?' She picked her way through strewn canes where Ted was sorting them into different lengths.

'There's nothing wrong,' he said. 'I were just talking to Debbie . . . saying how well she's done this past week.' He didn't want to get the lass in trouble because when all was said and done, she was doing her best, and nobody could expect more. 'To tell you the truth, lass, I'm amazed,' he confessed. 'When you said you wanted to give her more responsibility, I were against it as you well know. But you were right an' I were wrong, because she's taken to the job like a duck to water.'

Looking slim and attractive in an outsize white shirt and blue jeans, Lucy beamed with pride. 'I had an idea she might.'

Taking off his old cap, he mopped his brow with the back of one hand. 'I'm not saying she's got it right just yet,' he cautioned. 'Look what she did yesterday. A two-year-old would have known better than to stack plant pots forty high. Replacing that little lot'll cost us a pretty penny,' he moaned. 'Mind you, she's allus quick to apologise, and she *is* getting better,' he grudgingly admitted.

Lucy chuckled. 'You mean she hasn't drowned the petunias, or suffocated any of your seedlings?'

'If she does that again, I'll drown and suffocate her!' It would be many a year before he forgot *those* little incidents.

As Lucy turned to leave he called her back. 'I've not really thanked you,' he said softly. 'Signing them partnership papers like you did – well, it's taken a real load off my mind.'

'No, Ted,' she corrected him. 'It's I who should be thanking you. I know how much you love this place, and though you'll never admit it, I know what it must have cost you to take me on like you did. This is still your place, Ted, and it always will be. All I'm doing is helping you take care of it.' Her grey eyes sparkled. 'So no more thanking me, eh? We need each other, that's the top and bottom of it.'

He saw the pride in her eyes and his old heart warmed. 'You're bursting with plans, aren't you, lass?'

When she laughed, her face filled with sunshine. 'You could say that.'

'What have you got in mind?'

'Wonderful things,' she revealed. 'I'm putting all my ideas down on paper. When they look something like, and I've got them in some kind of order, I'd like you and me to sit down and talk things over. I promise I won't make any changes unless you agree.'

He gazed round the yard: at the muddle of wooden trays leaning against the greenhouse, and the pile of earth that had been brought from the new greenhouse site. He noticed how untidy everything was; how there were no proper places for the tools, and how the watering-cans were inadequate for the long green-houses which were packed with plants at various stages of development. Lucy had already made a move towards bringing some semblance of order by arrang-ing all the trees and shrubs in straight lines behind a wooden rail; each tree or shrub bore its own little label containing a short description of its character-istics and cultural requirements. They were all neatly priced and tagged. To Old Ted, that little corner, with its long orderly rows and wide paved walkway between, was a promise of things to come.

'I've always known you'd fetch new life to this tired old place,' he told her now. 'You'll spruce it up and get the folk pouring in, I know you will, lass. And that's how it should be.'

Lucy felt as though a great weight had been lifted from her shoulders. 'And you don't mind?'

He shook his head. 'Mind, lass?' His old face crinkled into a smile. 'The minute I took you on, I knew it were only a matter of time before we saw some drastic changes round here. 'Course I don't mind. Matter o' fact, I'm looking forward to it.'

'It might mean moving the office and replanning the whole area,' she warned. 'I think we should set the bigger plants out in long open beds, with paved walkways between so the customers can browse and choose . . . we'll need trolleys too, so they don't have to struggle carrying them by hand. Apart from the plants being easily damaged that way, there's the problem of customers getting dirt on their clothes and hands. Ideally, we'd do the carrying, but we're not always on hand, and people tend to get impatient.' Enthused, she went on, 'Of course, we'll need someone to man the till all the time, because once we get it all under way, I can see us doubling . . . even trebling . . . our turnover. And I've got other ideas . . . but we might need to approach the planners, and that's bound to be a real tussle. If you want, I'll deal with all that. So long as you're in agreement you can leave the messy bits to me.'

'By!' Scratching his head, Ted stared with astonishment. 'I can see you've been giving it a lot of thought.'

Fearing she'd gone too far, Lucy apologised. 'Oh, Ted, I'm sorry. You think the changes are too drastic, don't you?'

He looked at her a moment longer, thinking what a pretty young thing she was, with her shining dark hair and those expressive grey eyes the colour of a racing pigeon he'd once had. 'Shall I tell you something, lass?' he said softly.

'Yes,' she murmured, thinking he was about to scold her.

'You're the best thing that's happened to me in many a long year. What's more, I want you to take this place by the scruff of the neck and make what you can of it. It'll be a wonderful surprise, and I don't get many of them these days. I don't even want to see the plans. Because, whatever you do, lass, I know it will be for the best.'

Too choked to utter even one word, she leaned over to kiss him on the cheek. That one gentle gesture told him what was in her heart.

'You're a good lass,' he muttered, then thrust his hands into his trouser pockets and stared at her for a while. The sun was in his face, highlighting his silver-grey whiskers. He had meant to shave that morning, just as he meant to shave every morning but somehow never had the time. He'd have a shave tonight, though, when it was cooler and the razor wouldn't cut his skin.

His wrinkled old face crumpled into a grin. 'Let the world and his friend come in, I won't care a bit.' His expression darkened. 'So long as one devious bugger keeps out!'

Lucy was in no doubt as to who this 'bugger' was. 'Have you heard from him, Ted?'

'Not a dicky bird.' He gritted his teeth. 'But that don't mean nothing.' Suddenly he was smiling again. 'Let the bugger come, though, eh?' he suggested with a grin. 'Let him come, and he'll get a bloody shock, so he will. When that son of mine finds out we've got one over on him, oh . . . I'd give a year's takings just to see the look on his face!'

The day sped by without Lucy's realising.

When she looked up and there was Debbie, all ready to go home, Lucy was astonished. 'Staying here all night, are you?' her friend asked. Her face was grimy and there were twigs poking from her hair. 'I've been stood here talking to you for ten minutes. Have you gone deaf or what?'

Closing the accounts book, Lucy leaned back in her chair. She stretched her aching back and groaned like an old, old woman. Giving Debbie a sideways glance, she laughed. 'Look at you! Anybody would think you'd been dragged through a hedge backwards.'

'I have!' Debbie explained. 'Ted's new dog ran off with my yard brush, and I had to chase the bugger through a blackthorn bush to get it back.'

'Where's Ted now?' She hadn't seen him since they'd had those few words earlier on. She'd thought then that he looked pale and tired. 'He's working too hard,' she said. 'Never knows when to stop.'

'That makes two of you.'

Seeming not to hear, Lucy asked again, 'Where is he now?'

'Gone for his tea. He said you were to go home and he'd lock up later.'

'What about the others?'

'Robert was just putting the tools away. I expect he's gone by now.'

'What do you think to him, Debs?' Lucy had a reason for asking.

'I don't think nothing. Why d'you ask?'

'No reason.' Lucy didn't know why, but she had a bad feeling where Robert Johnson was concerned. At only sixteen years old, he was big and strong, with a quick mind and a thorough way of going about his work that left no room for criticism. Because Ted had taken the lad on, Lucy had tried very hard to like him. But there was something about him that made her flesh creep.

However, Ted was right on one point. Robert was not afraid of hard work, and he never back-chatted. So far he hadn't given her an excuse to pay him off. But she would watch him. Like a hawk!

'What about Sophie?'

'She left about a quarter of an hour since.' Throwing herself into the nearest chair, Debbie sighed wearily. 'It's time we were off an' all,' she said. 'Do what you've got to do an' I'll sit here and rest me legs.'

While Lucy went round the grounds, checking that all was secure, Debbie used the office cloakroom. She splashed her face with cold water and renewed her make-up. 'Never know whether you're likely to meet anybody on the way home,' she said on Lucy's return.

'Such as who?' Locking the filing cabinet, Lucy dropped the key into her purse and ushered Debbie outside. 'The only man you're likely to see on the way home is the petrol attendant when I stop to fill up.'

While she talked she locked the office door and walked with Debbie to the car. 'And he's old as Methuselah, bald and toothless, with a dozen grand-children. Don't tell me you're that hard up?'

Debbie climbed into the passenger seat. 'This petrol attendant, is he rich?'

Starting the engine, Lucy eased the car towards the gates. 'He's as poor as a church mouse,' she answered.

'Hmm!' Debbie was disgusted. 'Don't want him then.'

'Happen he doesn't want *you*.'

'Then he doesn't know what he's missing.'

'What about Alfie?' As they came nearer to the gates, Lucy applied the brakes.

Preparing to get out and open the gates, Debbie seemed surprised by her question. 'What about him?'

'He asked you to marry him, didn't he?'

'So?'

'Will you?'

'Depends.'

'On what?'

'On whether I'm drunk at the time.' She winked as she got out of the car. 'Alfie looks better when I'm drunk.'

Laughing, Lucy told her to open the gate: 'Or we'll still be sitting here tomorrow when Ted comes to open them!'

She watched Debbie walk across the yard. 'At least you're smiling again,' she murmured. For some long time after Debbie claimed to have hurt herself falling down while drunk, she was unusually quiet. Time and again Lucy had been tempted to voice her suspicions with regard to Debbie's father, but she never did. It seemed too intrusive. As always, Lucy hoped the time was not too far away when Debbie would turn to her.

As she opened the gate, Debbie began whistling. In her trousers and checked shirt, and with her mouse-coloured hair tucked under a peaked cap, she looked like a little boy. 'Come on, you!' Pushing back the heavy gates, she secured one by dropping the bolt into the ground; the other she held back with her body. 'Get a move on, you bugger! I don't get paid for standing here all day.'

Suddenly she looked up. 'Christ Almighty!' she yelled, hopping round as though she'd been stung. 'LUCY! QUICK!' Letting the gate go with a clatter, she ran towards the car. 'You'll never believe it!' she cried, stumbling and tripping. 'Come and see!'

Lucy was just about to move the car forward when she was alarmed by Debbie's cries. Wrenching on the brake, she flung open the door and ran to meet her. 'Whatever's wrong?' For a minute she wondered if Debbie had hurt herself, but when she saw the excitement on her face, felt puzzled. She hoped it wasn't anything too expensive because last week she'd flung the gate back so hard it fell off its hinges. Lucy dreaded to think what had happened now.

Catching her in her arms, Debbie swung her round. 'Look at that!' she cried, pointing to the sign above the gate. 'I knew the bugger were up to summat. He were down here all bloody morning . . .

shooing me off whenever I came near. The crafty article!'

Intrigued and worried all at the same time, Lucy's curious grey eyes turned upwards, towards Old Ted's precious sign. And there it was, in big bold black lettering against a white background:

NOLAN AND BECKENDALE
NURSERIES OF FINE REPUTE

Lucy was speechless. Old Ted had not only put her name on his coveted sign, he had placed it before his own.

'Yer famous now, gal.' Debbie slapped her on the back. 'It'll soon cost a pound to talk to you.'

Lucy could only stand and stare. She had never seen her name displayed before. 'Nolan and Beckendale,' she murmured. It was hard to believe.

To those who didn't know how proud and passionate Ted was about his sign, it might have seemed a small, unimportant thing. But to Lucy it was a turning point in her life, a dream come true, and the emotions that swept through her on seeing what Ted had done were indescribable.

Debbie saw those feelings written all over Lucy's face. She saw the tears fall from her pretty grey eyes, and she too was immensely moved. 'You've done it, gal,' she whispered. 'And I couldn't be more proud.' Again, she patted Lucy on the back, then hugged her, then complained loudly when Lucy asked if she would wait while she went to see Old Ted.

She didn't have to go far because when she turned he was standing right behind her. 'I wanted to see your face,' he told her, beaming from ear to ear. 'I've been waiting all day for this minute.' He held out his arms. 'Come here, lass,' he said. 'Give an old man a cuddle for doing something right, eh?'

And, with a glad heart, that's just what she did.

Together they looked up at the sign, and for a long moment nothing was said until Debbie chimed in, 'Are we going home or what? I'm bloody starving!'

'Thank you, Ted.' Lucy held his hands for a while. 'I know how much that sign means to you. I don't deserve to have my name up there with yours, but I'll *earn* the right. Just give me time.'

'You get off and see that young man of yours away. And don't worry about it, because he'd have to be out of his mind not to come back for you as soon as he can.' He grimaced. 'Mind you, I'll not thank him when that day comes, because then we'll have to talk again, won't we, eh?'

As they drove away, Debbie glanced out of the back window. 'The silly old bugger's still standing there, staring at the sign like it's the most precious thing in the world.'

'It is to him,' Lucy answered. 'He's built up a business from nothing. When he took on the land it was dust and rubble. Nobody else wanted it. He's worked his fingers to the bone and brought it alive. He has every right to be proud of that sign. It's a symbol of what he's achieved.'

'There's no getting out of it now, gal.'

'What's that supposed to mean?'

'It means you've got to prove he was right to take you on. It means you owe him. And now you're fighting his fight . . . keeping the land out of his son's greedy mitts.'

For the first time, Lucy suffered a pang of doubt. 'What if I'm not up to it?' she wondered aloud. 'What if I haven't got the guts to see it all through? All the plans we've made . . . all the promises? What if it all comes to nothing, and I let Ted down? Oh, Debs, I'd never forgive myself if his son got the better of us after all.' Not when George Beckendale sounded such a nasty character.

Debbie had no such doubts. 'From what Old Ted says, his son's a right bastard. But I'll tell you what, gal. If I know you, and George Beckendale tries to get the better of you, he'll be the one sent packing with a bloody nose!'

They fell into a deep silence, with Debbie thinking of home and praying the evening would not be spoiled by arguments and fighting, and Lucy too feeling a little sad, thinking about Jack and how bleak it would be with him gone.

Her thoughts materialised as she spoke. 'Maybe I'm a fool not to be going with him.' The question had been paramount in her mind all day. It haunted her during the daylight hours and invaded her dreams at night. One half of her said: To Hell with it all, go with him. The other half was more cautious . . . loving him, wanting him, yet praying their love would be all the stronger for the parting.

Shaken out of her darker thoughts, Debbie turned to look at her. 'Go? With Jack, you mean?'

Lucy nodded, her grey eyes troubled. 'To tell you the truth, I don't know if I'm doing right or wrong.' Slowing the car at a junction, she gave Debbie a worried glance. 'If I don't go with him, I might lose him. Everything . . . the nurseries . . . my chance to fulfil a dream . . . most importantly my promise to Ted . . . none of it would be worth losing Jack for.' At that moment, when she feared it might be a real possibility, she was ready to follow him to the ends of the earth.

'If you want my opinion, for what it's worth, I think you're doing right in staying. Bugger me, gal! It's not like he'll be all that far away, is it? And you know what they say. "Absence makes the heart grow fonder".'

Lucy had told herself the very same thing, again and again. 'You could be right,' she conceded. 'Since Jack and I met, we've seen each other almost every day.'

'There you are then.' Though she would never admit it, Debbie envied Lucy's closeness to Jack. 'If he goes, and you stay, it'll give you both time to stand back and be sure you really are ready to settle down and have a dozen brats.'

Lucy knew beyond a doubt. 'I'm sure now,' she said, the soft glow in her eyes betraying her depth of feeling for the man she had promised to marry. 'Jack feels the same way, but we want to wait a year or so before we walk down the aisle. We're young enough, and have a lot to do before then. I'd like to make a success of the nurseries and make sure Ted's all right. And Jack wants his own hotel. That won't happen overnight.'

Debbie wasn't so sure. 'I wouldn't count on it. Your Jack is a very ambitious man.' Grabbing her handbag from the back seat, she took out a handkerchief and blew her nose. 'Got a bleedin' cold coming. Serves me right for not securing that hosepipe. When the bugger started flying about, I got soaked to the skin.' She patted Lucy on the shoulder. 'Stop worrying, gal,' she said. 'The Isle of Wight is only across a narrow stretch of water. You can be there in half an hour on the ferry. Like you say, neither of you is in a great hurry to get married, though I know that day will come soon enough, the way you feel about each other. Meanwhile, Ted's counting on you to help him out of a bad situation.'

'I know that.'

'You've got a once-in-a-lifetime opportunity to carry out all your ideas for the business. I expect you'll soon be earning more money than you know what to do with . . . Jack too. And he'll be working so hard, he'll have no time to spend it.' Taking her life in her hands, Debbie taunted, 'Unless he takes a fancy to one of them street-girls who'll have his pants off in a minute, and his wallet too.'

Lucy gave her a wry little smile. 'Thanks. That's cheered me up no end.' In her heart she believed Jack would never be unfaithful. She wondered then, if he was ever tempted to go with another woman, would she be able to forgive him? It was a sobering thought, and one that made her feel very lonely.

'Naw.' Debbie leaned back in her seat. 'Jack wouldn't want no other woman, not when he's got you to come home to. What! He worships the ground you walk on.' She glanced at Lucy, admiring the handsome profile with its small straight nose and wide, full lips, the smooth creamy skin with a natural healthy glow to the cheeks, and those sweeping dark lashes that fringed her beautiful dove-grey eyes. Her dark, shoulder-length hair was tied back, but numerous wayward curls had escaped from the thin blue ribbon to frame her pretty face like a picture.

The remarkable thing was that Lucy didn't even realise how lovely she was. By nature, too, she was good and caring, and Debbie counted herself very lucky to have her as a friend.

Negotiating the corner, Lucy commented wearily, 'I won't be sorry to get home and have a nice hot bath – I'm shattered. It's been a hard week for all of us, what with turning out the old greenhouse and preparing the ground for the new one. Thank God it's not due to be delivered until Monday week. Now that we've got all the urns of pansies done and ready for sale, there's bound to be a rush on.'

'Hmm. I thought Ted would never stop ... forty urns, twenty-two tubs, and three hundred trays of plants to be labelled! I carried every one of them trays from one end of the greenhouse to the other. It's a wonder I'm not bow-legged! And what about you? Not only did you have the office work to do, phones to answer and customers to see to, you spent most of the day running wheelbarrows from the greenhouse foundations to the mound of earth at the back of the sheds. Christ Almighty, gal, them bloody barrows must have weighed a ton. Not only that, but I saw you helping dig the foundations. It's no wonder yer bleedin' well shattered!'

'We all did our fair share.' Turning the corner into Debbie's road, Lucy gave her a little smile. 'Anyway, once I've had a long hot soak in the bath, I'll feel like a new woman.'

'Seeing Jack tonight, are yer?'

The thought of him made Lucy smile. 'Hell or high water wouldn't keep us apart,' she murmured. 'It'll be our last night here together before he goes.'

'Going out on the town, are you?'

Lucy shook her head. 'Not tonight. Mam's a bit upset about him going away, so she's making a special dinner for us.'

'Bleedin' Hell. It's like the last supper, eh?'

Lucy laughed. 'I'll tell her what you said.'

'She wouldn't be offended if you did. Your mam's one of the best. Like you.'

'You won't say that when I stop you half a day's pay for that window you broke in the greenhouse.'

Debbie's face fell a mile. 'You wouldn't!'

'No, 'course I wouldn't,' Lucy assured her. 'It was as much my fault as yours. I shouldn't have left the ladder where it could be knocked over.'

'Thanks for not telling Ted. I'm in enough trouble with him as it is.'

Lucy's thoughts turned back to Jack, and their imminent parting. 'I'll miss him, Debs.'

'Who, Ted?'

'No. *Jack!*'

'I expect you will, gal. But it won't be for too long, you'll see. Sooner or later he'll get his own hotel, then the two of you will be swanning off and I'll be the one left behind.' She hated the idea.

Lucy hated it too. 'Do you really think I'd leave you behind?'

'Take me with you, gal, and I'll do anything. I'll wash dishes and sweep the floors . . . and . . .'

'You're capable of better than that.' Lucy knew

how lonely Debbie felt, and how desperately wrong
her home-life was.

'You mean, you'd trust me with a responsible job?'
She was beginning to get excited now.

'Why not? You're doing a responsible job now, aren't
you?'

'I suppose so, yes.'

'And the customers like you, don't they?'

'So the buggers should! I have to walk round the
greenhouses with them, answer all their silly questions, and then the cheeky sods want me to carry
the stuff to their cars!'

'Get Robert to do it.'

No answer.

'Debbie?' Lucy sensed something was not right.

'What?'

'I said . . . why don't you get Robert to carry the
purchases to the customers' cars?'

Again, no answer.

Lucy slowed the car and looked at her. 'Have you
asked him and he's refused?' If so, this was her
opportunity to get rid of him.

'I don't want him to do it. I'd rather do it myself.'

'What's wrong, Debs?'

A pause, then, 'I just don't want to ask him, that's
all. He's got his own work to do.'

'You don't like him either, do you?'

'That's got nothing to do with it.'

'If he's done anything to upset you, or anyone else,
I want to know.'

'When he upsets me, I'll tell you. All right?'

'All right.' But she wasn't satisfied. Debbie's mood
had changed the minute she mentioned Robert.

It was obvious they'd had a run-in of sorts.

A short silence, then, 'I only wish I could get a man to look at me the way Jack looks at you.' Anticipating Lucy's next words, Debbie put in, 'Don't even say it!'

Lucy had a soft spot for poor Alfie. Like a puppy, he followed Debbie round, hoping for a nod and a kind word. 'I was only going to say that Alfie feels the same way about you.'

'Yes, well.' Plucking at a frayed thread on the cuff of her shirt-sleeve, Debbie answered mournfully, 'If Alfie was only half the bloke your Jack is, I might give him a second glance. As it is, he gets right up my bleedin' nose. You'd think he'd want to ravage me, but no, it's always me who has to ravage him, the daft sod!'

Truthfully, Debbie was grateful for the night he'd taken her home drunk, and even more grateful that he hadn't taken advantage of her. But, whatever he did, Alfie would always be inadequate in Debbie's eyes. 'He's got no style, d'you see?' she moaned. 'And no guts. I mean, look at your Jack . . . he's off to make his fortune. It won't be long before he'll be back to sweep you off your feet. You'll be going down the aisle in a beautiful wedding dress, then he'll fly you off to some exotic place for a wonderful honeymoon. He's working his balls off so he can buy you a big house with a swimming pool, and a butler to answer the door.'

'I'll answer my own door, thank you.' And it would be an average sort of door, with pretty curtains at the windows beside it and the noise of children's laughter coming from the garden.

Sighing, Debbie said, 'I'll be stuck with Alfie in a two-up-two-down, with four snotty-nosed kids running round me arse. I'll have to make me own wedding dress, and think meself lucky if we get to Blackpool for a honeymoon.'

'Oh, I see.' Lucy managed to keep a straight face. 'So you do mean to marry him after all?'

'Do I Hell as like!' She stared at Lucy in horror. 'I'd rather jump off Blackpool Tower than marry Alfie Burrows.'

'You could do worse.'

'Hmm! If I can't do better than Alfie, I'll not get married at all.'

'That's not fair.'

'Why not?' Debbie was puzzled.

'Because if you don't get married, I'll never get to be a bridesmaid.'

'Shame.'

They burst out laughing.

'All right then,' Debbie promised, 'I'll get married. But not to Alfie, I'm not that desperate.'

Slowing the car to a halt outside Debbie's house, Lucy apologised. 'I do know how lucky I am,' she said, 'and I should be counting my blessings instead of fretting.' She would miss Jack, she couldn't deny that. But they would see each other often, and at the end of the day, they would still have each other.

After getting out of the car, Debbie poked her head in again. 'I don't suppose you'd like to swap Jack for Alfie, would you?'

'No.'

'Didn't think you would.' One last question. 'What time are you leaving for Lymington?'

'About five in the morning.'

Debbie gasped. 'Five? Jeez! That's the middle of the bleedin' night.'

Smiling, Lucy explained, 'We daren't leave any later than five o'clock or we'll miss the morning ferry.'

Winking cheekily, Debbie teased, 'Staying overnight in a hotel at the seaside, eh? Naughty, naughty! Mind you don't get pregnant, gal, or you might have to get married a bit quicker than you think.'

Lucy was patient as ever. 'Cheerio, Debs. And give Alfie a ring. I'm sure he'd love to go dancing tonight.'

'Well, he can go dancing with somebody else. I've got other things to do.' In fact, after what had happened last time she went out, Debbie was planning on spending a weekend indoors.

At least then she wouldn't be beaten black and blue when she got home.

Sensing the change of mood, Lucy's old suspicions rose to the surface. 'What's wrong, Debs?'

'Nothing.'

The half-smile didn't fool Lucy. 'We've been friends a long time,' she said quietly. 'If there is ever anything wrong, you can talk to me, you know that, don't you?'

This time Debbie's smile was quick and bright. 'There's nothing wrong, I tell you!' But behind that smile lay a touch of sadness that couldn't be disguised. 'Anyway, if there was it would be your fault, you bugger!'

'Oh, and how would that be?' Lucy's smile too was forced. She realised she had dug a little too deeply.

'You've got me thinking about Alfie,' Debbie answered, 'and now I'm all miserable.' Looking towards the house, she licked her lips. 'Me stomach thinks me throat's cut. I hope Mam's got the tea ready.'

Lucy pushed the gear stick into first. 'I'll be off then. Mind how you go now, and try not to drive poor Ted out of his mind while I'm away.'

'As if.' Rolling her eyes innocently, Debbie slammed shut the door, yelling through the window, 'Cheerio then, gal. Have a smashing time on the Isle of Wight, and don't be late for work on Monday morning, you bugger!'

'And don't you wreck the place before I get back, you bugger!' Lucy retaliated.

She was still smiling as she drove away, then laughed out loud when she saw Debbie making rude gestures through the back window. 'Debbie Lately, you'll never change,' she murmured, shaking her head. 'And thank God for that.'

There was no denying there were times when Debbie could be a real trial, but Lucy wouldn't change her for the world.

'You look lovely, lass.' Mike Nolan beamed with pride as he gazed at his daughter.

'Your dad's right,' Sally commented, her gaze travelling over Lucy's slim figure. 'You've always looked lovely in cornflower blue, and that dress shows you off a treat.' Fitted at the waist and flared from the thighs, the swirling hem fell just below her calves. The white high-heeled shoes with the crossover bar showed Lucy's shapely ankles to perfection, and tonight, because the evening was sultry, she had decided to leave off her tights. Her legs were lightly tanned, as were her arms and face. Round her neck she wore the small gold cross and chain which her parents had bought her for her last birthday. On her finger she displayed the beautiful opal ring which Jack gave her just two weeks after they met.

'Thank you, you two.' Lucy kissed her parents in turn. 'And I'm proud of you both.' Mike looked smart in white shirt and grey trousers, and Sally seemed years younger than her age in a straight white skirt and her favourite pink short-sleeved blouse.

'Jack will be here any minute.' Sally glanced at the mantelpiece clock. 'I think we'd better take the salads out of the fridge.'

As she turned, Lucy offered to help. 'I'll see to the meats,' she said, following her mother to the kitchen. 'And what about the trifle? When I checked it earlier it still wasn't set.'

'It'll be set now,' Sally told her. 'I turned the fridge up to number four.'

They laughed heartily when Mike called out, 'While you're doing that, I might help myself to a small beer.'

'He's probably searching for the biggest glass he can find,' Sally chuckled when they closed the kitchen door behind them. 'But he deserves a pint, bless him. It's been hot and tiring in the shop today. The customers never seemed to stop pouring through the door. Nobody's cooking meals . . . they're all living on salads.'

'I'm not surprised.' Crossing to the fridge, Lucy checked the trifle. 'It's too hot to eat cooked meals,' she said, dipping the tip of her finger in and making sure it was ready.

'Hey!' Sally tapped her on the knuckles with the wooden spoon. 'Hands off, my girl. You'll get your fair share when we all sit down at the table.'

'Sorry, Mam, but it's delicious. Nobody makes a sherry trifle like you do.'

'That's no excuse.'

Sally was about to put on her pinafore before arranging the salads in various bowls. She paused to study her daughter. 'You've done your hair differently.'

'I didn't think you'd noticed.'

Sally smiled affectionately. 'Of course I noticed,' she declared indignantly. 'I wouldn't be a woman if I hadn't. But there's no point mentioning it in front of your father. Men can't be bothered with that sort of thing.'

'As it's a special occasion, I thought I'd try a new style,' Lucy explained. 'What do you think?' Her mam's opinion was always important to her.

'Hmm.' Sally pursed her lips and cocked her head to one side. Lucy's dark brown hair was brushed away from her face; the thick fringe was full and casual, with little wisps of hair deliberately teased out around the temples. 'Turn round, lass.'

Lucy turned round then back again. 'Well?'

Sally's pretty blue eyes grew moist. 'Aw, lass. I'm that proud of you. Your hair looks lovely. *You* look lovely.' Suddenly she was crying into her pinafore. 'I've never told you before, but you're the best daughter a woman could ever have.'

'Hey, now!' Shocked, Lucy hurried across the room. Gathering the little woman in her arms, she asked tenderly, 'What's all this about, eh?' In all her life, she had never seen her mother cry.

'Oh, I'm just being silly.'

'You're never silly, Mam.' In fact, Sally could always be counted on in any crisis.

Content to remain in Lucy's arms for the while, she wiped her eyes. 'It's just that, well ... you and Jack and everything. I expect I've only just realised that you're a woman. A mother doesn't like to admit that to herself, you know, and it comes as a shock, I can tell you.'

Lucy tried hard not to sound amused. 'Mother, I'm twenty-two!'

'That's what I mean, and soon I expect you'll be leaving me and your dad ... getting married and having children of your own.' She laughed softly. 'I'll be a grandmother. Think of that.'

Relieved, Lucy feigned disapproval. 'Oh, I see. So you're not worried about me leaving? You're only worried about being a grandmother ... think it might cramp your style, is that it?'

That did the trick. 'Cheeky devil!' Drawing away, Sally wiped her eyes again. 'I'll have you know I'll make the best grandma in Lancashire!'

'I bet they all say that.' Lucy looked at her mam, at that dear, familiar little figure and those pretty blue eyes, and her heart ached. She recalled what her mother had said just now, about her being the best daughter a mother could ever have. 'You and Dad have been wonderful parents to me,' she said, 'and even if I left to get married, I'd never be far away. Miles couldn't part us, you know that.'

'I know, lass.'

'I do love you, Mam.'

Beneath her daughter's soft gaze, Sally couldn't hold back the tears. Lucy was a woman now, and she had no right to make her feel guilty for that. 'I love you too, sweetheart,' she said.

Jack arrived at half-past eight as arranged, looking handsome and relaxed in a pastel shirt and beige trousers. He kissed Lucy in a way that only a man in love can kiss. 'Like your hair,' he said, admiring her from top to toe, and Lucy was so delighted she would have walked over hot coals for him.

'Something looks good,' he remarked as she led him into the front room. 'Hope your mother hasn't gone to too much trouble on my behalf?'

'She's pushed the boat out,' Lucy laughed. 'So God help you if you haven't worked up a big appetite.'

The meal was wonderful: a variety of mixed salads, all beautifully presented; a selection of cold vegetables; small new potatoes still in their jackets; soft juicy peas; succulent chicken cooked to perfection, ham off the bone, and half a salmon bought from the fishmonger that very morning.

'It's a spread fit for a king!' Jack exclaimed, tucking in and enjoying himself.

'Fit for my daughter and her intended,' Mike announced, with a puffed chest and a smile that would melt an ice-cap.

They talked at great length about this and that, mainly the forthcoming trip to the Isle of Wight, and the new venture that Jack was undertaking. 'It could well lead to my own hotel,' he told them. 'I mean to keep my eyes and ears open. The minute any opportunity comes up, I'm after it.'

They talked about Lucy's plans for the nurseries, and everyone said how pleased they were that Ted had entrusted such a task to her. They denounced his estranged son George, and decided that if he ever dared show his face, he should be sent well and truly packing.

At twenty-five minutes to eleven, Mike opened the bottle of champagne he had been keeping for such an occasion. They all toasted Jack and Lucy, and Ted too. And when Mike sat down again, he said, to Lucy's surprise, 'This afternoon I phoned to ask Old Ted if he'd join us tonight, but he said he wasn't happy eating in front of other people, even those he knew and liked.'

'Some older folk are like that,' Sally interrupted. 'I think it's all to do with being made to sit at table when they were little, and being told they should be seen and not heard.'

Mike agreed. 'Anyway . . .' he was addressing Lucy now . . . 'me and your mam are going to see him tomorrow night, and we're taking another bottle of champagne with us.'

Lucy thought that was marvellous, and so did Jack. 'He's a fine man,' he said, raising his glass to Old Ted.

And that seemed as good a note as any on which to end the evening.

At five o'clock on Saturday morning, Jack arrived at the house in a taxi.

Dressed in beige trousers and a long-line black overshirt for the early-morning trip in the ferry, Lucy was watching from the window. Her hair was tucked beneath a patterned scarf which was tied at the back in a gypsy knot.

While Jack was getting out of the taxi, she ran like an excited child to meet him. 'Morning, sweetheart,' he laughed as he caught her in his arms. 'You look bright as a button.'

'You don't,' she said, drawing back to regard him more closely. His eyes looked tired, and beneath them were faint shadows. 'What's wrong, Jack?'

Clasping her round the waist, he took her back towards the shop. 'What could be wrong?' he said, kissing her on the mouth when she looked up. 'I'm off to build an empire, aren't I?'

'But?' She drew him to a halt.

'All right.' With arms still round her waist, he looked down at her with serious dark eyes. 'I'm disappointed that this time tomorrow I'll be on the Isle of Wight and you'll be on the mainland, that's all. Other than that, I'm raring to go.'

In actual fact he felt like the tail end of an ox's tongue, having spent an almost sleepless night, turning everything over in his mind: the daunting, almost impossible, task he had set himself in resurrecting a dilapidated building which had long ceased to be a business, and which he had vowed to transform into a thriving hotel of enviable reputation.

Far more important, and closer to his heart, was the fact that soon he and Lucy would be parting. Jack was not a man to be afraid of anything, but he was afraid now. Afraid that somehow, along the way, he might lose her . . . that she might find someone else, or maybe would grow resentful that he had accepted a challenge that took him from her. Losing Lucy was not a price he was prepared to pay.

Turning to her now, he asked softly, 'Would you rather I stayed?'

For a moment she wasn't certain she'd heard right. 'Stayed?' she repeated. 'You mean, stayed on the mainland ... not take up the new job?'

'That's exactly what I mean.'

Lucy was tempted to say yes, she wanted him to stay. She could imagine herself saying it. Oh, yes! Please stay, Jack. I don't want you to leave me, not for a minute or an hour ... it may only be a narrow stretch of water between us, but it might as well be an ocean. She wanted to say the words. Wanted to keep him with her.

Wisely she closed her mouth and forced herself to think it through.

If she asked him to, he would stay, and then he would come to regret it. Jack was a pioneer; the kind of man who constantly pushed himself to the limit. He needed challenges. He had to have a mountain to climb, a river to forge, a challenge that would satisfy his drive and draw every ounce of energy from him. He had a vision. He saw a failure and wanted to make it a success. He reached one peak and searched for another. He saw his dream and nothing on this earth would stop him striving towards it.

Nothing, that is, except the woman he loved. Lucy knew that if she pleaded hard enough, he would stay. But, in the end, his spirit would die and she would be responsible.

No, his staying could not even be considered. Jack could not stop now, any more than she could go back on her word to Old Ted. 'I don't want you to stay,' she lied. 'You have a job to do, and so have I. It won't be long before we're together. We can wait for that,' she said tenderly. 'We have to, don't we?' He would never know how much it cost her to say that, but she kept smiling, and he loved her all the more.

'You're some woman, Lucy Nolan,' he whispered, brushing her neck with his lips.

'And you're some man.' For a while she was lost in his embrace. When the breeze swirled round them and made her shiver, he suggested they should go into the house.

'Good thinking,' she said, her face wreathed in a smile that didn't quite reach her heart. 'We'd better make tracks. Or I might change my mind and ask you to stay after all.'

Ten minutes later, they were ready to leave. Lymington was a long drive and they had a ferry to catch.

'Drive carefully, you two.' Mike and Sally were at the door to see them off.

Lucy kissed them both. 'You should have stayed another hour in bed,' she chided. 'It's not as though we're going to the other side of the world.' She had to smile to herself because they were the very words Debbie had used to pacify *her*. 'Besides, I'll be back tomorrow night.'

'I couldn't sleep,' Sally confessed. She had been lying awake for some time. 'And, anyway, it's only proper that your dad and me should see our future son-in-law safely away.'

Putting his arm round her, Mike hugged his wife close. 'And once your mam's awake, there's no hope of me sleeping,' he chuckled. 'She's like a cat on hot bricks . . . fidgeting and fussing . . . turning one way then the other.' He shivered as though to make a point. 'One minute I've got the bedclothes over me, and the next I'm lying there, exposed in my underpants, and trembling like a jelly.'

Digging him in the ribs, Sally joked, 'Perhaps you'd rather have some other woman in your bed?'

Drawing her closer, he murmured, 'Never!'

'Stop complaining then.' Bestowing a wink on him, she coaxed, 'Treat me nicely and I might even make you a fresh cup of tea and a slice of toast.'

A naughty expression crossed his homely face. 'What d'you mean . . . treat you nicely?'

Her pretty blue eyes sparkled with fun. 'Mike Nolan! Behave yourself,' she chastised. 'We're in company.' She actually blushed when Jack smiled at her. 'What I meant was . . . fetch my slippers, will you, love? My feet are freezing.' When he hesitated, staring down at her feet, unaware that she'd come out without wearing slippers, she twiddled her toes and gave him a little shove. 'Go on then! Before my feet turn blue and drop off.'

While Mike went to fetch her slippers, Sally had more motherly instructions for Lucy. 'Give me a ring when you get there, so I know you've got across on the ferry all right. And be careful when you're driving home tomorrow,' she warned. 'There are some weird characters roaming the roads these days.'

'Stop worrying, Mam.' Lucy was used to her mother's fretting. 'I'll be home tomorrow, with lots to tell you.'

'All right. And there's nothing you've forgotten, is there? Have you got enough money? Did you pack your nightdress? Toothbrush?'

Mike's voice sailed over her shoulder. 'Oh, and don't forget your slippers,' he laughed, handing a pair of fluffy red things to his wife.

Watching her mother slip the furry red slippers over her feet, Lucy suddenly remembered. 'Debbie rang late last night . . .'

Sally tutted. 'I wondered who it was at that time of night.' A look of concern appeared on her face. 'She's not in trouble, is she?'

Lucy shook her head. 'No, she's not in trouble.' Funny how everyone automatically assumed Debbie was in trouble. 'She'll be round for my blue shoes some time today. Apparently she's decided to go dancing after all.'

Mike told her not to worry about anything. 'Your mam will see to Debbie,' he promised. 'Just enjoy your time with Jack, and we'll see you tomorrow night.'

Jack shook hands with him. 'I'll take care of her,' he promised.

Placing a fatherly hand on Jack's shoulder, Mike was struck by the strength of his handshake. He felt immensely proud of that fine young man, and deeply moved by the quiet sincerity in those dark green eyes. 'I know you'll take care of her, son,' he answered. 'And I know she'll take care of you. You and Lucy, well . . .' For one minute he faltered, but then continued, 'You're our future too, mine and Sally's, and we're proud to have you in this family.'

'That means a lot to me,' Jack declared. Taking Sally into his arms, he embraced her. 'Don't worry,' he whispered, 'Lucy will be safe enough with me.'

Reassured, she led the way to the car, and they

all chatted as they walked: Sally and Jack in front and Mike behind with his beloved daughter.

At the car, Lucy gave her parents another hug. 'Now go on inside,' she urged. The early-morning breeze was spitefully keen, and they were wearing only dressing-gowns over their nightclothes. 'You'll catch your death out here.'

In a minute she and Jack were seated in the car, Jack in the driving seat and Lucy happy to sit alongside. ''Bye, then,' she called as they drove away. 'I'll call you when we get there.'

Sally and Mike waved them out of sight. 'I'm so lucky,' Lucy remarked as she settled back in her seat. 'I've got wonderful parents, a marvellous job that I love, the chance to help Ted and show what I'm capable of at the same time.' Feeling emotional now, she took hold of Jack's hand. 'And I've got you, Jack Hanson.'

A shiver ran through her, making her cry out.

He turned to glance at her. 'If you're cold, there's a sweater on the back seat.'

'It's okay.' She forced a smile. 'It wasn't the cold that made me shiver. It was fright.'

He laughed. 'That's your mam putting the frighteners on. She only means for you to be careful when you're on your own, and quite right too. But *I've* got you now, sweetheart,' he murmured. 'So have no fear. If anyone tries to hurt you, they'll have to get through me first.'

Lucy still felt unsettled. 'I didn't mean that kind of fear.'

He gave her a sideways glance. 'What *did* you mean then?'

'I'm not really sure. It's just that I have so much to be thankful for, I just wonder if there might come a day when somebody up there . . .' She raised her eyes to the morning skies; the clouds were gathering and there was a certain sinister beauty all around them. 'I mean, do you think somebody up there might decide I've had more than my fair share and take it all away?'

'Whatever makes you think that?' he asked, giving her a reassuring squeeze of the hand. 'That "somebody up there" chose to give you good parents, and as for what you've achieved at work, that's down to you and your dedication. None of it was handed to you on a plate. Besides, you give back as much as you get. You've been a good daughter. You're the best friend Debbie could ever have, and so far as I'm concerned, it's *me* who's fortunate in having you. So let's hear no more of having it all snatched away.' Risking a quick glance, he gave her a warm smile. 'Love you,' he whispered.

Leaning over, she nestled against his shoulder for a minute, quietly contemplating.

His words made her think. He was right. She had worked hard to get where she was. Debbie gave her a lot to worry about though most of it was not her fault because, however much she might deny it, Lucy still believed she was being beaten by her father. That in turn created other problems . . . like the drinking, and the accidents and the fact that she was becoming unable to form a steady relationship with any man, or more particularly with Alfie. He was the best thing that could happen to Debbie, and in a strange way she knew that, but for some reason she could not let him into her life in a serious way. It was a great source of concern to Lucy, and before too long she would have to do something about it, though what exactly she wasn't certain. This was a delicate issue, and by rights it was for Debbie to take the first step by talking about it to someone she could trust. Lucy hoped that would be her.

'Hungry?' Jack's voice woke Lucy from an uneasy snooze.

Sitting up, she stretched her limbs and groaned with pleasure. 'Starving,' she told him. 'What about you?'

'The same. I've made good time, so we can stop here if you like. Or we can have breakfast on the ferry. What do you think?'

'I think it would be romantic to have breakfast on the ferry.' Never having been on a ferry, she wanted to make the most of it.

He laughed. 'I think you've been looking at the adverts for cruising on the super liners . . . where all the pretty young women stand by the rail with the wind blowing in their hair, tall handsome waiters vie for their attention, and rich women with little yapping dogs stroll lazily up and down the decks.'

While he talked, he flicked on the indicator and slowed the car. 'Okay, breakfast on the ferry then,' he agreed. 'But I'm afraid you'll have to settle for me as a waiter, and there'll be a queue a mile long. But I can join it while you stand out on the deck and scour the horizon. You can pretend you're en route to the Caribbean. How does that sound?'

'Sounds all right to me.' Lucy settled down into

the seat and closed her eyes, all manner of thoughts assailing her.

She thought about her parents, her friend Debbie, and her darling Jack. She thought about everything that was good in her life, and the wonderful things that were already promised.

And suddenly, for no reason that she could fathom, she was desperately afraid.

When they got to the ferry terminal there was already a line of cars waiting to board. 'We'll be loading in about ten minutes,' an official told them. 'If you go to the shop or restaurant, make sure you're back in plenty of time.'

Lucy took the opportunity to stretch her legs. In the little shop she bought a magazine and a packet of mints. Afterwards she and Jack spent a few minutes watching the small boats coming in and out of the harbour. 'It's a different world,' she remarked, cuddling up to him and loving every precious minute.

In no time at all they were driving on to the ferry. The officer flagged them towards the bow, where they parked the car and afterwards made their way upstairs to the refreshment deck. 'See what I mean?' Jack smiled, pointing to the queue that was already forming at the buffet.

Lucy offered to get their breakfast but Jack would hear none of it. 'I'll do that,' he said. 'You go and have a look round.'

'Are you sure you don't mind?'

Feigning impatience, he ordered, 'Do as you're told, woman!'

'Thanks, Jack.' She was itching to look round. 'What do they do for breakfast?'

'Whatever takes your fancy.'

She tried to see to the head of the queue, but couldn't. Finally she gave up, asking him, 'What are you having?'

They shuffled forward, another long queue forming behind them. 'I'm having the works,' he said. 'Eggs, bacon, tomatoes and sausages. Oh, and I might have toast and marmalade to top it off.'

'Pig.'

He laughed. 'A *hungry* pig.' Leaning down, he nibbled her ear. 'If I could have you right now, I wouldn't need breakfast,' he whispered.

A hearty chuckle made them look round. The woman was in her late forties, big and brassy, with a wide, delightfully toothless smile. 'You're a right pair o' lovebirds, an' no mistake. Off for a dirty weekend, is it?' she giggled. Looking at Lucy, she imparted in a low intimate voice, 'Still, it don't hurt now and then, to leave the old man at home and sample the goodies, if you know what I mean?' Giving a suggestive wink, she giggled. 'An' I should know 'cause I've done it often enough in me time.'

Smiling to himself Jack turned away.

Lucy didn't quite know what to say, but then the woman pushed her way forward. 'You carry on canoodling,' she declared, forcing them aside, 'I just want me breakfast.' With her elbows out and head forward, she thrust ahead, totally oblivious of the moans and protests of other passengers.

In a minute or so, she returned with a plate of food that would satisfy a navvy. 'This'll keep the fire burning,' she said, cocking a triumphant glance at Lucy as she went.

Lucy was tickled pink. 'I never knew travelling on a ferry could be such an experience,' she laughed as the queue shuffled forward again.

Jack looked down on her glowing face. 'Now you've seen that woman's breakfast, I expect you want the same?' he said with a straight face.

'You dare!' Digging him in the ribs, she chided, 'You can have the works if you want.' Not having been on a ferry before, she wasn't sure how her stomach would take it, and there was always the possibility that they could have a rough crossing. 'I'm playing safe,' she decided. 'Eggs on toast, if you please.'

While Jack got the breakfast, Lucy explored the vessel. Like a child in wonderland, she roamed around, in and out of the bar, the lounge, and every nook and cranny which wasn't 'Private'. She smiled and chatted and had a thoroughly lovely time.

Finally she came to some children playing the game machines. 'Which way to the upper deck?' she asked a little fellow.

'Up them steps there,' he told her in a surly manner. 'Don't you know nuffink?'

Out on the deck the August sunshine bathed her face; the wind was mischievous now, milder than before as it whistled in and out of the railings, while below the water spun like playful dolphins in the wake of the craft's passage.

Leaning over the rail, Lucy cast her eyes to the shore. Minute by minute the outline grew fainter and fainter, swallowed up by the morning mist. For one fleeting moment she felt lost and lonely, imagining how it must have been for loved ones parted for months or years, sometimes for ever.

Again, it overwhelmed her, the strangest premonition, that something awful was waiting to happen . . .

'Get yourself together, Lucy Nolan,' she muttered, bracing herself against the breeze. '*Nothing* awful is going to happen.' She tried to convince herself, but the feeling persisted. That deep-down anxious feeling that somebody was about to decide she had been given someone else's share of good fortune, and now they wanted it back.

Seeking reassurance, she ran down to the refreshment deck where Jack was setting the food on the table. 'Thought I'd have to come and find you.' Taking her breakfast off the tray, he put it before her then poured her a cup of tea, noticing how quiet she seemed. 'Everything all right, sweetheart?'

'So long as I'm with you, everything's just wonderful,' she murmured. So long as she had Jack, life could do its worst, and she would cope.

There was a moment then, as he looked at her with such love in his wonderful green eyes, when it seemed as though they were the only two people on board.

At that very minute the toothless woman swept by with her empty plate and a naughty wink just for them, and the moment was gone. They burst out laughing. 'Best tuck in or it will get cold,' Jack urged, pointing to her breakfast. 'Before you know it, we'll be there.'

Lucy was pleasantly surprised. Not only was her breakfast delicious, but the crossing was as smooth as silk. When they were called to 'Return to your vehicles', she felt refreshed and exhilarated. 'How far is it to Ryde?' she asked as they drove off the ferry.

'Nowhere's very far on this island,' he said, checking the traffic before turning off. 'Twenty minutes . . . half an hour at the most.'

It took them a while longer because Lucy kept asking him to stop the car so she could see the magnificent views across the island. 'I never realised it was so beautiful,' she breathed, her arms round his waist and her face turned towards a sparkling sea.

There was something timeless about the island: sweeping valleys and busy harbours filled with boats of every description; the picturesque cottages with their thatched roofs and colourful gardens, and the friendly people, passing the time of day as they went by. Even the sun seemed brighter.

Ryde itself was delightful. There was a long, sunlit promenade and quaint little cafés where the tables spilled on to the pavement. And there, right in the heart of all the bustle, was the Maybourne Hotel where they were to stay.

It took only minutes to park the car, a few more to unload and climb the steps to the front desk, and there was the proprietor, a smiling little figure in a pretty flowered dress, waiting with pen in hand ready to sign them in. 'Mr and Mrs Hanson,' she said, searching for their names in the ledger. 'Ah, yes!' With a swift tick of her pen she was ready to take them up. 'Wait a minute, though,' she said, turning to ferret in the pigeon holes. 'There's a package for you, Mr Hanson.'

There was a letter from Larry Moore, Jack's new employer, along with a bunch of keys. 'He was supposed to meet me on site,' he reminded Lucy, 'but he's been called abroad. I'm to see his accountant first thing Monday morning. Everything is to be done through him until Larry returns.'

'Is that a problem?' Lucy asked.

'Nope.' Jack was as confident as ever. 'Larry Moore or his accountant, it makes no difference. I'm contracted to do a job, and that's what I'll do.'

'You've got a lovely room.' The proprietor led them up another flight of stairs. 'It's got the best view in the place.'

And so it had.

From the window, Lucy could see right across to the harbour. 'All the same, you're a devil, Jack Hanson,' she reprimanded when the woman had gone. 'I'm a decent woman with my reputation to think of. How dare you book us into the same room?' Her voice was stern, but her grey eyes twinkled.

He held up his hands. 'All right, I realise I shouldn't have booked us in as man and wife without asking you first.' His handsome face flushed with guilt. 'I assumed that was what you wanted too, but I had no right.' When she didn't answer but continued to stare at him accusingly, he sighed and nodded. 'I'm sorry, sweetheart, I shouldn't have taken you for granted like that.' He reached for the bedside telephone. 'I'll ask her to book you into another room.'

'There you go again,' she murmured. 'Doing things without asking me first.'

Putting down the receiver, he crossed the room to her. 'I'm forgiven then?'

Enfolded in his strong arms, she would have forgiven him anything. But this time there was nothing to forgive. 'Of course I wanted to be with you,' she confessed. 'I wouldn't have liked being in a room by myself with you down the corridor. I would only have crept in with you when everyone else was asleep.'

'You would, eh?'

'You know I would. You and I belong together,' she murmured. 'Tonight, and every night. And, as you say, if all goes well, it shouldn't be too long before we really are man and wife.'

He stroked her hair, losing himself in the soft, warm feel of her face against his. 'What will I do without you?' he whispered.

'You won't be without me,' she replied softly, her mouth against his, and the tears never far away. 'Even after I leave tomorrow, I'll still be here with you . . . every minute of every day and night, until we're together again.'

With no words left to say, they gazed at each other, their thoughts and hearts as one.

Gently he took her by the hand and led her to the bed. Here he caressed her until her every sense ached for him. One by one he took off her clothes, then his own, and all the while he was touching her. His hands stroked her skin, following her every curve and lingering on her breasts. His tongue touched hers, his lips gently pressing and nibbling until she felt herself afire.

'You're bad, Jack Hanson,' she whispered. Her fingers reached down, following the strong manly curves of his body. Tender, trembling fingers excitedly exploring. Full, soft lips eager to be kissed. Now he was murmuring in her ear, his soft persuasive voice reaching deep inside, exciting her, thrilling her. Stirring bitter-sweet emotions. 'Love me,' she pleaded softly. 'Love me.'

It was midday when they left the room. Showered and fresh, they had put away their clothes and were feeling peckish. 'What do you want to do first?' Jack asked as they came out of the hotel. 'I've got the keys so we could see the old place I'll be renovating, or find a pleasant little café to eat.'

So far as Lucy was concerned there was no question. 'I'd like to see where you'll be working,' she told him. 'I need to know it's worth the sacrifice.'

Hidden from view by overgrown shrubberies and tall unkempt trees, the old hotel was the very last building along the promenade. It was a big, sad old place, with roof tiles missing and windows hanging off their hinges; the path was littered with weeds and broken glass, and the vast expanse of land all around was pathetically neglected.

'It'll take a lot of hard work,' Jack said as he walked through the filthy rooms, 'but I never thought it would be easy.'

Lucy looked up at him, at the squareness of his jaw and the light in his eyes, and knew he would make a success of it. 'You wouldn't have taken it on if it was going to be easy,' she said proudly.

Laughing, he swept her into his arms, swinging her round and making her squeal with delight. 'Sometimes I think you know me better than I know myself,' he cried. 'Come on, I want to show you something.'

Rushing her across the hall to the wide, formerly grand stairway, he held her hand while going up the steps two at a time. 'It's all right,' he assured her. 'The stairs are safe. I've had them checked out. No worm. No rot. They're as good as the day they were built.' He sniffed the air. 'But there is a suspicion of damp. That will have to be treated straight away.'

Running to keep up, Lucy was curious. 'How old is the house?'

'At least sixty years.'

Upstairs he ran her down the long dusty landing and into the west wing. Bursting into one of the bedrooms, he clasped his arm round her waist and swung her towards the window. 'Look at that, sweetheart,' he said, breathless and excited. 'Have you ever seen anything so beautiful?'

The view was stunning. From where they stood the land fell away across the rocky beach to the Solent. With the sunshine shimmering on the water, it looked like a cloak of silk, rippling in the breeze. 'Oh, Jack, it's wonderful!' Raising her eyes, Lucy could make out the mainland. For a long moment she was mesmerised. 'I'm glad you're doing this,' she whispered. 'There's something magical here.' Waving her arms, she encompassed the room. 'It's as though this old lady wants to live again . . . to be part of all this beauty.'

He kissed the top of her head. 'You have the heart of a poet,' he said. 'And you're right. I felt exactly the same when I first came up here.'

They wandered about, content in each other's company, while Jack outlined his plans. 'Here there will be a pool and leisure complex,' he explained, taking her down to the basement. 'There'll also be a gymnasium and a squash court. You see, I'm not only catering for tourists but also for the locals and the many businessmen who frequent the island.'

'Seems like you've done your homework.' Lucy was impressed.

'You bet I have.' His excitement grew as he took her all over the old place. He was full of ideas, brimming with plans, and itching to get started on it all. 'I would imagine the accountant will have been given full control over the project,' he explained.

'Does that change things? I mean, with the owner being away and you being accountable to someone else?' Lucy had seen how his face fell when he'd read the letter that Larry Moore had left.

'I'd rather he was here,' Jack confessed. 'But I don't think it will hold things up. The money is allocated, and Larry told me so long as it doesn't break the bank, and he can see a good return for his investment, I'm to have a free hand. I expect the accountant has been ordered to watch me like a hawk, but I don't mind that so long as he gives me the go ahead. And the sooner he does that, the better.' He grinned. 'I don't intend to give him a minute's peace until he does.'

He had that glint in his eye. Lucy knew what it meant. 'I feel sorry for this accountant,' she laughed. 'The poor devil doesn't know what he's let himself in for.' The odd thing was, she and Jack were two of a kind. When their hearts were set on something, they went for it, hook, line and sinker.

When they left the house, Lucy glanced at her watch and was amazed. 'It's nearly four o'clock!' she exclaimed. 'We've been in there for ages.' And yet it had seemed only a few minutes.

'The house is like that,' he murmured. 'It draws you in, and won't let you go.'

They stood for a moment, looking back at it, in their mind's eye seeing it as it would be when Jack was done. 'Look,' cried Lucy, pointing to the two narrow windows to either side of the door; the sunshine was filtering through, giving out a soft, pretty light. 'The house looks as if it's smiling.'

'So it should,' Jack declared, curling his arm round her waist and walking her down the weed-strewn path. 'So it should.'

Dinner was a long, leisurely affair. Seeing how much in love they were, and suspecting they were not married at all, the proprietor seated them at a candlelit table in the farthest corner. The window overlooked the gardens from where the heady smell of summer blossom wafted in as they ate and talked and made their plans for the future. 'Once I've got this project up and running, I can turn my mind to our own hotel,' Jack said. 'I still don't know how I'll raise the cash, but I will, I promise, sweetheart. Somehow I'll make it happen.'

Lucy had no doubts. 'I know you will,' she said. 'Meantime I'll be saving every penny I can.' Her dove-grey eyes glowed in the candlelight. 'I want the most beautiful wedding dress, so that when I walk down the aisle towards you, you'll be so proud of me.'

'I'm proud of you now,' he answered softly. 'It wouldn't matter to me if you walked down the aisle in rags.'

She laughed. 'It would matter to me!' she said. But it wouldn't, because when she walked down that aisle, all she would see was Jack, tall and handsome, waiting to make his vows with her.

After dinner, they strolled along the promenade, arms entwined, so much in love they only had eyes for each other.

For a time they were silent, as lovers often are. Then they began to talk, excited about the future and what it promised. They sat on the bench and watched the Solent in the cool of the evening. People walked by and smiled at them, and they were so very content. 'I wish I didn't have to go back tomorrow,' Lucy whispered when he bent to kiss her.

'Don't go back then,' he murmured, his mouth on hers.

'I have to, Jack. You know I have to, don't you?'

'Yes, I know,' he admitted regretfully. 'Our time hasn't come yet, but it will, sweetheart. Soon there will be a time for us, and nothing will part us then.'

Lucy kept that thought in her heart.

When they made love that night, she remembered what Jack had promised: 'Soon there will be a time for us.'

In the early hours she woke with his words in her mind. While Jack slept unawares, she stood by the window gazing out at the quietness of the deserted promenade, and marvelling at the beauty of the night. 'Please God, keep him safe,' she whispered. 'He means everything to me.'

The next day was pure delight. Jack took her on a tour of the island. They stopped for lunch at a quaint old inn, and afterwards walked for miles in the lovely countryside.

Like all good things, the weekend eventually drew to a close and they had to make their way to the ferry. Lovingly, they parted company. 'Take care of yourself, sweetheart,' Jack murmured, holding her close. 'Don't forget to ring me the minute you get home.'

'I won't,' she promised.

They stayed together for as long as they dared, and then he had to let her go. The moment before she left, he dug into his pocket. Taking out a small package, he pressed it into the palm of her hand. 'Don't look at it now,' he ordered. 'Open it when you get home. You can tell me if you like it when you call.' His dark green eyes were smiling in that familiar mischievous way, but there was something else shining there too: love and a kind of pride.

'What is it?' Lucy couldn't recall when he might have sneaked away to buy her a present.

But she had to go or be left behind. 'Love you, Lucy Nolan,' he said as their hands slid apart. 'Safe journey, sweetheart.'

From the upper deck she watched him, that tall familiar figure, dark hair blowing in the breeze. ''Bye, my love,' she murmured, waving to him as the ferry moved slowly out. 'I'll be back to see you before you know it.' She meant to make regular visits as and when work allowed. There was so much she and Jack still had to say. So many plans to make.

With a little smile on her face, she undid the package he had given her. Inside was a small leather box. When the lid was opened, she gave a gasp of astonishment, for nestling there was the most beautiful ring she had ever seen: a slim band of gold surmounted with a solitary sparkling diamond. In the sunlight, the stone glistened every wonderful colour of the rainbow. Beneath the ring was a note. She read it:

> Happy engagement, darling
> Hope you like it
> Love, Jack

Overwhelmed, she slid the ring on to her finger. It was a perfect fit. Jack had already spoken to her mother who was in on the little secret. 'Oh, Jack!' Thrilled, Lucy hung over the rail, waving and shouting, 'IT'S BEAUTIFUL, JACK! THE RING IS BEAUTIFUL!'

She could just make out his answering words. 'You weren't supposed to open it until you got home!'

The young woman beside her got caught up in the excitement. 'YOU KNOW WHAT WOMEN ARE LIKE!' she yelled, cupping her hands round her mouth. 'IMPATIENT BUGGERS, EVERY ONE!'

Soon Jack was lost from sight and Lucy was surrounded by enthusiastic fellow passengers, all keen to get a look at her brand new engagement ring. 'Men are strange creatures,' said a middle-aged lady with a fistful of gold rings. 'You'd have thought he'd want to put the ring on your finger himself. But then, they can be so self-conscious when it comes to emotional displays.'

Lucy felt she knew why he had not given her the ring before. 'I think he was just worried in case I didn't like it,' she said.

The young woman who had called out to Jack was enthralled, turning the ring round and round on Lucy's finger, sighing. 'How could he think you wouldn't like it?' she asked. 'It's absolutely beautiful.'

Later, during a conversation over a cup of tea, it emerged that the young woman had twice been jilted, and now wondered if there were any honest men left in the world. 'But it seems like you've found one,' she said. 'Hold on to him for all you're worth.'

If Fate was kind, that was exactly what Lucy meant to do.

Debbie was curled up in a shop doorway when her father found her. 'Come home, love,' he pleaded. It had taken him two hours to discover her and now he looked haggard and remorseful. 'It won't happen again, I swear to God.'

Staring up at him with a tear-stained face, Debbie was defiant. 'Go away! I hate you!'

'No, Debs. Don't hate me.' When he moved closer she visibly flinched, her face twisting in disgust.

'If I wasn't worried that somebody might get really injured . . . even *killed* . . . I'd move out tomorrow.'

'I've told you, Debs, it won't happen again.'

She shook her head. 'I can't believe what you say any more. How many times have you promised it won't happen again? How many times have I come back, and it's the same all over . . . the beatings . . . the questions . . . always the same. I'm frightened. It's getting so I daren't go to bed . . . afraid I might be murdered in my sleep.'

He laughed, but it was an ugly sound. 'That's silly and you know it. Things would never get that bad.'

'They will! Can't you see how bad they are now?'

'Trust me, Debs. Trust me.'

'Will you see somebody?'

'What do you mean?' There was real fear in his voice.

'You know very well what I mean! It's got to stop.'

There was a long silence. Then: 'All right. If that's the only way to get you home, I'll see somebody. I'll even let you make the appointment.'

There was another brief exchange before the two of them walked out of the alley together.

When, mistaking her for a prostitute, a drunken man made advances, Debbie's father was all ready to smack him to the ground. 'No, Dad,' she said, pulling him away. 'No more violence.'

They made a sad sight, the two of them, as they went away, arm in arm. But there was still a reservoir of love between them.

Only love, and patience, and the keeping of promises, would be their salvation.

PART TWO

1987

Looking Back

Chapter Five

Too excited for sleep, Lucy had been up since four o'clock that morning. Now it was ten minutes to eight and she was due to open the gates at half past.

'Bet you can't believe it, can you, gal?' Debbie stood between her and Ted, all three of them looking towards what used to be the old nurseries.

'No, I can't,' Lucy admitted. 'To be honest there were times when I thought we'd never see the day.' It was a year and eight months since she and Ted had entered into their partnership. All that time she had worked hard towards this day. They had *all* worked hard, and now the day was here, it was a thrill for everyone.

Ted was philosophical. 'Get away with yer, Lucy Nolan,' he chided. 'There was never a minute when you didn't believe it would happen.' He sucked on his old pipe. 'You've done a grand job, and I'm proud of yer.' Chuckling with merriment, he reminded her, 'The best day's work you've done so far was to see off that no-good son of mine, when he turned up a few months back.'

'He got what he deserved,' Lucy recalled. 'And if he comes back, he'll get more of the same.'

Ted reached down to stroke the Alsatian licking

his hand. 'That were a good idea of yours to get a guard dog,' he said. 'I don't know why I didn't think of it before. There's allus been a lot o' money tied up in these 'ere nurseries. More than ever now it's been all poshed up and restocked with more expensive shrubs and the like.'

Digging into his jacket pocket, he took out a small juicy bone. 'There y'are, fella me lad,' he said, sliding it between the dog's teeth. 'Look after the property, an' we'll look after you.'

Lucy shook her head and smiled. 'You spoil him,' she declared. But the dog was a real character and they all loved him. 'Anyway, Jake was bought to look after you first, and the property second,' she reminded him. 'I'd rather the thieves stripped this place bare than harmed you.'

'He's a good sort,' Ted chuckled. 'Thanks to you, he showed that bloody offspring of mine the way out, didn't he, eh?'

Stepping forward, Debbie ruffled the dog's neck. 'You're right, Ted, he is a good sort,' she agreed. 'He saw both the buggers off, didn't he, eh? That fancy solicitor fella your son brought with him nearly wet his pants when Jake had him pinned in a corner.'

Ted's face hardened to a frown. 'Nasty sort, that solicitor. Cunning devil, looking for every which way he could turn me out on the streets. Me own son were no better neither . . . the pair of 'em going on about how old I were, and how difficult it must be for me to keep a place like this going. Telling me I ought to sign responsibility over to George.' He blew out his cheeks in disgust. 'Bloody cheek!'

'You're not to worry,' Lucy told him. 'They went

away with their tails between their legs, and with luck they won't dare show their faces again.' Secretly, she wasn't so sure. Ted's son seemed determined to pursue his claim. When she'd closed the gates behind him, he'd accused her of cheating him out of what was rightfully his. 'The old man's gone senile,' he'd sneered. 'This land is worth a bloody fortune for development, and well you know it. You might think you've got away with your clever little plan, but I'll be back,' he'd threatened. 'And when I do, it'll be no more nurseries, and no more you, because the lot of you will be out on your ear!'

'They were after me blood,' Ted recalled, 'but they were no match for our Lucy and this one here, were they?' Stroking the dog's neck, he cackled with delight. 'Soon sent the buggers packing with their tails a'tween their legs, didn't we, eh?'

Lucy recalled the incident. She had taken an instant dislike to George Beckendale and the fellow he'd brought with him. Before she'd intervened, poor Old Ted was being frightened out of his wits by their persistent bullying. 'They were a pair of sharks and needed telling,' she said. 'If they show their faces here again, it won't be the dog I set on them, it'll be the police.' If George Beckendale wanted a fight, she was ready to oblige.

Tapping out his pipe and making sure the embers were well and truly out, Ted licked his lips. 'Have we time for a cup of tea, d'yer think, lass?' he asked her. 'If your hard work and advertising pay off, it'll soon be the Charge of the Light Brigade, then we shan't have time to breathe, let alone have a drink.'

'We'll *make* time,' Lucy promised. 'The gates aren't

due to open for another half-hour. I saw Mrs Roman getting ready for the rush just now as I came down. I'm sure she won't turn us away, and besides, I think it's only right that we should be the first customers in our brand new cafeteria.'

As they made their way down the trellised walkway and past the rose beds, Ted couldn't get over it. 'If somebody had told me two years ago that the old nurseries could look like this, I'd have said they were talking out of the back of their head. What! You've done wonders, Lucy me darlin'. And you've still left me part of the old site where I can hide away in me own little garden and dig me own potatoes. I've got the best of both worlds, and George can't get his mitts on either of 'em!' At the foot of the steps leading up to the terrace and cafeteria, he paused, a tear in his eye as he told her softly, 'I'll never know how to thank you, lass.'

'It's I who should be thanking you,' Lucy said. 'Anyway, I thought you were dying of thirst.'

'I am!'

'You'd better get inside then, before the kettle goes off the boil.' She didn't want Ted to feel obliged to her in any way.

'You're a good lass,' he replied. Then he gave a merry whistle and went on his way with the faithful dog at his heels.

'I'll be along in a minute,' Lucy called. 'I want to have a quick look round, to make sure everything's ready.'

He didn't turn but kept walking. 'That'll be the tenth time in as many minutes,' he chastised. 'If it ain't ready now, it never will be.'

Lucy asked him to warn Mrs Roman there would be another four for tea, herself and Debbie, and the two youngsters, Sophie and Robert. 'You were wrong about him, weren't you?' Debbie commented as they made their way to the conservatory. 'He's never yet put a foot out of place.'

'Maybe I *was* wrong,' Lucy had to admit. 'We'll see.' Robert had worked at the nurseries for over two years now, and as Debbie said, she couldn't fault his work or his manners. But there was still something about him that made Lucy's flesh creep. The way he smiled. The way his eyes seemed to watch every little thing. Even the way he tore into his work, with an insatiable energy. Yet she couldn't sack him for that, could she?

Sophie was in the dried flower department, her back to them as they went in. 'You can leave that if you like,' Lucy called as she approached. 'We're all congregating in the cafeteria for a well-earned cup of tea before the rush.'

Sophie seemed not to have heard. Unsuspecting, Lucy touched her on the shoulder. 'You and Robert go on, while Debbie and I check that everything's okay.'

Visibly startled, Sophie swung round. 'Oh! You gave me a fright.' But her hair was dishevelled and her eyes were red as though she'd been crying.

Reaching out to tuck a stray lock of hair away from the girl's white, frightened face, Lucy asked, 'What's wrong, Sophie?' Instinctively she glanced about for Robert but he was nowhere in sight.

'Nothing's wrong.'

'Have you been crying?'

'No. It's the dried flowers. I'm allergic to them.'

It was obvious to Lucy that the girl was lying, but she didn't want to press the matter in front of Debbie. Instead she saved Sophie's face by telling her compassionately, 'You should have told me you were allergic to the dried flowers. You and Robert will have to swap. He can come in here while you go on the outside till. Will that suit you better?'

Obviously relieved when Lucy seemed to believe her story, the girl nodded. 'Thanks,' she said in a small voice, 'I'd like that.'

A moment later it was arranged. After sending the girl for her tea, Lucy searched out the young man who was busy labelling the last few apple trees. 'What's been going on here?' She came right up to him and blocked his escape.

Unruffled, he looked her in the eye. 'What do you mean? Nothing's been going on that I know of.' He was quietly arrogant, and very sure of himself.

Lucy stared at him for a long moment, eyes searching his for some sign of guilt. But there was none. All the same she sensed something bad in this young fellow, and it made her feel deeply uncomfortable. She realised that if she persisted he would only deny any knowledge of why Sophie was upset, and would do it with such assurance she would make herself look foolish by insisting. Besides, it might make matters worse for the girl. Yet her instincts told her he was guilty of something, and that it would be folly to let the matter go uninvestigated. 'This is a small family business,' she informed him. 'If it's to be successful, we all have to work as a team. If anyone can't live with that, they should say so now.'

His face broke into a smile. 'That's why I like working here,' he said jovially. 'Everyone's so easy to get on with.'

'Go to the cafeteria,' she told him stiffly. 'We're taking a ten-minute break.'

As he walked away, Debbie conceded quietly, 'You know what, gal, I think you might be right about him after all.'

'He's a devious bastard,' Lucy said through gritted teeth. 'And I haven't finished with him yet.'

Debbie was shocked. 'Jeez! I've never heard you use that language before. He's really got under your skin.'

He had, too. And Lucy meant to speak to Sophie again at the first opportunity.

'You can go and have your break, if you like, Debs,' she said. 'I just want to have a last look round before I open the gates.'

Debbie was adamant. 'We'll look round together,' she insisted.

And that was what they did. They went from the open beds in their orderly rows, to the barrows of plants and the pergolas hung with climbers. Then they checked the trellises, the fencing and the hardware store with its array of garden tools and machinery. 'It was clever of you to charge for people to sell their goods from here,' Debbie told her. 'What made you think of that?'

'It just came up when that salesman wanted us to buy lawnmowers. I told him we couldn't lay out the capital, but that he could rent an area for so much a month and sell his own goods. He tried to make it a deal on commission instead, but I spoke to Ted and we agreed. You see, Debs, if there were no machines sold, then we'd get no commission and he would be using up good floor space that we could put to better use. Whereas this way, by renting him a space, we get paid whether he makes any sales or not.'

'I've got to hand it to you, gal, you can drive a hard bargain when you put your mind to it.'

'You're not so bad yourself, Debbie Lately,' Lucy said, patting her on the back. 'For all my bartering, I could never create a wonderful sight like that.' They were at the front gates now, looking up at the most delightful display of trailing plants. They tumbled over the pillars and down the walls, and smelled indescribably beautiful.

'It were nothing.' Debbie blushed with pleasure. 'It only took me a few hours.' All the same, she had excelled herself. The profusion of blooms with the amazing riot of colour cascaded down on either side of the gates, twined around each other, filling the air with the sweetest scent. It was the most beautiful display Lucy had ever seen.

'It's a work of art,' she exclaimed, draping an arm round Debbie's shoulders. 'You've found a talent you never knew you had.'

Debbie smiled confidently. 'I had to do justice to the new sign, didn't I?'

Figured in wrought iron and straddling the pillars, it stood proud and pretty:

NOLAN AND BECKENDALE
GARDEN CENTRE

This time the sign had been designed by professionals and erected just two days before the grand opening.

On the way to the cafeteria, they talked about this and that. 'Is everything all right at home, Debs?' Lucy enquired casually.

"Course it's all right,' she replied sharply. 'What are you insinuating?'

'Whoah! Hold on a minute.' Lucy was shocked by her vehement reaction. 'I'm not insinuating anything. I just wondered, that's all. You said yourself you haven't been out for weeks. I know you haven't seen Alfie though he's asked you umpteen times.'

'How do you know that?'

'Because he phones here all the time. He's desperate to see you, Debs. When I spoke to him last week, he apologised for ringing the office but said it was the only way he could speak to you. He said whenever he rings you at home, your dad growls down the phone at him.'

Lucy was worried. Debbie was becoming more and more of a recluse. She wouldn't even go out with Lucy any more. It was a bad situation. 'I thought maybe you'd had a row.'

Wide-eyed with fear, Debbie stopped dead in her tracks, her voice angrily raised as she demanded, 'What makes you think I row with my dad?'

Realising she had struck a sore point, Lucy assured her, 'I wasn't talking about your dad, Debs. I was talking about Alfie. Have you and *he* had a row?'

'Oh!' Relieved, she walked beside Lucy again. 'No, we ain't. And I'm sorry I yelled, gal.' Things were no better at home, but they were no worse either.

Her father had not kept his promise to go and see someone, and nothing Debbie could do would persuade him. So, in order not to cause trouble, she had lived like a recluse, not going out, not talking on the phone, having no contact with Alfie whatsoever, and staying in her room from the minute she left the dinner table to the time she rose in the morning to go to work. She was living an unnaturally quiet life but it seemed to be working. The violence had diminished and so, in a way, Debbie felt it was worth the sacrifice.

Lucy cursed herself for having said the wrong thing. Trying to make amends, she suggested, 'Why don't we go out on Saturday? We can celebrate the opening of the Garden Centre.'

'Better not.'

'All right, it's up to you, but if you change your mind, that's all right too.'

'Thanks, gal.'

Both subdued by their exchange, they strolled a little way in silence.

'What about Jack?' Debbie asked presently.

'What about him?' They were coming up the steps to the cafeteria now.

'The hotel's open and doing well, ain't it?'

'Yes.' In fact it was doing more than that. Every room was fully booked for the coming season, and the owner was thrilled.

'The owner's given him a big bonus, ain't he?'

'That's right.'

'So! When's the wedding?'

'Close.'

'How close?'

Lucy's eyes shone. 'Jack rang last night. He's coming over the week after next.' She crossed her fingers. 'I think he might have something special to tell me.'

'Such as what?'

'He wouldn't say, but I know Jack, and I know he was excited about something.'

'I'll bet he wants you to set the date.'

'Maybe.' Lucy couldn't be certain, but she suspected that was exactly what Jack did want. Oh, she did hope so!

'And will you? Set the date, I mean?'

Lucy nodded. 'I've been thinking about that a lot. You know how much I've missed him since he's been gone. Oh, I know we've seen each other a dozen times, but it's not the same. When you keep having to say goodbye, it only makes the parting that much harder.' Now she thought about what it would be like being Jack's wife and having him around all the time, and the thought made her smile. 'Yes, Debs,' she answered, 'I'm ready to set the date if that's what Jack wants.' Sometimes you made decisions and had to live by them. But in the end, nothing was worth paying a price that took away your happiness.

Debs was just the tiniest bit jealous. 'What about the garden centre? And Ted? And all the reasons why you made Jack wait in the first place?'

Lucy had spent many a sleepless night, wondering about that. 'Now that the Garden Centre is underway, and Ted is safe from his son, I hope I can think about me and Jack and our future together. The thing is, I'm not certain how being married to him will change things. I don't even know whether Jack will want us to buy a place round here, so I can go on working with Ted. Whatever Jack and I decide, I owe it to Ted to talk things over with him.'

'If it's wedding bells, don't forget I'm chief bridesmaid.'

Lucy laughed. 'As if you'd *let* me forget!'

It seemed they'd no sooner got their tea and sat down than it was time to go. 'Cor, bugger me, gal,' Debbie moaned, 'I ain't had time to wet me whistle.'

'Take it with you,' Lucy suggested. 'You can sip it between customers.'

She'd noticed how Sophie kept her distance from Robert. She'd also noticed how frightened the girl looked when he walked by and brushed against her.

Still deep in thought, she opened the main gates before making her way to the till by the far door. Everyone else was at their stations: Debbie in the standard rose and shrub department, Robert in the dried flower area, looking decidedly uncomfortable, Sophie outside, and Ted waiting at the door with the vouchers, one for each of the first fifty customers. The voucher would entitle them to one of Ted's potted chrysanthemums. When the vouchers were issued, he'd make his way to the greenhouse where he could hide from the crowds and tend his beloved seedlings.

'Do your worst,' Lucy murmured, waiting apprehensively for the doors suddenly to burst open and let in the first wave of customers. 'We're good and ready for you.'

Half-past eight came and went, then nine o'clock, and still there was no sign of any customers. 'Where the bleedin' Hell are they, gal?' Debbie asked, hurrying up the aisle to Lucy. 'I've drunk me tea and now I'm dying to spend a penny. Am I safe to go, d'yer think, or will the buggers come rushing in when me back's turned?'

'You might as well go,' Lucy told her. 'It's still early yet.'

Ted strolled over. 'Don't worry,' he consoled her. 'Folks are fickle. They'll come when they're ready, an' not afore.'

Lucy was bitterly disappointed. When the minute hand crept round the clock-face and it was twenty past nine, she began to despair. 'Maybe I've been over-ambitious,' she admitted to Ted. 'If I've persuaded you to go into this and wasted your money, I'll never forgive myself.' She'd been so certain people would come.

Through a toothless grin, he reprimanded her. 'Away with yer! If I've spent me money it's because I know a good thing when I see one. You're too hard on yerself, lass. They'll come, you'll see.'

His confidence in her was gratifying. 'Bless you, Ted.' She gave him a hug. 'I'd better get back to my station then.'

And that was what she did.

But still the minute hand ticked away, and not one single customer came through the doors. 'You've blown it, Lucy girl,' she muttered. 'You're all hot air and fanciful ideas, and now you've spent the best part of that dear old man's savings.' She would pay him back though, if it took her the rest of her life.

Disheartened, she glanced at Ted. Then she glanced at the doors, as if willing them to open.

She looked away, heard a sound, and when she

looked up again, the doors were flung open and in poured a stream of people. 'By! Doesn't it look grand?' Red-faced and determined, a rather large lady led the charge.

In the rush for the vouchers poor Ted was knocked sideways. 'Hey! This ain't a cattle sale,' he cried. 'Have a bit o' sense, will yer!'

Within minutes the place was in uproar, with people surging down the aisles, grabbing up the pretty plants and earthenware pots, cramming their trolleys full. One man collected a wheelbarrow and filled it with every conceivable garden tool. 'I've just moved back from abroad,' he told an astonished Lucy. 'I have to start from scratch.'

She was thrilled. The tills didn't stop ringing all day. Every now and then she would see Ted talking about a plant, or explaining the proper way to bring it on once it was taken to its new home. There was no greater authority on the rearing of plants, and people respected his expert knowledge.

He showed the customers round his emporium, he laughed and smiled and altogether had a wonderful time. About three o'clock in the afternoon he informed Lucy, 'I'm just taking this dear lady for a cup of tea in our new cafeteria.' She was a woman of about his age, with a lovely smile and a dog-headed walking stick which Ted immediately took charge of, while offering her his arm to lean on.

'You romantic old devil,' Lucy murmured as the two of them went away, chatting and laughing as though they were old, old friends.

At four o'clock there was a lull. 'Thank God for that!' Debbie came over to where Lucy was cashing up. 'I feel like I've been run over with a bleedin' steam-roller.'

'I know what you mean.' Lucy bagged the notes and entered the amount in the ledger. 'I hoped it would be a success, for Ted's sake more than mine, but I never dreamed it would be this good.' It was more than good. It was unbelievable. Already the takings in her own till had exceeded four hundred pounds. But that in itself created a problem. 'I'd better do the rounds,' she told Debbie. 'How busy are you over there now?'

'Quiet. You go on. I'll keep an eye on things here, and anyway Sophie's on hand if anybody comes to my till. Go on, gal,' she urged. 'I know how you worry when the money's not locked away.'

Gathering the money-bags from the bottom drawer, Lucy took firm hold of them. 'I'll be as quick as I can,' she promised.

'Hey! That Ted's a randy old bugger, ain't he? After the mad crowd cleared off, I sneaked a bottle o' pop from the cafeteria. Ted and his lady friend were still in the corner, gazing into each other's eyes as though the world was about to end.' Winking meaningfully, she whispered, 'Between you and me, gal, I reckon the old bugger's on a promise.'

Laughing at Debbie's turn of phrase, Lucy was happy for the old ones. If they found comfort and pleasure in each other's company, that was wonderful. 'Good luck to them,' she declared sincerely. 'Like my man said, why *should* it be only the young who fall in love?'

'You old romantic.'

'That's what keeps me going.' What actually kept

her going were memories of herself and Jack together, during her last trip to the island. They had made love on a secluded beach, and swum beneath the stars. Afterwards they had strolled along the promenade and talked about their future, about marriage and children, and how desperately they wanted to spend their whole lives together. It had been the most wonderful time of Lucy's life. She had lain in Jack's arms all night long, and in the morning, when the sun came shining through the window, she woke with a delicious feeling, just to know that he was there alongside her. For an age she had lain there, content to gaze on him asleep, admiring that strong, handsome face and the way his dark hair tousled over his eyes. She imagined the laughing dark green gaze that at any minute now would meet hers. He didn't wake, not then. What he did was to reach out and enfold her in his arms.

It was a moment Lucy would cherish for ever. A beautiful, private moment which she could relive when the world became too lonely without him.

It took half an hour to empty and reset the bulging tills. The day had been a tremendous success, and it wasn't over yet.

Lucy was just about to lock the office when a voice startled her. 'If you'd asked me, I'd have carried the money-bags over for you.'

Leaning against the door-jamb, his piercing blue eyes fixed on her, Robert was an unsettling sight. 'Judging by the number of customers we've had today, them bags must have weighed a ton.' He took a step forward as if to come inside.

Striding across, Lucy cunningly blocked his way. 'The takings are for me to worry about,' she said, brushing aside his comment. 'What did you want anyway?'

'I thought you asked to see me.'

'When I want you, I'll come and get you. Meanwhile I'd like you to get back where you're supposed to be.'

'You're the boss.'

'Exactly.' She wondered if he'd been drinking. His voice seemed a little slurred, and he was smiling like a man not in his right senses. As he walked away, his gait seemed just the slightest bit unsteady. She couldn't be certain, but at the first real hint that he was drinking on the job, that young man would be out on his ear so fast he wouldn't know what day it was!

Debbie was relieved to see her again. 'I've had half a dozen customers through here,' she told Lucy, 'and not one o' the buggers tall and handsome.'

'Thanks, Debs.' Lucy's mind was elsewhere.

'What's up with you? You look like you've lost a pound and found a penny.'

'Hmm.' As Debbie stepped out, Lucy took up her position behind the till. 'That young man worries me.'

'Oh, Lucy. You're not going on about that Robert again, are you? You're becoming obsessed with him. He's all right, I tell you. He's the best worker we're ever likely to get . . . doesn't mind whether the job's clean or mucky. He's smart and presentable, polite to everyone, and you've only to ask him to do something and it's done before you can turn round.'

161

'I know all that.' In fact Lucy still couldn't fault his work. And it was true the customers liked him. He took the time to chat, and made them feel welcome. And, like Debs said, he didn't mind how hard the work was, and never complained. Yet, there was something about him that worried her.

Debbie knew from experience that Lucy's judgement was usually sound, but on this occasion she wondered. 'You don't really believe he had anything to do with Sophie's being upset, do you?'

'Yes, I do.' All her adult life, Lucy had learned to follow her instincts. Now, those instincts told her that Robert Johnson was a bad lot. 'I *know* he frightened her,' she quietly insisted, 'and later I mean to get at the truth.'

'Rather you than me. You could be in real trouble if you accuse him and he didn't do anything.'

'We'll see.' Nothing Debbie said would make her change her mind about that deceitful young man.

After the initial rush of customers there was a steady flow through all departments until, at four minutes past six, Lucy closed the main gates.

'The bleedin' place is almost empty!' Debbie declared, her pretty blue eyes rolling heavenwards. 'I'm glad it's Robert and Sophie who'll be re-stocking the shelves tomorrow, and not me.'

'Double time if you want it?' Lucy asked hopefully. She was already thinking it was a mistake to let those two work here unsupervised, especially if there was trouble between them.

With things the way they were at home, Debbie was half-tempted. 'Will *you* be working?'

'I'll be working, yes,' Lucy confirmed. 'But it'll be at the suppliers. I miscalculated the amount of stuff we'd shift this weekend. There isn't one single earthenware pot left, most of the dried flowers have gone, and we've only two watering-cans left on the shelves.'

'And there are no more o' them pretty china vases left. That woman from the chip shop down Armitage Street bought six. They've opened the back room as a little café, and she reckoned the vases will look nice, one on each table.'

'She's right too,' Lucy agreed. 'In fact I bought one for my mam.'

'That's all right, you live in a decent area, but that lot down Armitage Street would have your leg off and sell it at the meat stall on the market. I told that chip shop woman, I warned her . . . that rough lot round there will nick the buggers the minute your back's turned, I said, but she took no notice.'

'Good.' Taking Debbie by the arm, Lucy propelled her towards the building. 'Stop trying to frighten away the customers,' she said. 'If the chip shop woman wants to buy six vases, she can buy six vases. And if they get nicked, she either won't replace them or she'll be back here for more. So, just in case, I'd better get another dozen.'

'Lucy Nolan, you're a cruel bugger!'

'And you're very generous.'

'Generous? Why?' She gave Lucy a suspicious look. 'Hey! It's no good asking me because I'm not giving to charity. I've got enough bleedin' charity at home.'

'I didn't mean that.' Lucy was enjoying herself. 'I

mean, the way you tried to talk that woman out of buying the vases, I admire that. You see, if the customers don't buy, you don't get paid. Money in, money out, if you see what I mean?'

Debbie was speechless. Until Lucy grabbed her and burst out laughing. 'You bugger, Lucy Nolan!' she cried, relief flooding her face. 'I've a good mind to clip your bleedin' ear.'

Ted looked ten years younger. There was a spring in his step and his back seemed straighter. There was also a twinkle in his eye that Lucy had not seen the like of before. 'I want you to meet Mabel Parkinson,' he said, coming up the pathway. Turning to the woman by his side, he introduced her to them. 'This is Lucy Nolan,' he explained. 'You remember I told you all about her?'

Mabel was a small, round woman with a fuzz of white hair and one of those faces that made people feel they'd known her all their lives. 'Ted thinks a lot of you,' she said, smiling warmly at Lucy.

'He's a lovely bloke,' Lucy replied. Seeing with astonishment how Ted blushed a delicate shade of pink, she called attention to Debbie. 'This is Debbie Lately, our supervisor.'

The older woman chuckled. 'Ted says you're accident prone,' she remarked innocently. 'You look safe enough to me.'

'I'm improving,' Debbie replied, giving Ted a narrow-eyed glance. 'At least I haven't had the roof down round our ears, so that's summat to be thankful for.'

Wishing he'd kept his mouth shut, Ted quickly

changed the subject. 'Mabel and I went to school together,' he revealed. 'O' course, I were a few years older than her, so we didn't see each other in lessons, but I used to watch her in the playground, thinking what a bonny lass she were.' He looked fondly at her and, just for a moment, the two of them seemed lost in thoughts of long ago.

'He was such a quiet young man,' she declared, keeping her gaze on his face. 'He hardly ever mixed with the other children. Sometimes he'd spend the whole playtime standing against the gym wall, reading his comics. I liked him even then. I so much wanted him to speak to me, but he never did.'

'Well, you've done a lot of talking today,' Lucy remarked. 'I thought I'd have to lock up with the pair of you still in the cafeteria.' It was really heartening, she thought, but then she cautioned herself. Mabel was probably married and only thinking of Ted as an old friend – although judging by the look in her eyes when she gazed at him, as she was doing now, it was more than friendship that drew her to him. 'Isn't it strange, though, how you've found each other again?'

'It's Fate,' Ted declared. 'Mabel told me she hardly ever buys the local paper but this week, for some reason, she did, and she saw my name in the advert.'

Mabel took up the story. 'I knew Ted's father was a nurseryman because my dad used to buy his tomatoes and lettuce from old Mr Beckendale. So when I saw the advert about this opening today, I just wondered if the Beckendale in the advert was the same Ted Beckendale I knew from school.' Her homely face spread into a girlish grin. 'Funny thing is, I recognised him straight away, because he looks just like his old dad.'

Debbie couldn't help herself. 'So his dad was bald and toothless an' all then?'

She burst out laughing, but was surprised when Mabel told her in a stern voice, 'As a matter of fact, Ted's dad was a good-looking bloke. Just like Ted.'

'Whoops! I think you've put your foot in it again, Debs,' laughed Lucy.

Sheepishly, she crept away. 'One o' these days, this bleedin' tongue'll get me hanged.'

Behind her the other three were chuckling. 'I told yer she were accident prone, and now you know what I mean,' Ted told Mabel.

'Perhaps it was my fault for leaping to your defence,' she replied. 'I didn't mean to make her feel guilty.'

'Oh, she's all right,' Lucy assured them. She knew Debbie as well as she knew herself. 'Anyway, I'd better go. Looks like we've got some last-minute customers.' Out of the corner of her eye she'd noticed a tall, brown-haired man approaching. He was accompanied by two children, one a dark-haired young man of about sixteen and the other a tall willowy girl with thick fair hair down to her waist. She looked to be in her early teens.

'That's one of the local doctors, ain't it?' Screwing up his eyes to get a clearer look, Ted confirmed his first suspicions. Addressing Lucy, he said, 'I've never had cause to see him myself, but folks say he's all right.'

She took a closer look. The man had seemed familiar, with that very slight stoop and the way he combed his thick hair straight back. Successful and well dressed, Steve Ryman was the kind of man a woman might look twice at. He was also very pleasant. 'I'd better go and see if I can be of any help.'

While Lucy went one way, Ted and his friend went the other. 'Steve Ryman's fairly new to these parts,' he explained. 'He lives in a big old house on Park Road. Seems a lonely kind o' fella. He's a widower, d'yer see? Left to bring up two children on his own these past eighteen months.'

'I thought I'd come and see what you had to offer.' While his two children explored the centre, Steve Ryman strolled through the rose garden with Lucy.

Gesturing towards the flowerbeds and garden furniture, she smiled into his pleasant brown eyes. 'What you see is what you get,' she said. 'All on special offer today, and all first-class stuff.'

'What would you recommend?' His eyes studied her closely; inquisitive eyes that missed nothing, sad, proud eyes.

'That all depends.' She glanced down at his smartly pressed trousers and the clean fingers with their perfect nails, and straight away assumed he paid a gardener to do all the dirty work. 'If you're after garden furniture we have some wonderful beech loungers,' she said, 'or how about a conservatory? We don't keep them on site, but we can order one 'specially.'

'I see.' The brown eyes still stared at her. 'So you've branded me a lounger, have you?' Drawing in a long deep breath, he released it again in a sigh. 'You don't think I might be the sort to bend his back doing a little digging or planting a few flowers?'

Lucy was embarrassed. 'Sorry,' she apologised, 'I didn't mean that.' She *did* mean that, but wasn't about to admit it to him. 'Really, Dr Ryman, you've got me all wrong.'

'Does it matter?' He was smiling at her again.

God! He was actually flirting with her, she realized with a jolt.

'You're right, though.'

'Oh?'

'I'm not used to planting flowers and the like. When I was growing up, I'd play in the most beautiful garden but my parents hardly ever walked the grounds. They were designed by a landscape firm, and tended by an old gardener whose name was Joshua. My father was a barrister and my mother a doctor. Busy people with no time to spare, more's the pity. Now it's my turn to be busy, and while it would be wonderful to be on my knees setting out the prettiest garden in the neighbourhood, I simply do not have the time. I'm ashamed to say, until I moved here, *I* had an old gardener myself . . . only he went by the name of Liam. He was a red-headed Irishman, with a frightening temper and a colourful vocabulary, but let him loose in the garden and he would work magic.'

'I see. And when you moved here to Blackburn, he didn't want to come with you?'

'Couldn't. He went home to Kilkenny . . . to die in Heaven, or so he said.'

'I can understand what he meant.' Lucy had visited the Emerald Isle many years ago with her parents. The memory had stayed with her. 'Ireland is a beautiful country.'

'Very true. Unfortunately Liam preferred to be there than with me. I did manage to hire a young lad to keep up the garden when I first moved to Park Road, but he left in January and now the place is a complete shambles.'

'What you need is a plan.' Lucy liked him. He was easy to talk to.

'What I need is a miracle, you mean.' He stopped in mid-stride, his brown eyes intent on her again. 'I don't suppose *you* would help a fellow in distress?' He laughed. 'Or rather, a *garden* in distress?'

'What exactly did you have in mind?'

Reaching into his jacket pocket, he produced a brochure. It was one of the advertisements Lucy had sent out to many households. Opening the brochure, he found the words he remembered seeing. 'It says here you can offer advice on gardening problems.'

'We do our best,' Lucy confirmed. 'Ted's the plant expert, I'm the designer.' Offering advice had been her idea. It had occurred to her that most of Ted's time was spent answering people's questions anyway, and she'd forgotten the number of times she'd helped a customer by designing a garden layout on the back of a till receipt. Before working with Ted, she hadn't realised that not everyone was a natural gardener.

Steve Ryman was delighted. 'There you go then!' he declared, stuffing the brochure back into his pocket. 'I need someone to design my garden before I can hire someone else to plant it. So when can you come and take a look at the jungle around my house?'

Lucy wondered if she'd be letting herself in for something she might wish she'd never started. But

169

it was a simple enough request. 'You don't waste time, do you?'

'Not on something as important as this.' Not when it was as important as getting Lucy Nolan interested in him, he thought.

Lucy could see she had little choice. He was obviously in need of help, and he was a nice enough man. And, after all, it was part of their service here. Steve Ryman was a customer, and customers were the life-blood of a business. 'Okay, Dr Ryman. If the garden is as bad as you say, the sooner we get started the better.'

Now he'd got her this far he meant to speed things up. 'How about tomorrow afternoon?' he asked eagerly. 'It'll take you at least an hour to get to grips with the wilderness. After that you can stay to tea.'

Lucy was flattered, but not keen on the idea. 'Thanks all the same but—'

'Please!' Lowering his head, he looked at her like a little boy lost. 'Won't you indulge a lonely man? Apart from talking to my patients in the surgery, I really don't get much adult company.' His smile was infectious. 'Don't say no,' he begged. 'Besides, my daughter bakes the most wonderful scones.'

How could she refuse? 'I'll be happy to redesign your garden, but I can't promise I'll stay for tea.' It might be an enjoyable experience; Steve Ryman was good company. And besides, where was the harm in having one of his daughter's scones over a cup of tea? We'll see, thought Lucy. We'll see.

Mike Nolan had just finished sweeping the pavement outside the shop. 'Hello, love,' he said as

Lucy got out of the car. 'You look shattered.'

'Well! Thank you very much,' she laughed. 'You really know how to buck a girl up.' Coming up the path, she pecked him on the cheek. 'It's been a long day,' she admitted wearily. 'But we've taken a small fortune. Honestly, Dad, I've never seen so many people in one place.'

'That's good, sweetheart. Didn't I say you'd do well, eh? You and Ted have worked hard and now it's time to reap the rewards.'

By the time Lucy had washed and changed and returned to the kitchen, the tea was set out and her parents were already seated at the table. 'Oh, Mam! You should have started,' she chided. 'You needn't have waited for me.'

'Nonsense, we don't mind at all,' Sally answered. 'Anyway, you know how I like the three of us to enjoy our meals together.'

Having done his bit by waiting patiently, when his nose was assailed by the delicious aroma of Sally's steak and kidney pie, Mike was soon tucking in. 'I were just telling your mam about there being so many people at the garden centre.'

'And why wouldn't there be?' Sally asked proudly. 'You and Ted have done wonders with that place. Mrs Barclay tells me she bought the prettiest vase there this afternoon, and it didn't cost her a fortune neither by all accounts. She had a sandwich and a cup of coffee at the cafeteria and says she hasn't spent such a pleasant afternoon in a long time. According to her, the place was crowded.'

'And she was right. Once they started coming in, there was no stopping them. They almost emptied the shelves. In fact, I've had to ring the suppliers for more stock. I'll have to start out early in the morning. I would have left the car at the nurseries and brought the van home, but I was hoping you'd look at the nearside tyre. I think it's got a slow puncture.'

Mike swallowed the last of his meat pie. 'Don't you worry, lass. I'll take a look at the tyre after we've had us tea,' he promised. 'If it is a puncture, I'll run it over to the garage while you give your mam a hand with the dishes.'

Sally gave him a withering but naughty look. 'Anything to get out of the washing up, eh?'

'Is there any custard to go with that apple crumble I saw in the pantry?'

'Have you earned it?' Sally was a devil for teasing, but he loved it.

"Course I've earned it! I managed to stop them two old biddies from ripping out each other's throats, didn't I?"

Lucy was all ears. 'What old biddies?' She knew most people round here, but couldn't think of any who might want to rip out each other's throats.

'You don't want to know,' Sally said. 'The argument was over a man.'

Lucy polished off a potato. 'You're wrong,' she said, a gleam in her pretty grey eyes. 'I *do* want to know.' She could do with a juicy little tale to take her mind off punctured tyres and bargain vases.

'You'll have to wait.' Standing up, Sally went across the room and returned with the apple crumble and a jug of custard. 'There you are, Mike Nolan.' Dishing up a generous helping, she put it down in front of him. 'That should keep you quiet for a minute.'

While he enjoyed his sweet, Lucy told her mam about Ted's new woman friend. 'Apparently they were at school together, although she's younger than Ted . . . about sixty I reckon.'

Sally was fascinated. 'What's she like?'

'She's got a lovely personality, and she's very pretty – white hair, round figure – and she's really nice to talk to.'

'Are they in love?'

Lucy smiled at that. 'They look into each other's eyes a lot, if that's what you mean.'

'I'm glad for him. Ted's a nice man, he shouldn't be on his own at his time of life.'

Mike had something to say, but it was through a mouthful of apple crumble. 'Mmmm! This pudding melts in your mouth, Sal. If Ted's woman can cook as good as you, he should marry her tomorrow.'

Sally winked at her daughter. 'I see,' she said, addressing Mike. 'And here was I thinking you married me for my beauty and brains, when all you wanted was my pudding!' The words weren't out of her mouth before she realised how that comment could be construed.

Lucy had to cover her face with her napkin to hide her giggles, while Mike looked from one to the other, eyes shining with mischief. When all three burst out laughing, the house seemed to sing with joy.

'You'd better go and look at that tyre,' Sally suggested, 'before you make me say something else that might appeal to your perverted sense of humour.'

With him out of the way, they had a minute or

two to talk. 'Is there something troubling you?' Sally knew her daughter well enough to know when something was wrong.

'It's that young man Ted took on some time back. I don't trust him.' More than that, she was even a little afraid of him. 'Sophie was crying today. I'm certain he had something to do with it, but when I questioned him, he denied all knowledge.'

'And you think he's lying?'

'I *know* he is!'

Sally would have pressed the point, but Mike appeared. 'It's a puncture all right,' he confirmed. 'I'll get it over to the garage now.'

'How long will it take?' If she was to make an early start tomorrow, she needed to go back for the van tonight.

'An hour at the most.' Mike's family was the most important thing in his life. 'You say you're going back to the nurseries tonight? I'll come with you. You never know who's hanging around in the dark.'

Lucy thanked him but said, 'The only person hanging about will be Sophie. She's saving for a holiday and wants as much overtime as I can give her. There was so much clearing up to do today, I told her she could work on for as long as she liked, and that I'd run her home when I got back. As for Ted, I dare say he's still pottering about.'

'Unless he's gone off with his woman friend,' Sally pointed out.

'It won't matter,' Lucy said. 'I'll be all right.'

'So you don't need me to come with you?'

'No, thanks all the same, Dad, I'll be fine.' Anyway, she wanted another word with Sophie.

* * *

It was nine-thirty when Lucy drew up outside the big gates. The lights in the main building were blazing. 'I thought Sophie might have got fed up waiting and decided to take a bus home,' she mused, 'but I'm glad she's still here.' A frown darkened her face. 'With Robert out of the way, she's more likely to tell me the truth about why she was crying.'

After driving through the gates she decided to leave them open. It shouldn't be too long before she was on her way out again, she thought, and anyway it was safe enough because, in spite of what her dad said, there were very few people wandering about at this time of night. Ted's nurseries were situated a little way out of town and there were not many houses round about, though of course it was on a main bus route and only a short drive away from the centre of Blackburn.

Getting out of the car at the main entrance, Lucy glanced at her watch. 'Sophie shouldn't be working this late,' she muttered, angry with herself for not having sent the girl home earlier. But then, it was Sophie herself who had asked to stay on, wanting to swell the coffers of her holiday fund. 'I need as much overtime as you can give me,' she'd urged. Well, she's certainly earned herself a nice fat wage-packet this week, Lucy realised with a little shock. Let's hope she hasn't worked herself into the ground doing it.

Coming up the steps, she saw that Ted's cottage was in darkness. 'Out on the razzle, eh, Ted?' she chuckled. 'And why not?'

Suddenly her sixth sense told her to be cautious. She could almost smell the danger, and suddenly there it was. The dog came bounding out, its back up, narrowed eyes glittering in the light from the building. As it ran forward it growled, low and threateningly.

'Easy, fella.' Remaining quite still, Lucy spoke soothingly. 'It's only me.'

At first the dog wasn't too sure. Crouching low, it moved towards her in a weird snaking crawl, head down, ears back, still growling, dangerously suspicious.

To anyone other than Lucy it would have made a frightening sight. 'Good dog,' she called softly. 'Come here, Jake . . . come on.' She held out her hand. The dog paused. There was a moment when it seemed he would either run away or attack. Suddenly he stood up on all fours and wagged his tail. 'Good dog.' Now he was dancing towards her, great head moving with the rhythm of his long body. Like a baby he nuzzled up to her. 'You were doing a grand job there,' she told him, deeply relieved. 'I'm glad I wasn't a burglar.'

Pressing his huge, hard body close to hers, the dog licked her hand. 'Where's Sophie?' asked Lucy. 'What have you done with her, eh?' When he merely stared up at her, she caressed his huge head between the palms of her hands. 'You big ugly brute,' she chastised. 'For a minute there I was sure you'd have me for dinner.'

A far-off noise alerted them both. Coming from the other end of the grounds, it sounded like the gates being closed. 'It's probably Ted,' she told the dog. 'But you'd better go and see anyway. If it's a burglar, do your stuff and see the bugger off!' Not for one minute did she think it might be an intruder.

In a minute the dog was gone, bounding away towards Ted's place, soon lost in the darkness. 'Ted need never worry with him around,' muttered Lucy. It had taken her a long time to persuade him he needed a dog around, but now he thought the world of Jake.

There was something wrong.

It was clear to Lucy that Sophie had done all that was asked of her. The floors were scrubbed and the shelves were tidied, though they were badly in need of re-stocking. All the tills were covered, and every door closed.

But there was something very wrong.

She called out: 'Sophie?'

No answer.

She walked down the aisle towards the back room. 'SOPHIE!'

Still no answer.

She paused, looking every which way. There was no sign of the girl. No sound. No sight. Only a strange, eerie emptiness that made her flesh creep.

Going into all the different departments, she soon realised that Sophie was not in the building. 'Where the Hell is she?' Her handbag stood beside the till, and her coat was hanging up in the staff room, so she obviously had not gone home.

Worried now, Lucy wished she hadn't sent the dog away. Don't be silly, she told herself. You're letting your imagination run away with you. She's probably in the loo. Of course! She hadn't thought of that.

A quick search told her she was wrong.

The only place left was the cafeteria. *That's* where she'll be. She's finished her work so she's gone for a well-deserved drink. But another nagging thought voiced itself. So why didn't she take her handbag with her? Like most women, Sophie took her bag wherever she went.

Instinctively Lucy picked up the bag and went in search of its owner.

Her hopes faded when she neared the cafeteria. The lights were out. Sophie wouldn't be in there. All the same, instinct urged her to take a look. I'm sure the lights were on when I came up the drive, she thought. She couldn't be certain, but in her mind's eye she seemed to see the lighted windows.

A little smile lifted the corners of her mouth. I expect she was in there when I arrived, and now we keep missing each other. But if that was so, why hadn't Sophie answered her call? Odd that. Lucy didn't like it. Not at all.

As she opened the door, Lucy thought she heard a scuffling sound. 'Sophie, are you in there?'

No answer.

She searched for the light switch, then her eyes were temporarily blinded by the rush of light. Slowly her gaze was drawn forward, to the kitchen area. A small spiral of steam rose from behind the counter screen. A great surge of relief rushed through her as she started forward, tracing a meandering path round tables and chairs.

Though she couldn't see the girl, Lucy sensed she was close. 'Sophie? What are you doing in the dark? I've been looking everywhere for . . .' Her voice froze, and her eyes opened wide with horror as she looked beyond the counter. She tried to speak but could only shake her head in disbelief.

The girl was stark naked, mouth sealed by means of a wide, dirty piece of cloth. The gag was stretched so tightly that it dug into her skin, making her eyes pop. Dark with terror, the eyes stared back at Lucy. HELP ME! they seemed to scream. PLEASE HELP ME!

Bound hand and foot, she was held flat against the wall by means of a rope tied to a beam above her, forcing her arms way above her head. Her legs were slightly parted and secured to the legs of two tables standing either side. Both the girl's ankles were encircled by a ring of blood where the ropes ate into the flesh.

Into Lucy's horrified mind came the image of Christ being crucified.

Recovering from her shock, she rushed forward.

Suddenly he appeared out of nowhere. Blocking her way, he slammed the flat of his hand against her chest. 'You shouldn't barge in here like that.' His voice was virulently hostile, piercing blue eyes holding her fast. 'You could so easily have caused an accident.' Laughing, he held up his other arm to show he was holding a kettle. 'But now you're here, you might as well stay.' He laughed softly in her face.

Steam from the spout spiralled into the air, causing all kinds of images to blur in Lucy's mind. Of course! That was what she had seen when she first switched on the light. *The kettle was filled with boiling water!*

In a quiet firm voice that belied the turmoil inside her, she appealed to him, 'Don't be a fool, Robert. Put the kettle down. Let me go to her.'

With one movement of his immensely strong arm, he hit out to send her reeling backwards. Falling amongst the chairs with a sickening thud, she rolled to the floor. Momentarily dazed and disorientated, she struggled to clamber up but had no chance as he grabbed her by the scruff of the neck, plucking her out as though she was no more than a rag doll.

Throwing her into a chair only a few feet away from the girl, he smiled, a slow, evil smile that told Lucy he was quite mad. 'You really are naughty,' he said, wagging a finger. 'You ought not to have come in here uninvited, especially when Sophie and I haven't even finished our little discussion.'

Daring to challenge him, yet still acutely aware that he was holding the kettle of boiling water very near her face, she pleaded, 'Let her go, Robert. She's done nothing wrong.'

He laughed, raising his eyebrows in disbelief. 'How can you say that?' he demanded, voice deepening to a growl. 'She told you I made her cry, didn't she?'

'No! She told me nothing.'

'You're a liar!' As he spoke he tipped the kettle over her foot. The boiling water seared through her shoe and into her skin, making her gasp with pain. 'Dear me,' he moaned. 'Now see what you've made me do.'

Anger surged inside her. 'You bastard! If you hurt that girl, I'll see you put away for a long, long time!'

Bending forward, he laughed in her face, holding the kettle over her neck. 'You shouldn't have said that, you bitch!'

She wanted to strangle him with her bare hands. The idea must have been visible in her face because without warning he took her by the throat. 'I ought to choke the life out of you here and now.' He sighed with a strange kind of pleasure. 'But I won't, because you see . . . I want you to watch.'

While he talked his voice grew lower and lower, thumbs pressing harder and harder, like two bolts driving through her neck. The pain was excruciating. Worse, she felt herself losing her senses. Like a tiger she clawed at him. Suddenly his hands loosened and, while he laughed insanely, she gasped air into her lungs, choking and coughing as she breathed.

When she was able to focus on him, he was standing beside the girl, one hand stroking her hair, the other raised to her throat. The kettle was discarded nearby. Now he had a long steel meat-skewer in his hand.

Touching the cold steel against the girl's throat, he moved it from side to side, drawing just the tiniest trickle of blood. When she began to whimper, he kissed her face. 'It's your own fault,' he sighed. 'You promised you wouldn't tell anyone about our little encounter the other night. I didn't mean to hurt you. If you hadn't been so unwilling in the first place, there would have been no need for me to force myself on you.'

'I knew it!' Lucy was on her feet. She felt sick to her stomach with pain, but such was her fury she kept advancing towards him, wanting to hurt him as he'd hurt her. As he'd hurt Sophie.

'THAT'S FAR ENOUGH!' his voice boomed out, stopping her in her tracks. The voice became a menacing whisper. 'Unless you want me to run her through.'

Knowing he meant every word, Lucy stood quite still, her eyes staring into his for a moment, and then she was looking into the girl's terrified face. The brown eyes stared back. Like two round, still pools they seemed strangely beautiful in that stark-white face. Her every limb was trembling as she silently pleaded with Lucy to stay back.

From that moment on, Lucy did as she was told. Her every instinct told her that Robert wouldn't think twice about killing the girl, and probably her too if she goaded him enough.

He smiled. 'Sit down, Lucy.' When she turned for the nearest chair, he ordered, 'NO! Sit on the floor.'

After momentarily hesitating, she sat down, the cold from the tiles striking deep into her bones. She was frightened now. Very frightened, for herself and for Sophie.

He smiled again. 'Good. That didn't hurt, now did it?'

Appealing to any shred of decency left in him, she quietly persisted. 'Think what you're doing, Robert. You've no reason to hurt Sophie. She didn't tell me anything. Why don't you let her go? Please!'

'KEEP QUIET!'

Lucy's gaze went to the girl. She half smiled, nodding her head in silent encouragement. The girl's eyes closed. When they opened again, tears hung like plump raindrops on her long lashes before spilling over and meandering slowly down her face.

Robert scowled at Lucy. 'You see how you're upsetting her,' he accused. 'We were all right before you came in.' Turning to the girl, he kissed her on the forehead. 'I'm sorry,' he moaned, 'but I can't send her away. Not until we've finished here . . . you and me.' Putting out his tongue, he licked her face. 'She thinks I want to hurt you,' he murmured. Keeping the tip of the meat-skewer against her neck, he let his other hand wander over her body, touching her breasts and thighs. When she shivered with terror he stroked one hand down her arm. 'Shh,' he whispered, 'I don't want to hurt you. I love you.'

For one heart-stopping moment he let his arm slide down with the meat-skewer hanging loose against his side. 'You love me too, don't you?' he pleaded. 'Say it, Sophie. Say you love me too.' He sounded desperate, softly crying as he urged her to say she loved him. Over and over he begged her, in his madness not realising she was gagged and unable to speak even if she'd wanted to.

Lucy would have used that moment to scramble up, but he turned suddenly. 'Don't try it,' he warned.

Striding across the floor, he dragged Lucy by the scruff of the neck to a place where he could see both her and Sophie at the same time. Pressing the skewer to the girl's throat again, he used his other hand to undress himself. 'Now,' he said, grinning into her face, 'you've kept me waiting long enough.' There was no mistaking his meaning.

With surprising dexterity, he removed first his shirt, then his trousers. 'She pretends not to like me,' he told the fearful Lucy, 'when she wants me all the time.' He laughed, that awful sinister sound that turned her stomach over. 'You mustn't mind if we make love now,' he jeered. 'After all, you weren't invited to watch, were you?'

Lucy thought she was in some kind of nightmare.

Here was Sophie, trussed up and tied like a pig about to be slaughtered, and now he was blatantly undressing with the intention of raping the girl before Lucy's eyes. Repulsed beyond words, she screamed, 'I WON'T LET YOU DO IT!' With a great roar, she scrambled up, and oblivious to her own safety, launched herself through the air towards him.

Taken by surprise he took the full force of her attack, stumbling back spreadeagled with Lucy on top, hitting out and yelling like a thing possessed.

Suddenly there were other voices. A long dark shadow knocked her aside as it made for its intended victim. With a loud thud it landed square on his chest. Excited by his terrified screams, it tore into him. There was a mad scuffle, with the young man screaming and Sophie struggling to release herself. In the mêlée, Lucy was almost smothered by Robert and Jake as they fought and rolled about, one on top of the other.

Fighting her way past, Lucy was able to release Sophie. Gently she untied the gag and the ropes. 'It's all right,' she comforted her. 'You're safe now.' And so was she. The enormity of what had taken place here was only now beginning to dawn on her.

Old Ted's voice rose above the din: 'HERE, BOY! HERE!' Reluctantly, the dog gave up its quarry.

While Ted secured the dog, Lucy's father took hold of the young man. 'I should let him finish you off, you bastard!' he hissed. He had witnessed the dreadful scene and been shocked to the core.

Lucy was still cradling the sobbing girl in her arms when she heard her father's voice. 'Will she be all right, Lucy?'

She shook her head. No one, not even Lucy, could imagine how such an experience would affect the girl's mind. All the same, for Sophie's sake she answered, 'She'll be fine, Dad.' Her voice was husky with gratitude. 'Thanks to you two.'

Mike nodded. He understood. 'Come on, you!' he snapped at Robert. 'The police will want to deal with you. Though if I had my way, you'd get your just deserts right here and now!' But it was enough for Mike to know the women were all right. Besides, it gave him a deal of satisfaction to see how the dog had mauled the young man. 'Painful, is it?' he asked, jabbing a finger at the wound on Robert's shoulder and making him cry out. 'Now you know what it's like to be on the receiving end, eh?'

Later, when Robert was locked in a shed, with Ted and his dog standing guard until the police arrived, Mike explained how he'd been worried about Lucy, and that when he'd driven out, he and Ted had mounted a search. 'It was a father's instinct that brought me out here,' he told her. 'I only wish we could have got here a bit faster.'

By the time the police arrived, Lucy had plied Sophie with endless cups of strong sweet tea. She'd brought her clothes, and helped her dress, and coated her ankle wounds with antiseptic cream from the first-aid box. 'You're safe now, sweetheart,' she murmured, cradling her tightly. 'He won't hurt you, ever again.'

Though, as he was marched to the police car, the young man's voice could be heard raised in fury: 'Can you hear me, Nolan, you bitch? I'll have you for this. Don't think you can sleep easy in your bed at night.'

Lucy accompanied Sophie to hospital where it was advised she should stay at least overnight. 'She's in shock,' the doctor told her worried parents. 'But apart from the ankle wounds and grazes to her wrists, there is no physical damage.'

He was not qualified to comment on the extent of her emotional trauma. Only time would tell.

Chapter Six

Stern-faced and anxious, Jack paced the room. He was a man with a purpose, a man with a sweetheart too far away from him. Enough time had already been wasted and his patience was at an end. 'So what's the situation?' he demanded.

The other man was also impatient, aching to be left alone on his weekend off. 'We'll talk tomorrow.'

'We'll talk *now*! Or not at all.'

'What's the rush?'

'What "rush"?' Jack's voice hardened. 'You put a very sound business proposition to me some months back, and I accepted it. I think you've had time enough to consider it, and now I need to know which way you're going.'

'Bugger off, Hanson!' he groaned. 'Come to the office in the morning. We'll talk it through then.'

'Won't do.' Jack was adamant. 'I'm booked on the ferry out today, and if I don't have a firm decision now, I may well not come back. My business here is finished. I've done what I set out to do. Now I'm looking for new challenges.'

'Like your own hotel?'

Jack had paced to the window and was staring out across the Solent. The April sun was shining, but his heart was shadowed by thoughts of Lucy. He missed her. God, how he missed her!

At the other man's remark, he swung round and strode across the room. 'Yes, my own hotel,' he confirmed. 'That's always been my aim, and that's the only reason I'm here.'

'You're a stubborn bugger, I'll give you that.'

'And a good businessman.' Jack felt he had him right where he wanted him. 'You're a good businessman too, or you wouldn't have approached me.'

A small smile. A nod. But not a single reassuring word.

As he leant over the desk, Jack's angry green eyes bored into the other man's. 'You came to me, and I liked your idea enough to feel I could make it work for both of us.' In fact the idea had excited him so much he'd lain awake half the night, thinking and planning. 'But I won't be played along,' he warned. 'Either you want to go ahead with the plan or you don't.' Suspicion edged his voice. 'If you're having second thoughts, you'd better tell me. I don't like being kept in the dark.'

Prosperous, plump and quietly aware of his own importance, Cecil Dayton didn't even look up. Instead he drummed his fingers on the desk, mouth pursed into a multitude of tight little lines, his whole body swaying back and forth as he considered his answer.

Careful in everything he did, Cecil was irritatingly single-minded when considering business matters. He took his time. But people were prepared to wait for his opinion, because when he reached a conclusion, the result was usually money-spinning for all concerned.

A first-rate accountant, Cecil had an enviable reputation; a status which reflected itself in his exorbitant but well-justified fees.

When he spoke it was with the same deliberation he applied to his thinking. 'I'm *not* having second thoughts.'

'What then?' Jack wondered if he would ever understand the man.

'I like to do things in an orderly way ... in the office, between nine and five, Monday to Friday. I do not take kindly to being badgered in my own home on a Sunday afternoon.' But his irritation was tempered with respect because, like himself, Jack had an eye for a solid business venture. He also had a unique talent for making money. There were very few men about of the calibre of Jack Hanson, so the last thing Cecil wanted to do was alienate him.

Jack had heard enough. Without a word he turned and made for the door. Pity, he thought. The idea had been good, but it wasn't worth kow-towing for.

Cecil summoned him back. 'Don't be an arsehole!' he called out. 'You've caught me in a foul mood, that's all.'

Not easily placated, Jack told him, 'You're not the only one with a busy schedule. I didn't need you before, and I don't need you now. Remember that.' Whatever he had to do, he could do it on his own.

The other man regarded him with a kind of pride. He liked Jack, admired the set of his jaw and the steely glint in those dark green eyes. Most of all he liked the idea of making money hand over fist. Jack would repay an investment ten times over, and Cecil was not about to let him go. 'Over there,' he said, pointing tiredly to the walnut cabinet. 'I could do with a drink. Get yourself one.'

While Jack retrieved the whisky and glasses from inside the cabinet, Cecil went on, 'I've had a bad night. Like a fool I let myself be talked into going sailing yesterday. It was hard work and I'm aching all over. And I mean . . . all over!'

Smiling, Jack handed him a glass half-filled with whisky. 'All over?' he repeated, trying not to laugh.

'My legs, neck and arms are killing me, I tell you.' After taking a sip or two of the burning liquid, he leaned back in his chair and chuckled heartily. 'Even my arse aches!'

Jack raised his glass. 'To your arse,' he said, solemnly.

'You heartless bugger!'

But the ice was broken and a more amicable atmosphere prevailed. 'So you're away to the mainland tonight?'

'That's right,' Jack confirmed.

'Done the job you came to do and now it's back to the lovely lady?'

'Right again.'

'Last time she was here, I got a glimpse of her in the hotel foyer. Mmm!' The tip of his tongue came out to wet his lips. 'I can see why you're in a hurry to get back to her.'

Jack had been seated. Now he stood up, determined to keep Lucy out of the conversation. 'The business proposition,' he growled, 'is it on or off?' He had no time to waste.

'It's on.'

Jack's heart turned somersaults. 'Everything as we discussed then?'

Cecil nodded. 'Exactly as discussed.'

'The money?'

Again that knowing little smile. 'The money's already earmarked. I saw to that last week.'

Jack's delight was tinged with anger. 'Then why the Hell did you keep me waiting 'til now?'

'It's a lot of money. I had to be certain.'

'Of what?'

'Of you.'

'Been checking up on me again, eh?'

'Check and double check, that's always been my creed.'

'Okay, so you've checked. The money's there. So when can I get started?'

'Just say the word, and it's all systems go.'

'Everything's ready,' Jack confirmed. 'It's just a matter of getting it all into gear.' In fact, he had worked his tail off these past months, and now he was raring to go.

'When do you hand over the running of the hotel to the new manager?' Caught up in a rush of excitement, Cecil was busy making notes.

'Friday week.' It couldn't come soon enough for Jack. As long as he had Lucy with him, he wouldn't care if he was off to the other side of the world.

'And after that?'

'A few loose ends to tie up, that's all.'

'And then?'

Jack made a few quick mental calculations. 'All being well, I reckon I'll be on my way in a fortnight.'

'That's what I like . . . a man with a purpose. We'll do all right, you and me.'

Still cautious, Jack warned him, 'I want no interference.' He'd rather go it alone than be answerable to another lord and master.

'You'll get none. What do I know about the running of a hotel? I'm perfectly content to let you treble my investment.'

'As I've already said, I make no promises. It's as much of a risk for me as it is for you.'

'On a somewhat different scale of investment, though.'

'All the same, I'm putting in every penny I've got.' It was hard-earned money, got by blood and sweat. 'My entire savings.'

Cecil nodded with approval. 'That's what swung it in your favour,' he revealed. 'The fact that you were prepared to sink everything you'd got into the venture. With confidence like that, I'd have been all kinds of a fool not to get involved.'

'As I said, you may not see any return on your money for some years.'

'I'm prepared for that.'

Jack raised his glass again. 'To the new hotel.'

Cecil's smile filled his fleshy face. 'To *us*.' Then he took a great gulp of whisky, and instantly regretted it.

When he had stopped choking, they shook on the deal. 'Bloody midges!' Grabbing up a rule, Cecil frantically scratched his itching back.

Deeply satisfied with the outcome of this meeting, Jack stood up to leave. He felt good. At long last he could see it all coming right.

While they shook hands he said, 'You know, in the end I would have done it on my own.'

Seeing the determination in those striking green eyes, the other man realised again he had backed the right horse in Jack. 'I don't doubt it for a minute,' he conceded. 'But this way you get it all off the ground a bit quicker.'

'If all goes well, this is only the first of many.'

'I don't doubt that either.' Cecil's voice was filled with genuine admiration. 'I'm sure, in years to come, we'll see a whole string of Hanson hotels right across the world. And here I am . . . part of that budding empire.'

'Glad to have you along.' The easy, boyish grin twinkled in Jack's eyes. 'So long as you remember your place.'

Falling back in his chair Cecil returned the smile. 'Don't be late for the ferry,' he said. 'You shouldn't keep a girl like Lucy waiting.' Catching the gleam in Jack's eyes, he chuckled. 'Looks like you're in a celebratory mood.'

'And why not? You see before you a happy man,' Jack replied. 'A man with *two* dreams. I have one of them within my grasp. The other is waiting on the mainland.' In two strides he was across the room. 'I'll be back in a few days to finalise matters,' he promised. 'And by the way, I'll thank you to keep your avaricious eyes off my future wife.'

As he ran down the steps outside, he felt like a man released. 'Well, Lucy, I'm on my way, sweetheart,' he murmured. 'You'll never know how much I've missed having you near, but now we can be together at last.'

A great tide of love washed over him. 'I hope to God we'll never be parted again.'

Lucy saw the ferry arriving and her heart leaped.

It seemed she had been waiting a lifetime for it to appear and now it was only a matter of minutes before Jack was striding towards her. With a feeling of great joy she fell into his arms and stayed there for what seemed an age. Being close to Jack, with his arms around her, was the most wonderful feeling on earth. 'It's so good to see you,' she murmured, hugging him to her.

Swinging her away, he kissed her full on the mouth. 'Anybody would think I'd been away for months.' He smiled. 'But I know what you mean, and it's good to see you too, sweetheart.'

As they drove home, with Lucy relaxed in the passenger seat and Jack at the wheel, she thought it was time she learned what all the excitement was about. 'You still haven't told me, you devil.'

'*What* haven't I told you?' He had so wanted to keep his secret for a more intimate moment.

'Stop teasing!' She gently tweaked his ear. 'When you rang the other night, you said you had something to tell me.'

'So I have.' This was a big moment in their lives. 'Well?'

Hopefully, he glanced at her. 'Sweetheart, will you do me a favour?'

'All depends.'

The warmth of his fingers spread through hers when he suddenly reached out to touch her. 'Can you wait until this evening? What I have to say is too important to discuss while we're driving along.' He was bursting to tell her, but this wasn't really the time or the place. 'I want to be looking into your eyes when I tell you.'

She knew then that it was something very important. Something wonderful, to do with their future together. Convinced he was about to ask if she would name the wedding day, she told him, 'I can wait. But only until this evening!'

Another quick glance. 'Love you, Lucy Nolan,' he murmured, his fingers squeezing hers.

'Love you back,' she whispered. And she did. More than he would ever know. 'Now take your hands off me and pay attention to the road, or we won't make it to this evening!'

But they did, and that evening turned out to hold the biggest surprise of her life.

Unknown to Lucy, Jack and her mother had been planning a night out at a club, with dinner and dancing, and afterwards her parents would go one way and she and Jack would go the other.

Sally knew Jack meant to ask Lucy if she would name the day, but had not been told of the other exciting news. He was determined that Lucy would be the first to know.

'You look beautiful,' he said as she came into the front room to greet him that night. She was wearing a simple blue dress and bolero. On her feet she wore her favourite blue shoes; around her neck a single string of pearls. She wore no earrings, and her hair was brushed loose and free. Her eyes had only the merest hint of shadow, and her mouth a touch of warm red lipstick. Lucy was just an ordinary girl with ordinary tastes but an extraordinary kind of beauty. One that shone from her soul.

There was something about her that crept right inside him, inspiring him to great things. 'You'll turn every man's eye in the place,' he breathed, thrilled to be home. Thrilled to be with her.

'Thank you, Jack.' She quietly studied him.

Jack always looked smart, but in his dark blue suit, white shirt and narrow tie, he looked incredibly handsome. 'I won't see another man,' she assured him. With Jack beside her, why should she?

Sally's happy voice cut into their intimate moment. 'What about me?' she demanded, twirling round in her black skirt and shimmery top. 'Do I look lovely, or don't I?'

'You look good enough to eat,' Mike said, emerging from upstairs in a dark suit, looking nothing like a greengrocer. 'Let any other man eye *you* up and he'll end up on the floor.'

Sally beamed. Winking at Lucy and Jack, she said hopefully, 'Sounds like I might have a jealous husband.'

'You can bet on it.' Taking her by the arm, Mike led her to the door. 'Now, if you please, your carriage awaits.'

The 'carriage' was a white chauffeured Jaguar, hired by Mike at no small expense. Lucy had half-heartedly protested at the extravagance, especially when she suspected they would need every penny to pay for the wedding.

On this occasion, though, Mike had swept aside her protests. 'This is a very special evening, sweetheart,' he said. 'Probably the only evening like it we will ever have in our lives.'

And how could she argue with that?

It was the most wonderful evening, one which would stay with Lucy until the day she died.

The club was packed, the band playing music of a more romantic era, and at their candlelit table, Lucy looked at those she loved until her heart ached with happiness.

All around them people were having a wonderful time. Peals of laughter rang through the air, the music played softly in the background, and altogether there was an atmosphere of celebration.

The meal was splendid but Lucy was so excited she couldn't do it justice, though her parents tucked in and thoroughly enjoyed themselves. 'Haven't had a feast like this in ages,' Mike declared, gratefully sipping the claret. Sally told him not to overdo it: 'Or you'll suffer with indigestion in the morning.'

That slowed him down because she was right.

When the meal was over, Jack took Lucy on to the dance floor. 'Enjoying yourself, sweetheart?' he whispered in her ear.

'It's a marvellous evening,' she replied. 'I wish you'd tell me what it's all for?' She had already guessed, but needed to hear it from him.

Suddenly, he brought her to a halt. Gazing down into her soft grey eyes, he asked, 'How much do you love me, Lucy Nolan?'

It was a moment before she answered, for how did she put into words all that she felt in her heart? In a tender voice, she replied, 'You *know* how much.'

'Enough to marry me?'

'Oh, Jack!' She thought she knew what was coming. 'You don't have to ask that.'

'Enough to marry me inside a month?'

Speechless, her grey eyes shining with happiness, she could only nod.

He smiled, then he laughed, then he swung her round and kissed her. All round them dancers had heard the conversation and now stopped and stared. Smiling and laughing as though they were a part of it, they watched as Jack grabbed Lucy's hand and ran her across the floor to the stage.

Taking her by the waist, he swung her up first before following with one easy leap. By now people were crowding round, with Mike and Sally up front. The band stopped playing and he was given the microphone. 'Listen, everybody!' Drawing Lucy close, he embraced her with one hand while juggling the microphone in the other. 'I want you all to know . . . Lucy and I are going to be married!'

The place erupted, with laughing and clapping and shouts of 'Congratulations!' Then the band struck up a Nat King Cole number and everyone started to dance. Sally and Mike lingered a moment, smiling up at the happy couple through moist eyes, before they too mingled with the others: to dance, and think, and reflect on their own happy life together.

Jack took Lucy in his arms and they danced round the stage. 'I love you,' she murmured, and it seemed all of her life had been leading to this very special evening.

At half-past midnight, Jack and his party decided to leave. 'It's been right bloody grand!' Mike declared,

red-faced from the wine. 'Me an' my Sal, dancing the night away.'

'Come on, you daft devil,' she chuckled. 'Let's get you home and off to bed.' Though, as she and Mike bundled into the Jaguar, she reiterated his comment. 'It's been one of the best evenings we've ever had,' she told Jack. 'It's a bit of a shock . . . you and our Lucy getting wed in a month! I thought it would be some time yet, I really did.' She laughed. 'Don't make me a grandmother too soon, will you, eh?'

Thrusting his face forward, Mike declared, 'Tek no notice. Have a dozen kids and we'll be thrilled to bits, won't we, our Sal, eh?' Nearly falling out of the car at the house, he shook hands with Jack. 'But, my word, it's been a grand evening. Aye, a right bloody grand evening. Thank you, son. Next time the treat's on me.'

But the evening was not over yet.

After dropping off Mike and Sally, Jack stretched out a hand to stop Lucy from stepping out of the car. 'No, sweetheart, we're not going home,' he said. 'We need to talk.'

She was pleased but curious. 'Where are we going?'

'Wait and see,' he murmured. Then, leaning forward, he instructed the driver.

A short time later the car was parked down Penny Street, with the driver gently snoozing, while Jack and Lucy strolled alongside the canal. 'There's something else I have to ask,' Jack began to explain. 'About *after* the wedding.'

Without knowing why, Lucy was anxious. But she made no comment. Instead, she waited for him to go on.

'You know I'll be handing over the hotel to its new manager soon?'

'Yes.' Her curiosity heightened. 'And you've already found another, is that it?'

'In a way.'

'Oh, Jack, that's wonderful. I knew you'd be searching around, but I'd no idea you already had something in your sights. Another rundown place, is it?'

Down by the water, the cool air seemed damp, filtering right through her bolero. When she shivered, he pressed her close to him. 'There's only one way to tell you,' he said. 'You know how much I've always wanted my own hotel? How I've always worked towards that end, keeping it in mind, day and night? A dream, sweetheart, a dream for you and me to share.' In his excitement, the words tumbled out, one over the other. 'Well now, thanks to a certain man . . . or rather *two* certain men . . . I can make that dream come true.'

He then went on to explain how Cecil had been so impressed by his work at the hotel that he was prepared to back him to the hilt. 'It was one of those chance meetings . . . a businessman on holiday got drunk, talked a lot about how he was on the verge of going bankrupt. Apparently, he'd bitten off more than he could chew and was desperately looking for a buyer for this half-built property in Cyprus.'

'*Cyprus!*' This was the first Lucy had heard of it and she was more than a little shocked. 'Why did you never mention it?'

'Because I honestly believed it was pie in the sky. Drink makes some people talk a lot of nonsense. I needed to make enquiries . . . get him checked out, go there and see for myself what was on offer.'

'You mean you actually went to Cyprus?'

Guiltily, he bowed his head. 'I know I should have told you,' he admitted. 'I wanted to, but it might all have come to nothing.'

'Now I know why I couldn't get you on the phone for three days.'At the time she hadn't worried because he always left a message saying he was here or there, and that he would ring her back when he got a minute. She was up to her neck at the nurseries and, what with one thing and another, it didn't seem too urgent and the time flew by. 'I never knew you were so devious.'

'Am I forgiven?'

'All depends what else you've got to tell me.'

'Remember the accountant who was looking after my boss's interests?'

Lucy remembered. The man hardly took his eyes off her when they were introduced in the hotel foyer. 'Cecil . . .'

'Dayton,' Jack added. 'Cecil Dayton, a man with so many fingers in so many pies it's a wonder he has enough hands to go round! But he's a clever, shrewd fellow. He's well respected and trusted by every businessman on the Isle of Wight. When he says jump, they jump, and they're a whole lot richer because they listen to him.'

'I can believe that.' He seemed like a man who knew what he was doing.

'He offered to come to Cyprus with me, and I took him up on the offer. I knew he would spot a fraud a mile off, and as he had certain business interests

there, he had already gone through the legal mine-
fields before.'

'When he saw this half-built property, what did
he think?'

'At first he was a bit jittery. But when he saw I
was committed to going ahead, he wanted in.'

Lucy couldn't believe her ears. 'Jack Hanson, are
you saying you've got yourself into debt for a hotel . . .
in Cyprus?'

Gripping her by the shoulders, he turned her to
face him. 'This is it, Lucy!' he said in a harsh, jubilant
voice. 'This one is *ours*! It's big and beautiful. It's
right on the beach, and the price is open to negotia-
tion. You see, there are so many hotels going up,
nobody wants to take on somebody else's failure. I'll
take it on, though, and it will be the start of many
more.'

'When is all this supposed to happen?' The consequences were only now beginning to dawn on her.
'And if this accountant is backing you, won't the hotel
be partly owned by him?'

'Only if it all goes wrong, which it won't.'

Lucy was thrilled. 'I've never seen you like this
before,' she told him. Jack was always confident, but
this time it was as though he held the world right in
the palm of his hand.

'I've never felt like this before.' He smiled. 'I
promise, Cecil won't get to touch what belongs to
you and me. It's all agreed. He'll get his money back,
with a fat profit, when the hotel is up and running,
and that's it. Once the money is repaid, he has no
hold on me or the hotel.'

'So it's like a mortgage?'

'But not so restrictive. He's investing in *me* rather than in the business. And, don't forget, I do have money of my own.'

'Where do you go from here?'

'Day after tomorrow, I have to be back on the Isle of Wight. I need to tie up a few loose ends. Then I'll be flying out to Cyprus. There I'll meet up with the owner, then it's solicitors' meetings, that sort of thing . . . make sure everything is legally watertight. After that, I'll be back to make you my wife. Then a honeymoon wherever you want to go. Next stop Cyprus, and a new life.'

In the lamplight his eyes shone with such excitement it was infectious. 'What do you say to that, my love?'

'I don't know what to say.' Suddenly she was smiling. 'I didn't expect to live in Cyprus after I got married. I've never even thought of going there.'

'Oh, Lucy, it's beautiful! Clear blue skies, turquoise seas and a setting sun such as you've never seen. Oh, and you'll love the people. They're so friendly.'

In the cold she snuggled up to him. 'It sounds like Paradise,' she whispered. 'But then, Paradise will always be where you are.'

'You mean it, sweetheart? You don't mind moving so far away from your family?'

'How long does it take to get there?'

'Three and a half hours . . . four at the most.'

'So, it's not the other end of the world?' She would miss her mam and dad, but they would always have each other. And she would probably worry about Debbie, but four hours wasn't too far away.

Besides, as she told Jack now, 'So long as we're

together, I'm content.' But then there was Ted. She would have to think that through.

Lucy wasn't too astonished when the Jaguar sped away from town and into the countryside. 'I suppose this is all part of the surprise?' she said, giving him a wary glance.

'Give you a taste for honeymooning.' He smiled, kissing her soundly on the mouth. 'Why? Would you rather go home?'

She kissed him back. 'No. Surprise me.' She was getting used to being 'surprised'. What with Jack buying his own hotel in Cyprus, and the two of them going to live there after they were married. Now she was being driven away to God knows where to acquire a 'taste for honeymooning'. Where would it all end? she thought. But then, she didn't want it to end. She wanted it to go on and on.

The hotel was a beautiful quaint inn along the Preston New Road. Set beside the River Ribble, it had old oak gables and lead-lighted windows, and little flowerbeds all along the front.

'Pretty, eh?' Getting out of the car, Jack held out his hand to her. 'We're booked in for one night,' he said softly. 'I hope you like it.'

Looking up at the gable ends, Lucy read the name aloud. 'The Tickled Trout.' She smiled. 'What a strange name.'

'Apparently that's because it fronts the river. The fishermen flock here, hoping to catch trout.'

'How did you know about this place?' Lucy had never heard of it.

His boyish grin always delighted her. 'I'm not in

the hotel trade for nothing,' he said. 'At one time I actually had my eye on this place.' It had come to nothing, he didn't have the money or the backing to pursue it, so like most enterprises it didn't even get off the ground.

'You're a deep devil, Jack Hanson.' Lucy's gaze fixed on him. 'What else don't I know about you?'

'What you see is what you get,' he answered. 'Now let's get inside. It's blowing a bit chilly.'

There were two rooms booked in the name of Jack Hanson; one double en-suite for himself and Lucy, and a single room for the driver. 'Shameful extravagance,' she teased. 'I hope you're not trying to buy me?'

Throwing his overnight bag on the trestle, he grabbed her by the waist. Seated on the bed, he stood her before him, his wonderful dark green eyes looking up at her. 'We could always leave and sleep in the car,' he said with a smile.

'That would be cosy... you, me and the driver. He might be a snorer.'

'Or a Peeping Tom.'

She pulled a serious face. 'Are you implying there might be something for him to peep at?'

'I'm hoping so.'

'In that case, I think we'd better stay here.'

Suddenly he was serious too, his gaze melting into hers and arms tightening around her waist. 'I do love you,' he murmured.

For a time she gazed down on his face, that handsome, familiar face she had come to know and love so much. It wouldn't matter to her whether he was a bus-driver or swept the streets, she would love him just the same. He was her once-in-a-lifetime love. He was the man she wanted above all others; her yesterday, today and tomorrow. Jack was her life, and there were no words to explain how she felt towards him. 'I love you' never seemed enough.

'Cat got your tongue?' His smile enveloped her.

She laid her hand on his face. 'Oh, Jack Hanson.'

In that very special moment something bound them together, some unseen thing that was delicate as life itself, yet stronger than any force on God's earth.

Suddenly she was crying, warm, gentle tears falling down her face. She was so happy it was almost unbearable.

He understood.

Tenderly he reached up, wiping her tears with his thumb.

With a slow, surprisingly gentle touch, he took off her bolero and laid it on the bed.

When she was naked, he laid her alongside him.

Through his trousers, she could feel the hard erect member against her thigh. Wanting him, needing him, she undid them and slid them down. He took off his shirt, revealing the whole of his magnificent body: the wide dark chest, slim waist and hard curved buttocks. The touch of his skin on hers was soft and rough at the same time. And all the while he gazed at her, those wonderful eyes whispering of deep oceans and deeper emotions.

Astride her now, his hands following the curves of her body, he savoured his woman, coaxing and caressing, awakening wild savage needs within her. 'Don't, Jack!' Her voice was low and needful, her arms around his neck then down below, pushing, urging. When he burst into her, she gasped with pleasure, every nerve-ending alive and tingling.

He was on top, then she was, moving together, bound by the same all-consuming passion, loving each other in the way it should be. Wilder now. Frenzied. Nothing could stop the wave of passion that carried them up, up to unbearable sensual pleasures – until, exhausted and thrilled, they clung together for what seemed an endless time.

They showered together, washing each other. Calmer now, wonderfully satisfied.

Wrapped in a towelling dressing-gown, Lucy was about to clean her teeth when she suddenly realised she had no toothbrush. 'Surprises are all right,' she said, 'but I've got no nightie, no toiletries, and God knows what I'll look like in the morning without my make-up on.'

'You'll look lovely,' he promised her.

'Oh, yes, with a shiny nose and yucky teeth.' Running the tip of her tongue over them, she frowned. 'I'll ring the desk and see if they can provide a toothbrush.'

Getting his overnight bag, Jack unzipped it. 'See what you can find in here,' he said with a little grin.

Inside the bag she found another, smaller overnight bag, containing her toiletries and fresh underwear, a favourite blue silk nightie, and even a change of clothes: brown cords and a long-sleeved blouse. 'As I said before, you're a devious devil, Jack Hanson.'

He slid in between the covers. 'Organised, that's

what I am.' Winking, he urged her to hurry up: 'So I can give you a big cuddle.'

After she'd put on her nightie, cleaned her teeth and brushed her hair, she returned for her big cuddle.

Jack, however, was fast asleep, one arm across her pillow, the other over his face. 'You're right,' she chuckled, gently removing his arm and kissing his mouth. 'It's been a long day.'

Just as she was about to slide in beside him, a thought crossed Lucy's mind, making her sit up. 'Mam!' In all the excitement she'd forgotten to call Sally. 'She'll be worried sick.' Picking up her wristwatch from the bedside cabinet, she was horrified to see what time it was. 'Two o'clock. I don't know if I dare ring her now,' she mused. 'What if she's asleep? What if she's already guessed that Jack and I are staying elsewhere?' She couldn't be certain. 'She's probably pacing the floor, worried out of her mind. Oh my God! I hope she doesn't call the police.'

She laughed, a soft reproachful sound. 'Don't be so melodramatic, Lucy,' she chided herself. 'Your mam's no fool.' But she knew from experience that Sally was a born worrier. I'll have to let her know we're all right, she decided, or I won't get any sleep either.

Very quietly, so as not to wake Jack, she picked up the receiver and dialled '9' for an outside line, then the number. It seemed to ring for ever. She began to panic. 'Come on, Mam, where are you?' She let it ring, on and on, until at last a tired voice spoke at the other end. 'Who's that?'

'Mam?' Relief flooded through her. 'It's me, Lucy.'

The voice sharpened. 'Lucy! Whatever are you ringing for at this time of a morning? Is everything all right? What's happened? Is something the matter?'

'For Heaven's sake, calm down, our mam.' Lucy was confused. 'I'm only ringing because I thought you and Dad might be worried about us. You see, Jack sprang another surprise on me . . . well, *two* to be exact, but I'll tell you about that when I see you. You're not to worry anyway because we're staying at The Tickled Trout along the Preston New Road.'

'And you got me out of a warm bed at two o'clock in the morning, just to tell me that?'

'Well, yes.' Now she was even more confused, and just the tiniest bit hurt. 'I thought you might be worried.'

'Well, I'm not.'

'Oh.'

'And the reason I'm not worried is because I knew where you were. Jack got me to do the booking for you. What's more, who do you think packed your overnight bag?'

Lucy felt foolish. 'Oh, Mam, I'm sorry. I shouldn't have got you out of bed.'

'No, you shouldn't. Your father kept me awake with his blessed indigestion, and now it'll take me ages to get off again.'

'I didn't know.' She glanced at Jack, sleeping like a babe. 'It's Jack's fault. He should have told me.'

Sally gave a little laugh. 'I expect he's been too busy. And I don't think it's indigestion that's kept you awake 'til this hour, so it must have been something else!'

Lucy couldn't help but smile. 'Goodnight, Mam. We'd both better get some sleep or we'll be fit for nothing in the morning.'

'Goodnight, love.'

It was some time before Lucy fell asleep.

She felt restless, excited by all the news, yet slightly apprehensive. So much had happened in such a short space of time, and now she felt as though she was being swept along, when there were so many things to be taken into account. Married in a month. God! Was that all? So much to organise . . . get her wedding dress . . . talk to Ted. Oh, Ted! What would he think? But she'd paid her debt to him, and he'd known all along that this day would come. The garden centre was up and running, and now that his grasping son was out of the picture, he shouldn't have to worry. As for her share of the partnership, they could always sort that one out.

When she finally fell asleep, it was a deep, peaceful slumber with no fears and no nightmares.

Chapter Seven

April was already easing into summer when the call
came from Jack. It was Friday. He and Cecil had
arrived in Cyprus. 'We've got a business meeting in
half an hour,' Jack told Lucy. 'I thought I'd give you
a quick call now, because I've no idea how long it
will go on.'

Lucy was just relieved to hear from him. 'Knowing
you, it could be well past midnight,' she laughed.
'And if it is, I'll be in my bed fast asleep.'

'Ring you tomorrow then?'

'If you don't, I'll be over on the next plane.' She
was already missing him.

'In that case, I don't think I'll ring,' he teased.

They talked for a quarter of an hour about the
forthcoming meeting and what Jack expected to
achieve. They discussed the flight and he reiterated
how he hated being up there in the sky with no
control over his own destiny. And finally they got to
talking about themselves. 'Tell me what you'll be
doing this evening,' he pleaded. 'Then, if the meeting
starts to drag, I can turn my thoughts to you.'

Lucy knew him too well. 'The meeting won't drag,'
she said. 'You won't let it. As for what I'll be doing, I
expect I'll be here until eight o'clock. It took me over

an hour to put up a special display of seed-packets . . .
six feet tall and double width, it was. Now it's lying
all over the floor, on top of the ceramic flower pots it
crashed into.'

His laughter made her smile. 'I'm only guessing,'
he spluttered, 'but it sounds like Debbie had one of
her little accidents?'

Believing it best to let sleeping dogs lie, Lucy
changed the subject. 'Try and ring early tomorrow,
if you can. Debbie and I are having a girls' day out.'

'Shopping for the dress, is it?'

'Dress . . . *es*,' she corrected. 'Don't forget we have
to get Debs's as well.' She knew the list by heart.
'We also have to get headdresses and shoes. I need
something blue – I've already got something borrowed
and something new. And I have to get a little trinket
for Debs. I thought maybe a pretty gold locket, but
I'll have to be discreet about that because she clings
to me like glue.'

'Hmm! Sounds to me like it'll be a long day.'

Lucy could have kicked herself. 'Oh, Jack, I'm
doing it again. You don't want to hear all this. Not
now.' She was so excited about the wedding and
everything, she did tend to go on a bit. 'Who's coming
to the meeting?'

'Cecil and the bankrupt owner. His solicitor and
accountant, and a legal contact of Cecil's.'

'Sounds formidable.' She was not concerned,
though. Where Jack's future was at stake, he would
go for the throat.

'We're all men of the world,' he reminded her, 'and
we're all there for the same purpose. They want to
offload an albatross, and I want to turn it into a swan.'

212

His voice dropped to a whisper. 'You're wrong, you know, sweetheart.'

'Wrong about what?' She'd been about to say something very important and now she'd lost her train of thought.

'About me not wanting to hear all your plans. It's my wedding too, you know.'

'All right. Do you think I should get a pink or a blue nightie?'

'Neither. I like you in the raw.'

'No problem then. I'll just get a pair of blue bedsocks.'

'Got to go.'

'Knock 'em dead!'

'I don't think I need go that far. It's all in my favour. Right now, they want me more than I want them.' He'd almost forgotten. 'Did you decide where you want to go for our honeymoon?'

'Scotland, I think, or maybe Ireland. I haven't made up my mind.'

'I'm easy. What about doing a week in each?'

'We'll talk about it later. There's plenty of time. It's not like we'll have to book a flight or anything like that.'

'I really have to go, sweetheart. I'll ring you tomorrow. Love you.'

A few more intimate words and then silence. Lucy replaced the receiver, her thoughts still with him. 'You're a lucky woman, Lucy Nolan,' she told herself. 'Now go and clean up Debbie's little accident.'

Debbie was just sweeping up the last of the broken pots. 'I know you said I was to leave it,' she started, 'probably because you thought I'd do even more

213

damage, but, well, it was me who knocked it over, and it's only right I should clear it all up.' She looked pale and worried. 'Anyway it's done now.' Stepping back, she waved her arm to show the clean floor and tidy display cabinet. 'How's that, boss?'

'Hey!' Even before the accident, Lucy had been worried about Debs. She had been unusually quiet, and looked as if she hadn't slept a wink all night. 'Since when do you call me boss?' It was a term she had never liked and until now it had never been used on her. Apart from that, the way Debbie had said it just now sounded too much like an insult.

Debbie was mortified. 'I'm sorry, gal,' she apologised, 'I got up in a ratty mood this morning.'

Lucy was ever patient. 'I noticed,' she remarked thoughtfully. 'But that's no reason to take it out on me or the furniture.' She couldn't help but notice the shadows beneath Debs's eyes and the stoop to her shoulders. 'You look like you had a bad night.'

'You could say that, and now I'm bloody knackered.'

'Debs, you're not slimming too hard, are you?' Lucy was really worried. Debbie was changing by the day. Her face wasn't so round, her bust not so plump, and there was a lean, hungry look about her that made her seem almost a stranger.

Like a flash, Debbie gave a smile that lit up her face. 'Got to look beautiful for the wedding, ain't I?' she answered brightly. 'I don't suppose I'll ever be the bride, but I mean to be the best bloody bridesmaid who ever walked down the aisle.'

'Alfie's still waiting.' Lucy knew in her heart that he would make Debbie a contented woman, if only she would let him.

'Let the bugger wait then. I'm keeping myself for a better man.'

'Have you seen him lately?'

'No.'

'I know he's asked you to go out tomorrow night. Will you go?'

'Might. Might not.'

'It's a wonder you don't drive him mad.'

'I'm trying my best.' She giggled. 'If I drive him mad, they'll put him away and he won't bother me any more.'

Lucy shook her head with frustration, her voice heavy with anxiety as she asked quietly, 'Is everything all right, Debs?'

'Right as rain.'

Lucy knew it wasn't. 'I can't make you out.'

'Can't make meself out at times.'

'What about tomorrow? Are we still going shopping or what?' Debs was so unpredictable that, like poor Alfie, Lucy never knew where she stood these days.

''Course we are. I'm looking forward to it.' A haunted look flitted across her face. 'So long as we're back before Dad gets home at six o'clock.'

'We'll be back,' Lucy promised softly. 'Don't worry.' Her quizzical gaze met Debs's, and in that very special but brief moment there was a unique understanding between them. Lucy held her breath, sure that now Debs would open her heart. But the moment was too swift, and like the haunted look in Debs's face, was soon lost.

'Are you picking me up?' That was the usual way. Lucy would drive to Debs's house, and afterwards drop her off there.

'Can't,' she explained. 'The car's in for a quick service. I'm taking it to the garage tonight, and it won't be ready until five tomorrow. I thought we might go to Manchester on the bus. Is that all right?'

Debs shrugged her shoulders. 'Like I said, so long as I'm back before six, we can go by Shanks's pony or ride bareback on a shire.' She made a naughty face. 'Should be a tickling experience, what with me being bare and the horse being hairy.'

Lucy laughed aloud. 'Debbie Lately, you're disgusting!' But the idea was interesting. 'You on a shire horse?' She groaned. 'I daren't think what chaos you'd cause.'

They went away together, laughing, and it seemed, for a while anyway, that Debbie's problems were set aside.

During the course of the afternoon, Lucy kept a close eye on the new recruit; at only sixteen, Paul was a big boy with wide shoulders and an outgoing personality. Lucy had taken him on because she felt him to be right for the job. Not only was he a delight to the customers, but he was strong as an ox, open and honest. Lucy and every other member of staff liked him enormously.

The most surprising new recruit was Mabel. Motherly and efficient, she worked wherever she was needed, showing remarkable business skill that both surprised and delighted Ted. Her talents were demonstrated on a certain busy day when a particularly irate customer burst through the door.

Red-faced and threatening to sue everyone in sight, the customer had come in to complain about a mower which he'd bought some time ago, and which, he claimed, had given him trouble from day one. Even Lucy could not placate him.

However, within minutes of Mabel's taking him under her wing, the man was chatting as though he hadn't a care in the world. When he finally went on his way, it was with a new and more expensive mower, and a further twenty pounds' worth of goods which he had not intended to buy.

'Where did you learn to deal with people like that?' Lucy was deeply impressed.

'My father had a general store for many years,' she explained. 'We sold everything from bacon to step-ladders. I worked there for twenty years and loved every minute of it. My main responsibilities were stock-taking, ordering, and keeping the cash-ledger up to date for the accountant. But I served behind the counter whenever I could, and believe me, we had our share of irate customers.'

Ted also was filled with admiration. 'There's more to you than I reckoned,' he remarked thoughtfully. But then, as he took her away for a well-deserved cup of tea, he could be heard complaining, 'I reckon the bugger fancied yer. If he sets foot in here again, I'll have him out the door before he can say "How d'yer do?"'

The incident set Lucy thinking. For some time now she'd been trying to work out how she could ease Ted back into the driving seat because, when she and Jack were married and living in Cyprus, she would have to relinquish her role in the garden centre. 'Mabel, you might have just provided me with an answer,' she murmured.

A little bird told her that Ted had set his cap at

Mabel, and that it might not be too long before wedding bells were ringing in that particular direction.

To Lucy's romantic young heart, the idea of Old Ted and the homely Mabel spending their twilight years together was delightful.

'Old hearts, young love,' she sighed. A few moments later, her voice raised in song, Lucy resumed her work before the day came to an end.

Manchester's largest department store was heaving with people. 'Jeez! There ain't room to swing your arse,' Debbie grumbled.

'Stop moaning.' Lucy waited for her to catch up. She too was footsore and weary, but wasn't about to let it get her down. Instead, she just kept hoping that once they got to the bridal department, it would be much quieter and a little more dignified.

'Hmm!' Debbie came off the escalator at a run. 'It's all right for you,' she growled, glaring as though she could commit murder. 'You ain't just been squashed between two fat cows halfway up the escalator.'

One of the women overheard. 'Who are you calling a fat cow?' she demanded, swinging her shopping bag at Debbie.

'If the cap fits, wear it,' she jeered.

'Why, you cheeky young devil!' This time the bag caught her on her side.

Incensed, Debbie advanced threateningly towards the apple-faced woman. 'Do that again, and I'll tip you over that bloody rail,' she warned, and judging by the look on her face, she meant every word.

Lucy thought it was time to intervene. 'Come on,'

she urged, taking her friend by the arm and rushing her away. 'We'd better find somewhere and get a bite to eat, before one of us gets arrested.'

The 'somewhere' was a quiet corner in the second-floor restaurant. 'Here, get that down you.' Lucy offloaded the tray on to the table: two pots of tea, a double bacon buttie for Debbie, and a cheese and tomato bap for her. 'Just what the doctor ordered,' she sighed, taking a wonderful long sip of tea. As the warm sweet liquid flowed down her throat she felt herself begin to unwind. There was still so much to do, but at least in here they were far enough away from the pressing crowd to get their heads together and plan the next move.

Debbie too began to unwind. 'I'm sorry, gal,' she muttered sheepishly. 'I shouldn't have yelled at her like that. The poor old cow ain't done me no harm.'

Now that it was over and they were out of harm's way, Lucy could see the funny side of it. 'Well, she did hit you with her bag,' she spluttered, grinning at Debs over the rim of her teacup. 'That wasn't a very friendly thing to do.'

Debbie chuckled heartily, but when she spoke there was a measure of regret in her voice. 'I'm really sorry, gal. I showed you up, didn't I?'

'If you say so.'

'Honest to God, I don't know why you put up with me.'

This time Lucy was determined. 'I know there's something wrong at home, Debs,' she said quietly. 'I'm no expert, but I'm sure it would do you good to talk about it.'

A flicker of fear crossed Debbie's face. She lowered

her gaze, then looking up, replied in a whisper, 'I've wanted to tell you, but I was too ashamed.'

'Don't be,' Lucy said, laying her hand over Debbie's. 'We've been friends for too long. Besides, you know whatever you tell me will never be repeated. I just want to help, if I can.' She felt so close, so very close, but one wrong word and she knew Debbie would clam up, and if she did that, there would be no getting to her again.

'What is it, Debs?' she insisted softly. 'You can tell me.'

Debbie was in turmoil. She knew Lucy would never say anything to a living soul, and trusted her implicitly. But the shame was crippling, the awful shame, and the terrible feeling of helplessness. Yet she had to tell somebody because if she didn't, it would drive her crazy. 'It's me mam and dad,' she began nervously. 'They're always at each other's throats, and I'm not sure if it's me who's causing it.'

Sensing her pain, and knowing it was an ordeal for Debs to talk like this, Lucy reminded her, 'Married couples do have their bad times, you know, Debs. My own mam and dad are the same.'

'No.' Debbie shook her head. 'Your mam and dad aren't like mine.' Her voice fell to a whisper, becoming almost inaudible. 'Sometimes I think there'll be murder done in our house. I'm frightened, Lucy . . . really frightened.'

'Have you told them how you feel?'

Her words came out in a scornful stream. 'They know how I feel, but they don't seem to care.'

Lucy was uncertain how to deal with this. She wanted to comfort her friend, to reassure her in some way, but she didn't know how. If there was real animosity between Debbie's parents, there wasn't much anybody else could do. 'That's why you don't want to move out, isn't it?' she asked now. 'That's why you won't let Alfie come to the house . . . why you don't want to get too fond of him?' She could understand now, and it made her feel humble.

Debbie shrugged her shoulders. 'Alfie's all right, I suppose. But I can't think about myself. Not when there's a danger me mam and dad might split up.' She shivered visibly. *'Or something worse.'*

'What do you mean, something worse?' There it was again, that sinking, frightening feeling.

Debbie made an effort to retrieve what she had implied. 'That's a silly thing to say. I didn't mean anything by it. Only they do love each other, gal. They fight and argue, and it frightens me, but they love each other too much to go their separate ways.'

'Can't you persuade them to see a counsellor? I know it isn't the answer for every couple in distress, but they might be able to help in some way.'

'It isn't as easy as that.'

'Why not?' Again Lucy sensed something deeper, something sinister.

'Don't be bloody daft,' snapped Debbie. 'It ain't marriage counselling they need.'

Taken aback, Lucy apologised. 'I'm sorry, Debs. I didn't mean to pry.' She knew by the look on Debbie's face that she had said all she was going to say.

'No, gal. It's me who's sorry.' It had almost spilled out. All the shocking truth about what was really happening at home. But, as always, Debbie couldn't bring herself to tell. She could *never* tell. 'I know you want to help,' she acknowledged, 'but you can't. Nobody can. Don't worry, I'll deal with it.' When she saw Lucy about to speak again, she stopped her. 'I shouldn't have said anything. Please, Lucy, I don't want to talk about it again. I'm asking you to forget what I've said. Can you do that? For me?'

Lucy's heart was aching. She was desperate to help and yet she didn't know how. There must be a way, though. It was hard to stand by and see how all this was ruining Debs's life.

'Please, Lucy?' Her voice was trembling now. 'Promise you won't mention it ever again?'

Lucy had no choice. 'If that's what you really want.'

'You see, I'm the only one who can do something about it. I've been putting it off and putting it off, hoping they'd sort themselves out. But now I know they won't, so I'll have to do something myself. And I will.' Her voice became harsh. 'I'll have to, before something bad happens.'

Lucy gave her word she wouldn't mention it again. 'But I'm here if you need to talk things over, don't ever forget that,' she said.

Debbie thanked her, and for the while the subject was closed though each of them stayed subdued for different reasons: Debbie because she knew the time was coming when she would have to take things into her own hands; Lucy because she knew how unhappy Debs was, and it irked her that she could not do a single thing about it.

'Come on, gal,' Debbie urged, collecting her shopping bags from beneath the table. 'No more long faces. I've said I'll deal with it and I will. For now, we've got a wedding round the corner so get a move on. I want the best bridesmaid's dress in town and no expense spared. All right?'

Lucy was relieved to see Debbie seemed to have put the problem behind her for the moment. 'All right,' she agreed. Taking up her own shopping bags, she followed her out of the restaurant. 'The best bridesmaid's dress we can find. If that's what you've set your heart on, that's what you shall have.'

Without another word they set off for the bridal department.

It was a bewitching hour.

'Oh, Lucy, you look like a fairy princess!' Goggle-eyed and filled with admiration, Debbie stared at the vision of loveliness before her. 'Oh, yes, I like that one best of all.'

It was the third dress Lucy had tried; a splendid creation of lace and silk and floating gossamer net, it came in at the waist and out at the hip, and showed off her smooth, creamy shoulders to perfection.

She twirled around and turned to see herself in the full-length mirror. As on the two previous occasions, she gave a resounding: 'No. It's not me, Debs.' Then it was back to the dressing room with the attendant following.

A few moments later she emerged yet again to search through the seemingly endless racks of beautiful gowns. Dresses were tugged out then quickly returned. Eager and excited, Debs showed her this and that, but Lucy saw nothing to satisfy her. They were all wonderful, but not for her. 'I'm sorry,' she told the assistant, 'I can't find what I want.'

Suddenly her eye caught the hem of a dress

peeping from beneath a curtain. 'I haven't seen that one, have I?' she asked, intrigued.

'I'm sorry, dear. That particular gown was damaged in transit. It has to go back for repair.' The assistant had been given strict instructions that no one should try on the dress. 'Our reputation is at stake,' the manageress had warned before she took herself off to the hairdresser's. 'Have it sent straight back.' Unfortunately the day had gone too quickly, the assistant had been run off her feet. The dress would not now be returned until the morning. 'It would be more than my job's worth to let you try that gown.'

She had not reckoned with Lucy's determination. Within seconds the curtain was flung back and the dress brought out. 'See?' The assistant pointed to where the delicate strap was frayed at the point where it joined the shoulder. 'Now do you see why I can't let you try it?' Afraid the manageress might return at any minute, she kept the gown clutched tightly in her hands.

Debbie was mesmerised. 'Wow!'

Lucy was silent for a moment, her gaze taking in the gown's every little detail, lovely grey eyes sparkling with the wonder of a child on its first Christmas. 'It's beautiful,' she gasped. 'Please, won't you let me try it?'

The dress was everything she had dreamed of. No lace or gossamer but all of smooth, shimmering silk, it had a V-neckline, a low back, and the daintiest, prettiest straps. The body of the dress was slim-line, with scalloped hem and a discreet slit from ankle to knee. It was pure, unashamed elegance. The kind of dress every woman wants to wear but daren't.

With both Lucy and Debbie pleading, and the dress being Lucy's size, how could the assistant say no? 'If the manageress comes back and sees you with it on, you're to say you took it without my knowing.'

The dress might have been made for Lucy.

When she emerged from the dressing room, Debbie was visibly moved. 'Oh, Lucy! Lucy!' Her pretty blue eyes filled with tears of joy. Clapping her hands to her mouth, she stared and stared, temporarily lost for words, and wondering if there would come a day when she too might be trying on a wedding gown.

Lucy felt like a million dollars. The dress fitted her like a second skin; following the gentle curves of her upper body, it somehow made her look taller and slimmer. The back was low, the neckline discreet, and the fine figured straps accentuated the straight line of her shoulders. From just below the hips, the material fell in tiny pleats of silk that moved when she walked and clung in just the right places. 'Oh, Debs, isn't it wonderful?' she murmured, twirling and turning in front of the mirror. 'I really love it.'

Filled with awe, and dreaming of her own wedding day many years before, the assistant was soon caught up in the excitement. 'You're the prettiest bride I've ever had in this shop,' she said truthfully. Then she brought a long trailing veil in the sheerest lace, together with a small round headdress which was finished in tiny slivers of mother-of-pearl. 'Let me see you in this, dear,' she said, fastening the veil in place while Lucy stood very still.

The whole ensemble was stunning. In the doorway a small group of shoppers had gathered to see. 'Oh, lass, you look beautiful,' one little woman sighed.

'Makes me wish I were young and slim again,' said another.

'Gerraway, Dora Clegg, yer were *never* young and slim!' argued her friend.

A good-natured uproar broke out, but they were all in agreement that Lucy had to have the dress.

It was quickly arranged. The veil and the dress, which would be repaired, were reserved in Lucy's name.

Then it was Debbie's turn.

She tried on a big blue thing, then an outrageous mass of tulle and lace, both of which were swiftly rejected. She pranced about in a light green horror that made her look seasick, and finally, when Lucy decided it was time for her to step in, tried on a straight-cut, ankle-length dress in a pretty shade of cornflower blue which brought out the colour of her eyes. The dress had short sleeves and a gathered waist, and was absolutely perfect. 'Oh, yes!' she cried, seeing herself in the mirror. 'It makes me look really pretty.'

'That's because you *are* pretty,' Lucy said, and she meant every word.

On the way home the bus was crowded. 'I can't wait to see Jack's face when he sees me in my wedding gown,' said Lucy.

Debbie smiled. 'It wouldn't matter if you wore a sack, he'd still think you were the most gorgeous girl in the world.'

In reflective mood, Lucy murmured, 'I'm really lucky, aren't I, Debs?' She never stopped thanking the good fortune that had brought her and Jack together.

'You deserve it, gal,' Debbie answered from the heart. 'You're the best, and you deserve the best.'

'It will happen for you too,' Lucy warmly assured her. 'Whether it's Alfie or some other fella, you'll be the next one walking down the aisle.' She had to believe that, for Debbie's sake.

The conversation quickly moved on to other things. They talked about Lucy's last visit to the priest, and how the next one would take place when Jack got back.

Debs's voice fell to a whisper. 'To tell you the truth, gal, I've been thinking of going to see him. My mam and dad might listen to a man of the cloth.'

'It might be worthwhile,' Lucy agreed, 'but I didn't know your parents were all that religious?' She was thrilled that Debbie seemed to be finding it easier to talk about them. Surely that must be for the better? she thought.

'They're not what you call "religious". Once upon a time, though, they used to go to church on a Sunday. They haven't done that for ages, but they always give to good causes when people from charities call round, so I reckon they still have some regard for the church and all that.'

Lucy thought it was a good idea, but just as she was about to say so, Debbie changed the subject again, as she always did whenever the subject of her parents came up. 'Have you heard from Jack lately?'

'This morning. He's still up to his neck in meetings and negotiations. Apparently the owner is trying to squeeze more money out of him.' She recalled how concerned Jack was when he'd called a few nights ago. 'He won't give in, though. He says the price was agreed and he's not shifting.' She gave a proud little smile. 'When Jack digs his heels in, he's a devil to move.'

Debbie saw that secret little smile and for a shameful moment let envy turn her tongue. 'Aren't you worried he might find a woman over there?'

Visibly surprised by Debbie's comment, Lucy gave her a curious glance. 'No.' She shook her head decisively. 'Jack would never cheat on me, and I would never cheat on him.'

Mortified, Debbie tried to make amends. ''Course he wouldn't,' she said. 'And if you'd wanted to cheat on him, you could have done it time and again these past weeks.' She gave a cheeky little wink. 'Steve Ryman fancies you rotten. Every time he looks at you, his trousers rise six inches.'

'You're crazy, Debs!' Lucy surprised herself by her own sharpness. 'The man's a customer, that's all, and well you know it.'

'Hey, I were joking!' She winked again. 'He's a bit of all right though, ain't he, eh? You've been round there a few times now, ain't yer? What's he like at home? What's his house like? Grand, I expect. I mean, he's not badly off, is he, eh? Steve Ryman . . . doctor . . . lonely and looking for a woman.' She pulled a sour expression. 'Not *any* woman though. A man like that, professional an' all, well, he'd want a woman like you. I don't suppose he'd look twice at me.'

'What's the matter with you?' Anger tinged Lucy's voice.

'Nothing. Why?'

'All this talk of Steve Ryman. The man means nothing at all to me, not in the sense you're implying.'

There could never be any other man for Lucy than her beloved Jack. For some reason Debbie was being spiteful, and that wasn't like her.

Slowly and deliberately Lucy spelled it out. 'I've been overseeing the landscaping of his garden, as you very well know. To hear you talk, anyone would think we were having an affair.' Giving Debbie an angry glance, she demanded, 'What's wrong with you this afternoon? If I didn't know better, I'd say you were trying your damnedest to rile me.'

A look of contrition appeared on Debbie's homely face. 'You're right,' she admitted. 'Sorry, gal. I can be a right cow when I put me mind to it.'

'Why?' Sometimes, like now, Debbie was hard to fathom.

'Jealous, I suppose.'

'Jealous? Of what?' Normally Lucy might have let the matter go, but this time she meant to have it out.

'Of you. You're so pretty, and nice, and everybody loves you. Your mam and dad love you. Ted thinks the sun shines out of yer arse. Jack worships the ground you walk on. And now the local doctor fancies you. Why can't I be more like you, Lucy? Why does everything go wrong for me?'

'God, you really have got it bad!' Lucy had never seen Debbie like this before. 'First of all, don't keep putting yourself down. My mam and dad don't think any more of me than yours think of you. All right, they might be having problems, but that doesn't mean they love you any the less.' She leaned forward, whispering so the other passengers couldn't hear. 'Jack does love me, yes, but Alfie loves you, so we're equal. As for Steve Ryman, he's a good man but he means nothing at all to me. If I go to the house, it's because I've agreed to do a job, and the man is paying handsomely for it to be done properly.' Gripping Debbie by the arm, she went on harshly, 'As for Ted, he's a kind old man who sees the best in everybody. Think about it, Debs. He even puts up with you, and you've come close to wrecking the place time and again.'

Debbie shook her head in disbelief. 'You're right, gal. I can't believe I put the fork-lift through the greenhouse wall again.'

Lucy had to smile. 'Neither can I. It's a good job we've got insurance.'

'I shouldn't have said all those things,' Debbie declared. 'Take no notice of me, gal. I can be a spiteful bastard.'

'I've noticed.' Lucy gave her a wry little look, but there was a smile lurking beneath. No doubt there were things going on at home that made her friend the way she was.

Debbie touched her hand. 'Friends?'

''Course we are.' Lucy's smile was reassuring. 'But it might be a good idea to think before you speak in future.'

Skirmish over, Debbie wanted to know, 'Do you think they'll get wed?'

'Who?'

'Ted and Mabel. Do you think they'll tie the knot?'

'I think they might.' It did Lucy's heart good to see how Ted had gained a new lease of life since Mabel came to work at the garden centre. 'I hope they do get wed, because they were made for each other.' A

darker thought crossed her mind. 'He had a letter
from his son the other day. Apparently, George
Beckendale wants his dad's forgiveness.'

'Bugger me, gal! What does Ted think?'

'That he's up to something, and so do I.' A softer
tone crept into her voice. 'It would be nice, though,
if he really did want to make it up with his dad. I
mean, Ted's got no other children, and I suspect deep
down he's broken-hearted at the way things have
turned out between him and George.' Like Ted,
though, she suspected there was a more devious
reason behind George's letter. 'George wants to come
and see him . . . to explain, he said.'

'Surely Ted won't see him, will he?'

'Mabel persuaded him to think about it, and I tend
to agree. After all, George does owe his dad an
explanation. There's always the chance he might be
genuinely sorry, though I doubt it. Anybody who could
threaten to throw his own father off his own land
can't be much good. On the other hand, what if he
really does want to make amends?'

'If I were Ted, I'd chop the bugger's balls off before
I'd let him through the door!' Debbie was in a dark,
unforgiving mood.

'That's for Ted to decide. I'm having no say in it.
But Mabel could be right, and besides, George can't
do much harm, not with my name on the deeds.' On
that matter Lucy had already exchanged a confiden-
tial word with Steve Ryman – the only professional
man she knew – who assured her that George
Beckendale had no claim unless he could prove that
his father was mentally incapable of looking after
his own affairs, which Ted clearly was not.

'Ted should have nothing to do with him.'

Lucy recalled the last incident when George Beckendale had shown his face. 'You could be right. When it comes down to it, he might chop off his son's balls instead of letting him through the door.' She smiled. 'And who could blame him?'

Sally washed the dinner things while Lucy wiped. 'Thanks, Mam. That was a lovely meal.' As she put away the last of the crockery, she sighed wistfully. 'It's been a fabulous day.'

Mopping the sink top, Sally suggested, 'We'll have a glass of wine to celebrate, and you can tell me all about it.' She had seen the glow in her daughter's face when she came in from shopping, and like any mother was filled with a sense of accomplishment. Secretly congratulating herself, Sally believed she and Mike had done a grand job of raising their only offspring. Lucy had been a good child, generous to a fault, and now she was a lovely young woman on the threshold of her life.

From the depths of the armchair, Mike spoke up. 'Is this gonna be women's talk?'

Crossing the room, Sally kissed him on the forehead. 'If you don't like it, you can always take a walk.'

'Happen I will.' Standing up, he folded his newspaper and laid it on the table. 'I've been meaning to see Harry Butler about that truck he wants to sell. I might do that, eh?' His face crinkled into a grin. 'It means I'll have to buy him a pint, but if I get the truck at a price I can afford, it'll be money well spent.'

Sally smiled, saying, 'And of course you'll have to buy a pint for yourself, eh?'

'You wouldn't want the poor blighter to drink on his own, would you? Bad manners, is that.'

She gazed at him fondly. Mike worked long and hard for six days a week. He was entitled to a Saturday night out. 'Go on then,' she murmured. 'Try not to be too late, love.'

'One pint, then I'll be off home.' He put on his cap and coat and returned to kiss the women in his life. 'You make me proud,' he told Lucy. 'I can't wait to walk you down the aisle.'

'Thanks, Dad.' Lucy's love for her parents was deep and abiding. There was nothing she wouldn't do for them.

When the front door slammed shut behind him, Sally laughed out loud. 'Women's talk,' she declared. 'That's a lame excuse for running off to the pub. Have you ever seen how the men prop up the bar and talk all night long? Greyhounds, pigeons and football, where would they be without them?'

Pouring out the wine, she brought the two glasses to the fireside where Lucy was seated. 'Now I expect it'll be talk of trucks and petrol consumption.' Shaking her head, she raised her glass with a smile. 'Anyway, here's to you and Jack, and the most wonderful wedding Blackburn town has ever seen.'

While they sipped their wine, Lucy wondered how she would approach the difficult subject of her and Jack living abroad. Taking a deep breath, she put down her glass and looked Sally in the face. 'Mam?'

Sally had been in the middle of a gulp of wine. She swallowed it quickly and looked at Lucy with quizzical blue eyes. 'Yes, love?'

'Would you mind if Jack and I had to move away?'

'I suppose I would, yes.' Now she was regarding Lucy with a frown. 'But you're a grown woman, and once you're married, you'll go where your man goes.' Something in Lucy's face told her she wasn't talking about moving to the other side of town. 'When you say moving away, what exactly do you mean?'

'Abroad.' There was no other way to say it but straight out. 'You know Jack's heart is set on owning a hotel in Cyprus and he's out there now, fighting to get it together?' Seeing the frown deepen on her mother's face, Lucy forced herself to go on. 'When we're married, he wants us to live out there, in Cyprus.'

'How long for?' Disappointment coloured Sally's voice.

'We haven't talked about that yet. Besides, there are residence permits to be got and that takes time.'

'Is it what you want, love?' Sally's expression softened.

Lucy had thought about it a lot, and now she gave her answer. 'Wherever Jack is, that's where I want to be.'

Sally understood. 'That's how I feel about your dad,' she revealed. 'When a woman falls in love, she hopes it's for keeps. That means being together, growing together, and raising your children as best you can.' For the merest moment she was young again. 'When I first set eyes on your dad, I knew, if he asked me, I'd follow him to the ends of the earth.'

Lucy had never seen that look on her mother's face before and it moved her almost to tears. 'I hope Jack and I are as happy as you and Dad,' she murmured. 'When we have children, I want them to have the same kind of parents I've had.'

The evening went all too quickly. For Lucy the special time she and her mother spent here, talking and planning, was one of the most memorable in her life. She and Sally had always been close, but because of Lucy's forthcoming marriage and the fact that Sally was seeing her only child spread her wings and fly away, something inexplicably wonderful bound them together for all time.

While they talked of wifely things and motherhood, of love and belonging, it was with the unique understanding that only a mother and daughter can share.

They chatted about Lucy's wedding gown, and Sally said it sounded beautiful. They talked of marriage and honeymoons and Jack's ability to become a very rich man. Lucy said she wouldn't care if he was a pauper, and Sally argued that love alone wouldn't keep them warm. Ted was discussed, and his son George, and the letter begging forgiveness.

Sally held the same opinion as Debbie. 'How could a son threaten his old dad like that? He must be a real bad bugger. I couldn't forgive him, not in a million years.'

Then the conversation moved inevitably on to Debbie.

'She was in a strange mood today,' Lucy explained. But she didn't betray Debbie's confidence, nor did she linger on the subject, except to describe the bridesmaid's dress, and to say how lovely Debbie looked in it.

'She's a pretty young woman,' Sally agreed. 'What with being bridesmaid, and that young man Alfie always asking her to marry him, I would have thought she'd be over the moon.' Intrigued by Lucy's comment, she asked thoughtfully, 'What makes you say she was in a strange mood?'

Lucy took a casual sip of her wine. 'I expect she's all excited about the wedding,' she said evasively. 'Come tomorrow she'll be right as rain.'

They talked for a while about the success of the garden centre. 'Have you and Ted discussed things?' Sally wanted to know. 'About what you'll do after you and Jack are married?'

Lucy had thought about that a lot, and even spoken to the solicitor who'd drawn up their agreement in the first place. 'It's a difficult one,' she confessed. 'I've got a number of options. I'm entitled to sell my share or give it away. Or I can be a silent partner.'

'What's that?' Though she and Mike had run a greengrocer's shop for many years, Sally had little idea of business.

Lucy explained, 'It means I won't be working there, but I'll be able to keep my share and take a percentage of the profits.' She had already dismissed that idea. 'I won't do that, though. Half the fun is working at the garden centre and seeing it grow. Besides, Ted gave me that partnership to get him out of a scrape so it really doesn't belong to me. By rights, I should just give it back. But that might put him back in the same position as he was before.'

'What will you do, then?'

'I'm toying with an idea.' She had to bide her time though. 'A lot depends on what Ted thinks.'

'I'm sure you'll do your best by him.' Sally had no doubts where her daughter was concerned. 'Now, if you don't mind, I'm off to my bed.' A quick glance at the clock told her it was quarter to eleven. 'I expect your dad's gone home with his mate.' She rolled her eyes heavenwards. 'Men! Once they get talking about trucks and such, there's no stopping them.'

After her mam had gone to bed, Lucy washed the glasses and put them away. She sat for a while by the empty firegrate, eyes closed and head back, her mind full of all kinds of things. She thought about Debbie and the way she had been today. She hated herself for not being able to help.

When she let her mind wander to thoughts of Jack, the loneliness was overwhelming. 'Oh, Jack, I wish you were here.' Her small voice was lost in the chiming of the clock. She smiled, bringing his handsome, loving face to mind. 'I got my dress today, Jack. Oh, it's so beautiful. When I walk down the aisle, and you turn to see me, I want you to fall in love all over again.'

The idea grew in her mind and wouldn't go away. She looked at the clock. It was half-past eleven. 'I can't ring him now,' she told herself. 'He's probably exhausted after a day of meetings and hard wrangling.'

She turned out the lights and went to bed. And still the idea wouldn't go away. She needed him badly; needed him to hold her, to reassure her that everything would be all right, because suddenly, and for no apparent reason, she was afraid. Sad, and desperately afraid.

At a quarter to twelve, she crept downstairs and telephoned him, astonished when he picked up the receiver after the second ring. 'Jack! Is that you?' His voice sounded different somehow, like someone deep in thought.

'Lucy?' Immediately his tone lightened. 'I was thinking of calling you, but I was sure you'd be in bed fast asleep by now.'

Lucy told him about her evening, and the conversation with Sally. 'We had a real heart to heart,' she said. 'I told her about us living abroad after we were married, and she understood.'

'That's good, sweetheart,' he said jubilantly. 'Because the deal is almost done. Tomorrow afternoon we have to sign all the papers, then it's all systems go. With a bit of luck, I should be able to get back in plenty of time to see the priest.'

'Thank God for that. I was beginning to get worried.' The real truth was, she missed him dreadfully. 'I got my wedding gown today.'

'I bet you look stunning in it.'

Lucy laughed. 'Debbie was speechless, so it must look good.'

'I'm only the groom, so I don't suppose you'll tell *me* what it looks like?'

'You suppose right.'

They laughed and talked and made love over the phone. Finally, they had to part. 'Take care of yourself, sweetheart,' he murmured. 'It won't be long before we're together.'

In her mind she imagined his face close to the phone, his mouth almost touching the receiver, his breath whispering into it. 'I love you,' she said.

In a moment, he was gone.

Lucy had been asleep for only a short time when she was rudely awakened by some sort of commotion outside her window. Swinging her legs out of bed, she sat on the edge for a minute, gathering her sleepy wits.

Flicking on the bedside lamp, she glared through bleary eyes at the alarm clock. 'For God's sake, it's one o'clock in the morning!' She was suddenly awake. 'What the devil's going on?'

Wrapping herself in her dressing-gown, she ran to the window and looked out. At first she couldn't see anything, but she could hear a lot of yelling and shouting, and angry neighbours who had also been woken by the noise. In the distance, parked beneath a street-lamp, she could just make out the shape of a large truck, surrounded by curious people.

When she came down the stairs it was to see her mam making for the front door. 'Your dad's not home,' she cried, flinging open the door and peering out. 'I kept awake as long as I could, and then I must have fallen asleep.' She sounded anxious. 'The noise woke me, all that shouting and swearing. What's going on, our Lucy? And where's your dad at this time of the morning?'

In fact, Lucy's dad was right in the middle of all the noise. 'I'm sorry, lass,' said Harry Butler to Sally. He was a big man with a round hairy face and a cigarette stub permanently glued between his lips. With great difficulty he helped Mike down from the cab. 'It weren't his fault,' he promised her, 'but the poor sod's drunk out of his head.'

Sally was shocked. 'I think you'd better explain.'

The cigarette stub danced up and down as he spoke. 'Me an' Mike were meking a deal on the truck . . . arguing the price, so to speak . . . an' somebody mentioned your Lucy were gerrin' wed. One fella bought him a pint. Well! Afore you know it, *everybody* wants to congratulate him, and there's a row o' pints laid out on the bar. Well, I mean, I helped him to drink a few, but he downed a fair number himself an' all.' He gave a gruff laugh. 'Buckled at the legs, he did. You can see he ain't used to the booze.'

Struggling with Mike's limp form, he laughed good-naturedly. 'Don't be too hard on him, lass. It ain't every day a man's daughter gets wed.'

Sally took a closer look at Mike, who was hardly able to stand up. 'What have you got to say for yourself, Michael Nolan?' she said. 'Drunk and disorderly on the street. Whatever will the neighbours say?' All the same, like Lucy who had never seen her father drunk before, she couldn't help but smile. Especially when Mrs Lacey from number three cackled and roared and told everyone: 'My Fred were the very same. Came home pissed as a newt the night afore our Mary got wed. He were sick as a pig and missed the bloody wedding!'

Mike laughed louder than anybody. 'That were nowt new for Fred,' he cried. 'He were *allus* bloody pissed!' He laughed so much he nearly fell over.

Harry Butler was full of apologies. 'We'd best get him inside,' he suggested. 'The state he's in, he'll sleep for a month.'

'Thanks for your help,' Sally declared, 'but me and our Lucy can get him inside. You take yourself off home or your wife will be worried out of her mind.'

'I don't think so,' he said gruffly. 'She ran off with a woman from Newton Street.' He scratched his head. 'I never could understand it.'

'I can!' called Elsie Armitage. 'She'd rather cuddle a woman than a hairy-faced bugger like you!'

That set folks laughing again. They were still chuckling as they closed their doors and returned to the comfort of their beds.

'Are you sure you can manage?' Harry felt like the messenger who had his head chopped off for bringing bad news. 'He's a bit of a weight for you two lasses.'

Taking the weight on to herself, Lucy thanked him for bringing her dad home. 'But we can manage all right, Harry. As Mam said, you should get off home now.'

Accepting he was no longer needed, he climbed back into the truck, where, spitting out the stub, he lit a fresh cigarette from the packet. 'I've nowt to go home to,' he told himself in the mirror. 'Not like you, Mike Nolan . . . with that pretty little wife o' yourn.' His lonely gaze followed Sally as she and Lucy struggled down the street with Mike between them. 'You're a lucky bugger,' he groaned. 'Some of us have to be content with a dog for company.'

Before setting off again he took a moment to savour the scene. Sally was quietly talking to Mike, who was stumbling and laughing and kissing her at every other step. Lucy was the strong one. With her arm about her dad, she took his full weight, edging him slowly and surely along the pavement towards the house.

Oblivious of the uproar he'd caused, Mike declared in a slurred voice, 'I've bought us a truck, Sal, my love. You're looking at a man who knows how to make a deal.' He laughed, and stopped, and kissed her.

Then he started up again. 'Made a bloody good bargain, I did. You'd be proud of the way I beat his price down. That Harry, the hairy bugger, he tried it on – oh, yes, he tried it on – but I weren't having it.'

He stopped again, weaving about as he looked her in the eye. 'Hey! You look right pretty, Mrs Nolan. How d'you feel about making love with your old man, eh? Right here in the street, and bugger 'em all. Eh? What d'yer say, me beauty?'

Lucy had to stifle her giggles, but Sally told him straight, 'The drink's addled your brain and loosened your tongue. What you need is a good night's sleep. I reckon you'll have some explaining to do in the morning.'

He appeared not to be listening. 'Hey!' Giggling like a schoolboy, he stuck out his chest. 'I've bought us a truck.' Swinging round, he looked over to where Harry was starting the engine. 'That's it!' he cried. 'What d'yer think to it, eh?'

'Tomorrow,' Sally told him kindly. 'You can tell me all about it tomorrow.'

They were two doors away from home when Harry wound down the window as he slowly passed. 'You've blotted your copy book, Mike, old son,' he called out. 'Give me a ring when your head's clear.'

'Hey! Come back wi' my bloody truck!' Struggling and thrashing, Mike threw up his arms. 'COME BACK, YOU BUGGER!'

It happened so quickly Lucy could never recall exactly when her mam fell. All she knew was that there was a moment of chaos as Harry Butler drove by. Her dad was yelling, there was a scuffle, and then her mam was rolling towards the rear end of the truck.

'JESUS, MARY AND JOSEPH!' Shocked and shaking, Harry Butler had leapt out of the truck and was staring down at Sally's small broken figure. Mike was on the ground, sobbing and calling her name, his hands smeared with her blood where he had frantically tried to drag her out from beneath the wheels.

While Harry took charge of Mike, a horrified neighbour called the ambulance. Others gathered round, stunned into silence, afraid and ashamed. Only a few minutes ago they'd been laughing. Now their heads were bowed and their hearts shaken.

On her knees, far under the truck, Lucy cradled her mam close to her breast. She couldn't believe this was real, that her lovely, pretty mam was lying in her arms, her life's blood running into the gutter. 'Mam,' she whispered in a soft, trembling voice. 'Oh, Mam!' Inside she was all in pieces. Outside, she tried to keep calm for her mam's sake. 'Open your eyes, Mam,' she pleaded. 'Please, Mam. Open your eyes.' While she spoke the tears began to fall, hot burning tears washing down her face. 'Don't die, Mam.' She could hardly speak. 'Please, Mam. It's Lucy. Open your eyes.'

In the light from the street-lamp, the eyes opened, struggling to focus; those pretty bright blue eyes that had so often smiled on Lucy and her dad. They smiled now. 'You're a good girl,' Sally whispered. 'You mustn't be afraid, love.' The voice faltered. 'Lucy . . .'

'It's all right, Mam, I'm here. The ambulance is on its way. You'll be all right.' Suddenly she felt her

mam's body shudder in her arms. 'MAM! MAM!'
Emotion was choking her. 'Look at me, Mam! Look
at me!' She couldn't hold back the sobs any longer,
great racking sobs that tore her apart. 'Oh, Mam,
Mam!' Slowly, ever so gently, she rocked the familiar
body in her arms, like a mother rocking a child. 'I
love you, Mam.' Some deep instinct told her that her
mother was losing the fight. 'Can you hear me, Mam?
I love you . . .' The words broke on a sob and she
could say no more.

While Lucy's tender fingers stroked her mam's cold
face, Sally opened her eyes for the last time. Taking
Lucy by surprise, she whispered, 'Promise me . . .
look after . . . your dad?'

Thrilled at the sound of her mother's voice, and
immensely relieved at the screeching noise of a siren
in the background, Lucy told her excitedly, 'The
ambulance is here, Mam! Hold on, sweetheart. You'll
be all right.' In her heart she offered up a prayer:
Dear God, don't let her die. *Don't let her die!*

'Promise?'

Wiping her eyes, Lucy gazed on her mother's face.
In the half-light, it seemed a ghastly colour. 'Oh,
Mam?'

The blue eyes were pleading. 'Look after him.'

'You'll be able to look after him yourself, Mam.'
She refused to believe Sally was never coming home
again.

With astonishing strength, her small hand closed
over Lucy's. 'You have . . . to . . . *promise.*'

Lucy was shocked. 'Shh! All right, I promise.
I'll look after him. But only until you come home,
eh?'

Blue eyes were smiling, the most beautiful smile Lucy had ever seen. Then they closed.

And all was quiet.

When they took her away, Mike and Lucy went with her; he was sober now, and crippled by a terrible grief. His sobs could be heard in every house as the ambulance drew sedately out of the street.

There was no hurry. Sally Nolan was gone.

Empty inside, Lucy held them both close, adoring them so much, the parents who had given her such love and security; these two people who had taught her the meaning of generosity and compassion. Because of them she was strong of heart, and understanding of those less fortunate than herself. But she could not understand what was happening to them now.

Until her dying day she would never understand.

Only a short time ago they were laughing and chatting, and now they were silent except for their tears.

They were a family devastated.

A family that would never be the same again.

On the last day of May, 1987, Sally Patricia Nolan was laid to rest.

St Peter's Church was packed. There were people who had known Sally and her family for many years; there were those who had known her only because they shopped at Nolan's the greengrocer's; and there were others who knew her through her cheerfulness as they passed her in the street or said good morning while waiting in a bus queue – ordinary, caring people, who knew what it was like to lose someone you love, and whose hearts went out to Lucy and her father.

In spite of her own terrible grief this past week, Lucy had been a tower of strength to Mike. She cried silently, in her bed, or walking the streets with tears pouring down her face, and often in Jack's loving arms. During these times, when she thought her heart would break, Lucy was never friendless.

Her father wept openly. Day and night there was no consoling him. He would not, could not, accept what had happened, believing that at any minute his darling Sal would walk through the door. 'It's my fault,' he would cry, over and over. 'It's my fault.' And no one could persuade him differently.

Today was the hardest day of all. Throughout the service, he sobbed uncontrollably in Lucy's tender embrace. And afterwards, when Sal was lowered into the ground, it was Jack whose arms kept him safe; Jack who spoke softly to him. 'Shh, Mike, we're here for you,' he whispered. 'Hold on to yourself.'

As they walked back to the cars, the sun beat shamelessly down. Only Lucy and her father lingered at the graveside. Two lost souls, in their hearts imagining Sal's dear face, hearing her voice, her laughter, her gentle teasing. And for Mike, it was all too much.

He sobbed like a child all that day. He sobbed all through the night, and when the morning came, fell ominously silent.

From that day on, Mike Nolan never again cried. And he never again spoke another word.

* * *

Doctor Barrimer was sorry: 'But we've done all we can. He isn't responding to treatment, and the only other solution is to admit him to a clinic.'

'Are you saying he's mentally ill?' The words stuck in Lucy's throat. She looked haggard. Because her father had refused to go upstairs to his bed, she'd stayed down with him, going without sleep for nights on end, talking and coaxing, her own grief smothered by her concern for him.

'Not mentally ill as you might think of it,' he explained, 'but his mind has closed, and he doesn't want to face reality.'

'I won't have him put away.' Her hands gripped the chair arms so tightly it hurt. 'If he can be treated, it will have to be in the security of his own home,' she said flatly. 'He couldn't cope with strangers.'

'Very well. But as I've already explained, there is little we can do. Your father's illness is emotional. He really needs to talk to a psychiatrist.'

'We could never get him to do that.' Lucy had spent hours trying to persuade him to talk to someone who could help, but he merely shook his head and went to sit in the garden. 'I can't force him,' she said now. She was desperate, but not desperate enough to drive her father over the edge. 'If I can get him to talk to me, will he get well?'

'It will be a start.' That was all the commitment he could give. Michael Nolan was convinced he had killed the wife he adored. Only God above knew how a man's soul could be affected by such a thing. 'If you need me, or if you change your mind about the clinic, you know where I am.'

The drive home from the surgery was like a dream.

Mentally and emotionally exhausted, Lucy let her mind wander over the past weeks. Even now she could hardly believe the course of events, with her mam gone, and her dad only a shadow of his former self. The shop was closed, and she hadn't the heart or the stamina for work, even if it was possible, which it was not. Not with her dad taking up every minute of her time, night and day. Then there was Jack. Oh, what a friend he had been through all this. But he was another source of worry, because the wedding had had to be cancelled and it seemed unlikely another date could be set with her father as he was. But Jack had been so patient, showing a depth of compassion she had never before seen in him. 'Where would I be without you, Jack, my love?' she sighed.

For a fleeting moment, the idea that she might have to do without him stunned her. Frightened at the enormity of such a prospect, she brushed away the idea, pretending it had never occurred to her.

He was waiting at the door. 'How did it go?'

Lucy shook her head. 'They want to put him in a clinic, but I would never let them do that.'

Jack seemed shocked. 'Why? What can they do in a clinic that they can't do at home?'

Lucy had asked the very same questions and still had no answers. Close to tears, she shrugged her shoulders, kissing him on the mouth before he could question her further. 'Thanks for looking after him,' she said gratefully. 'Has he been all right?'

'No trouble at all.' Taking her by the hand, he led her through the sitting room, to the back window, where he pointed to a huddled figure in an armchair.

'He wanted to sit in the garden. I made him some tea and he's well wrapped up.' Smiling, he put his arm round her shoulders and drew her close. 'I brought a blanket off his bed, and tucked him up so tight he couldn't move if he wanted to.'

Lucy's grey eyes studied her dad where he sat, his face turned towards the small flowerbed which he and Sal had planted such a short time ago. The daffodils were truly over now, and the tulips were bowing their heads.

'He and Mam used to sit out there of an evening,' she explained. 'They'd be like two sweethearts, laughing and chatting and making silly plans for the future.' A wistful smile raised the corners of her mouth. 'Mam always said she would cruise round the world when she got the time. Not Dad though. He said he'd rather have a conservatory and grow tropical plants. Somehow they never got round to either.'

'We'll get him a conservatory if you like? Maybe it will give him a purpose in life.'

'Oh, Jack.' She reached out, touching his face with the tips of her fingers, the tears swimming in her eyes. 'You're so good to me.' He was more than good. Jack was her strength. Through all these dark days, he was the reason why the sun came up for her in the morning.

Taking her in his arms, he murmured, 'You look tired, sweetheart. Why don't you get some sleep? I'll stay with your dad.'

She shook her head again. 'We have to talk, you and I.'

'I know.' Leading her to the settee, he cupped her

face in his hands. 'While you were gone, I've been thinking about so many things.' Looking into her sad grey eyes, he went on softly, 'I can't bear to see you punishing yourself. You've done everything that's humanly possible, and I love you for it. But now you're making yourself ill and it's tearing me apart. It was right to postpone the wedding, and I do know how hard it is for you to think about us ... our future. But we can't put it off for ever, sweetheart.'

'I'm sorry, Jack.' But he was wrong, because during those long lonely nights when she sat with her father, she'd thought of nothing else but herself and Jack. And the more she thought, the more disillusioned she became. How could she grasp at her own happiness when her father was so desperately ill?

When she looked at him with stricken eyes, he groaned. 'I can't even begin to understand what you must be going through. But we have to decide what's to be done, sweetheart. Look, I think I've found the answer. We'll get married ... a quick, no-fuss ceremony if that's what you want ... then we'll take your dad with us to Cyprus. In the sunshine, with a new life and us beside him, he might be able to forget.'

Lucy smiled as she had not done for many a long day. 'You're a good man, Jack,' she said. 'And, yes, the idea of taking Dad with us had crossed my mind, but I wanted it to come from you. I need to know that it is what you want as well.'

He held her close, enjoying the moment, believing that everything would be all right after all. 'It *is* what I want,' he assured her. 'I'm fond of your dad too, you know.'

For the first time in ages, Lucy felt the smallest

glimmer of happiness alight inside her. Now, at last, she could see a brighter future. 'Let's go and ask him.'

It was Jack who put the proposal. 'So what do you say, Mike?' he asked eagerly. 'I'll see to everything. There's a lovely little villa high on a hill, overlooking the beach at the front and the mountains behind. We'll be happy there, the three of us. A clean sweep. It's what you need, Mike . . . a chance to breathe. Time to come to terms with everything. So what do you say?'

While Jack outlined the idea, Lucy held her father's hand, silently willing him to say yes. Suddenly he turned and stared at her, his once laughing eyes filled with a terrible sadness.

Gripping her hand so hard she felt her fingers grind one into the other, he shook his head, slowly, deliberately, eyes hardening like frozen pebbles.

There was a moment when she thought she saw a flicker of hatred in his face, but the moment was quickly gone as he continued to gaze on her, talking to her with those sad eyes, silently pleading with her not to take him from the home where he and Sal had known such happiness.

'Give it a chance, Dad,' she urged desperately. 'We'll keep the house and the shop on. It will always be here for you.' She was afraid now. Afraid that she might lose Jack. Afraid that her future had died with her mother. 'Please, Dad,' she begged. 'You could at least give it a try.'

He continued to stare, and to squeeze her hand so hard she felt the blood draining from it. When he suddenly laid his head on her shoulder, she sensed his desperation. 'All right, Dad,' she murmured. 'Don't worry.' She stroked his head and was astonished to find that he had fallen asleep. Gently, Jack took him in his arms and carried him into the house where he laid him on his bed. 'It's a terrible thing,' he said. 'A man like Mike Nolan, come to this.'

He turned then, and when he saw the look in Lucy's eyes his heart fell to his boots. 'Don't say it,' he pleaded. 'There has to be a way. There has to be a time for *us* too.'

She smiled at him sadly. 'I'll always love you, Jack,' she whispered, 'but I can't leave him. I won't. Not while he's like this.'

'Then I'll come back. We can live here if you like. So long as I'm with you, that's all I care about. Nothing else matters.'

She shook her head. 'No, Jack. You can't do that. You have a business to look after, and interests that would only suffer if you came back here.'

'Sod the business!'

'No, Jack. It wouldn't be fair. I know what that hotel means to you. It's everything you've worked so hard for. For years you've struggled and planned, and now it's all happening for you. You can't throw it all away. I won't let you.'

Gripping her by the shoulders, he shook her hard. 'It's all been for you! It means nothing if I haven't got you beside me.' He had never cried in his life but he cried now, silent tears glittering in those wonderful ocean-green eyes. 'I love you so much,' he murmured, 'I won't leave you.'

The next words she spoke were the hardest she had ever uttered. 'You have to,' she said coldly. 'I don't want you here, Jack. You were meant for better things, a man who climbs mountains because they're there, remember?' He had told her that a lifetime ago. 'If I were to agree, and you came to live here with us, you'd be like a man in a prison. You would only grow to hate me. You'd blame me, without even knowing it.'

'No! You're wrong. I could never hate you. Never! I can let the hotel go. I can always sell it, or I might even be able to find somebody to manage it. It doesn't have to be the end of everything.'

Lucy was adamant. 'It wouldn't work, Jack. You know as well as I do that you could never hand it over to someone else. Besides, I don't think your backer would agree. As you said, he's not investing in a particular project, he's investing in *you*.'

'I'll talk to him. He's not an ogre, for God's sake!' His emotions were churning, but his brain was like cold steel as he frantically sought a way out.

Lucy saw the light of realisation in his eyes. 'Don't lie to me, Jack,' she said in a hard voice. 'If he knew you were backing out, wouldn't he do the same? He might even sue you. After all, he's a businessman first and foremost. The papers are all signed. You're both committed, you can't deny that.' When he hesitated, she insisted, 'I'm right, aren't I, Jack? If you were to back out now, all Hell would be let loose.'

He knew that was the truth. 'All right,' he conceded, 'he might well pull the rug from under me. But if he does, I'll just have to start over. I've done it before. I can do it again.'

'But he could sue you, couldn't he?'

'Maybe. As you say, he's invested a lot of money.

I'll talk to him. Once I've explained the situation, I'm sure he'll understand. Give me time, Lucy. I'll work something out.'

'No, Jack. I can't ask you to destroy your dream.' She knew that in doing so, she would destroy him too. 'Go to Cyprus. Do what you set out to do. When Dad's better, then we can make plans.' Her heart was in her mouth. 'If you still want me?'

'God Almighty! If I still want you!' He took hold of her then, raining kisses on her face and mouth, whispering all the while, 'You'll never know how much I want you. I can't leave it like this. I'll be back for you, Lucy Nolan. You can bank on it.'

After he'd gone, she realised just what she had lost. 'You can't come back,' she murmured. 'Not yet. Maybe never.'

She went to the sideboard and picked up Sally's photograph, clutching it to her breast and remembering. 'Help me, Mam,' she whispered. 'Dad needs me, and I need Jack. I don't know what the answer is any more. I'm tired, and hurting, and oh, I do miss you so.'

After a while she went to her dad and curled up beside him on the bed. She lay there, gazing at his sleeping form, the tears rolling down her face. Soon, exhausted and spent, she drifted into a long, deep slumber.

Chapter Eight

The young woman was darkly beautiful. Her long black hair and striking dark eyes were typical of her Greek origin. She was slim and elegant, dressed in a white blouse and loose cream-coloured trousers, and turned all eyes in this beach-front restaurant.

But while the other patrons admired her, she had eyes for only one man. That man was Jack Hanson.

For some minutes now she had been watching him, noting how his quiet green eyes stared out over the ocean. He hadn't touched his iced drink. Instead he absent-mindedly rolled the long glass between his fingers, his thoughts many, many miles away, in a little house down a narrow street in England, with his darling Lucy.

Only now was he beginning to realise that he had lost her for good. He had tried so hard. Sometimes he believed it was his own fault. In the circumstances, with the burden she was made to carry, and the heartache she had already endured, maybe he had tried *too* hard.

Maria read his thoughts, resenting his preoccupation with this other woman whom he had often talked about. She had known him only a short time, but had come to see the strength in this good and lonely man. She had grown to admire and love him, though it was a love she could not speak of. Not while his heart was so far away. 'You still think of her, don't you?' she asked softly. 'You still torture yourself.' She sipped her drink through a slim pink straw, her black eyes betraying the love she felt.

Her words jarred on him, shattering the image of Lucy's lovely face with those wonderful grey eyes. He was a man accomplished in so many ways, yet he felt like a man starved. Success, and the money that came with it, had brought him nothing worthwhile. Only Lucy was worthwhile. Only the love they had shared, the laughter and the tears. Only *that* had been worthwhile.

He turned to face the woman, his green eyes dancing in the bright sunlight, a quick, easy smile belying the heartache inside. 'Yes,' he answered simply, 'I do still think of her.'

'You still love her, don't you?' she insisted. She hoped he might refute it, that after all these months he might turn to her.

He could never deny it. 'Yes, I still love her,' he murmured, shattering her hopes when he added firmly, 'and I always will.'

She drew hard on the straw, letting the cool liquid slither down her throat. 'Will you go back?'

The answering sigh came from deep within his heart. 'If I thought she still wanted me, I'd catch the next flight home. But she doesn't want me, not any more, so no.' His smile stiffened. 'I won't be going back.'

'What went wrong, Jack?' She couldn't let it go. 'Why doesn't she want you?'

He stared at her, hating this intrusion into his private thoughts. 'Life,' he answered wisely. 'Life and its cruelties, that's what went wrong.' His smile was bitter. 'Who am I, Maria?' he asked philosophically. 'What's it all for... all of this?' He waved his arms to encompass the elegant restaurant, the white sandy beach and the expensive car parked a short distance away. 'What does it matter, any of it?'

'It matters.' She leaned back for a while, gazing at him, trying to assess his thoughts, and feeling frustrated when she realised she was not part of them.

He shook his head. 'No.' For one delicious moment he closed his eyes and thought of Lucy again. The thought was unbearable. 'Here I am, a big success,' he said cynically. 'I've achieved what I set out to achieve. The hotel is all I wanted it to be, and soon my debt to the backer will be paid. The hotel will be mine, lock, stock and barrel.'

'You've worked hard enough for it.'

'Other men work hard,' he reminded her. 'All their lives they chase a dream striving to better themselves, but something always gets in the way. Not me, though. Everything I touch seems to turn to gold. I run an expensive car, I eat at all the best places, my expertise is sought by anyone who's anyone, and if things continue to go on the way they are, it won't be too long before I make my first million.'

'That's wonderful, isn't it?' Maria liked money. She craved material things, and had set her heart on Jack from the first moment he arrived in Cyprus.

'It might have been,' he conceded, 'with Lucy.'

'Is it really too late?' she asked hopefully.

'It seems that way,' he replied sombrely. 'Maybe it was all my fault. Maybe I should have given her more time to come to terms with what happened. Maybe I should not have gone back, again and again, trying to hold on, trying to persuade her father that he would have a good life out here, in this beautiful Paradise.' He laughed, a harsh, hollow sound. 'I always thought Paradise was made for two.'

'It is.'

He gave no answer. His thoughts were in that little house in a narrow street. With his lovely Lucy.

After months of calls and letters that had gone unanswered, he was forced to leave Lucy alone. If she had stopped loving him, there was nothing he could do; though, if it were in his power, he would do anything to right what had gone wrong between them.

'It's time we got back,' he said, glancing at his watch. 'Don't forget we have a meeting in an hour.'

'I haven't forgotten,' she said, following him to the car. 'I have the designer coming before then. I still can't decide on the material for the new curtains in the Conference Room.' Maria loved her work. Being responsible for the soft furnishings in a brand new hotel gave her a feeling of power.

'Don't look to me for help on that one,' he said, opening the car door for her. 'You're responsible for that kind of thing. After all, you're the one with the expertise in soft furnishings, and that expertise is what I pay you for.'

As they drove away, Jack was captivated by the magnificence of the Troodos Mountains. 'This is a lovely place,' he murmured, 'Lucy would have loved it.'

Maria appeared not to have heard. Settling back in the plush seat, she discreetly regarded him. With that strong, square jaw and those brooding dark green eyes, he was the most handsome man she had ever met. Considerate and fair, he was well liked and respected by all who dealt with him. He was single and, so far as Maria was concerned, he was available. He was also very rich.

I want you, Jack Hanson, she thought covetously. If I have my way, you will never see your precious Lucy again.

It was the week before Christmas.

Lucy was at her wits' end. 'Come on, Dad, you must eat.' For the umpteenth time she tried to coax him into sipping some vegetable broth. 'You know what the doctor said . . . you don't want to go into hospital, do you? Just one sip, eh? That won't hurt you.'

When, with immeasurable patience, she put the spoon to his lips, she really thought he would open his mouth. Instead he pushed it away, spilling it down her clean blouse.

He didn't speak. Nor did he look at her. As always, he stared unseeing at the floor, eyes so sad it broke her heart. 'What am I going to do with you, eh?' she asked, sitting back on her heels and forcing a little brightness into her voice. 'You should be ashamed, Dad. Here it is, Christmas, and you won't even help me dress the tree.'

Pointing to the tree in the corner, she made him turn and look at it. The tree was six feet high and planted in a wide sturdy base which she had filled with sand in order to keep it from toppling over. 'I had fourteen trees in the shop, and as soon as I saw this one I knew you'd like it. I kept it back for us, Dad.' She'd had a real struggle with that tree. 'I'll tell you what, though, I could have done with your help when I brought it through from the shop. It weighs a ton. I honestly don't know how I managed to get it upright and into the bucket. But it's a lovely tree, don't you think, Dad?' Her grey eyes shone with tears – tears for her mam, for her dad, but most of all for what she and Jack had lost. 'You put the fairy on, and the lights . . . and I'll do the rest,' she murmured brokenly. 'What do you say?'

For just the briefest instant, she thought she detected a flicker of awareness. Astonished and thrilled, she wrapped her arms round him, her face touching his and a rush of overwhelming love coursing through her. 'Oh, Dad, I do love you.'

Day after day, since her mam had died, Lucy had tried to get through to him, to jog his memory, to make him ashamed. She tried pleading, shocking him, and when she was at her lowest ebb, she even threatened to let the doctors take him away. Afterwards she was mortified with guilt, but it didn't matter what she did or said, he wouldn't let her near, and now she was running out of hope.

Holding him tight, with the tears running down her face, she murmured softly, 'Dad, do you remember when I was little? How you would always be the one to dress the tree? No one else was allowed near. First you'd put the fairy on top, then you would arrange all the little coloured lights along the branches. When that was done, you and Mam would lay out the decorations on the floor, choosing the biggest ones for the middle and the smaller ones for the outside.'

In her mind she could see the finished Christmas tree. It always stood in the corner of the sitting room as it did now, close to the window, so the lights could be seen from outside. The memory was painfully raw. 'Oh, Dad!' she breathed. 'It was so beautiful, and you were so proud. Remember, you'd come into the kitchen where Mam and I were getting the food ready. You'd make us close our eyes and you'd lead us into the room. "No peeping, you two!" you'd say. And we never did, did we, eh? We never did peep until you said: "READY!"' Describing it made her feel like a child again.

He looked at her then, his face twitching as though he was struggling to remember.

'That's right,' she urged. 'You remember now, don't you? The Christmas tree and the way you used to decorate it. Oh, Dad! Will you do that for me now? Will you? I've invited Debbie and Alfie over for Christmas. Remember, I told you? And Ted . . . and Mabel. They're all coming to share Christmas Day with us.'

A flush of anger darkened his face.

'Oh, Dad, don't be angry. We can't hide ourselves away. I've signed over my interest in the garden centre. It was always Ted's, and now it belongs to him and Mabel. I had no right to keep it. But I'm not lonely, am I? I've got you, and since I've reopened the shop, I've got all your old customers back. I work from morning to night, and I'm here when you want me, aren't I? I've finished with Jack.' Her gaze fell to the carpet. When she spoke again, it was in a quiet forlorn little voice. 'I'm sorry, Dad, but there's nothing else I can do.' She looked away, unable to go on.

A surprising thing happened then. For the first time in a long, long while, he wrapped his thin fingers round hers and squeezed them tight, eyes looking into her face, a world of sorrow in his gaze.

Lucy's voice trembled. 'Oh, Dad! Dad! If I could bring her back, I would, you know that. Don't you think I miss her too? Don't you think I wish that night had never happened? But it wasn't your fault, any more than it was mine.'

She had to make him believe that. 'Please, listen to me, Dad. It isn't for us to say who goes and who stays. I'm not God. And I'm not our mam. There's nothing I can do but love you, and I will. You and Mam gave me so much. You were always here for me, and now it's my turn. I promised her I would look after you, and I will. But you have to help yourself, Dad. You can't go on like this. She's gone and she's never coming back!' Saying it, actually saying those words, was like stabbing herself through the heart. But she needed to say them out loud. She needed him to realise the truth.

Her words struck home.

Getting out of the chair, he walked slowly to the door, his shoulders hunched like an old man's, footsteps painfully slow. When she cried out again, 'Why can't you accept it? SHE'S GONE AND SHE'S NOT COMING BACK!' he turned to stare at her. Just a moment, that was all.

But it was a moment that left her shocked, for in that all too revealing moment she knew he wanted to leave her.

She couldn't see how, or when, but she knew, as sure as she knew night followed day, he would never rest until he found his darling Sal again.

Going into the kitchen, she looked out of the window. He was sitting in the garden, in the same spot that was always his and her mother's. 'It's cold out there,' she said decisively. 'Like it or not, he's coming in.' Without further ado, she put on her coat and went to do battle.

Chapter Nine

Something was very wrong.

When she heard the doorbell jangle and looked up to see Debbie standing there, Lucy was intrigued. 'Debbie! What are you doing here?' she asked in a surprised voice. 'I thought you and Alfie were going out tonight?'

'We were, but we're not now.' She sounded weary and a little afraid. 'I need to talk to you, gal,' she said. 'How long before you shut up shop?'

Lucy was serving Mr Cartwright. He could be difficult at the best of times, and right now he was being more so than usual. 'Can you give me a minute?' she asked. There were times when she could strangle Mr Cartwright.

'Don't worry, gal.' Debbie began pacing the floor. 'It ain't that important.'

Judging by the look on her face, Lucy wasn't so sure. 'You've come this far,' she said, 'so now you can come a bit further... round this counter, if you please. We can talk while Mr Cartwright is making up his mind.'

Patiently smiling, she rolled her eyes in the direction of the fellow in question. 'I'm sure he won't be much longer,' she suggested in a firm voice. 'ISN'T THAT SO, MR CARTWRIGHT?'

He swung round, cupping his ear and staring at her. 'What's that you say?' He was old and bent, and had been a regular customer in her parents' shop ever since it opened. That was the only reason Lucy put up with his rude and cantankerous ways.

She shook her head, sighing when he continued his tiresome little routine. The old fellow was wandering round the shop, dropping things into a little wire basket then taking them out again. He'd been doing that for the best part of ten minutes, and any minute now Lucy would have to show him the door.

'If you put the kettle on,' she told Debbie with a wink, 'I'll have the shop shut before the water's boiled. A word of warning though. Try not to make a noise. Dad's taking a nap in the front room.'

'I'll be quiet as a mouse.' Debbie was relieved to be here. After all these years, Lucy was still the only one she could turn to. 'Anyway,' she added compassionately, 'you look as if you could do with a cuppa.'

'You don't know the half,' Lucy sighed. It was five minutes before closing time, and she'd been run off her feet all day. She was about to shut up when old Mr Cartwright had appeared. Though her heart fell to her boots, she didn't have the heart to turn him away. Now she just needed to fall down and never get up again.

She said as much to Debbie a few minutes later when she came into the kitchen. 'Of all the people to turn up at the midnight hour, it had to be Mr Cartwright!'

Debbie brewed the tea. 'How did you manage to get rid of him?'

Lucy's grey eyes twinkled. 'He couldn't make up

his mind between two cabbages, so I gave him the pair for nothing. Honestly, Debs, he went out the door as though I'd given him the world.' She felt ashamed. 'I shouldn't really be impatient with him, but he does try me to the limit sometimes.'

'Hmm! If it were me, I'd ban the old bugger from the shop. Tell him to get his bleedin' cabbages somewhere else.' Going to the fridge, she got out the milk. 'You've got the patience of a saint, gal,' she said. 'You deserve better.'

Debbie's words triggered another source of guilt. 'I'll go and make sure Dad's all right,' she said, already halfway across the room.

Mike was as she had left him, fast asleep on the settee and comfortably snoring. 'Tired, eh?' she murmured, bending to kiss his forehead. 'You sleep now. Later I'll bring your tea, and we can have a chat, eh?' It was her dearest wish that she and her dad could 'have a chat'. But he was too far away, with Sal. There was nothing he wanted in this world any more.

She stayed with him for a moment, gazing down on his face and thinking how much he had changed. He was thinner, more haggard, and there was a lost, desolate look about him, even when he was asleep. It was a sad sight, and one which gave Lucy endless anxiety.

When she came back to the kitchen again, her bright smile belied the darkness in her heart. 'Dad's still asleep,' she said. 'I'm glad because he was awake all night, pacing the floor.' He did that a lot lately.

Falling into the armchair that had been her mam's, Lucy eased off her shoes. 'Oh! That's better,' she sighed. 'I began to think they were glued to my feet.'

Pouring out two cups of tea, Debbie asked, 'That woman you've taken on, why doesn't she stay with him all day?'

'Because I don't want her to. She comes in four hours of a morning, and the rest of the time I manage to keep an eye on him myself. Polly Craig is a dear soul, and she's always here when the shop is busiest. I'm thankful for her, but I don't need her any longer than the time she's already here.' The words stuck in her throat. 'You see, Debs, I don't want Dad to think I've deserted him altogether.'

'Why don't you let her serve in the shop so you can be with your dad all the time?' She poured in the milk, then stirred in sugar; four spoonfuls in her own cup, and one in Lucy's.

Lucy smiled. 'As I said, Polly's a good woman. She can cook and clean, and she knows how to look after a sick man, but put her behind a counter, and face her with a constant stream of people, and she'd probably have a fit.'

'Get somebody else behind the counter then.' Everything was black and white to Debbie.

'No.' Lucy was adamant. 'I'd rather things were kept the way they are now.'

Serving behind that counter on her own was very demanding, but it gave her time to breathe, space to stretch her mind. More importantly, she saw it as a labour of love. That shop had been her parents' livelihood, a place they had chosen and where they had worked together. It was where they had known some of the happiest years of their lives, and now keeping the shop alive was important to Lucy. When she made that promise to look after her dad, it seemed to her that looking after the shop was part of it.

'I expect you're right.' Debbie came across the room. 'It would be expensive an' all. I don't suppose a greengrocer's shop can provide for too many folks.' Setting Lucy's teacup on the floor beside her, she sat herself in the other chair.

'Oh, I'm all right for money,' Lucy confided, gratefully sipping at the hot soothing liquid. 'You know how Ted insisted on making me a settlement when I signed over my share of the garden centre to Mabel.'

'Yes, I do, gal. But he'd have given you more if you hadn't battled him down.' She tutted loudly. 'I mean . . . you could have had the full value of your share, and what do you do? You settle for an income linked to takings.' She tutted again. 'I said then you were a silly ass, an' you were.'

'The arrangement suits me.'

'Suits him more like.'

There was a certain bitterness in Debbie's voice that prompted Lucy to ask, 'What's wrong, Debs?'

She sipped her tea. 'Nothing's wrong.' Just now, when Lucy came back from making sure her dad was all right, when she fell into the chair like an old woman and took off her shoes with such bliss, Debbie had been riddled with shame. She had not realised just how hard life was for Lucy, and now didn't have the heart to burden her further.

But Lucy had known Debbie too long to be put off so easily. 'Don't tell me nothing's wrong,' she chided, 'I know there is. You didn't come here on a social call. Something's worrying you, and I won't rest 'til you tell me. So out with it.'

Debbie knew she meant every word. 'I don't want to bother you with my troubles when you've got enough of your own.'

'You're bothering me more by not telling me.' Lucy's voice softened. 'Is it your mam and dad? Have they decided to split up, is that it?'

'In a way.'

'Go on.'

'It's not that simple, gal.'

'Nothing ever is.' And she should know. Not too long ago she'd had a wonderful man, a wedding day all set and a future in Paradise. Now her mam was gone, her dad didn't want to know her, and her future was tied to a greengrocer's shop. She stood behind a counter all day long, six days a week. On the seventh day she did the stock-taking and brought the accounts up to date. In between, she cared for her father the best way she knew how.

She had no time for socialising. She fell asleep in front of the television, dragged herself upstairs to bed at night, and lay awake, listening for her dad, praying he might get better when in her heart she knew he never would.

When she wasn't thinking about all that, she was thinking about Jack: about how she loved him more with each passing day, and how she had turned him away time and again, until now he too didn't want to know her any more.

Most nights she cried herself to sleep. Every morning a new day dawned and she was a day older, a day wiser, but nothing had changed. Debbie was right. Nothing was ever simple.

But in spite of her own troubles, she still could

not see Debbie unhappy without trying to help. 'Well?' She put down her cup and turned to Debbie, grey eyes regarding the other young woman with determination. 'I'm waiting.'

Debbie hesitated, but in the end she was desperate. Taking a deep breath she let it spill out, all of it, every little detail; all but one, and that was too secret, too shameful. 'I've been seeing more of Alfie. It's a funny thing, gal, but I've really come to like him.' Beneath Lucy's grey quizzical gaze, she actually blushed. 'Oh, I'm not saying there's any thought of wedding bells or owt like that, but, well, I like him, and it's a start.'

Lucy's voice was soft, her emotions in turmoil as she thought of her own wedding bells. 'Oh, Debs, I'm glad,' she said warmly. 'I knew all along he was the man for you.'

'That's all very well,' Debbie explained, 'but there's Hell to pay at home. Me mam and dad have been fighting again . . . yelling and screaming like two banshees. Last night me dad threw a vase at me mam and she had to have three stitches in her forehead.' Her voice trembled. 'I'm frightened to stay and frightened to go. I don't know which way to turn, gal. I daren't take Alfie to the house, and if I'm seen to be getting ready for a night out, the sparks start flying.'

Lucy understood. 'You're caught in the middle, eh?' She would have comforted her, but suspected that was not what Debbie wanted right now.

Gulping hard, she looked up with tearful eyes. Rolling up the left sleeve of her jumper, she bared a scar; a thick, jagged one, reaching from elbow to wrist.

'No!' She put up a hand to stop Lucy, who had leaped from her chair in horror. 'Don't, gal. Sit down. I ain't done yet.'

Lucy did as she was told. 'All right,' she murmured. 'Go on.'

Debbie continued, 'I've begged 'em time and again to go and see somebody, but they won't. Things are going from bad to worse. If they keep arguing all night, I know me dad will lose his job and then God knows what will happen. Sometimes I think it might be my fault. I can't help feeling it might be better if I got out. Besides, if I stay any longer, I think I'll go stark staring mad!' She took another deep breath. 'So I was wondering, gal . . . could I come here to live with you and your dad?'

Lucy hadn't expected that, but she had been about to tell Debbie how, if the worst came to the worst, there would always be a home here for her. ''Course you can,' she answered. 'If that's what you really want.'

They sealed the deal with a cuddle. 'You can make a start by helping me to get the dinner,' Lucy told her cheerfully. 'I peeled the vegetables at lunchtime while the shop was shut, and made the meat pie last night after Dad fell asleep. I'll get the oven going while you set the table.' Funny, she felt as though a great weight had been lifted from her shoulders. Debbie had been a constant worry. At least now Lucy would be able to keep an eye on her. Reading between the lines, Debbie's dad was getting more and more violent. When it got like that, a woman could either leave or stay. Debbie's mam had apparently chosen to stay. In that situation Debbie had made the right decision, to leave, and let them battle it out between themselves.

Lucy was closing the oven door on the meat pie when Debbie spoke again. 'There's summat else I ain't told you, gal,' she began sheepishly.

Stripping off her oven gloves, Lucy turned to face her. 'Sounds serious.' But then, what could be more serious than a violent father, and a mother who refused to stand up to him?

With Lucy looking at her and waiting for an explanation, Debbie didn't know how to say it. In the end she came straight out with it. 'I've lost me job, and I wondered if I could work in your shop? I'll be living here, so I'll not have to pay bus fare, and me shoes will last that much longer so I'm prepared to take a cut in wages. I mean . . . I can't expect you to pay me what Old Ted was.'

Somehow, Lucy wasn't too surprised. 'How did you come to lose your job?' she started, then went on before Debbie could answer, 'No, don't tell me . . . let me guess. You lost control of the forklift and demolished the house?' In her mind's eye she could see it all.

Debbie was mortified. 'I did no such thing!'

'All right, so you ran over a whole batch of pots?'

'Give me credit for some sense. I only ever did that once, and it weren't my fault. Somebody left 'em in the wrong place.' She was angry now and it showed. 'Anybody would think I were allus having accidents! This one weren't my fault neither! It were a bloody silly place for Mabel to be anyway. How was I to know she were bending down behind the compost? What! It gave me the fright of me life when I stuck the pitchfork in. There was this almighty scream, and she came running out of there like the devil were after 'er. I'm telling you, gal, it put the wind up me.'

Lucy suppressed rising laughter. It was unbelievable. 'Are you telling me you stuck a fork into poor old Mabel?'

'I didn't feel a thing so I can't say for sure, but when she came flying out o' there she were holding her arse, I know that much.'

Lucy stared at her, biting her lip to keep back the giggles. 'Mabel came rushing out *holding her arse?*'

'And screaming.' Debbie was taking it all very seriously. 'She weren't hurt though. I mean, she said herself she weren't hurt. Even when her and Ted tripped over the plant-pot display afterwards, and that were all Ted's fault for making such a fuss. What! He came out of that office like a bull at a gate. It were no wonder he lost his balance and took her with him.'

It was all too much for Lucy.

In a small, slowly rising voice, she repeated the story. 'You rammed a fork into the compost and Mabel came running out screaming . . . *holding her arse?* Then Ted came rushing out of the office and the two of them fell over the plant-pot display?' With every word she found it more and more difficult to hold back the laughter. Try as she might to behave seriously, she could feel the tears rising in her eyes and the knot of laughter filling her throat.

Debbie giggled. 'It were like summat outta the Keystone Kops,' she said. ' "Piss off you," he told me, so I did.'

Lucy looked at her.

Debbie looked back.

Soon they were helpless with laughter.

'You're a walking disaster!' Lucy spluttered. 'I must be mad, letting you move in here.'

'What about a job, eh?'

'Why not? You've made me laugh for the first time in ages. You can serve behind the counter for a pound an hour, with food and board thrown in.'

'That'll do.'

'On one condition.'

'What's that?'

'Don't fetch the house down round our ears.'

'Aw, gal, would I do that?'

Their laughter rang through the house, stopping when the pan boiled over and the oven timer went off.

A few moments later Lucy went to bring her dad to the table. Astonishingly, he had slept through the uproar.

While she walked him back down the hallway, the sound of a plate clattering to the kitchen floor made her pause. 'I must want my brains tested, having Debbie here,' she groaned.

Yet she felt happier than she had done in a very long time. Debbie and she understood each other. When all was said and done, it was good to have a friend.

Chapter Ten

Lucy was enjoying the first quiet moment in a hectic day when the knock came on the door. 'No peace for the wicked,' she muttered, scrambling out of the chair. She hurried to answer the door before her dad woke up. He desperately needed his rest. Come to think of it, so did she. But life doesn't always work out the way we want it to, she thought wryly.

For just a fleeting second when she opened the door, the light from the street-lamp blinded her. 'Yes?' Narrowing her eyes, she leaned forward to see better but his face was bathed in darkness. She almost spoke his name but wasn't quite sure. It looked like him, but he was wearing a hat against the cruel wind. She had never seen him in a hat before.

When he took off the hat, she knew straight away. 'Steve, what are you doing out on a night like this?'

Since she'd left the garden centre, Steve Ryman had become a frequent visitor to the house. He made pleasant company and was welcome so long as he kept his place, which she'd had to remind him of on more than one occasion. At last he seemed to have got the message and now they were firm friends. 'Come in, for goodness' sake, before you catch your death of cold.' She inched the door open just wide enough to let him pass.

Seeing her peering out, looking for his children, he informed her, 'They're not with me. I'm footloose and fancy free until the New Year.'

Closing the door softly, for fear her dad might hear, she took his overcoat and hung it on the hallway peg. Afterwards, she led him into the sitting room. 'It's wicked out tonight,' she said, gesturing for him to sit down in her dad's armchair. 'Been visiting a sick patient, have you?'

His smile enveloped her. 'No, I've come to see you.' He made no move to sit down.

'Oh!' Intrigued and a little worried, she asked cautiously, 'And what have I done to deserve that?'

Lucy wished he hadn't come here. Not tonight. Not when she was alone for the first time in ages. She made him feel welcome all the same, because she had come to respect him. He was a friend, but nothing more than that.

Hell would have to freeze over before he could take Jack's place. Even then he could never compare. But into this hard, lonely life she had inherited, Steve Ryman had brought a little cheer and comfort. He had an easy, likeable manner. His practised charm and confidence were the hallmark of any good doctor, and he had that uncanny knack of being in the right place at the right time; like the day when he called into the shop just when her dad took a nasty tumble down the garden steps. He'd taken charge of it all, and Lucy had never forgotten that.

Momentarily ignoring her question, Steve sug-

gested cheekily, 'If you want *me* to sit down, you'll
have to sit down first.'

'I can't.'

'Why not?'

'Because I wouldn't be much of a hostess if I didn't
offer you a hot drink to chase out the cold.' Inclining
her head to one side, she told him, 'It'll have to be
tea or coffee. You know I don't keep anything stronger
in the house.' Except for the bottle of brandy in the
understairs cupboard, but that was kept only for
emergencies.

'Coffee then. It'll give me false courage.'

Suddenly suspicious, she stared at him. 'Why
would you need false courage?'

'Coffee first?'

'Coffee can wait. Why are you here, Steve?'

She gave him a withering look. 'I hope you're not
starting all that romance stuff again?' He was standing too close. Uncomfortable, she stepped back a pace.
'We've been through all that, and you know how I
feel.'

'Yes, I do know how you feel,' he said, the warmth
of his smile belying the annoyance he felt at her
remark. 'And I wouldn't dare start "all that romance
stuff again".' He moved closer. 'Not that I wouldn't
like to,' he admitted, 'I just wouldn't dare.' Not yet
anyway, he thought cunningly. He meant to make
Lucy his wife, but he must tread carefully because
she was still hopelessly in love with Jack Hanson,
more was the pity.

Lucy visibly relaxed. 'Good. I'm glad we've got that
out of the way.' She turned towards the kitchen.
'Coffee, you said? Strong and black?'

He followed her into the kitchen. 'There's something I want to ask you,' he explained. 'With the children away, I thought this was as good a time as any.'

Keeping her back to him, she put the kettle on. Taking two china mugs from the cupboard, she asked guardedly, 'As good a time as any to do what?'

'To tell you how lonely I am.'

'Don't start that again, Steve. I know how lonely you are. I'm sorry, but all I can do is be here when you need to talk something over.' She could feel his breath on her neck. It was very disconcerting. 'Two sugars, wasn't it?' Deliberately she edged away.

This time he didn't follow. 'I'm trying to be good.' He put on his 'little boy lost' expression.

A wave of remorse washed over her. 'I'm really sorry, Steve. I don't mean to be sharp, but I don't want anything more than friendship. So long as that's understood, you're always welcome in this house.'

'It's understood,' he conceded. Inside though he was as determined as ever. With her lovely looks, proud, loyal nature, and hard-working philosophy, Lucy was the ideal woman for him. The ideal wife, and the ideal mother. The fact that she had shown no interest in him with regard to romance or matrimony did not deter him. On the contrary, it only fired his enthusiasm.

When the coffee was made and they each had a mug in their hands, they remained in the kitchen with Steve standing beside the cooker and Lucy leaning on the table. 'Why *did* you come tonight?' She made a pretence of sipping her coffee. She didn't really want it. What she wanted was to return to the quietness of the sitting room, on her own, alone with her most intimate thoughts.

Hesitating, he bit his lip then drank some of his coffee before revealing with a sheepish grin, 'I was hoping you'd have dinner with me, that's all. Nothing grand. Just a friendly, enjoyable hour or two in town. Will you, Lucy? I haven't had a good meal in ages, and I really am feeling in need of some intelligent adult company.'

He asked so nicely she might have said yes, but she couldn't. 'I'm worried about Dad,' she admitted. 'I can't leave him, not even for a couple of hours.' She was ashamed even to think it, but sometimes she felt as though the promise she had given her mother had become a life sentence.

He didn't give in easily. 'I'm sure Debbie will keep an eye on him.'

'She probably would, but I can't let her do that.'

'What's the problem?' He wore his doctor's expression. 'Your father is so much better now, isn't he?' Though he was not the attending doctor, he knew the case well enough, and bitterly resented it. If it wasn't for Lucy's father, he might have had more of a chance with her, he thought.

Her troubled gaze grew distant. 'He does seem a lot better,' she admitted. 'He's eating without too much bother, and taking more care of himself. There are times when he seems just like the old Mike Nolan, and I start to think, This is it, he's getting better.' She smiled, a sad little smile that touched his heart. 'One minute I'm sure he'll be all right, and the next, I don't know what to think.' She voiced the question that had been on her mind for some time now. 'Do you think it's my fault, Steve?'

He appeared startled. 'That's a silly thing to say. Of course it's not your fault. Why should you say that?'

She seemed not to have heard. 'He doesn't talk, or smile, or cry, yet I know he has so many things to say, so much to ask. He's still grieving for Mam, and I don't know how to help him any more.'

'The simple truth is, you can't.' Being a doctor, he was hardened to these things. 'Grief is a very personal experience. No one can help you through it except Mother Nature and the strength within yourself. Until your father comes to terms with his loss, there is nothing anyone else can do.'

'All the same, I have to be here when he needs me.' Thinking of her dad's pain brought tears to her eyes. 'He still has such terrible nightmares, you see. If I wasn't here when he woke from a nightmare, I don't know what would happen.'

'And you don't think Debbie could cope?'

She looked up, not wanting to hurt him but realising he knew very little about human nature. 'You don't understand, do you?'

Afraid he might spoil his chances with her, he quickly apologised. 'Sorry, Lucy. I always seem to jump in with both feet. Of course you know best, I do understand.' Wearing that 'little boy lost' expression again, he sighed. 'I shouldn't have asked you.'

Relieved, she explained, 'It would have been lovely, though. I haven't been out to dinner in a long time.' Not since Jack took her out, in fact.

'I'll just have to settle for my own company.'

A thought occurred to her then. It would be some

kind of consolation for him. 'Why don't you come here for Christmas dinner?'

His face lit up like a beacon. 'Why, thank you, Lucy. That would be wonderful!'

She suddenly remembered. 'But what about the children? Aren't you spending Christmas Day with them?'

'Can't.' He grinned, obviously thrilled at the prospect of spending some time over Christmas with Lucy. 'Unfortunately I'm on call all over Christmas, and as their grandmother lives in the south . . . four hours' drive away. . . I can't go that far. But I can come to you in the evening, and leave this number for emergencies. If you don't mind, that is?'

Delighted that she hadn't completely ruined his visit, Lucy assured him, 'I don't mind at all.' Her warm smile made his heart leap. 'With a bit of luck, no one will get sick and you can enjoy your meal in peace.'

'Let's hope so,' he said. 'I wouldn't want any evening with you ruined.' Rolling his eyes to the ceiling, he sighed, 'Christmas dinner with all the trimmings . . .' The dinner would be wonderful, he was sure, but being with Lucy was the main reason for his accepting.

She felt the need to remind him, 'It will be a full house. There'll be me, Dad, Alfie and Debbie. Not to mention Mabel and Ted.' Oh, how she was looking forward to it.

'I won't even see them.' With Lucy there, how could he have eyes for anyone else?

Momentarily lost for words, she shrugged her shoulders. 'I don't suppose Dad will join in the festivities. He has no interest in anything.' She looked up, smiling bravely. 'I'm not sure how to deal with him any more,' she confessed. 'I feel guilty yet I don't know why, and I'm . . .' she searched for the right word, '. . . frightened.'

'What do you mean, frightened?' he asked. 'What are you frightened of?'

'What he might do next. You were here when he tumbled down the steps, and it wasn't the first time.'

'I understand.' He had seen it all before. Michael Nolan was a wretched soul without purpose, unaware of the harm he could do himself and totally oblivious of the sacrifices his own daughter was making on his behalf. 'You mustn't feel guilty,' he told her. 'None of it was your fault. Besides, haven't you forgotten something very important here?'

She gave no answer because she couldn't see what he was getting at. More than that, she was suddenly very tired, willing him to leave. Yet she wanted him to stay because if she had learned one thing, it was this: there could be nothing worse in the whole world than loneliness.

Seeing how quiet she was, he strode across the room towards her. Taking hold of her hands, he was surprised when she gave no resistance. 'Listen to me, Lucy. Your father isn't the only one who's grieving. You've suffered a loss too. You've been deprived of a mother you loved, and while you are here to help your father through it, who's here for you?'

Her grey eyes swimming with tears, she looked up at him. 'I never thought of that,' she murmured.

'Then you should. You say you feel guilty but don't know why. There's nothing sinister or worrying about

that, and it has little to do with your father. It has
to do with you, Lucy, and your own special loss. Feeling guilty is a natural reaction. Because you have
your father to care for, you've bottled up your own
needs. You don't talk about your mother, and you're
too proud to ask for help. In my experience that's a
recipe for disaster.'

Every word he spoke was the truth, but now, when
he said it aloud, it only made things worse. 'I'm tired,'
she said evasively. 'If you don't mind, Steve, I think
I'll have an early night.'

Having got what he came for, he could afford to be
generous. 'That's a very good idea,' he said, giving her
a doctor's look. 'You're right. I'd better be on my way.'

She walked him to the door. 'I hope you don't think
I'm throwing you out?'

'Well, aren't you?' Taking his coat from the peg,
he brushed against her and, not for the first time
that evening, she felt deeply disturbed.

Suddenly he was staring at her, his brown eyes
intense. 'If you threw me out, I'd only come back
again and again until you had to shoot me.'

'You'd better leave now or I might just do that.'

'You wouldn't?'

'Don't count on it.' There was the merest ghost of
a smile on her face, but the grey eyes were defiant.

He put up his hands. 'All right!' he said, backing
to the door. 'I've overstepped the mark and I'm sorry.'

As he drove away he congratulated himself. He
wasn't sorry at all. He was glad. For some inexplicable
reason, he felt he was drawing closer to the day when
he could ask Lucy to marry him, and she would have
no alternative but to say yes.

Turning out of Penny Street, he began whistling, and continued all the way home.

Mike Nolan was not asleep as Lucy thought. He had heard the conversation on the doorstep, and now he watched as Steve Ryman drove away.

He stayed by the window until the car was out of sight, then walked sedately to his bed where he turned back the eiderdown and reached an arm beneath the mattress.

Having located the small bundle of letters, he sat on the bed and untied them. Setting them out like a deck of cards, he thumbed through each and every one. Finally he opened one. This had been the last, delivered three weeks ago, and like all the others scooped up and secreted away before anyone realised.

Holding the open letter between trembling fingers, he ran his eyes over the words:

My Darling Lucy,

This is the hardest letter I have ever written.

After all that has been between us, I was sure you would write to me, but I can't seem to get near you any more. My letters go unanswered, and now I find you've gone ex-directory so that's another line of communication closed.

Sweetheart, I don't need to tell you how I feel about you, because you know all too well by now.

I don't know what to say, my darling.

I can't stop loving you. Every minute of every day and night, I'm thinking of you . . .

can't get you out of my mind. Everything I do, everything I've ever done, every small achievement, has always been with you in mind.

I understand how hard it must be for you, and my heart goes out to you. But I can't help feeling angry.

I was prepared to give it all up for you, sweetheart. I wanted to be with you, and still do. I know why you turned me away. It's the kind of person you are, putting others before yourself. You thought I would come to regret throwing it all away, and I must admit I was uncertain at first. Like you say, I have worked hard to get where I am.

But I want you to know that where I am is a very lonely place without you.

I love you so much, too much to force myself on you. So, I'm giving it one more try. Let me come back, Lucy.

It's you I want. If I have you, I have everything.

You know my number. You have my address. I'll be waiting for your answer.

If I don't hear, I'll know there is no point in writing to you again. Please, sweetheart, don't let's throw it all away.

With all my love,
    Jack

Carefully Mike folded the letter. Tying the batch neatly, he then returned it to its hiding place. Stealing the letters had been easy. Sometimes he waylaid the postman, and other times he merely wandered into

the shop and collected the post while Lucy and Debbie
were busy serving a customer.

It had been the phone which proved to be more
difficult. Twice he had picked it up when Jack called.
Each time he had flicked the receiver cradle to make
it seem as though there was a fault. Then, after much
deliberation, he had written to the telephone company, saying they had received nuisance calls, and
could they be made ex-directory with a new number?

When Lucy got the letter informing them that they
had been issued with a new number he had been
afraid it might give the reason why. Thankfully, it
didn't. Neither did it mention the fact that they had
gone ex-directory. That confirmation came later, when
he was able to hide it away from her.

Being run off her feet with other, more important
matters, Lucy merely accepted the new number. She
informed her suppliers, and nothing more was ever
said about it.

Mike Nolan had no regrets about deceiving her.

He had done it because he loved her; because he
couldn't bear the idea of her being hurt, as he had
been hurt. Better never to love than be hurt the way
he had been.

Love was a terrible, merciless thing. His greatest
wish now was that Lucy should never know the pain
it brought.

Chapter Eleven

It was Christmas Eve.

All day long the snow tumbled from the skies until by mid-afternoon the pavements were covered in a thick layer of crispy white frost that crunched underfoot and filled the children with joy. 'My kids have been out since eight o'clock this morning,' Madge Tyler told Lucy as she bought her last-minute groceries. 'I haven't seen hide nor hair of 'em, but I'm not bothered. Their bellies will fetch 'em home for their tea, you can be sure o' that.' She chuckled as she left, and it wasn't long before the next customer took her place.

That's how it had been since early morning. When Lucy opened the shop door at eight o'clock there were three customers waiting, and there had been a steady stream all day. Now they were turning up in droves, finishing their last-minute shopping before the Christmas holiday.

'Busy, ain't yer, dear?' enquired the landlady from the public house. 'Your turn now and my turn later, eh?' She bought eight huge Spanish onions, and a whole carton of beetroot. 'For the Christmas Eve buffet,' she explained. 'We allus do summat special for Christmas.'

'Waste o' time!' Angus Long sniffed back a juicy dewdrop from the end of his long nose. 'Give 'em a cheese sandwich with their pint and they'll be happy as Larry.' Angus was never one for fancy food.

Lucy kept well out of the argument. All she wanted was to serve the customers and lock the doors for a long, well-deserved weekend. She had hoped to shut early, but it didn't seem likely because no sooner had she got rid of one queue than there was another. 'Debbie run out on you, has she?' The little woman from Ackroyd Street had two rows of pink gums, a runny nose, two bright pink eyes and an insatiable appetite for gossip. Leaning over the counter she asked in a murmur, 'That Debbie, eh? I expect she's off on personal business. They say her parents have been rowing morning, noon and night, and now they're thinking of splitting up.' She leaned further over the counter, her bright eyes open wide with expectation. 'You can tell me, lass, 'cause I'm not one for gossip. Is it true? Are they really splitting up?'

Lucy was fuming, but made little of the comment. 'You shouldn't believe everything you hear,' she answered, throwing half a dozen apples into the woman's shopping bag. 'My mam used to say people who spread gossip about other people must have more to hide themselves.' Her grey eyes twinkled mischievously. '*You're* not hiding anything, are you?' she whispered intimately. 'No secret lovers or anything like that?'

Slamming a pound coin on to the counter, the little woman blushed carrot red. 'Don't know what you're talking about,' she said. Then she grabbed her change and departed in such a crashing hurry that she tripped over a sack of potatoes and landed in a heap.

'You silly old bugger!' Mr Entwhistle helped her to her feet. 'When will you learn not to poke your nose in other folk's business?'

'Huh! And when will *you* learn to keep your trap shut, you old windbag!' She wasn't a bit grateful for his help, and flounced out of the shop with a chip on her shoulder as wide as a barn door.

It didn't bother old Entwhistle. 'Shame on you, Lucy Nolan,' he chuckled. 'Fancy asking if she'd got a secret lover! I shouldn't think she's ever had a lover in her life.' For an old man, he gave a young and cheeky wink. 'I have, though. What! There was a time when every woman in Lancashire was beating a path to my door.'

Lucy could well believe that. Though he was now in his seventies, Mr Entwhistle was still a fine figure of a man; tall and distinguished, with a sprightly walk and twinkling green eyes, he was quite handsome. Like Jack might be when he's that age, she thought. It only made her sad, so she shooed the thought away.

Half an hour later she was able to shut up shop. 'Thank God for that,' she sighed, leaning against the closed door and taking a long, deep breath. She still had to sweep and clean and sort out the shelves, but that could wait. A cup of tea, and a few quiet minutes on my own, she decided. Before Dad wakes up. Mike had been upstairs in his room since midday. When she'd crept up to see him at one o'clock, he had been sleeping like a baby.

As she made her way to the kitchen, there was a knock on the front door. 'Surely to God Debbie hasn't forgotten her key again!' On weary feet she went to let her in, swearing under her breath when she tried to switch on the hallway light, and realised she still hadn't changed the bulb.

The visitor was George Beckendale, Ted's estranged son.

He was leaning on the door-jamb, his face half turned to the street-lamp. At first glance, Lucy was shocked. He seemed older, thinner and more haggard. The way his shoulders stooped they might have been carrying the weight of the world. 'I hope you don't mind my coming here?' His dark eyes stared at her, mouth trembling as he gave a half-smile.

It pleased Lucy to see he was not so cocksure of himself as he had been the last time she'd seen him. All the same, the sight of him here, at her own front door, naturally made her suspicious. 'What do you want?' Her voice was hostile. She still hadn't forgotten the way he'd treated Ted.

His face fell. 'I didn't expect a welcome,' he admitted, 'but I did hope you might hear me out.'

'I asked . . . what do you want?'

He hesitated before going on with increasing confidence, 'I've been a fool, and you've every right not to want me on your doorstep. If I was in your place I'd tell me to shove off too, but I hope you won't. I hope you'll let me speak first?'

Lucy had to remind herself that he was Ted's son. 'I'm listening,' she said, though she couldn't trust him.

'I don't want my father to hate me.'

'You should have thought of that before you threatened to throw him out.' She had no sympathy for him.

'I know, but I've come to realise my mistake and now I want to make it up with him.'

'So why are you here? Shouldn't you be saying all this to your dad?'

'I'm ashamed.'

'So you should be.'

'Will you talk to him for me?'

'I don't think so.' Bloody cheek!

'You have a father, don't you?' he asked pointedly. 'You love him, don't you?'

He had touched a sore point. How dare he talk about her relationship with her dad? 'Goodnight, Mr Beckendale.' She stepped back to close the door.

'No. Wait!'

She waited but only long enough for him to plead, 'I got it wrong, and I'm sorry. He's all I've got and I've only just come to realise that. Dad and me, we've never really got on, but what I tried to do was unforgivable and I want him to know I understand that now. Please! Talk to him. He'll listen to you. Make him understand, before it's too late.'

Something in his voice moved her, but she was still wary. 'If you really are sorry, then it's best you tell him yourself.'

'He's a stubborn old bugger, and always has been.'

She smiled. 'You've got that much right.'

Her smile encouraged him. 'I've tried to tell him how sorry I am, but he won't listen.'

The smile hardened on her face. 'Then you'll just have to try again, won't you?'

He nodded, turning away. 'I shouldn't have come here.'

She would have closed the door, but her conscience wouldn't let her leave things like this. 'Mr Beckendale!' she called.

Hopefully, he turned. 'Will you talk to him?'

She shook her head. 'No, I won't do that. I haven't forgiven you yet.'

'I understand.'

'Talk to Mabel. Ted listens to her.'

He nodded gratefully. 'I will. Thank you.'

Lucy gave him a hard stare. 'Be warned, though, she's nobody's fool.' If he was lying for his own ends, Mabel would know and she would protect Ted to the bitter end.

Lucy shut the door. 'I don't know what your game is, George Beckendale,' she muttered, striding down the passage to the kitchen, 'but if you're up to your old tricks again, you won't get very far.' She wondered whether she should call Ted, but decided against it. He could take care of himself. Besides, with Mabel by his side, they made a formidable pair.

Lucy managed to get a whole hour to herself.

During that time she crept back upstairs to check on her dad, who had hardly moved an inch. She banked up the fire and sat in front of it with her shoes off and her feet up. She sipped at a mug of warming cocoa, and in the gentle heat, willed herself to stay awake.

The silence was golden. The mantelpiece clock ticked merrily away, and only her thoughts were disturbing; thoughts of Jack, of what had been and was no more. She closed her eyes. Oh, Jack! Jack! You'll never know how much courage it took for me to send you away.

She could see him in her mind's eye as though he was right here before her: that wonderful strong face, with its caring smile and striking green eyes. 'Where are you, Jack!' she murmured lovingly. 'Do you have someone else? I wonder if she loves you like I do?' The idea that he might have someone else stuck in her heart like a knife. 'I won't blame you,' she told him. 'I wouldn't want you to be lonely. Not like me.' And, oh God, she was so very lonely. 'It's true I have my dad, and now there's Debbie. But she has her own life, and Dad . . .' Lucy sighed deeply, a terrible sense of guilt and hopelessness washing through her. 'He has no life at all,' she whispered. 'No love, no purpose . . . no hope. Only me. And I can't desert him.'

It was heartbreaking to see her own father pining away, but there was nothing she could do. While her mother lay dying in her arms she had made a promise and, however hard or unfair that burden was, she would honour that promise, come what may.

Rested now, she returned to the shop where she scrubbed the floor and emptied the shelves, putting the good fruit and veg in the cold cupboard and the rest in the sacks which she prepared to take outside. A farmer from Samlesbury would collect them later for his animals, if the neighbourhood cats didn't get to them first.

When it was all done, she stood in the doorway and took one last look across the shop area. It always seemed bare when the shelves were empty, yet there was a feeling of history, a sense of family in this old place, which was hard to ignore.

The longer she stood there, the clearer she could see her mam and dad as they were not too long ago, her dad laughing and joking as he weighed the purchases, and her mam chatting as she served.

Enjoying the memory, Lucy smiled. 'I miss you, Mam,' she murmured. 'And if you've got any influence up there, try and help our dad.' She gulped back the tears. 'Because he's lost his way without you.'

A few minutes later she stood at the bedroom door, gazing at his sleeping face. 'Just look at you, Dad,' she sighed. 'What are you doing to yourself?' The thought flickered in her mind: And what is he doing to *you*, Lucy? Ashamed, she thrust the thought away, mortified that, for a fleeting minute, she had harboured a sense of anger.

The quick rush of bitter resentment receded. Don't blame your dad, she told herself. You're old enough to make your own decisions. But she wasn't *free*. Not free to leave her dad, and not free to go to Jack. 'Funny how things change,' she muttered as she went downstairs to prepare dinner. Fate can be cruel, and like it or not, we're all playthings in its hands.

It was half-past nine when Debbie got home. Her voice sailed through the front door with a blast of cold air. 'PISS OFF, YER LITTLE SODS! IF I CATCH YOU MAKING FACES BEHIND MY BACK AGAIN, I'LL KICK YER ARSES 'TIL THEY'RE BLACK AN' BLUE!'

In the kitchen Lucy glanced up with a smile. 'Sounds like she's had a good time.'

She was right.

The front door slammed shut and in came Debbie, drunk as a lord and waving her hand about. 'Look at that, gal!' she screeched, crashing in through the door. 'That little squirt Alfie's done for me now.'

Wiping her hands on the tea-towel, Lucy led Debbie to a chair. 'Sit down before you fall down,' she told her.

Debbie's eyes opened wide with horror. 'Ooh, I'm sorry, gal, coming in screaming and shouting like that. I expect I've woke your dad up, ain't I?'

'Don't worry,' Lucy said, returning to the sink where she was straining the vegetables. 'Dinner's nearly ready. It's time he was awake anyway.'

Debbie followed, leaning on the cooker and trying to stand upright with difficulty. 'It were them bloody kids,' she groaned. 'They made me that mad . . . trailing me from the end of the street, hiding in doorways when I turned round and coming out to torment me when me back was turned.' Her mouth twisted like a sailor's rope. 'If I get me hands on the little sods, I'll hang for 'em, I will!'

'Kids are kids.' Lucy studied her friend, a little smile playing at the corners of her mouth as she saw the state Debbie was in. Her hair looked as if she'd been in a force nine gale, her bright crimson lipstick was all over her face, and her tights were laddered in three places. Lucy laughed out loud. 'I'm not surprised the kids followed you down the street,' she said. 'It's a wonder the dogs didn't pee up your legs!'

Debbie was affronted by that. 'What! Just let 'em,' she cried. 'The first dog as pisses up *my* leg won't piss up anybody else's, I can promise yer that.'

Lucy knew exactly what she meant. 'Anyway, where've you been? More to the point, who have you been with who would fetch you home looking like that? Honest to God, Debs, you look as if you've been dragged through a hedge backwards.'

'I *have*!' The look on her face gave it all away. 'Well, in a manner of speaking. Y'see, me an' Alfie had a bit under the hedge. Jeez! It were bloody cold to me arse, I can tell yer that!' She roared with laughter. 'That Alfie though! He's a bugger, ain't he, eh? I'm tellin' yer, Lucy gal, I've been and gone and done it now.' She raised her arm and fell against the cooker, knocking a pan of hot water sideways. 'I'm pissed as a newt, gal,' she chuckled, 'and me head feels like ten.' She went a deathly shade of pale and sagged at the knees. 'It were worth it, though. By God! It were bloody well worth it.' She laughed so much she couldn't stand up straight.

'Right!' Lucy had no alternative. 'It's bed for you, my girl.' Sometimes she felt she had two children, one here and the other upstairs.

Debbie tried to push her away. 'I ain't going to bed.'

Lucy's patience was sorely tested. 'You bloody well are, my girl.' Tucking one arm round Debbie's waist and taking her arm with the other, she inched her across the room and up the stairs, where she dumped her unceremoniously on her bed. 'I think you'd better sleep it off.'

Regretful eyes looked back. 'I ain't much use to you, am I, gal?'

Lucy smiled. 'No, you're not.'

'D'yer hate me?'

'Don't be daft.'

'You should.'

'What did you want to show me?'

'Look, gal.' Raising her left arm, she wiggled her fingers. 'That bloody Alfie . . . he's talked me into getting engaged.'

Lucy was thrilled. 'Oh, Debbie, that's wonderful!' She hugged her tight. 'I know he's right for you. I've always known that.' Tears of joy filled her eyes. At least her friend would find happiness.

Debbie's voice softened. 'I shouldn't have told you, gal.'

'Why not?'

'Because of you and Jack, and everything.'

'It doesn't matter,' she said. But it did matter. It mattered like Hell.

'D'yer like me ring?' Stretching out her hand, she spread her fingers in front of Lucy's face. 'Alfie said he saved for a whole year, 'cause he were sure I'd say yes in the end.' She blushed. 'Cocky sod!'

Taking hold of Debbie's finger, Lucy lovingly stroked the ring. It was the prettiest thing – an oblong sapphire surrounded by tiny diamonds. Jack had given her a ring but now it was hidden away from prying eyes. Sometimes she took it out and cried herself to sleep, but that was when she let herself think too deeply. Lately she had learned not to punish herself like that.

'Well? D'yer like it or don't yer?'

'It's lovely,' murmured Lucy. 'You and Alfie are made for each other. He'll make you happy, I know that, and you must look after him, Debs.' A wave of regret swept through her. 'I know what it's like to lose a good man.'

Before Debbie could reply, she went on, 'And you're not to worry about me. This is your day, and I'm so happy for you.' She was, too. Though in the tiniest corner of her heart, she wished it could have been her.

Debbie gave her a long fond look, then, in the blink of an eye, lolled over and fell into a deep sleep.

Lucy left her there, snoring like distant thunder and in between chattering in her sleep. 'It ain't fair. Lucy's lost her fella and I've found mine . . . the world's a topsy-turvy place.'

'You never spoke a truer word.' Lucy closed the door behind her. Topsy-turvy described her life, all right. Upside down, all messed up, and not even a light at the end of the tunnel. 'Stop feeling sorry for yourself, Lucy Nolan.' She went down the stairs and into the kitchen. 'You'd best get a move on. There's a meal spoiling in here.'

As she set out the plates, she took a minute to wonder about Christmas dinner. I'll flay that Debbie alive if she ends up legless, she threatened. I want Christmas to be special . . . like it used to be when Mam was here. Her heart skipped a beat. How can it be special? she asked herself. When Jack is so many miles away and I'm never likely to see him again?

It was a sobering thought, and one which stayed with her for a very long time.

Chapter Twelve

'Not too early, am I?' Steve was the first to arrive.

Lucy wasn't surprised when she opened the door and there he was, twenty minutes ahead of time. In fact she would have been more surprised if he had not been the first. "Course you're not too early.' She drew him in, quickly shutting the door against the howling wind. 'The others should be here any minute,' she said. 'Debbie went over to Alfie's in a taxi. Ted rang only minutes ago to say he and Mabel were starting out, and Dad's in the kitchen, looking over some old photographs.'

'Is that wise? I mean . . . won't it upset him?'

'No, it isn't wise, and yes, it will upset him,' she conceded. 'But lately he's been showing a lot more interest in everything, so I'm hoping this is the first sign of a recovery.'

In fact Lucy had been thrilled and astonished earlier when her dad came into the kitchen and, without even asking, had gone to the dresser and taken out the lovely lace tablecloth her mam always brought out at Christmas. He laid it over the dining-table and went back and forth, setting the table with all the lovely things her mam had used: the pretty silver condiment set, the crystal wine glasses and the best set of cutlery. He even placed a pair of favourite candlesticks at either end of the table and dressed them with red candles and ribbons, in the very same way her mam used to do.

When he was finished, he took Lucy by the hand and showed her. The table was set with such loving care, it brought tears to her eyes. 'It's beautiful, Dad,' she murmured, cuddling up to him. 'What made you think to do that?'

He didn't answer.

'Does that mean you might dress the tree as well?' she asked hopefully. 'I've got the box out . . . all the trimmings and everything.' She still had not dressed the tree, and she wouldn't. Dressing the tree was her dad's job, and if he didn't do it, then it would have to stay bare.

He still gave no answer. Instead he looked at her with a proud expression before going into the kitchen where he sat at the table, poring over old photographs of his beloved Sal.

He had been there ever since.

Lucy wisely left him to his memories. 'They say things get worse before they get better,' she told Steve now. 'Maybe we've had the worst, and from now on it can only get better.'

'Let's hope so,' he said.

'Thank you for that. You've been a good friend to me, and I won't forget it.'

Suddenly he was more intense, his eyes regarding her longingly. 'Is that all you'll ever allow me to be, Lucy . . . a friend?'

Ignoring his comment, she said firmly, 'Let me take your coat. Make your way into the sitting room and I'll get you a drink . . . it'll help to keep out the cold while you're waiting for the others.' She liked Steve a lot, but she didn't love him. In her book, love and marriage went together, and she had no intention of marrying anyone but Jack. And if she couldn't have him, then she didn't want anybody.

'You look very lovely.' Her grey eyes were stunningly beautiful beneath that dark fringe. She had on a straight blue skirt and white blouse, and her thick dark hair was brushed until it shone like fallen chestnuts. 'It isn't right that you should hide such beauty behind a shop counter.'

She smiled. 'There are more beautiful women than me behind shop counters.' She held out her arms. 'Let me hang your coat up before the damp soaks through to your bones.'

'Let's *both* have a drink to keep out the cold,' he suggested. Reaching into his coat pocket, he drew out a small bottle of brandy. 'You will join me, won't you?'

She shook her head. 'I'm not a brandy drinker, but I'll take a sherry with you.'

He visibly relaxed. 'That's good enough for me.'

'The coat?'

Quickly shrugging out of the overcoat, he gave it to her. 'Sorry if I spoke out of turn.'

'So am I.' She hung the coat on the rack and the two of them went through to the sitting room where she poured him a brandy and herself a small sherry. Normally she didn't keep drink in the house, but this was a special occasion.

When she turned it was to see him banking up the fire with a shovelful of coal. 'You don't mind, do you?' he asked, replacing the shovel on the stand. 'Only I'm so used to doing everything for myself at home, I did it without thinking.'

She gave him his drink. 'I don't mind a bit,' she admitted with a twinkle in her eyes. 'When you've finished banking up the fire, there's a pile of dirty saucepans in the kitchen, and a three-course dinner to dish up.'

He laughed. 'Hey! Hang on a minute. I don't recall saying I *enjoyed* domestic chores.' He chinked his glass against hers. 'Happy Christmas anyway.'

'Happy Christmas.' She sipped the sherry, loving the warm sensation as it trickled down her throat.

Going to the window, she looked out. The world was white, and cold, and astonishingly beautiful. 'White Christmases are wonderful,' she breathed. 'They make me feel like a child again.'

He came to stand beside her. 'You're right,' he agreed, peering over her shoulder. 'There is something very special about a white Christmas.' He was so near he could smell the freshness of her hair. He needed her badly yet she was forbidden to him. It made him almost crazy. He wanted to touch her, to kiss that lovely neck, to place his hands on her shoulders and swing her round to him. He wanted to look down on her eager, upturned face, see a hungry light in her soft grey eyes as she waited for his kiss. He wanted her. Craved her. Dreamed and ached and longed to have her. Yet she was still forbidden to him.

That's how it was. For now.

But the night was still young.

And Lucy was a lonely, vulnerable young woman . . .

* * *

The dinner was a wonderful success.

Ted said he had never tasted roast turkey like it. Mabel loved the mince pies and wanted to know how Lucy managed to make such deliciously light pastry. Everyone laughed when she admitted they were shop bought, and Debbie told her she was a fool not to take the credit. 'I wouldn't have told the truth,' she declared, and meant it.

It was a happy time for Lucy. She laughed and chatted and glowed with contentment. She had her dad here, and her friends, and there were people in this world who had neither, she told herself, whenever she began to feel lonely for Jack.

Ted revealed that his son had been in touch again. 'I don't know why he bothers,' he said angrily. 'After what he tried to do, I prefer to think I haven't a son at all.'

Mabel didn't agree. 'Keep an open mind, Ted,' she pleaded quietly. 'However hard-hearted he's been, he should be given a second chance. After all, he is your son . . . the only family you've got.'

Whether it was the drink, or the idea that maybe George really was sorry for the way he had treated his old dad, Ted's eyes filled with tears. Taking Mabel's hand in his, he told her, 'You're wrong, lass. He's not the only family I've got. *You* are.'

Blushing with pleasure, she replied that was a lovely thing for him to say. Looking round the table, she revealed, 'Ted means to make a decent woman of me. We plan to marry on Easter Saturday next year.'

Everyone cheered and drank their health, and

Lucy thought they were so well suited they should have married years before. 'God bless you both,' she said, kissing them in turn. 'And may you have many long years of happiness together.'

While everyone chattered with excitement, she let herself think back to when she and Jack had planned their wedding, and prayed that nothing would go wrong for these two lovely people.

As the evening wore on, and the food and wine diminished, it transpired that Mabel was to be made a full partner in the business. 'She's much like you,' Ted told Lucy. 'Works like a maniac, and enjoys everything she does. The customers adore her, and she has a natural knack of keeping everybody happy.' He chuckled with delight. 'It seems like I've lost one angel and found another.'

Later on, Alfie and Debbie gave out the news that they too were planning to wed, and there was another round of raised glasses filled to the brim with wine. 'I ain't pregnant neither!' Debbie assured everyone. 'I know I allus said I'd never marry the scraggy bugger, but he wouldn't take no for an answer.' Her face was flushed from an earlier bout of booze, so she limited her drinking, and confided in Lucy while the two of them were fetching the coffee from the kitchen. 'I know you wanted me and Alfie to sleep here tonight, and we're very grateful for that, but we've decided to stay in a hotel . . . for a bit of wild nooky, if you know what I mean?' She winked and Lucy knew exactly what she meant. 'So, yer don't mind, d'yer, gal?'

Lucy enjoyed Debbie's happiness, so her answer was a simple, 'What do you think, you daft arse?'

She hiccuped and giggled all in one breath.

Debbie stared at her. It wasn't often Lucy swore like that. She noticed the flushed face and misty grey eyes, and that slight lean when she walked across the room to the sink. 'Lucy Nolan!' She gaped in disbelief. 'You're drunk!'

'I am not.' In fact Lucy hadn't realised she'd drunk too much wine until she got up from the table to walk into the kitchen. That short familiar distance suddenly felt like climbing Mount Everest.

'Sit down, yer bugger.' Pushing Lucy into a chair, Debbie made her a cup of strong black coffee. 'Get that down yer, and don't stop 'til it's all gone,' she ordered.

Feeling dizzy and ashamed, Lucy did as she was told. Afterwards she felt sick. 'We're a right pair and no mistake,' she laughed. 'But it is Christmas, after all, so what's wrong with letting our hair down, eh?' Suddenly she was crying, great big tears rolling down her face. 'Isn't it wonderful news . . . you and Alfie, and now Ted and Mabel? I'll have to treat myself to a new outfit, with *two* weddings to go to.'

Coming to sit beside her, Debbie suddenly understood. 'Two weddings . . . but not your own, eh? And you're the one who deserves a slice of happiness.'

Lucy was too choked to answer straight away. She felt disgusted with herself, but at the same time couldn't help yearning for the way things were. 'You're wrong, Debs,' she whispered. 'We *all* deserve a slice of happiness, me no more than anyone. Ted and Mabel have had their share of troubles, and so have you. I'm thrilled for you all, don't ever doubt that.'

'Why don't you ring him, gal?'

The grey eyes looked puzzled. 'Who?'

'You know who.'

Lucy's heart melted. 'Jack,' she murmured, 'you want me to ring Jack?'

'Do it now.'

Lucy shook her head. 'I can't.'

'Why not, for Chrissake?'

'Because it's been too long, and because I can't offer him any more than I did before.' If only Debbie knew how often she had begun to ring Jack, and put down the receiver before anyone could answer. 'He's making a new life for himself, and I've no right to give him false hope.'

'What about you? Shouldn't you have some measure of hope?'

Sensing that they were getting on to dangerous ground, Lucy stood up. She felt better now, more in control, though her head still felt like two. 'We'd better get this coffee in, before they come looking for us.'

'I see. End of subject, eh?'

'That's right, Debs, and I must ask you not to contact Jack in any way. If and when the time is ever right, I'll go to him, but until then, I have to be the one who decides. All right?'

Debbie had seen that same look of determination on Lucy's face many times, and she had learned not to argue. 'All right.' She made a gesture. 'Scout's honour.'

They took the coffee in and nothing more was said on the matter.

Lucy was delighted with the way her dad had

remained at the table throughout, listening to the conversation though not joining in and seeming to enjoy the meal she had cooked for him. At any minute during the evening she had expected him to nod an apology and make himself scarce, but he didn't. And, for the first time in an age, she began to believe he was coming to terms with his loss.

They finished their coffee and chatted round the table for a while. It had been an easy, casual affair and now it was almost over. Lucy felt sad about that.

At eleven o'clock, the party started to break up. 'Us old-timers had better be off,' Ted suggested.

Mabel reluctantly agreed. 'When you get to our age, you need your beauty sleep,' she told Lucy.

Ted declared Mabel was 'beautiful from morning to night', and they went away holding hands like young lovers.

Not too long after that, Alfie and Debbie made their excuses and left. 'Leave the dishes in the sink, gal,' Debbie called out as she went. 'I'll help you wash up in the morning.'

In fact, the way Lucy felt, light-headed and full of wine, she decided she might just do that.

'Don't worry about the dishes,' Steve remarked, 'I've got a good strong pair of hands, and I can do wonders with a dish-cloth.'

Lucy was grateful. 'But it's late, Steve. I can manage if you want to go.' Worried that she had in fact drunk too much wine, and feeling the old loneliness already creeping up on her, she thought it might be safer if he left now. 'Dad will help me,' she said, glancing over to where her father had been only minutes before. 'You'll give me a hand, won't you, Dad?'

But her dad wasn't there.

Steve was secretly delighted. 'I thought you knew... he left the room with Ted and Mabel. It's been a long night for him, I expect he's gone to bed.' He came across to her, gazing at her intently. 'Looks like you're stuck with me, after all.'

What did it matter? she thought. So he fancied her. It wasn't the first time a man had fancied her, and hopefully it wouldn't be the last. She was a grown woman and had always been able to handle herself. If he started any hanky-panky, he'd be the sorry one.

'All right,' she conceded. Why should she feel afraid of him? He was just a friend. 'If you're so keen on helping with the dishes, you can scrape the leftovers into that plastic bag by the sink. While you're doing that, I'll go and see where Dad's got to.'

Instinct took her straight to his bedroom.

As she mounted the stairs she felt dangerously unsteady on her feet. 'Debs is right, you drunken slut,' she giggled, catching hold of the banister when she lost her balance. 'You've had one over the eight, and if you're not very careful, Steve will try and take advantage of you when you're not looking.'

At first when she opened the bedroom door she didn't see him, but he was there, she could tell. She flicked on the light, and instantly her gaze was drawn to the window. Mike Nolan was seated in the high-backed chair, his face half turned to the night, but his head bent, as though he was crying. He didn't look up, but at the sudden light his shoulders stiffened and his hands unclenched on his lap. He had obviously been deep in thought when she came in, and maybe now he resented the intrusion. Certainly

310

she got the feeling that she wasn't altogether welcome.

Lucy wasn't sure how to deal with him when he was like this. In fact, she had never seen him the way he had been today. There was something very different about him, a strange, quiet strength that touched her heart. She came towards him. 'Dad, are you all right? I didn't see you leave, I'm sorry.'

He turned then, his eyes brighter than she had ever seen them. And then he did something that took her by surprise. He held out his hands; those big strong hands that had nursed her when she was small, and wiped away her tears as she grew from child to woman. His gaze never faltered as he silently called her to him.

As she went to her father, Lucy felt like a child again, safe and warm in his embrace. 'Why don't you talk to me?' she softly pleaded. 'I miss you talking to me. I miss the sound of your voice, and the way you laugh, and oh, I so much want us to be a family again.' Her voice fell to a whisper. 'Jack's gone, you must know that. That was the hardest thing I've ever had to do in my life, Dad,' she confided for the very first time. 'You see, I made a promise to our mam, and I had to send him away. But it isn't your fault. It isn't anybody's fault. It's just the way things turn out sometimes.'

Suddenly she wasn't talking to her father. She was confiding in someone else, someone who wasn't there, and yet maybe they were. 'I'm lonely, you see,' she went on, her troubled grey eyes searching the dark night through the window. The ledge outside was thick with hardening snow. 'I love Jack still, and I'll go on loving him for all time, but he'll never be mine. Not now.'

The wine kept her talking, and the wine made her cry. 'I expect he's got another woman, and who could blame him, eh? He's a good-looking, wonderful man ... and probably very wealthy by now.' She laughed softly. 'There are women who will chase him just for that. I hope he has more sense than to fall for one who's after his money. She'll only make his life a misery. I wouldn't care if he was penniless,' she murmured. 'So long as I had his love, that's all I'd ask.'

Suddenly she felt cold. She shivered, acutely aware that she had said far more than her dad wanted to hear. 'Hark at me!' she declared, drawing away from his embrace. 'It's the wine, I'm not used to it. A few glasses and my tongue runs away with me.'

She was astonished, and a little amused, to see that he'd fallen asleep. 'Well, I never!' Fetching a blanket from the bed, she tucked it around him then placed a cushion behind his head and made sure he was comfortable.

On tiptoe she went away, softly closing the door. 'I'll be back soon,' she promised. 'Then we'll get you into bed.'

As she went downstairs, she thought: It's just as well you fell asleep. Some of the things she had said were not for her father's ears at all.

Steve proved to be a godsend. Half an hour later the dishes were all washed, stored away, and now to her amazement he was offering to leave. 'Well, that's the work done so I'll be off.'

With mixed feelings, Lucy walked him to the front door. 'I owe you an apology,' she said, helping him on with his coat. 'I really thought you offered to help with the dishes because you suspected there might be a chance you'd get your wicked way with me afterwards.'

His eyes twinkled as they always did whenever he saw his little game working in his favour. 'Well now, that just shows how wrong you can be.' He kissed her briefly on the mouth, opened the door, and hurried away in a whirl of snowflakes.

After closing the door, Lucy leaned on it for a long, long time, her heart aching, while the loneliness in that sad little house pressed in on her. Upstairs her father was sleeping. Ted and Mabel were probably tucked up in front of their fire or cuddling in bed, while Alfie and Debbie were no doubt making love at this very minute.

Going into the kitchen, Lucy poured herself another sherry. 'Who cares if you get drunk?' she asked herself. 'Not your dad. He doesn't care about anything any more, and not the others, or they would have stayed and kept you company.' She gulped down the drink and poured another. 'No, I mustn't blame them,' she decided. 'They've got each other, and that's how it should be.'

All the same she felt just the tiniest bit sorry for herself. Angry too. 'If you're alone, it's your own fault,' she reminded herself. 'Steve would have stayed. All you had to do was ask, and he would have stayed for as long as you wanted him to.'

But did she really want him to stay? she asked herself. And back came the resounding answer that, yes, she did want him to stay. Anything was better than being alone on Christmas Night. Anything was better than being alone on *any* night.

'Sod it!' She drank the sherry and was just about to pour another when she thought she heard a noise.

She listened at the foot of the stairs but it wasn't her dad. As she turned she heard it again, and realised there was someone at the front door.

Gingerly, she opened it. 'I've been sitting in the car,' said Steve, 'I hate the idea of going back to an empty house.'

The sherry was beginning to cloud Lucy's judgement. 'I was hoping you'd come back,' she confessed reluctantly.

The look on his face should have told her he'd planned the whole thing, playing on her loneliness and making certain he left her just long enough for her to need his company.

He knew she didn't love him.

But liking was a start. The rest would follow.

Chapter Thirteen

They made love on the rug in front of the dining-room fire.

With controlled lust, Steve gently took off her clothes. 'I have always loved you,' he murmured. But he didn't know what love was. Not the kind of love that grew between a man and woman and lasted a lifetime; not the kind that gave instead of took; and not the kind of warm, binding love that still existed in Lucy's heart for the only man she could ever really care for.

Steve knew only the insatiable demands of his own body. He knew lust, and he knew how to take, but he would never know how to give. 'Say you need me.' Stripping off his clothes, he lay on top of her slim, warm body. 'Say it, Lucy,' he whispered. 'You and I . . . we belong to each other.'

In the flickering glow from the fire, her grey eyes were soft and serious, clouded by the effects of wine, and darkened by the loss of her man. Her thoughts were confused, rambling one way then the other. What was he saying? No, he was wrong. *Jack* was her man. Jack.

'Jack!' The name trembled on her lips. But Jack wasn't here. Only Steve. *He* was here, holding her close, kissing her mouth, stroking her body and loving her. Yes, Steve was here, and now she didn't feel quite so lonely.

Winding her arms round his neck, she clung to him, aroused because she was a woman needing to be loved. When he entered her, she felt a momentary rush of pain but then it was wonderful.

His hands moved to the small of her back, curving her towards him, merging her body with his while he thrust feverishly, backwards and forwards, firing her senses and drowning all the regrets.

She let herself enjoy him. Thrilling. Participating. After all, she was a woman.

Mike stood at the door, his shocked eyes taking in the scene before him. His daughter, his lovely girl, naked and willing in this man's arms; a man he had taken an instant dislike to; a man who had no love for Lucy, and never would, because he didn't know how to love any woman. Another man could tell. Mike could tell. And it broke his heart all over again.

He watched for a moment, watched Lucy with her head back and her eyes closed, and the man pushing into her, devouring her like a wild beast. Suddenly he could watch no longer.

Lucy didn't see him there. She did not hear him walk away, nor did she hear the sharp click of the front door as it closed behind him. For one mad, unthinking moment she had put it all behind her, all the heartache and the longing, the tears and the loneliness. Just for once she let the anger rage within her, allowing herself to be carried along against her better judgement. What did it matter? Why should she keep herself for a man who was never coming back?

But deep down she knew. Sometime, somewhere along the way, she would be made to pay the price for this one momentary lapse.

Mike pressed on. Without a coat to keep out the bitter cold, and with the neck of his shirt wide open, he was at the mercy of the elements. 'Why did you leave me, Sal?' The tears fell down his face, merging with the snow and freezing against his skin. 'I'm sorry . . . I'm so sorry.'

At the top of the hill he paused. On a clear summer's day he and Sal had been able to see the whole of Blackburn town from here. He screwed up his eyes against the wind, peering down, desperately searching for some fragment of memory. But the snow blinded him. 'It's gone!' his pathetic cry rang against the wind. 'Oh, Sal . . . Sal, I can't see it any more.'

Filled with a terrible urgency, he began running, stumbling, losing his way and finding it again. He was so cold. But he could see her now. He could see her, and daren't stop, even for a moment.

Lucy felt ashamed.

'Are you all right?' They were dressed now, and Steve was pouring her a drink.

She looked up with a little smile, hiding her shame, wishing herself a million miles away. 'Yes, I'm fine,' she answered. 'Why?'

When he handed her the glass of wine, she placed it on a side table; she had drunk more than enough for one evening, she decided bitterly. More than enough for a lifetime.

He knelt at her feet, sipping his wine, eyes glowing with unusual tenderness. 'No reason,' he said. 'You seem very quiet, that's all.'

Touching the lock of hair that had fallen across his eyes, she swept it back. 'Just thinking,' she murmured. 'But I'm all right ... really.' What she had done was shameful, but the blame was hers not his. Any man would take what was on offer, and she had made no resistance. In fact, she had even enjoyed it, to a certain extent.

He picked up her glass, and held it out to her. 'Aren't you drinking with me?'

She shook her head.

For a moment he didn't know what to say. Putting down the glasses, he sat beside her. With the same tenderness as before, he said softly, 'Look at me, Lucy.'

Now the regrets were beginning to tell. They showed in her grey eyes and betrayed themselves in her voice when she suggested kindly, 'It might be better if you left now.'

Something very strange had happened to him. When he first met Lucy she'd triggered off a need in him, a certain lust, a yearning to have her for his own. But it was not love. Not then.

Tonight, though, he believed he really did love her. He felt different, warmer, softer, wanting to take care of her, like any man in love would want to take care of his woman.

He told her as much now. 'I'll go if you really want me to,' he said, 'but I would rather stay. Neither of us need be alone any more. I want to marry you, Lucy. I love you.'

She didn't want to hurt him. 'I like you a lot,' she said honestly. 'But I—'

'Don't say it, Lucy. I'm offering to marry you. Think about it, that's all I ask.' He took hold of her hand. 'I have money. We can have a good life.'

Standing up, she asked him again, 'Please go, Steve. We can talk tomorrow.' She wanted to make certain her dad was all right. He had gone suddenly from the table and she didn't know what he was thinking. She never knew what he was thinking.

'All right, but I'll be ringing you tomorrow. Think about what I said.' Standing before her, he cupped his hands around her face and raised it to his. His gaze was that of a man in love. He felt like a man in love, and didn't want to leave. 'One more kiss for the road?' he asked, already bending his head to her.

She didn't pull away. Instead she let him kiss her. When it grew passionate she drew away. 'We'll talk tomorrow.' Without further ado she turned from him and made her way down the passage to the front door. Here she took down his coat and held it open while he made his way towards her. 'Goodnight, Steve,' she said with a warmer smile.

He merely nodded, put on his coat and left, turning once to tell her, 'I'll be in touch.'

'Drive carefully.'

He has not drunk too much wine. Not like me, she thought. But the effects were beginning to wear off now. Making love with Steve had been a sobering experience.

She was amazed at how deep the snow had become.

'Will you be all right?' she called after him.

He grinned. 'Are you offering me a bed?'

'No.'

'Then I'll have to be all right, won't I?'

Closing the door on him, she made her way up to her dad's room. Fast asleep, I expect, she thought with a smile. He's had a long, busy day, bless him. She had seen such a change in her father these past hours, it was heartening.

She was astonished, on checking his bedroom, to find he wasn't there. The bedclothes were hardly crumpled, looking as though someone had sat on the bed, not slept there. 'Dad?' She checked the bathroom. He wasn't anywhere upstairs.

For some reason she couldn't fathom, she felt fearful. Maybe it was guilt. But then, why should she feel guilty because a man had made love to her? Anger resurfaced. 'Dad? Where the Hell are you?'

Convincing herself that he must be asleep in the sitting room, she ran down two steps at a time, calling his name with every step.

Just as she reached the foot of the stairs, loud insistent knocking on the front door startled her. 'Dad?' Running to the door, she flung it open, bitterly disappointed to see Steve standing there. 'I can't start the bloody thing,' he groaned. 'If you won't find me a bed, you'll have to let me use your phone. Either way you could be stuck with me for a while longer, I'm afraid.'

She was in no mood for chit-chat. She wanted to tell him to go away and leave her alone, but now there was her dad to think of. 'Come in. You're letting in the cold.' Staring out, she saw the snow was taking a real hold again. 'God! It's coming down with a vengeance now.' Pointing to the hall table and the phone there, she left him to it. 'I'm sorry, Steve, but I've got to see to my dad.'

He wasn't in the sitting room, but when she opened the door it was like opening the gates to Heaven. The whole room was bathed in soft illumination; pretty coloured lights danced from the walls and made fairy-like patterns on the ceiling.

Lucy gasped with wonder, her wide eyes drawn to the tree in the corner. 'Oh, Dad!' The Christmas tree was all dressed up, and she was a child again. The fairy on top looked wonderful in its pink dress and silver tiara. Now, as she gazed up, it waved its magic wand and smiled at her, just as it had done over many, many Christmases before.

'I've made the call,' Steve's voice was close, 'but the rescue service is up to its neck. I'll have to wait some time . . .' He saw the look on her face and was surprised. 'Lucy, what's wrong?' His gaze followed hers, and he too was struck by the beauty of the Christmas tree. Draped with silver tinsel, coloured decorations and glittering ornaments, it looked wonderful. Like Lucy, he was mesmerised. 'And to think we made love in the dining room, when we could have had all this.'

She wasn't listening. Going across the room, she felt she had to touch the tree. She needed to know she wasn't dreaming. 'Isn't it beautiful?' she breathed, smiling at him, as the fairy was smiling at her, with kindness and understanding. 'This is the first time the tree has been dressed since our mam . . . since . . .'

When she trembled he put his arm round her. 'I

understand,' he whispered. 'Dressing the tree like this means you're coming to terms with it at last.'

'You're so wrong,' she murmured. 'It isn't me who hasn't come to terms with it, it's Dad. He always dressed the tree, you see, but now Mam's not here, he refused to do it. And now look.' Her eyes shone with pride. 'He's beginning to get over it at long last.'

She daren't even think what that might mean for her and Jack. It was too soon. Too delicate still. One thing at a time, she cautioned herself. Right now she had to tell her dad how wonderful it all was.

Suddenly the fear returned. 'But where is he? I can't find him!' She fled from there to the kitchen and then to the dining room. 'He's not here. Dear God, where can he be? He can't have gone out in this weather...' She checked the coat rack. 'He hasn't gone out. His coat's still here,' she said, greatly relieved that he must still be in the house somewhere.

Steve helped her to check every single room, every nook and cranny, and even the garden. Lucy was frantic. 'I'm going to find him,' she said, running to get her coat and wellingtons. 'Phone the police. Tell them he's not in a fit state to be out at all, let alone in this weather and without a coat.' Where was he? What in Heaven's name had driven him out on such a wild, cruel night? The guilt swept through her, and she couldn't shake it off.

'You're not going anywhere.' Steve took hold of her, shaking her until she realised she was beginning to get hysterical. 'You won't find him,' he told her. 'Not on your own.'

Choking back the fear, she spoke in a low, almost

inaudible voice. 'I have to find him,' she said brokenly. 'Don't you see? I have to find him!'

'We'll find him together.' He pressed her into a chair. 'Sit still while I phone the police.'

She heard him describe himself as a friend of the family. 'I'm a doctor. Mike Nolan is very ill,' he explained. 'He suffered a breakdown some time ago. So far as we can tell, he's gone out wearing only a thin shirt and house-shoes. His daughter and I are going out now to try to find him, but we need help.' He listened for a moment, obviously concentrating on what the person at the other end was asking.

Lucy could stand it no longer. Leaping out of her chair, she held out her hand for the phone. 'While we're wasting time here, he could be lost . . . hurt . . . anything. It's blinding out there, and there's no time to waste!' She paused. 'What?' They were asking for her dad's description. 'He's medium height, slim build, with brown hair and eyes. He was wearing a white shirt and blue tie.' She knew that because she had put them out especially for him to wear tonight. Then she gave the address. 'No, officer. I won't wait here for you. I have to go out and search for him. No, I don't know where to look, but I'm sure he can't have gone too far. Please hurry. I don't think we can find him on our own.'

Replacing the receiver, she turned, admitting to Steve, 'I'm frightened. I'm really frightened.' Without waiting for his answer she pulled up the hood of her coat and tied it beneath her chin. 'He might have gone to the top of Blakey Hill,' she said. 'He and Mam used to go there a lot.' Memories threatened to overwhelm her. 'It was Mam's favourite place.'

Squaring her shoulders, she collected her father's overcoat, a thick woollen scarf and a pair of heavy boots. After ramming all this into a bag, she took a torch from the cupboard. 'Please God we can find him,' she muttered, gratefully glancing at Steve who had never left her side.

'Here, let me take those.' He carried the clothes while she took the torch.

The wind had dropped slightly, but the snow fell thick and fast. Silently praying, Lucy led the way down the street, searching as she went, every doorway, every little niche. 'Have you seen my dad?' she asked three neighbours battling their way home. 'He's gone missing.'

The men hadn't seen Mike, but they had known him for many years and hated the thought that he might be lost, especially on a night like this. 'We'll help you,' they said. Not only did they promise to help, but once Lucy and Steve had set off again, they quickly rounded up a number of concerned neighbours, all keen to give their assistance. Armed with torches, flasks of hot tea and a strong length of rope, just in case, they spread out in pairs.

The women watched from their doorsteps. 'Lucy Nolan has had her fair share of bad fortune,' one said to another. 'I can't think what her dad were thinking of, to wander off like that.'

'That's just it,' replied the other. 'The poor soul ain't capable of thinking. He's been off his head ever since Sally were run over.' Making the sign of the cross on her forehead, she added harshly, 'God forgive me, but if they find him dead, it might be a blessing in disguise.'

Just then a police vehicle drew up, a heavy thing with huge tyres. 'They've gone searching,' one woman called out.

'I reckon he's tekken shelter in the church,' another suggested hopefully.

A third was certain. 'Unless you find him quick, it won't matter either way.'

They watched the two officers set off with a dog. Satisfied that everything humanly possible was being done, they returned to their cosy firesides and waited patiently for news of Mike Nolan's fate.

It was gone midnight when they found him.

After searching far and wide, Lucy was at her wits' end. 'I could have sworn we'd find him here.' She and Steve were standing at the very top of Blakey Hill. It was as if all Hell had been let loose. An icy wind cut across the hilltops, and the snow whipped against their faces. She was so cold her lips felt as though they were glued together, and the skin of her face was numb. 'There's only one other place I can think to search,' she said, already making her way down the hill. 'The church where he and Mam were wed. Not a single year passed when we didn't go to Christmas Mass there.' Her spirits lifted. 'Father O'Malley lives next door; he'll keep him safe if he's turned up there.'

Steve voiced the question, just as she was silently asking it herself. 'If your dad did turn up at the church, wouldn't Father O'Malley have rung you? He'd know how worried you'd be.'

She tried not to think about it. 'Maybe he did,' she answered hopefully. 'Maybe he phoned when we were talking to the police, and when he rang back we were already out of the house.' Maybe the lines had come down soon after, and he couldn't contact her. Maybe her dad asked him not to ring for some reason. Maybe her dad was in the doorway and Father O'Malley didn't even know. Maybe! Maybe! Too many maybes.

Father O'Malley made them welcome. 'But sure I've not seen yer father these many months,' he sympathised. 'But you must come in and dry them clothes or you'll be no use to him at all.' He was a large, round man with vivid blue eyes and a heart as big as an ox, but he had no family and couldn't really be expected to understand. If her dad was in trouble, Lucy would gladly run through fire naked to help him.

It was when they came out of Father O'Malley's house and started down the path that the idea came to her. Stopping in her tracks, she turned so quickly she almost knocked Steve over. 'Of course! Why didn't I think of it before?'

'What?' He was cold to the bone and aching to get inside to a warm fire. Just now when Father O'Malley had asked if he wanted to stay and dry his clothes, he was tempted to say yes. Only the fact that Lucy would know had made him bravely refuse.

She set off at a run, her boots dragging her down, hope driving her on. 'I should have thought of it before,' she cried out. 'Don't let me be too late. Please God, don't let me be too late!'

As she rounded the corner into the churchyard, her frantic eyes sought out the tall white angel that marked her mam's resting place. She couldn't see him, but she knew. In her heart she knew this was where she would find him.

She ran, and fell, and struggled up, and searched the ground ahead, hoping . . . praying . . . that he would be all right.

At first glance she couldn't see him. The white shirt against the snow made him hard to find. It was his hair that drew her eye; that shock of brown hair speckled with snow, so incredibly young against his grey, quiet face.

'Dad?' Her voice sighed with the breeze as she fell to her knees beside him, cradling him, pressing his frozen face to her breast. 'Oh, Dad!' Turning to Steve, who was trudging through the snow, she screamed out, 'Hurry! Please hurry!' Yet something told her that he would not need his coat or the boots she had so lovingly brought. 'What were you thinking of, Dad?' she asked softly. 'What made you wander off like that?'

The answer came when she gazed up through the falling snow into the face of the angel; a gentle, quiet face, almost alive behind that falling curtain of whiteness. Could it be true that her dad had come to be with his beloved Sal?

Even if he had not been a doctor, Steve could have told they had arrived too late. 'I'm sorry,' he murmured. 'There's nothing we can do for him now.'

Lucy felt herself breaking up inside. 'NO!' she cried. 'I won't let him be dead! His coat . . . give me his coat!' She grabbed at the bag, tugging at the coat until it fell out. Visions of her mother lying beneath the lorry flashed through her mind. Now her dad. No! No! She closed her mind to everything but the fact that he was found. Her dad was found and he had to be safe.

Carefully, she wrapped the coat about his cold, still body, caressing him, rocking him backwards and forwards, and talking to him as though he could hear every word. 'Don't you worry, Dad. They'll be here any minute. We'll soon have you home and safely tucked up in bed.'

'No, no, child.' A pair of determined hands pulled her away. 'Don't torture yourself.' Father O'Malley had followed them to the churchyard. He, too, had wondered whether Mike Nolan had at last gone to meet the love of his life. 'Your father is in better hands now,' he promised her.

Many years ago he had married Mike Nolan and Sally in this very church. Later he had baptised baby Lucy, and more recently had read the service that laid Sal to her rest.

He had seen some wonderful and terrible things in his lifetime, but this, seeing Mike Nolan lying across the stone that bore his wife's name, was the saddest he had ever encountered. 'It's times like these when we need to believe in a greater being,' he sighed. 'God brings about his wonders in mysterious ways, and it will be many an age before we mortals understand.'

Lucy fell into his arms, her body racked with terrible sobs. Through the mist of her tears she saw Steve's face. She saw the compassion in his eyes, and in that moment knew how much he loved her. But when he held out his arms to her, she turned away.

It was the guilt. Always the guilt.

It was a few days later that Lucy found the parcel.

The shop was closed as a mark of respect and, after all that had happened, she vowed it would never open again. It was their shop, her mam's and dad's. Now they were gone, the heart of that little shop had gone with them. It was time to think about her own future now. Her parents were together at last, but Lucy was alone, and loneliness was a terrible thing.

On the night she and Steve had returned to this house, he had turned out the Christmas lights and she had not set foot in that room from that day to this; even when the mourners came back after the funeral, she stayed in the kitchen, busying herself making tea and cutting sandwiches. Being busy helped her to forget for a time. People were very kind. They would come and chat, but then they would leave. Only two remained constant, Debbie and Steve.

Debbie was with her now, the two of them seated in the cosy little kitchen where they had spent long hours, day and night, talking things through and looking forward as much as they could. 'You're looking a whole lot better today, gal,' Debbie said, biting into her toast and marmalade, swearing out loud when she spilled some down her front. 'I know it's been hard,' she admitted. 'And I know you're like a ship lost at sea just now, but it's all over, gal, an' there's better things to look forward to. So now mebbe you'll get on with yer life, and take better care of yerself.'

Lucy was used to Debbie's down-to-earth manner so she took no offence. However, there was something else about Debbie's remarks that made her suspicious. 'I hope you've kept your word about not contacting Jack? I don't want him to know about Dad. Not yet anyway.'

'When, then?' Debbie didn't intend to give up. She had kept her word about not contacting Jack, though the temptation had been almost too great to resist. 'Never mind about Steve. I know he's been a friend when yer needed one, but then so have I, and I'm not badgering yer to marry me, am I?'

A spiral of laughter rose in Lucy. 'I should think not!'

Debbie made a little face. 'Aw, an' I could'a sworn yer loved me.'

'I'll ring Jack when I'm sure I know what to say.' For the past twenty-four hours she had thought of nothing else. Jack was on her mind every minute, but it was too soon yet. If she were to ring him now, so soon after her dad's passing, it might seem as if she had been waiting until he was out of the way. Dear God! She couldn't deny the thought had crossed her mind; that if anything happened to her dad, she could go to Jack if he still wanted her. Yet the thought was merely one of those passing things that came in the dark and went in the daylight, never properly entertained.

Debbie was persistent. 'I don't care much for him.'

Lucy wasn't sure who she meant. 'Who? Jack?'

'No, yer silly ass . . . Ryman! I'm sorry if it hurts yer feelings, gal, but to tell yer the truth, I think our Doctor Ryman is a devious bugger.'

'He's been good to me though, Debs.'

'I know that, gal, and I could be wrong, but I just can't take to him.' Rolling her eyes with horror, she warned gruffly, 'If the day ever came when yer let that one put a ring on yer finger, it would be the worst day of yer life.'

Lucy smiled confidently. 'I've no intention of letting him put a ring on my finger.' Every time he came to see her, which was often, he asked her the same thing: 'Marry me, Lucy. Let me look after you, and I'll give you the world.'

Her answer was always the same. She couldn't marry him because she didn't love him.

Lucy was silent for so long, Debbie urged, 'Talk to me, gal. Tell me what's on yer mind right now. A trouble shared is a trouble halved, or so yer once told me.'

'Guilt.' It was still there. 'I keep thinking about that night.' It was like an old movie going over and over in her mind. 'Oh, Debs, every time I close my eyes to sleep, I can see it all so clearly.'

'Go on, gal.'

'Dad . . . wandering about in the dark in that bitter cold, and me with Steve . . . the two of us behaving like animals off the streets.' In her mind's eye she could see herself, stark naked, rolling about on the rug with Steve on top of her, and all the while her dad was out there, in the dark.

'You've got to close yer mind to it, gal, or it'll drive yer crazy. Why must yer keep putting yerself through all kinds of Hell? Who gave the order that yer had to be celibate for the rest of yer life, eh?' she demanded. 'D'yer really think yer dad would want yer to be lonely? He's gone to Sal, and his soul is at peace. Why can't yer see that? Oh, I know how hard it is for yer, gal. Don't think I don't know how much yer've lost, but it ain't all bad. Yer don't have to stay here, and yer don't have to be alone either.'

'I don't want to talk about that.'

'About Jack, yer mean. Come on, gal, say it. Say his name. Yer don't want to talk about *Jack*!'

'All right, I don't want to talk about Jack.' He had been on her mind constantly lately.

'So when will yer ring him?' Finishing the last of her toast, Debbie licked her fingers, smacked her lips, leaned back in her chair and tucked her chubby little legs underneath her.

Lucy sighed. She had Steve nagging her about one thing, and Debbie nagging her about another. There were times when she felt like a bone between two dogs. 'You don't give up, do you?'

'Nope. So . . . when *will* yer ring Jack?'

'When I'm ready.' She so wanted to hear his voice, to talk to him and have him near; to feel his strong arms round her and see those wonderful ocean-green eyes smiling down on her. 'Don't forget he hasn't tried to contact me in a very long time. I know I sent him away, but I thought he might write and see how I was getting on.'

Debbie chuckled. 'Ain't that just like a woman?' Her smile vanished as she reflected on Lucy's words. 'You're right though, gal. I'm surprised he didn't bombard you with letters. Jack Hanson didn't seem like the kind of bloke who would give up easily.'

'When you think about it, he had no choice. After all, I didn't give him any hope.' Deep down inside Lucy was afraid, dreading the possibility that he might have a new woman. She daren't think about it, but she must call him soon or go quietly crazy.

'When will yer be ready to call him?'

While Lucy took a moment to consider, Debbie discreetly regarded her. She was worried for her friend, and before Lucy could give an answer to her question, she had to say what was on her own mind. 'Don't leave it too long, gal, or I know you'll be sorry for the rest of yer life.' She sat up, her gaze travelling over Lucy's thin, pale countenance. 'Look at yerself! If Jack were to walk through that door now, he'd be sickened at the sight of yer.'

Lucy chuckled. 'That's what I call a real friend,' she said. 'Someone who gives you confidence when you need it most.' But Debbie *was* a real friend, and Lucy would be forever grateful for that. 'I do know what you're saying, Debs,' she confessed. 'And I appreciate the concern.' These past few days she'd had no interest in anything. It was hard enough just trying to come to terms with the catalogue of events that had befallen her; the way she looked, or whether she slept or ate, seemed to have little importance.

'You'll make yerself ill, that's what you'll do!' Debbie ranted on, unaware that Lucy was hardly listening. 'For days now, you've worked yerself into the ground . . . washing an' scrubbing everything in sight. Even painting the kitchen ceiling. You've changed all the beds at least six times, and turned out every single cupboard in every single room. You've washed all the curtains, shone the winders, and now this morning, I see you've been at the cooker. It looks that new, I won't dare fry an egg on it!'

'Stop exaggerating.' She wasn't, though. Working helped. It was when Lucy stopped that the world closed in on her.

'Have yer had any breakfast?'

'I'll have some later.'

'No, yer bleedin' well won't. Yer ain't had no proper

333

food for days, an' yer ain't slept hardly a wink.'

'I know, but I'll be fine, I promise you. Don't worry.'

'I don't suppose you've set foot inside that front room either?'

'Not yet, no.'

'For God's sake, gal, why not? Yer said you'd do that first thing this morning. There's no getting away from it, it's got to be done.'

'I know.' The thought of going in there was a nightmare. 'It's just that . . . the tree and everything. It must have taken a great deal of strength for Dad to dress that tree . . . to go through all the things that Mam had packed away in her box. It took so long for him to do it, and now I have to go in there and dismantle it all.' It was the end of an era, and that tree was symbolic. There would never again be one in that little room; there would be no lights to dance from the walls, and no coloured balls swinging in the breeze. 'I will take it down though,' Lucy said, with renewed determination. 'That's one of the things on my list for today.'

In fact it was the first of two things on her list. One was to take down the tree. The other was to ring Jack. To be honest, she wasn't certain which would be the more formidable task.

'D'yer want *me* to take the tree down, gal? Alfie ain't calling for me for another half-hour.' For all her bumptiousness, Debbie understood how hard it would be for Lucy.

'Thanks all the same, Debs, but it's something I have to do for myself.' It was a deeply personal thing. 'In fact, the sooner I do it the better.' Now that she had prepared herself for the ordeal, she wanted it over with. 'I'll do it right now!'

Debbie ran after her. 'That's the spirit, gal!' she cried, tripping over the rug in the hallway. 'I hope you've got a new rug down on that list o' yours an' all. That one's about had its day.' The rug was well worn. It cost ten bob out of Woolworths, and that was fifteen years ago. Lucy remembered when her mam had bought it. 'This rug will look pretty in the hallway, lass,' she'd said, and it had been there ever since.

The sitting room was in darkness. The curtains had been drawn shut on the night her dad went missing, and no one had been in there to open them up. Lucy opened them now.

The tree seemed to fill the room. All round its branches clung decorations in all shapes and sizes. The fairy on top was smiling. Suddenly, much to her astonishment, Lucy found herself smiling too. 'It is lovely, isn't it, Debs?' she asked softly. 'Dad was always good at making that tree come to life.' Two large tears rolled down her cheeks. She brushed them away. 'Better get on with it, eh?'

Debbie came to stand by her side. 'Do it quick, gal. Take it down,' she urged quietly. 'Yer dad's gone now. You can have a new tree next year... when Jack and you have your own special Christmas.'

'If God's good,' Lucy reminded her.

Debbie shook her head. 'God can't do it all on his own. You've got to help him along by ringing Jack. Tell him what's happened and that you want him home. What! He'll be on that plane before you've finished speaking.'

Lucy wasn't so sure. 'We'll see,' she said.

'What's the matter with you?'

'What if he's courting someone else? He might even be married. Or he might not want me any more. Have you ever thought of that?'

'All right. Men can be buggers, so it just might be possible. But yer won't know if yer don't try.'

Lucy's gaze turned to the tree again. 'First things first,' she said, and rolled up her sleeves. 'Thought you wanted to help,' she remarked, taking out a box and sliding it towards Debbie's feet. 'You pack the lights in there and I'll see to the ornaments.'

When Debbie hesitated, Lucy suspected it was as much of an ordeal for her. But there was no going back now. 'Come on, move yourself. If Alfie catches you without your make-up on, he might change his mind about wanting to marry you.'

Debbie would rather be hanged upside down than be caught without her make-up on. 'Hmm!' She grabbed at the box and began stripping off the lights. 'You know how to hit below the belt, yer bugger,' she groaned. But she was delighted to see a twinkle in Lucy's lovely grey eyes. It was the first in many a long day.

The twinkle vanished when Lucy caught sight of a small parcel wrapped in gold paper and tied with a big red ribbon. It was hanging high in the tree above Debbie's head. 'What's that up there?' she asked. 'Get it down, will you, please, Debs?'

Debbie reached up and plucked the present from its hiding place. Attached to the parcel was a tiny white card. 'It's got your name on it, gal,' she observed, turning the card over in her chubby fingers. 'Looks like you missed one of your Christmas presents.'

Making a face, she added grudgingly, 'From Steve Ryman, I expect.'

Lucy took the parcel. 'No, if you remember, Steve gave me that pretty bracelet. There were no more parcels left under the tree after we all sat down to dinner. I'd already given Dad his new pipe. You had your perfume and Steve had his scarf. Ted and Mabel took their presents home with them, and I know for certain there were no more presents left under this tree.' She handled the parcel gingerly. 'I honestly don't know where this came from, Debs.' She was loath to open it. Something about it made her flesh creep. She suddenly realised something. 'The wrapping paper is some that was left over from a roll *I* bought this year.' She pointed to the half-empty roll on the floor. 'See, I bought it especially to wrap *your* present in it, don't you remember?'

Realisation dawned. 'Open it then, gal.'

Reluctantly, Lucy opened the parcel, and when she saw its contents, she gave a little cry. 'I don't believe it!' There, nestled in the box, was a ring etched with tiny hearts. 'It's my mam's wedding ring. Dad must have put it here for me to find.'

'So that's what he was doing after he left the table.' Debbie recalled how Mike had disappeared from the dining room when Ted and Mabel left. 'But I don't understand. Why would he hide it like that? If he wanted you to have the ring, why couldn't he just give it to yer?'

Lucy took a moment to answer. She too had wondered that, but now it was all becoming clear. 'Because if he had given me this, I might have guessed what he intended to do,' she murmured thoughtfully. 'Our mam's wedding ring was his most precious possession. There's no way he would ever have let this out of his sight. Unless he knew he had no more need of it.' A great anger welled up in her. 'How could he do it?'

Debbie had seen the change come over Lucy, and it made her curious. 'What are you getting at, gal?'

It was hard for her to explain how she felt, but beneath it all she had held fast to the belief that her father had not deliberately committed suicide. Even when it was the unspoken conclusion on everybody's lips, she secretly chose to believe he had gone out without thinking and simply wandered away, coming to the churchyard and his Sal purely by accident. 'I should have known,' she whispered, almost to herself. 'I should have known he went out of this house with the intention of never coming back.'

'Does it really matter how it happened? Even Father O'Malley said yer dad was in better hands now. He's back with his Sal, and that was what he wanted. He didn't have no life the way things were, did he? I know it's a shocking thing to say, gal, but maybe it were all for the best after all. Maybe the Father were right when he said there's a greater being somewhere.' This was the first time she had realised that Lucy didn't accept that her dad had killed himself. 'I know the word suicide was never mentioned in the church service, and the coroner put it all down as an accident, but, well, everyone else had their suspicions.'

She looked at Lucy and imagined her pain, but didn't know how to deal with it. All she could say was, 'I'm sorry, gal.'

Rummaging first in the discarded paper and then in the box itself, Lucy was frantic. 'There isn't even a letter!'

The anger that followed was like a thick, black cloud suppressing every other emotion. 'He never talked to me when he was here, and even when he was wrapping that box . . . knowing what he intended to do . . . he couldn't even talk to me then. Why not, Debs? Why couldn't he talk to me?' she said harshly. 'All that time and not one single word . . . not once. He never smiled . . . never let me know what he was thinking!'

Her anger was so strong she had to pace the floor or throw something against the wall. 'He knew how much I loved him. I told him, time and again. I begged him to let me in . . . to let me help him. But he wouldn't.' Tears of rage spilled down her cheeks. 'Oh, Debs! How could he take his own life? How could he do that? I know he missed her. So did I. I was lonely too. But I was always there for him. I washed him and fed him. I kept him clean and cared for him as best I could. I put him above everything . . .' Her voice broke. 'I even put him before Jack. Dad knew that! He knew the sacrifices I made, and I would make them all over again if I had to. But now I know . . . none of it mattered to him, did it? DID IT?'

'We'll never know, gal. We'll never know how yer dad felt.'

'But I should have known! He knew how I felt, because I told him. I was there for him, morning, noon and night. I was there when he couldn't sleep, and during the day when he wanted me to hold his hand and comfort him. I was there whenever he needed me.' She swallowed hard, trying to shut out the pain. 'But he was never there for me, was he? I needed to share my grief with him, and he wouldn't let me. I spent hours sitting with him, trying to make him see that life was worth living. I told him I'd never leave him. But he didn't want me, did he? Not really. He showed me no friendship, no compassion.'

'Yer dad couldn't help the way he was.' And yet she didn't blame Lucy for being angry. It was as if her dad had used her, and then deserted her when she needed him most. 'Leaving you that wedding ring was his way of saying he was sorry, don't you think, gal?'

Lucy's sigh echoed from her very soul. 'Maybe,' she conceded. 'But why no letter? Just the smallest, simplest note would have helped me to understand.' She smiled, a slow, troubled smile that moved her mouth but didn't reach her eyes. 'Shall I tell you something, Debs?'

'If you like.'

There was a desolate pause. 'Every day, whenever I was near him, my dad looked at me and never even saw me.' She was laughing now, a soft, bitter sound, through her tears. 'Can you imagine that? MY DAD LOOKED AT ME AND NEVER EVEN SAW ME!'

When she buckled and the tears flowed into heart-rending sobs, Debbie went to her. 'Come here, gal,' she murmured. 'Come here to me.'

As she took Lucy into her fat little arms, she too was softly crying. 'Let it go, me darling. Yer never had time to grieve for yer mam, and now you've got twice the heartache. Yer mustn't blame yer dad. He found his own way, and now you've got to find yours.'

Torn apart, not knowing which way to turn, and suddenly overwhelmed by a terrible grief, Lucy cried herself empty.

When the crying was done, she felt better, stronger, able to carry on. As Debbie said, she had to find her own way now.

When Alfie arrived an hour later, apologising for being late, the tree was emptied and the boxes packed with all the paraphernalia. 'I'll put them in the loft later,' Lucy told her, but in truth she had other ideas.

'We'll stay in, if yer like?' Debbie offered, but Lucy would have none of it. 'You and Alfie go and enjoy yourselves,' she said. 'Anyway, I have things to do.' She gave Debbie a look that was filled with promise. 'I might even make a certain phone call.'

'Good gal.' She gave Lucy an approving wink. 'Me an' Alfie had better get off then, but I'll expect to hear all about it when I get back.'

Alfie was all ears. As they went down the street, he asked, 'What's all this about a phone call?'

A quick dig in the ribs was his answer, and a sharp rebuke that kept him quiet for the best part of ten minutes. 'Mind yer own business. If yer mean to pry into every little thing when we're wed, Alfie me boy, I'll have to think twice before I let yer put a ring on me finger, won't I, eh?'

Lucy picked up the receiver four times before she had the courage to dial. Even then she dialled only the first three numbers before replacing it yet again. 'Come on, Lucy,' she chided herself. 'You have to ring. You need to know.'

For a long time she sat on the arm of the settee,

nervously chewing her fingernails. Suddenly she leaped up and returned to the telephone.

There was a frantic moment when she twisted the piece of paper round and round in her hands before finally flattening it against the table top and, with difficulty, reading the numbers written there.

With great deliberation she redialled.

The ringing sounded so loud in her ears, on and on and on. 'Please let him be there,' she whispered. 'Please let it be all right.'

Eventually a woman's voice answered. 'Yes?' The voice was dark and sultry, sending a shiver through Lucy.

'Is Jack there, please? Jack Hanson?' She felt shy all of a sudden, but very determined.

'Who's calling?'

'This is Lucy Nolan. If you'll just tell him, please?'

'Of course.' The voice softened. 'He's not here right at this minute, but he shouldn't be too long. He went out for a bottle of champagne about half an hour ago. We're expecting guests for dinner and he forgot to re-stock the wine rack. You know what men are like.' A gentle tinkle of laughter. 'This is his wife, Maria. If you'll give me your number, I'll get him to call the minute he comes in. Hang on, I'll just get a pen.' There was a muffled click as the receiver was put down on a hard surface.

Lucy stopped listening. 'This is his wife, Maria.' The words echoed in her brain.

When the receiver was put down at the other end, Lucy replaced her own. 'No message,' she murmured. 'Except I wish him well.' Suddenly all the sorrow fell away, all the longing and loneliness of the past.

'So Jack married someone else?' She actually laughed out loud. 'Serves you right, Lucy Nolan,' she cried. 'What did you expect? That he would wait for ever?'

No, she hadn't expected that. But he could have written. He could have cared that much at least, she told herself. But he didn't. And now, in order to smother the emotions that might have suffocated her, she deliberately hardened her heart against him.

When, half an hour later, Steve arrived, Lucy opened the door with a smile. 'Come in,' she invited, opening the door wide to let him pass. 'I was just about to put the kettle on.'

He seemed taken aback. 'If I didn't know better, I'd say you were pleased to see me.'

'I am.' She led the way into the sitting room. 'See, the curtains are open and the sun is shining. The old year is over and it's time to look forward.' She gulped back the hard lump in her throat as she went on firmly, 'I've made up my mind. Soon this house and shop will be going on the market.'

'You're making the right decision,' he said approvingly. He approved even more when he slid his arm round her waist and she did not pull away, as she might have done yesterday or the day before. 'Dare I ask if you're in the mood to make another decision?' he asked hopefully.

She turned to look at him. 'Such as?' There was a bright mischievous gleam in her eye as she waited for his answer.

'Marry me, Lucy,' he pleaded softly. 'You know how I want you. Oh, I know you still love Jack Hanson, but he's not here, is he? And I am. I adore you, Lucy,

I always have. We could have a good marriage, you and I. You'll never want for anything, and I'll cherish you for ever.' When she hesitated he didn't dare to believe she might be considering it. 'Say yes, Lucy,' he urged in a whisper. 'Please ... say yes.'

'All right then ... yes, I'll marry you.' There was defiance in her voice. 'Why not?'

He was shocked, then elated, then he was swinging her round and shouting, 'I can't believe it! You've said yes. Oh, Lucy, you won't regret it, I promise you will never regret it.'

That evening, when Steve had gone and Debbie had returned, Lucy told her the news. 'Steve was here,' she said quietly. 'He asked me to marry him again, and I've said yes.'

'You've what!' Debbie was so dumbfounded she fell into the nearest chair. 'You must be bloody mad!'

Lucy's smile gave a lot away. 'Not mad,' she intimated. 'More like desperate.' She took a deep breath, letting the words flood out in a long sigh. 'I think I'm pregnant.' While Debbie reeled from that little snippet, she went on, 'At least, I could be. Normally my periods are as regular as clockwork, but I'm three days late now.' She pointed to her heart. 'In here, I just know I'm pregnant.' She smiled wryly. 'It's no more than I deserve after the way I behaved that night. But when you think about it, Debs, marrying Steve is the right thing to do.' She shrugged her shoulders. 'The baby has to have a name, and besides, what have I got to lose?'

Suspecting there was more to this than met the eye, Debbie asked, 'Did you ring Jack?'

'Yes.'

'Did you tell him about Steve? About the baby? If there is one, that is. Three days late don't mean much. Sometimes I'm as much as two weeks late.' She grimaced. 'Mind you, I've never been what yer call regular.'

Lucy answered her honestly. 'I rang Jack, but I didn't tell him anything because he wasn't there.'

'Ring back. Do it now. Baby or no baby, I bet he'd marry yer tomorrow.'

Lucy smiled. 'Then he'd be committing bigamy. His wife – a very pleasant lady by the name of Maria – answered the phone.'

It was all too much for Debbie to take in. 'Oh, gal, I'm so sorry.' But she was still adamant about one thing. 'I know it must have knocked yer for six, but I can't help feeling you'll regret it if yer marry Steve.'

Lucy was equally adamant. 'He's a good sort, Debs, and I do believe he really loves me. Besides, if I am having his baby, marrying him is the right thing to do.'

'Hmm!' Debbie would take some convincing. 'I just hope you don't come to regret it, gal,' she said.

Before the night was over, Lucy was already beginning to regret it. But taking everything into consideration, she had to believe it would all come right in the end.

Even so, when she lay awake until the early hours, it wasn't the baby or Steve who filled her thoughts. It was Jack.

And the love she felt for him was as strong as ever.

Jack consulted his notes. 'So it's agreed then? We

aim to start the extension within six months, to incorporate extra leisure facilities and an indoor pool.' He ticked off the items, returned the paper to his briefcase and dismissed the meeting. 'Hang on, Bob, I'd like a quick word before you go.' Young and enthusiastic, Bob Drummond was the finest architect Jack had yet come across.

'Everything to your satisfaction, I hope?' Sliding out of the chair beside Jack's, he placed his portfolio on the table and sat down.

'Everything's fine.' After he had put Bob's mind at rest, Jack turned to Maria. 'We'd appreciate some fresh coffee,' he suggested with a smile. 'Unless you're in a hurry?'

Uncrossing her long slim legs, she returned his smile. 'Coffee coming up,' she offered, 'I'm in no hurry.' Where Jack was concerned, she had all the time in the world.

Bob's eyes followed her to the door. 'Some lady!' he groaned. 'But she won't even give me the time of day.'

Jack was in no mood to talk of women. 'About the new cafeteria,' he began. 'Have you given my suggestion any thought?'

'Yes, and I think it's a splendid idea . . . a gallery that overlooks the pool will be a real winner.'

'Good. So I can expect to see it included in the amended plans?'

'In all its glory.'

'Tomorrow afternoon?'

Gulping hard, Bob stared at him. 'That soon?' he asked, scratching his head.

Jack looked surprised. 'Don't you always boast that you can deliver at the drop of a hat?'

'Yes, but—'

'No buts.' Jack stood up and prepared to leave. 'I'll see you tomorrow at four. Is there a problem?'

'No problem.'

'Good. Enjoy your coffee while it's hot.' He had already seen Maria enter with a tray. Without further ado, he strode out of the room and down the wide carpeted stairway, pausing only when she ran after him.

'I was hoping we could go somewhere for a bite to eat?' she suggested hopefully.

Jack shook his head. 'I've already got a meeting,' he lied. 'Sorry.'

'Tomorrow then?'

'Okay, we'll have lunch at the harbour, but it will have to be short and sweet. I've got the accountant coming in the morning, and I've already made arrangements to see Bob at four o'clock.'

She was grateful for any little crumb he threw her way. 'Lunch will be fine,' she said eagerly.

'Goodnight, Maria.'

'Meet you in the foyer at twelve. Does that fit in with your plans all right?'

'Like a hand in a glove.' He gave one of his cheeky winks. 'Bob's waiting. Go and put the poor devil out of his misery.' Before she could detain him any longer, he continued down to the hotel foyer.

'Goodnight, Jack.'

'Oh, just a minute, Maria.' He half turned. 'You left the meeting to answer a telephone call in my office. Was it anything I should know about?'

His striking dark green eyes, intent on her now, made her want him all the more, but as yet she had

347

not managed to break through that protective barrier he'd put up against the world. Still, it was only a matter of time. She never wavered from that belief. 'It was nothing important,' she lied. 'The receptionist put through a wrong number, that was all. It won't happen again.'

'Hmm.' He considered it for a minute then went on his way, leaving her sighing with relief.

'If I told you it was your precious Lucy, you'd be on the next plane home,' she muttered, hurrying back up the stairs.

Aware that Bob was lingering just for her, she preened herself in the mirror at the top. 'If I can't have you, Jack, I suppose I'll have to settle for second best . . . just for tonight.'

Bob was easy. He was short-term. Jack was a harder fish to catch, but the prize at the end would be worth all the effort.

Stopping at the reception desk, Jack called a young woman to one side. 'Barbara, I'd appreciate it if in future you could make certain there are no interruptions when meetings are going on upstairs. I understand a wrong number was put through.'

The young woman looked confused. 'A wrong number? I'm sorry, Mr Hanson, I don't understand. Your instructions were clear enough and everyone knew you were chairing an important meeting.' Her expression darkened. 'You can be sure I'll have something to say about this.'

'No need to create a bad atmosphere,' he told her. 'I just want your assurance that it won't happen again.'

'It won't.'

'Good. Then that's an end to it.'

* * *

Evenings in Paphos were often warm and sultry, even during the winter months. Tonight was one such, and when it was spent in a candlelit restaurant overlooking the pretty harbour, with its bobbing boats and illuminations twinkling, it was hard to believe there could be any lovelier place on God's earth.

'Enjoying the night air, eh?' The restaurant owner was a short, dark-haired man, with a smile as round and ruddy as a full moon. 'But you should have a woman to share such a night with,' he sighed. 'What good is a sky full of stars if you're all alone?'

Jack liked him, he was always good company, but tonight he needed to be alone with his thoughts. 'You're just an old romantic,' he laughed. 'I've got no woman, so I'll have to share the evening with one of your marvellous brandy sours. Okay?'

The restaurateur shrugged his shoulders and spread his hands. 'Whatever you say.' Wearing a broad smile, he delivered the brandy sour. He thought it a waste of a beautiful evening for Jack to be all alone, but kept his opinions to himself. After all, he was here to make his customers happy.

Jack was deep in thought. He had tried every way a man could to win Lucy back, short of breaking down her door and demanding that she come with him. But what would that solve? When and if Lucy came to him, it would have to be of her own free will.

Dear God! What was he to do? There was no happiness for him without her.

Raising his glass, he murmured wryly, 'To you,

my lovely Lucy, wherever you are.' Sadness washed over him. 'I miss you like Hell, but as you've made it clear you don't want me to come to you, all I can do is wait for you to come to me.' He took a great gulp of his drink then hung his head and closed his eyes as he brought Lucy into his heart.

'There's a man in love,' one diner said to another. 'He wants her, but she doesn't want him.'

'How can you tell?' asked his colleague.

'Because I've been there. And I'll tell you this much, I'd rather travel all the way to Hell than go through that again!'

Sensing their eyes on him, Jack glanced up.

When the two men looked guilty, he guessed what they were saying. It made him take another look at his situation and, with a surge of determination, he decided to have one last shot at happiness. 'I can't let you go that easily, my love,' he murmured. 'One more try. I owe us that much at least.'

Finishing his drink, Jack called out his goodnights to the proprietor. With a lighter heart, he strode out on to the street. 'I've finished with telephones and letters.' Suddenly he knew what he must do. 'I'm on my way home for you, sweetheart,' he said softly. 'And I'm in no mood for argument!'

Chapter Fourteen

Lucy was sitting alone when the knock came on the bedroom door. Startled out of her thoughts, she jumped up. 'Who is it?'

Debbie's voice answered. 'It's me! Who the devil d'yer think it is?'

'Just a minute.' Checking that there were no tear smudges, Lucy dabbed a powder puff over her face. 'Hang on!' she called again. 'I'm on my knees under the dressing-table.' Running a comb through her hair, she made herself smile then determinedly squared her shoulders and opened the door. 'Sorry, Debs, but I can't find my nail-varnish . . . that lovely soft creamy colour I bought in town the other day. The one we both thought would look good with the wedding gown.'

She wasn't lying about losing the nail-varnish because it really had rolled away beneath the dressing-table and she had spent ages searching for it. She still hadn't found it.

Losing the bottle of varnish was only another incident in what had begun as a bad day. Her eyes were puffed up like balloons after a restless night, and now she couldn't find the varnish bought especially for today.

Lucy brought herself up sharply. Today was her wedding day. She could hardly believe that, in less than an hour, she would walk down the aisle to make her vows with Steve. For all her brave face and determination, the prospect was daunting.

Oh, he was a good man, and he treated her well. He adored her, or so he kept saying. Everything pointed to their having a good life together. Yet she was deeply unhappy. Worried and not knowing why. Aching inside as though she had a physical ailment. Time and again these last weeks she had told herself not to be silly; to be grateful that she was loved by a good man. Any other woman would be eternally thankful, especially when Steve had promised she would want for nothing.

'Want for nothing'. That made her smile. Though he had turned his back on her now, and she could hardly blame him for that, she would spend her life wanting Jack.

All the same, the enormity of what she was doing had only just begun to sink in. It was a frightening thing, to be beholden to someone you could never love. Yet she had little choice. She was pregnant with Steve's child. That was the hard truth, and she had to face it. Whether she liked it or not, she was promised to Steve. He was her future. Jack was her past. It broke her heart to think that way, but for the sake of her sanity, she had to face the truth.

Now, with Debbie standing there, her arm draped with the most exquisite, expensive wedding gown money could buy, the realisation of what she was doing made Lucy tremble.

'Are you all right, gal?' Taking the weight of the

dress on to the hanger, Debbie hooked it over the wardrobe door before turning round to regard Lucy anxiously. 'You look as if you've seen a bleedin' ghost.'

Lucy closed the door and, gathering her wits, attempted to put Debbie's mind at rest. She had argued over and over with Debbie about this wedding, and hated the thought of yet another confrontation. 'You're imagining things.' She put on her brightest smile, sat before the mirror and asked disarmingly, 'Do I look all right?'

'No.' Debbie was never one to hide her feelings. 'Yer too thin an' pale.'

'Well, thanks for nothing.' Lucy couldn't blame Debs for saying what she thought, but reproached her nevertheless. 'You're supposed to be on my side.'

'I am, gal. That's why I'm begging yer to think twice before going through with it.'

Lucy sighed long and wearily. She knew all the arguments already. 'I thought we'd agreed to differ?'

'We did. I also agreed not to say anything today, but I'm a born liar so I'm saying what I think. Stop this wedding afore it's too late.'

'It's already too late.'

'Why? Because you're having his baby?'

'That's one good reason.'

'All right. I'll admit you're in a bad situation, but it ain't bad enough to throw yer life away for, is it?'

Already jittery, Lucy was desperately afraid her doubts would show. 'I'm not throwing my life away,' she argued. 'Steve loves me, and I love him . . . all right, not in the same way I love Jack, but he's gone and I'm pregnant. It's right for me to marry Steve. It's what he wants, and it's what I want.' That wasn't altogether true but there was one overriding reason for marrying him. 'You're forgetting, Debs, I have a moral obligation to the baby.'

'Baby or no baby, I don't want yer to do it, gal.' Debbie's voice was soft and trembling. 'I don't want yer to marry him.'

There was something in Debbie's worried words that echoed Lucy's own deeper sentiments. 'Why not?' she asked quietly. 'Tell me the truth, Debs. *Why* don't you want me to marry him?' She sensed there was more to Debbie's words than she was letting on. 'What is it? Do you know something I don't know?'

When Debbie remained silent, Lucy forced a little smile. 'I hope you're not going to stand up in church when the priest asks if there's anyone who thinks we shouldn't be married? Because if you do know something I don't, I'd rather you told me now.'

Debbie blushed to the roots of her hair. 'Don't be so bloody daft! As if I'd do a thing like that.'

'I wouldn't put it past you.' She knew Debs better than most, and standing up in church to protest wasn't beyond her capabilities.

'Don't worry, gal.' She smiled at Lucy, at this young woman who had been such a wonderful, loyal friend to her, and just for a minute she felt ashamed. 'I wouldn't do that to you, gal,' she promised. 'You don't deserve that.'

Lucy wasn't convinced. 'What then? Come on, out with it.'

'I don't like the bloke, that's all.'

'Why not?'

'I don't know why not. There's summat about him that gives me the creeps.' She visibly shivered. 'Don't

ask me what it is about him, gal,' she pleaded, ' 'cause
I don't know. I only know yer making a terrible
mistake.'

Lucy smiled wryly. 'I made the mistake when I
let him make me pregnant,' she admitted. 'But it
was *my* mistake, and I don't see why a little innocent
should have to pay for it.' Her mind was made up.
'This baby is going to have a name, and that means
marrying its father. So if you can't give me your
blessing, I'll have to be married without it.'

'Yer a stubborn bugger.'

'No more than you.' Lucy got down on her hands
and knees and began looking for the bottle of varnish.
'I'm getting married today, so you might as well get
used to the idea.' Peering up from beneath the
dressing-table, she asked pertinently, 'Well? Will you
help me, or won't you?'

Tugging at her petticoat, Debbie ordered, 'Get up,
yer silly ass. If you mean to go through with it, then
I suppose I'll have to help yer. Anyway, I've got to
get prettied up meself, so get yer dress on while I
look for the bloody nail-varnish.' She gave a sigh.
'The buggers downstairs are running round like
headless chickens. Honest to God, Lucy, I wish you
hadn't asked Old Ted to give you away. He's poncing
about like a bleedin' prima donna. Mabel's fussing
over him like he's the best thing since sliced bread,
and that neighbour of yours is causing a riot . . .
pinning the flowers on everybody, even before they've
got their jackets on! Speaking of which, did yer know
the silly pair've given me me old job back?' She threw
up her hands in a helpless gesture. Walking over to
the window, she laughed out loud. 'Blimey, half the

street's out, waiting for yer, and there must be five hundred kids lining the way. Anybody would think they were waiting for bleedin' royalty.' She turned, and tutted and moaned and shook her head, and said with a heavy sigh, 'Look at yer! Yer ain't even dressed yet. It'll be a miracle if we're ready on time.'

An hour later they were ready. 'By! Yer look lovely, gal!' Debbie was close to tears as she gazed at Lucy, at the shining grey eyes and fine features that seemed all the more beautiful because of her pregnancy. 'Nobody would ever know yer a few months gone with a baby.'

Her admiring eyes searched for the small bulge which was discreetly hidden by the cleverly cut gown; a classic style, with a sweetheart neckline and slim lacy sleeves, the gown fell gently from the bustline in a neat gathering of tiny folds. Simple and becoming, the beautiful creation brought out all of Lucy's best features. Her dark hair shone, and her grey eyes now looked wonderful, with the merest touch of shadow and a soft brushing of mascara. For weeks she had taken great care of her nails and now, thinly painted in the soft cream varnish, they were the best they had ever been. Lucy had always been a nail-nibbler, but she had promised herself that when she held out her hand for Steve to put on her wedding ring, she would not be ashamed.

At the church there was a mixture of familiar and unfamiliar faces. Old Ted stood proudly next to her, while Mabel smiled encouragement from the pews. In their best bib and tucker, they looked real dandies. There were a dozen good neighbours from the shop, two doctors from Steve's medical practice, four of his old college friends – only one of whom Lucy knew, and that was because he had stayed for two nights at the house, learning the ropes of being best man at Steve's wedding. Tall and thin with a military bearing, he had a sad smile and spoke very little.

Steve's children were there too. At sixteen years of age, Sam Ryman was a good-looking young man, blessed with thick dark hair pulled back in a ponytail, and brown and black speckled eyes that missed nothing. But this sullen, moody young man had taken an immediate dislike to Lucy, and nothing she said or did could endear her to him.

His sister Annabelle was as happy as her brother was miserable. A blonde beauty, she was fourteen years old, with a maturity that put most girls of her age to shame. Right from the start she had taken Lucy under her wing, though she'd graciously declined Lucy's invitation for her to be a bridesmaid. 'This is your day,' she'd told Lucy. 'Yours and Debbie's. I want to watch from the sidelines and take the best pictures for your album.' And that was exactly what she did.

Jack had been hammering on the door of the shop for some minutes when a neighbour came out to see what all the noise was about. 'It's no use you banging on that door,' she snapped, angry because he'd woken her from a deep dream-filled sleep, 'there ain't nobody there.'

Approaching her, he explained, 'I have to see Lucy. Please . . . it's very urgent. Can you tell me where I might find her?'

The woman scratched her sleepy head. 'Urgent, eh?' she repeated curiously. 'Well now, I expect you'll find her at the church. I'd be there meself only I've got this bad foot and can't walk far.' She tried to draw his attention to her bandaged foot, but gave up when she realised his mind was elsewhere. 'St Peter's,' she explained. 'You'll find Lucy at St Peter's Church.'

Jack fleetingly wondered what she might be doing at the church, but he didn't have time to ask. All he wanted was to find her, talk to her, take her back with him and make plans for their future together. 'Thank you,' he said, climbing back into the taxi. He smiled at the woman and thanked her again.

With her next words the smile was wiped from his face. 'I don't expect she'll have time to stop for a chat,' the fat woman called out good-naturedly. 'You see . . . Lucy Nolan's being married today.'

'Where to, guv?' The taxi-driver didn't realise the awful impact the woman's words had had on Jack, not until he glanced in the mirror and saw his ashen face. 'All right, mate?' he asked, more curious than concerned.

Jack nodded affirmatively. Slamming shut the door, his eyes glinted angrily. 'St Peter's Church,' he said. Somewhere in the back of his mind he prayed the woman was wrong.

When the taxi drew to a halt, Jack prepared to clamber out. But just as he reached for the door-handle, he froze in his seat. There was Lucy, half turned from him as she came out of the church with her new husband. Seeing her caused a pain like a knife slicing through his heart. His darling Lucy with a stranger. But she wasn't his darling any more. She was someone else's darling now.

Jack forced himself to look at the man beside her. They looked good together, he grudgingly admitted. His gaze was drawn to Lucy's face. She looked so beautiful. He wanted to call her name and see her smile at him. He wanted to rush over there and grab her away. But he had no right. Lucy had made her choice, and it wasn't him. If only he'd been able to leave Cyprus as soon as he'd decided to, he might have been able to change her mind . . .

'God bless you, sweetheart,' he murmured, his green eyes alive with pain. His gaze shifted to Steve. 'You're a lucky man, whoever you are. And God help you if you don't do right by her.'

The taxi-driver's voice was innocently cheerful. 'Want me to wait, d'yer, guv?'

'No.' Jack settled back in his seat. 'Better take me back to the hotel. I'll just be a minute, then you can take me on to the airport.' His hopes were finally shattered.

As the taxi pulled away, Debbie's inquisitive gaze followed it. 'Gawd Almighty!' she muttered. 'If I didn't know better, I'd say that was Jack Hanson!'

Lucy, too, had been watching the taxi draw away. When she heard Debbie softly mutter, she asked, 'Did you see who that was?'

Sorely tempted to reveal she suspected it might have been Jack, Debbie forced herself to keep the secret. There was nothing to be gained from telling Lucy now. 'No, I didn't see who it was,' she lied. 'Why?'

Lucy watched the taxi until it was out of sight. 'Nothing,' she replied thoughtfully, 'I just wondered who it was.' She thought it curious, that was all. The taxi drew up, and so far as she could see, drove off without anyone getting out. That was very strange, she thought. *Very* strange.

And somehow disturbing.

PART THREE

1988

After the Wedding

Chapter Fifteen

Sam Ryman had got up in a foul mood as usual. 'What the Hell's this?' He thrust the plate of eggs and bacon to one side. 'You can't expect me to sit exams after eating *this* rubbish!' Glaring at Lucy, who had been up since the early hours after a restless night, he told her harshly, 'How many times have I got to say it? I don't eat crap food.'

Lucy was at the end of her tether. 'Then you'll have to go hungry because I didn't feel well enough to do the shopping yesterday.'

'Having a baby too much for you, is it?' His voice was heavy with hatred. 'My mother had two children, and she was never heard to complain.'

Wisely, Lucy didn't rise to his taunts. In the few weeks since she had become Mrs Steve Ryman, stepmother to his two children and mistress of this big, fine house, she had learned when to speak and when not to. This morning particularly she felt unable to deal with this sneering young man.

Lately she hadn't been sleeping too well. Whenever she woke, restless and uncomfortable, Steve would complain bitterly, saying he worked a long hard day and might be called out at any minute. 'I need my sleep,' he told her. 'It's all right for you. You have little to do all day.'

Not wanting to get into yet another argument, she would quietly leave the bedroom and walk the kitchen floor, so he could get his precious sleep.

'Leave her alone!' Annabelle's voice rang out. 'Can't you see she's not well?' Annabelle had come to love Lucy dearly. Whenever there was an argument she would always take Lucy's side, even against her own father.

Hating the idea that she might cause a rift between brother and sister, Lucy gave the girl a warning glance. 'It's all right, sweetheart,' she said. 'I'm quite capable of looking after myself.' She was also capable of giving him a clip round the ear if he didn't get off her back. 'Eat your breakfast or leave it,' she told him. 'It makes no difference to me.'

Her comment brought a sly grin to the young man's face. 'I knew it! You've done this on purpose, haven't you? You deliberately put this breakfast in front of me because you knew I'd hate it.'

'That's a stupid thing to say.' Buttering her toast, Lucy gave him a withering glance. 'Why would I do such a thing?'

'Because you don't like me, that's why.'

There was no answer to that, so she gave none.

At that moment, Steve entered the room, rubbing his hands and licking his lips. 'Something smells good.' Going to Lucy, he kissed her soundly on the mouth. 'You look pale.' Placing his hand on her forehead, he remarked with a little concern, 'You have a temperature. Perhaps you'd better go and lie down. We don't want any harm to come to the baby, now do we?'

'No, we don't,' Lucy confirmed. 'But I'm fine. Just tired, I expect.'

'It's *him!*' Annabelle put the blame squarely on her brother. 'He thinks you married Lucy just so she can wait on him. Bring this, fetch that. Yesterday he left his tennis racquet out in the rain and blamed Lucy when it got spoiled. Now his breakfast isn't good enough. Tell him, Dad,' she pleaded. 'Tell him, Lucy isn't his personal slave.'

Attempting to defuse what she saw as a potential row, Lucy was quick to point out, 'I'm sure Sam doesn't think any such thing, Annabelle.'

Steve wouldn't leave it there. Eyeing his son with a hard expression, he demanded, 'Have you anything to say?'

'No.'

'Oh, but I think you have, and you're not leaving this table until you say it.' Standing straight as a ramrod at the head of the table, he reminded Lucy of something out of a Victorian melodrama. 'Well? I'm waiting.'

Sick to her stomach and tired of all this bickering, Lucy felt obliged to intervene. 'It's all right, Steve. Sam and I understand each other.' He hated her and there was nothing on God's earth she could do about it. That was the way of things, and all the wishing in the world wouldn't change it.

Ignoring her, Steve continued to glare at his son. 'I'm still waiting, Sam.'

He looked up. His hard gaze went from his sister to his father, and then to Lucy. 'I'm . . . sorry,' he muttered grudgingly.

She nodded, wishing the earth would open and

swallow her whole. This was a strange family, and she had come into it like a fly into a spider's web.

Steve, however, was not satisfied. 'What was that?' he said, eyes still focused on his son's face. 'I didn't hear. Say it again if you please . . . louder this time so we can all hear it.'

Sam's face darkened with anger, but he knew better than to get on the wrong side of his father. Taking a deep breath, he looked Lucy in the eye. 'I AM VERY SORRY.'

Every word was ground out with loathing.

Steve smiled. Either he didn't realise he was only worsening matters or he didn't care. 'That's better. Now perhaps we can all get on with breakfast.' Rubbing his hands, he promptly sat down, briskly addressing Lucy who was inwardly squirming with embarrassment: 'I woke up with a huge appetite. I could eat two eggs, lightly turned, with the yolk running. Oh, and if you've got any of that black pudding left, I'll have a round or two of that as well.'

Annabelle opened her mouth to protest, but Lucy gave her a sideways glance. 'If you've finished your breakfast,' she said, 'I wouldn't mind a helping hand in the kitchen.'

Sam made his escape while Lucy brought Steve's breakfast and the girl cleared away the unwanted dishes. In the kitchen she rounded on Lucy. 'You let them get away with too much. *I* could have brought Dad's breakfast. You should have stayed at the table and had something to eat . . . a cup of tea even.' She pointed to the untouched slice of toast on Lucy's plate. 'Look at that! You're pregnant. You should be eating for two, but you hardly eat anything at all.'

Lucy had to laugh. 'You're like a little mother hen. Stop worrying, will you? I'm strong as a horse, or so your father's always telling me.'

'My father's a good doctor, but he doesn't know everything.' Annabelle regarded her through loving eyes. She was worried about how thin Lucy was, and the dark shadows under her lovely grey eyes. She knew Lucy didn't sleep and lately had sensed an undercurrent of regret. 'Are you sorry you married him?' she asked with the innocence of a child.

Swinging round from her place at the sink, Lucy was astonished, not because of Annabelle's question but because she had been so perceptive. 'Whatever makes you think that?'

'Because he doesn't treat you right.' She came to stand beside Lucy, leaning her arms on the worktop and looking up into her face with a world of admiration. 'You're so pretty, and you always try to smooth things over when there's an argument. Sam gives you Hell, and still you try hard to be his friend.'

'That's because I don't want to end up his enemy.'

'Aren't there times when you'd love to strangle him?' She giggled, but her eyes sparkled with anger.

With Annabelle, Lucy could be honest without fear of being quoted. 'You know there are times when I want to strangle him,' she admitted. 'But what would that solve? Absolutely nothing. In this world you have to do the best you can with what you've got. It's a funny thing, sweetheart, but sometimes it's easier to turn the other cheek than it is to let your temper fly.'

There was a moment's thoughtful silence before Annabelle revealed softly, 'I can't stand it when Sam makes trouble for you. You don't deserve it.'

'All the same, I really can take care of myself. What's more, I don't want you falling out with your brother on my account.'

'I'd do anything for you, Lucy. You're like a real mother to me, and I love you.'

Wiping her hands on the tea-towel, she took the girl into her embrace. 'I love you too,' she said softly. 'You're a lovely, lovely girl, and I'll always be here when you need me. I want you to remember that.'

Now, when Annabelle looked up, her eyes shone with tears. 'You won't go away, will you, Lucy?'

'Why should I want to go away?' she asked, suppressing the emotion that even now churned in her stomach. She had no doubt that Steve loved her, he showed it in so many ways, but she missed that close affection she had enjoyed with Jack. Her heart turned over. It seemed never a single day passed without his name coming into her mind.

'When Sam's rotten to you, I'm always afraid you might leave.'

'Leaving isn't the answer,' Lucy said firmly. 'I'm a married woman, and I have responsibilities.' Responsibility. Duty. That was what it had come down to. In spite of the harsh reality, she would make this marriage work. She had to. 'Besides, we wouldn't want Sam to think he'd won, would we, eh?'

Annabelle wanted more. 'Promise me you'll stay?'

Into Lucy's mind came another promise. A heartfelt promise drawn from her in the heat of tragedy. She couldn't promise Annabelle, but she couldn't let her go on worrying either.

'Sometimes it's harder to stay and make things

work than it is to admit defeat and run away,' she answered wisely. And if she did run away, what was there for her? Steve was a bit bumptious, but he was a good husband in many ways, and she still believed he would make a good father to their baby.

'Why doesn't Dad cuddle you more often?'

'Because some men find it hard to show their emotions.'

'I hate him being a doctor.'

'Why? It's a fine profession.' Yet she knew exactly what Annabelle meant. Maybe that was why Steve couldn't show his emotions. Maybe his training had taught him that he must not get involved. Besides, it couldn't be much fun living your life by a timetable; being on call when you just wanted to put your feet up and watch a good film, or having to climb out of bed in the middle of the night when you'd rather be making love. 'Being a doctor is very demanding,' Lucy agreed, 'but it's what your father wanted to do. It's what he loves.' She nearly said it was what he loved most of all, but stopped herself in time. Yet it was true. Steve Ryman ... *Dr* Ryman ... put his profession above all else, even his family.

'Lucy?' The girl eased herself out of Lucy's arms.

'Mmm?'

'Can I ask you something?'

'Ask away.' Lucy had a special affection for this girl. If it hadn't been for Annabelle's loyalty and friendship, life here would have been very lonely. There were just over ten years between them, and Lucy found it hard to behave like a mother to her, but she had come to love her like a sister. 'What's on your mind now?'

'Do you love my father?'

'Of course.' It was not a lie, yet not altogether the truth. Love could be many things. It could also be a duty.

Quietly considering Lucy's half-hearted answer, Annabelle wisely decided not to press the point. 'I wish you'd eat more,' she remarked instead.

'I eat what I need.'

'You didn't have any breakfast. That was Sam's fault, wasn't it?' She couldn't forgive him so easily.

'I wasn't all that hungry, and anyway it had gone cold.' In fact, she might have enjoyed the toast, if only she had been allowed to.

'I'll make you another slice. What about a boiled egg as well? Dad's right, you do look pale, and I know you've not been sleeping. I can stay home from school if you like? You could have some food then go back to bed. Please, Lucy! You can't go without food or sleep. You'll only make yourself ill.'

'Whoah!' Lucy put up her hands. 'Stop worrying. And don't be such a bully.' Pecking Annabelle on the cheek, she insisted, 'Get yourself off to school, my girl. I'll have something to eat when I've done the housework.'

'Will you be all right on your own?'

'Yes. Now go on.' In fact she loved being on her own. She loved it when the door was closed and everyone was out, and she had the house to herself. It was the only time she could gather her wits and call her soul her own. 'I'm all right. Really.'

'Promise?'

The sound of the kettle whistling told her she ought to be getting on. 'By the time I've made the tea, I'll expect you to be on your way to school.'

'I'll do it, if you like?'

She would have done too if Lucy hadn't put out an arm to stop her. 'School!' she said, a little smile belying the firmness of her voice.

'Oh, all right, but I'll come and see you before I go.'

'I should hope so too.'

Lucy had taken a pot of fresh tea in to her husband, and was in the kitchen when Annabelle came back, dressed and ready for the outdoors.

'I can stay at home if you need me to,' she offered again.

'It's a kind thought,' Lucy acknowledged, 'but I'm not an invalid, and I'm not the only woman in the world to be having a baby.'

'Well, I don't want one,' Annabelle grumbled. 'Not if there's a chance it might grow up like Sam.'

They said their cheerios and a moment later the girl left for school. She didn't kiss her father goodbye. Instead she called from the door, 'See you later, Dad.'

Engrossed in his morning paper, he didn't look up. 'Mind you work hard,' he called out.

Shrugging her shoulders, Annabelle quietly closed the door and ran down the street to meet her best friend. 'I'm never getting married,' she declared sternly. 'When I grow up I'll be a nun.'

Her friend screeched with laughter. 'You can't be a nun!' she giggled. 'Nuns aren't allowed to have sex, and you've already had it with Richard Leadbeater.'

Annabelle stared with horror. 'How do you know that?' she gasped, blushing to the roots of her hair.

Glancing about to make certain no one was

watching, her friend proudly revealed, 'Me and Pat Clegg were watching.'

Annabelle groaned. 'Oh my God! Pat Clegg's the biggest gossip in the school. If she breathes a word to anybody, I'll kill the pair of you.'

'Don't worry.' The other girl winked cheekily. 'She already knows that if she tells about you, I'll tell about her.'

'What will you tell?'

'That she's had sex with John Arkwright . . . three times.'

'Ugh!' Annabelle made a grim face. 'Fancy going with John Arkwright. He's the pits!'

The other girl giggled. 'That's why she won't tell on you, because if I tell on her, she'll be a laughing stock.'

'All the same, I should still belt the pair of you.'

'I know we shouldn't have watched, but it were great.' She nudged Annabelle, her face alight with mischief. 'When are you doing it again?'

'Why? So you can watch us again?'

'No.' She could hardly keep a straight face. 'So I can charge the sixth formers a pound a peep.'

'You devil!'

Worried though she was, Annabelle began to see the funny side. 'If it was me, I'd charge them twice as much,' she chuckled.

By the time they got to the bus stop, they were in fits of laughter. 'Summat tickled yer fancy, has it?' asked the jolly bus conductor.

His innocent remark made them giggle all the way to school.

* * *

'You're a good cook,' Steve said as Lucy began clearing the table. 'Good-natured. Loyal.' Brushing his hand across her bottom as she passed by, he told her, 'I wouldn't get a better housewife if I scoured the country.'

Pausing in her work, she stared at him. 'Is that all I am to you?' she demanded. 'A good-natured, loyal cook who can keep house?' A spiral of bitterness rose in her. 'Because if that's all you see in me, I've made a terrible mistake.'

In an instant he was out of his chair and covering her in kisses. 'You know that isn't all you mean to me,' he protested. 'I love you. I always have . . . ever since I first set eyes on you. Of course I'm pleased that you can cook, and that I don't have to worry when we have guests for dinner. I'm proud of you, my love. Any man would be. But it wouldn't matter if you were the world's worst housekeeper, and if your pastry was like the sole of a shoe, I'd still want you for my wife. I could hire a cook and cleaner, but I could never replace you.' Chucking her under the chin he said softly, 'Sometimes I say things without thinking. You mustn't be offended.'

Past pretending, she answered honestly, 'I *am* offended.' Drawing away from him, she continued collecting the breakfast things from the table. 'Sometimes you can be very hurtful.'

'I don't mean to be.'

She paused, gazing at him, wondering . . . wanting to say all the things that were in her heart, but not being able to because of the kind of man he was. He was accomplished, respected throughout the community, intelligent and articulate, and yet in some ways he was more of a child than his own son.

What was the use? she thought. He would be sorry today and hurt her tomorrow, but, as he said, he didn't intend to. He was just insensitive. That was one of the traits in his nature she had failed to see before they were married.

'I know you don't mean to be hurtful,' she admitted, 'but I wish you'd think before you speak. I wish you'd realise I'm your wife. I'm helping to raise your children. I'm not just the cook or the housekeeper. I need to be respected too. I may be fat and pregnant, and I may not have much of a life outside these four walls, but I still need intelligent conversation just as much as you do.'

'I understand that.' Dropping his gaze, his brown eyes were like those of a puppy in trouble. 'Don't be angry with me.'

Oh, how she hated that hurt, little-boy expression. On some men it was endearing. On Steve it was nauseating. 'You'd better get ready to leave.' She wanted him out of here, away from her. Lately she found it hard to breathe when he was around.

Twining his arms round her waist, he whispered suggestively, 'I want you. We could go back to bed, if you like?'

The idea sickened her but she forced a smile. 'Sounds okay to me,' she lied, 'but won't it make you late for surgery?'

'Oh my God!' His eyes followed her gaze to the clock. 'I forgot I was on early surgery! Why didn't you tell me?'

'I'm telling you now.'

She watched him run about, looking for his black

'You shouldn't leave the door open,' she chastised as she came in. 'Any scoundrel could walk in.'

'A scoundrel like you, you mean?' Lucy ran to embrace her. 'You don't know how glad I am to see you, Debs,' she cried. 'I've missed you like mad. Her excitement bubbled over in a cascade of questions. 'How are your mam and dad? When are they coming home? Where have they gone? Is everything all right?'

'Bloody roll on!' Debbie wailed. 'It's like the bleedin' inquisition.' Glancing at the kettle, she asked hopefully, 'Is there a cup of tea going?'

Thrilled to have her here, Lucy hugged her again. ' 'Course there is,' she said, her grey eyes shining.

Flopping into a chair, Debbie kept hold of Lucy's hand. 'It's good to see you, gal.' Her inquisitive gaze went to the gentle rise beneath Lucy's skirt. 'It's only been a week, but you've really begun to show now.'

She looked at Lucy's flushed face and the dark shadows beneath her lovely grey eyes, and her voice hardened. 'Apart from your belly, you're too thin,' she commented. 'You've not been eating, have yer?'

'Don't you start. I've had all that from Annabelle this morning, and yes, I am eating. It just won't stay down.'

Eyeing her curiously, Debbie thought Lucy seemed unusually troubled. 'So? How's it all going then, gal?'

'Okay.' Lucy had a lot to tell her friend, but there was time enough for that later. 'You look tired, Debs. I'm sorry I bombarded you with all those questions. It's just that I'm really pleased to see you. I've been worried about you, and besides, good company is short round here.' Going to the kettle she boiled it up again and brewed the tea. 'I've made you some cheese and salad rolls, and last night I baked us a fruit cake . . . I had to hide it in case Sam ate the lot.'

'Doing me proud, eh?'

Lucy took the teapot and mugs to the table. 'Come on,' she urged, 'we can talk while we eat.' Crossing the room, she took Debbie's coat and hung it in the hallway. When she returned, Debbie was at the table, sipping her tea.

'You always did make a bloody good cuppa, gal,' she said. 'Now then, sit yer arse down and tell me what's been going on while I've been away.'

'Same as usual,' Lucy confided, dropping into her chair. 'You'll be pleased to know that the longer I'm married to Steve, the more I realise you were right when you said I'd live to regret it.'

Debbie shook her head, replying in a soft voice, 'I'm not pleased to hear that.'

'Oh, I'm sorry, Debs.' Angry because she seemed to be growing as insensitive as her husband, Lucy was quick to apologise. 'I know you're not pleased . . . you were right, and I was wrong, but I still don't know that I could have done anything else but marry him.' She patted her stomach. 'I had to put the baby first. I know I was right about that. It's just . . .' She didn't know how to say it. She searched for the right words, and somehow they spilled out. 'Steve's not a bad man, but he's harder than I thought . . . insensitive and bullish. He's almost impossible to please, and when there's a decision to be made, he thinks his opinion is the only one that matters.' She chuckled. 'I'm working on that one, though.'

Debbie listened, munching her roll and sipping

her tea in between. When Lucy had finished, she said perceptively, 'Am I right in thinking you two have got a bit of an argument going?'

'Yes, you are.' It was a great relief to be able to talk to Debs. 'Steve thinks I should have this baby at home, and I say no.'

Debbie seemed surprised. 'I should have thought you'd prefer to have it at home. I mean, he's a doctor, so you'll be well looked after.' She shuddered. 'Ooh! I hate hospitals.'

Lucy explained, 'If the circumstances were different, I would have preferred to stay at home, but not here, not with him.'

Something in her face told Debbie there was more to it than Lucy was saying. 'What else, gal?' she urged. 'Yer ain't telling me everything, are yer, eh? What's the real reason you'd rather go into hospital?'

'That's it,' Lucy assured her. 'Even though it's his idea that I have the baby at home, he would still manage to make me feel as though I was a burden. He has this way of turning blame around . . . starting an argument and convincing you it was your fault. He fusses too. At first it was flattering, having someone fussing over me all the time, but he doesn't know when to stop. Sometimes I feel as if I'm drowning. What's worse, I'm never sure if he's genuine or not. He's like a kid with a new toy. If I so much as *look* at a man, he goes crazy . . . he even accused me of flirting with the milkman.' She chuckled. 'You'd think I'd got enough on my plate without wanting more, wouldn't you, eh?'

'And did you?'

'Did I what?'

'Flirt with the milkman?'

Lucy laughed out loud. "Course I did. I dragged him inside, ripped off his trousers and threatened to get my milk elsewhere if he didn't see to me there and then.'

'Randy cow!' Winking mischievously, Debbie declared, 'I wouldn't mind a bit of that meself.'

'Oh? And what about Alfie?'

'Who says I can't have more than one bloke at a time?'

'You're a bugger.' Lucy's heart was happier than it had been in ages. They had been part of each other's lives for so long.

'What else, gal?' Popping a big portion of fruit cake into her mouth, Debbie muttered through it, 'Love yer fruit cake. I'm glad you hid it from the 'orrible Samuel.' Having finished her cake she licked her fingers, asking, 'What else then? I know you. There's summat else, so out with it.'

Lucy went on, 'You've got it right when you say "the 'orrible Samuel".' She paused for a moment, seeing the young man in her mind's eye and feeling as though, even now, he was watching her. 'He's a strange creature . . . always watching, picking fault, broody one minute and violent the next.' Suddenly she felt cold. 'Sometimes he frightens me,' she admitted.

'I don't like the sound o' that, gal. Has he ever threatened yer?'

'No. But he's one of the reasons why I'd rather go into hospital to have this baby. I can't imagine how he'd be if I was here, giving birth to his father's child. He's shown no interest in the baby . . . in spite of his

dad's ramming it down his throat at every opportunity ... or maybe he hates the baby *because* of
that. At any rate, he loathes the sight of me.'

Debbie considered what Lucy had said and she
agreed. 'From what you tell me, gal, I'm on your
side. You stick to yer guns, whatever yer old man
says.'

'Thanks for that, Debs.' Even Annabelle wasn't
on her side in this argument. Like the little mother
she was, the girl had decided she could keep a better
eye on everything if Lucy was at home. 'My mind's
made up,' she declared now. 'I intend to have this
baby in hospital. Steve can bully all he likes but so
far as I'm concerned, that's an end to it.'

'Good on yer, gal.' Raising her mug, Debbie went
on, 'Here's to you and the baby, and here's hoping
the miserable Sam will learn to love you like I do.'

Lucy smiled. 'You'll hope for a long time,' she said.
'That one doesn't know how to love.'

'Hmm.' Drinking her tea while keeping her gaze
on Lucy, Debbie asked after a moment, 'What about
Steve?'

'What about him?'

'Does *he* love you?'

It took a while before Lucy could answer truthfully.
'If love means always wanting me near ... *yes*. If
love is needing constant reassurance and craving
for sex every minute God sends, then *yes*. If it means
wanting to take over my life ... *yes* again.'

'That ain't my idea of love.' Debbie's face said it
all. 'Sounds like yer in prison to me.'

Lucy smiled. How right she was. 'But I can't deny
he's tender and generous too, and sometimes ...

though I think it would be better if he didn't . . . he takes my side against his own son.' She took a long, deep breath. 'All the same, I wish there had been some other way.'

'Do you love him?'

Lucy gave a small laugh, but it was tinged with bitterness. 'I thought I could learn to love him in the way a wife should love her husband, but I can't. I'll never feel that way about him. I don't like him making love to me. I don't even like him touching me any more.' She shivered involuntarily. 'But, as I say, he's a good, kind man, and my life here is better than most. When it comes down to it, I have no right to grumble. Annabelle is a delight to know, and I have the baby to look forward to. I live in a fine house and I don't go short of money. Steve makes me a very generous allowance, and because I don't go out much, I have a healthy bank balance. He's a good-looking man, yet he has eyes only for me, even though I'm getting fat and ugly.' She smiled at herself. 'Look at the state of me, Debs. I'm lucky to have a man at all.'

Debbie did look at her. She saw how thin Lucy actually was, and how shadowed her eyes were. She saw how the bulge beneath her skirt was becoming more pronounced, and how her hair had lost its sheen. Yet, at the same time, there was no denying Lucy's very special quality. The kind of inner beauty that shone from her dove-grey eyes and lit her face with an aura of gentleness.

Like all real beauties, Lucy was unaware of how lovely she was. She could see only her failings. She could not see what Debbie saw. She didn't feel that wave of warmth and belonging that touched anyone who looked into her kind and tender gaze. 'You could never be ugly,' Debbie told her now. 'It's Steve who's the lucky one, not you.' She couldn't stop the words from spilling out. 'Anyhow, it shouldn't be Steve with you. It should be Jack.'

At the mention of his name, Lucy's heart turned somersaults. Her gaze fell to the carpet and her face grew white. She couldn't deny what Debbie had just said because in her heart of hearts she had wished so many times that it was Jack lying beside her in bed . . . Jack who held her hand when she woke in a nightmare . . . Jack who shared her days, her nights, her troubles and joys.

When she raised her gaze, Debbie saw the tears in her eyes. 'I'm sorry, gal,' she said, 'I didn't mean to make yer feel bad.'

A bright smile replaced the tears. 'You didn't,' Lucy answered truthfully. 'I often think about Jack . . .' The smile faded. 'But he's married now. He might even be a father.'

Now Debbie's voice was harsh. 'Leave Steve, gal.'

Lucy was gazing into the blazing fire, her expression hard. 'And have him follow me to the ends of the earth . . . fighting for me . . . fighting for the baby? Making our lives a misery?' She shook her head. 'No, Debs. The reason I married Steve is still the same. And anyway, you're forgetting, it was Jack who turned his back on me. Leaving Steve isn't the answer, and you know that as well as I do.'

Reluctantly Debbie had to concede. 'I expect you're right, gal. Let's hope things get better, eh?' Thinking of her own parents, she muttered, 'Seems like marriage ain't a bed o' roses after all.'

Lucy hadn't forgotten. 'You haven't told me about your mam and dad. Are they all right?'

'They're sorting theirselves out.'

Lucy waited.

Debbie looked up. 'They've got a big problem, and they've gone away to see if they can get it together. Dad's got a temporary job in Aylesbury, and me mam . . . well . . .' She bit her lip and seemed embarrassed. 'All I can say is, the buggers are still together.' Her mouth lifted in a smile. 'Well, in a manner o' speaking they are.'

Lucy was philosophical. ' Your mam and dad love each other. They'll work it out, don't worry.' She was curious as to what the problem was, but guessed it had something to do with Debs's dad. There had been suggestions of drunkenness and violence for years now but it wasn't her place to pry, and as always she would wait until Debs felt able to confide more.

Debbie's smile broadened. 'D'yer know, gal,' she said almost jovially, 'I reckon yer could be right. They just might sort it all out, once and for all. We'll have to wait and see, won't we? Anyways, they haven't let the house go yet, so they must mean to make their way home at some time or another.' Having convinced herself that was the case, she asked cheekily, 'Yer ain't got more o' that fruit cake hidden away, have yer, gal?'

'I might be able to find some,' Lucy teased. 'I've also got a big box of chocolates. Steve bought them for next week. There'll be twelve people round my dinner table, and I have to play hostess. I have to wrap the chocolates in dainty little doilies and place them ever so prettily on a tray.' Her eyes glinted with mischief. 'Fancy one, do you?'

Debbie thought it a wonderful idea. 'Go on,' she enticed. 'Why not?'

Lucy brought out the remainder of the cake, and between the two of them they ate the lot. They also drank half a bottle of wine, and ate the entire box of chocolates. 'It's like a bleedin' party, ain't it, gal?' Debbie chuckled.

'Lovely, though, ain't it?' mimicked Lucy. 'And why the bleedin' Hell shouldn't we have a party, eh?'

They laughed and chatted, and when it was time for Debbie to go, Lucy clung to her for a long minute. 'Don't let my mistake put you off marrying your Alfie,' she urged.

'It won't,' Debbie assured her. 'I reckon it's time for me to give up working. Alfie wants kids. I reckon a dozen might do it.'

After Debbie left, Lucy was sick as a dog. 'Serves you right,' she groaned, splashing her face with cold water.

Briskly rubbing a towel over her face, she stared at herself in the mirror. 'Debbie's a bugger,' she laughed, feeling better already.

A bright smiling face looked back at her. With the tips of her fingers she traced its contours, but it wasn't her own face she was touching, it was Jack's. The smile fell away and in its place came a look of resignation. 'She was right about one thing, though. I don't belong with Steve. I belong with you, Jack.'

Turning away she murmured, 'You and me, eh, Jack?' Oh, how her heart warmed at the thought.

Glancing back in the mirror, she saw the sadness

in her smile. 'Wake up, Lucy,' she told herself. 'It doesn't do to dream.'

But then, if you can't dream, what else is there?

Chapter Sixteen

The phone had been ringing for some time before Lucy came rushing out of the bathroom, her hair soaking wet and wrapped in a towel. 'It's all right,' Annabelle shouted from downstairs. 'It'll be for me!'

Thankful, Lucy rushed back into the bathroom and threw off the towel. She was no sooner through the door than she heard an almighty argument. 'SAM, YOU BASTARD! PUT THAT PHONE DOWN.' It was Annabelle's voice.

Shocked to the core, Lucy raced out yet again, to see Sam leaning over the banister. 'Got something to hide, have you?' he taunted his sister. 'Been having it off with someone at school, is that it? And now you're frightened the old man might find out?' He waved the receiver of the upstairs phone at her. 'Go on, little sister, carry on talking. I don't mind getting it all second-hand.' Grinning like a fiend, he whispered into the receiver, 'This is Sam here. I know who you are, and I know what the two of you have been up to.'

Realising he was eavesdropping, Lucy grabbed the phone and slammed it into the cradle. 'What the devil's going on here?'

'I should have thought any fool could see that. Even *you*.'

'You should be ashamed ... listening in on your sister's private conversation.' His sneering face was only a few inches away, so near she could have smacked it hard enough to send him off balance. The temptation was overwhelming.

He sniggered in her face. 'You should try listening in on private conversations,' he muttered. 'You'd be surprised at what you learn.'

'You disgust me.' That one short remark betrayed all of her deepest feelings towards him.

For one brief moment he appeared shocked by the vehemence of her voice. However, the moment was short-lived because soon he was smiling again, voice trembling with delight as he told her, 'Well now, I've finally got through to you. You can't know how pleased that makes me. You see, Lucy Nolan, I *want* to disgust you. I want you to be so bloody disgusted that you'll leave this house for good. This family got on all right before you came, and we'll get on all right when you've gone.'

Pushing his face close to hers, he demanded in a harsh, threatening voice, 'Have you got that, bitch?'

Incensed, Lucy raised her hands to thrust him away, but just then another hand grabbed him by the scruff of the neck. 'I THINK YOU OWE MY WIFE AN APOLOGY!' Red-faced with anger, Steve shook his son hard. 'Well?'

Defiant as ever, the young man scowled at Lucy. 'I don't owe her anything,' he hissed. 'We don't need her here. She's trouble. She's been trouble from the first day.'

It was evident where Sam got his vicious nature from because in that moment, Lucy saw the very same trait in his father. Leaning forward to whisper in Sam's ear, he told him, 'Apologise now or I swear to God I'll beat you black and blue.'

Enough was enough. 'I don't want him to apologise under duress,' Lucy insisted. 'I'd prefer it if Sam and I worked this out ourselves.'

When they both stared at her as if she'd gone out of her mind, she insisted. 'I mean it, Steve. I don't want you forcing an apology from him. It wouldn't mean a thing to me.'

With a spiteful jerk of his arm, Steve released the squirming young man. 'Get out of my sight,' he rasped, pushing him so hard he almost fell headlong down the stairs. 'And think yourself lucky you don't feel the weight of my foot behind you.'

Lucy's gaze followed Sam down to the hallway from where he glared up at her, silent hatred burning in his eyes. 'I wish you hadn't done that,' she said to the man beside her. 'It can only make matters worse.'

'What are you saying?' Peeved that he'd been dissuaded from punishing the boy, Steve blamed her. 'You shouldn't let him talk to you like that. I won't have it, do you hear?'

'I can deal with it.'

'Like Hell you can! The next time he's disrespectful, it'll be *me* that deals with him. He won't get off scot free next time, I can promise you that.'

Lucy knew from experience it was no use arguing. From now on, she would just have to make certain she and Sam kept out of each other's way. 'I'd better go and get ready.' She glanced at the wall clock. It was almost seven. 'The guests will be arriving in an hour.'

When she turned to Steve again, he was smiling. That same self-satisfied smile that made her heart sink. 'An hour's a long time,' he whispered. Sliding his hand inside her dressing-gown, he toyed with her breast. 'I always want to make love to you when you're straight out of the bath.' He sniffed her hair. 'You smell lovely,' he groaned. 'Like a new baby.'

She turned away. 'I've a mountain of things to do. So have you.'

Escaping into the bedroom, she leaned against the door. 'Help me, Lord,' she murmured. 'Help me to love him like I should.'

Stripping off her gown, she stood stark naked before the mirror. 'Look at yourself, Lucy Nolan,' she said bitterly. Suddenly her mouth fell open. *You called yourself Lucy Nolan!* As Sam had done just now.

'Hmm.' The smile became a soft laugh. 'You and he *have* got something in common after all . . . you both wish to God you'd never married into this family.'

It was ironic. 'You're caught between the devil and the deep blue sea, my girl,' she told herself. 'You've done the right and only thing, and still you're looking for a way out. Face it, Lucy girl, there is no way out. Not unless you want to bring your child up without a father. Is that what you want? Do you think it would be a small price to pay for your independence? You've still got the shop. If you opened it again, you could earn a decent living. Neither you nor the child would go without. Think about it.' God! These past weeks she had thought about nothing else, but the answer was always the same. 'You can't do it. It wouldn't be you paying the price, it would be the child.' Besides, she still had a small affection for Steve; though there were times, like just now, when she was made to question her own judgement.

When she looked back on the twists of Fate that had brought her to him, it almost seemed it was meant to happen. 'It's a punishment on you,' she commented wryly. 'As your mam might say – you've made your bed, now you'd best lie on it.' All the same, she doubted whether even her mam would agree with her staying in a marriage that seemed to bring little happiness.

Naked and growing cold, she stared at herself. Her body was supple and firm, and apart from the rise of her stomach, she had the nymph-like figure of a young girl. The skin was smooth, the limbs perfectly shaped, and the breasts pert as ever. Little had changed, except the face.

Still lovely, still young, the face was that of a woman yearning for something more; the grey eyes were wiser, older, more serious now. There was a sense of sadness about the mouth, a harder line, where once it had been uplifted in a girlish smile. 'You look haunted,' she murmured as she turned away, a feeling of hopelessness washing over her.

She didn't hear him come in. It was only when his hands ran over her shoulders that she pulled away, startled. '*Steve!*'

He laughed softly. 'I should hope so.' There was a moment of silence, then, in a deadly serious voice, he murmured possessively, 'God help any other man who dares to lay hands on you.' He stared at her. 'You wouldn't want any other man, would you, my dear?'

She didn't like it when he was like this. It frightened her. With his eyes fixed on her, Lucy decided to bluff her way out of a desperate corner. Shaking her head, she answered convincingly, 'No other man, I promise.'

'I want you.'

'Maybe. But right now, I don't want you. I want to dry my hair and dress and be ready for our guests when they arrive.' Gently pushing him away, she advised kindly, 'I think you'd better get a move on as well, or they'll catch you with your trousers down.'

'Let them.' With a swift unexpected movement he threw her on to the bed. 'I can't wait all evening for you,' he sighed, lying on top of her. 'I need you now.'

'Steve, get off!' Frantic, she pushed at him with her hands, but he swept them aside as if they were not even there.

'When I came in just now,' he murmured, 'what were you thinking of?'

'Nothing.'

'That's not true,' he persisted. 'I heard you talking to yourself . . . or were you talking to someone else? Maybe you were holding a conversation with someone who isn't here.' He pinned her arms beside her, the weight of his body holding her down. 'Is that what you were doing, Lucy? Talking to someone who isn't here?'

'I don't know what you mean.' Yet she knew all right. She knew what he was getting at, and his next words confirmed her suspicions.

'Were you talking to Jack?'

'Don't be silly.' She felt her face growing hot

beneath his inquisitive stare. 'That's a crazy thing to say. Why should you think a thing like that?'

'Because I've always felt you still prefer him to me.'

'Let me go, Steve. You're hurting me.'

'Tell me then.'

'Tell you what?'

'Tell me you love me more than you ever loved Jack Hanson,' he said harshly, 'then I'll let you go.'

'For God's sake, Steve!'

'Tell me!'

'Let me up, or you can play host to your guests all by yourself.' Anger tore through her. 'I mean it, Steve. I'm cold, and angry, and you're hurting me.' He went to kiss her, but she turned away. She would have brought her knee up and caught him where it hurt most, but he had her exactly where he wanted her. Because she had suffered too many sleepless nights, and skipped too many meals, and because the baby seemed to be sucking away her strength, there was irritatingly little she could do about it.

'I don't want to hurt you,' he assured her softly, 'I only want to love you.' He fumbled with his zip and suddenly there was nothing between her naked body and his large erect penis. 'You must want me as much as I want you,' he whispered in her ear. 'It's been a whole week, and it's driving me mad. If I don't have you now, I won't be able to keep my eyes off you all evening.' Now he was straddling her, his weight beginning to bear down. 'Please, Lucy, let me. You know I won't force you to.'

It was true what he said. He would never force himself on her. But if she refused yet again, he would make it impossible for her. Dammit! she thought rebelliously. Why should I?

'Please, Lucy.' He was licking her breast, making her shiver. 'I want you so much.'

She hated him . . . hated herself. Turning away, she opened her legs and let him in.

Thankfully, it was over in a matter of minutes. He mounted her, thrust into her a few times, then jerked, shivered, and fell aside. 'You're wonderful,' he groaned.

Wonderful? In her disgust she had to smile.

She had done nothing wonderful.

She felt nothing wonderful.

All she felt was shame. And guilt.

The table had been in Steve's family for generations, as he never tired of telling her. All the same it was a beautiful thing. Constructed in solid oak, with a deep figured skirt encircling the top, and round, sturdy legs, it was a feat of early craftsmanship.

When dressed in a lace tablecloth and silver candlesticks – these ornate candlesticks also having been in Steve's family since as far back as he could recall – it was a sight to behold.

Lucy put the finishing touches to it. The table and candlesticks might have been Steve's but the dinner service had been her own choice: clear white china with a fine rim of blue forget-me-nots encircling each and every piece, it was her pride and joy. The service was a twelve-place set, and all of it would be in use this evening. Now she carefully set the last place before making the first pretty napkin fan. With deft fingers she fashioned the intricate creation and placed it gently in the centre of a plate.

Stepping back to admire it, she almost fell over Annabelle. 'Where did you learn to do that?' the girl asked curiously.

'What?' For one awful minute, Lucy thought it was Steve she had collided with. But no, he would be upstairs for some time yet, she reminded herself with relief. He would be preening himself, making sure he was the smartest, brightest thing at the dinner table. Sometimes he rehearsed his little speeches in front of the mirror time and again until he believed he'd got them right . . . smiling and frowning and joke-telling, according to what kind of speech he was planning. It would have been funny if it wasn't so pathetic, Lucy thought wryly. 'Where did I learn to do *what*?' she said, dropping into the nearest chair.

'The napkins? How did you learn to make them into fans like that?'

Lucy smiled. '*Lessons in Etiquette* . . . top shelf in your father's library.'

'You must be joking!' Annabelle exclaimed in horror. 'I'm not going in there. You know what he's like about his precious library. What! If I was to upset the order of things, I'd never hear the last of it.'

'Oh, come on. He's not all that bad.' But he was, she told herself. He was.

'Will you show me?'

Lucy laughed. 'Oh, I see. You want *me* to get it in the neck, eh?' She stood up. 'All right then, I'll find the book for you.'

'No, I didn't mean that,' Annabelle protested. 'I meant, will you show me how to do it?'

Relieved, Lucy showed her.

She used up several napkins before Annabelle thought she could do it herself. Several more before the girl cried jubilantly, 'I've done it!'

'So you have,' said Lucy. 'How would you like to do the rest?'

'Oh, could I?' Her brown eyes glittered with pride. 'Are you sure you can trust me?'

''Course I can.' All the same, tonight was especially important because it was medical colleagues and their wives. No matter, thought Lucy. I can always check the table again when Annabelle's not looking. She didn't want to hurt her feelings.

Leaving the girl to get on with it, Lucy went into the kitchen where a grey-haired woman was whisking up a bowl of cream. 'Is there anything I can do to help?' Lucy asked hopefully.

Occasionally, when he'd found he couldn't cope himself, Steve had hired this dear lady to help out, and now, whenever there was a dinner party of any real importance, he insisted she should be in charge of the kitchen. 'Not that I have any complaints about your cooking,' he always assured Lucy. 'It's only to take the pressure off you, so you can make yourself more beautiful for your guests.'

'There's nothing to do,' the woman answered. 'Everything's under control.' She regarded Lucy with kindly eyes, her gaze travelling from the thick shining brown hair to the becoming blue calf-length dress that Debbie had helped choose. 'You look lovely,' she said, smiling into Lucy's eyes. 'Being pregnant suits you.'

Lucy smiled back. 'Thank you,' she murmured

gratefully. When Steve told her she looked lovely, it was said with a certain aloofness, as though he was asking for the salt to be passed.

'The young miss was in here looking for you just now.'

Lucy was already on her way out. 'It's all right, Mrs Filey,' she answered, 'she found me in the dining room.' She remembered then that she still hadn't talked to Annabelle about the phone call, and the suggestion by Sam that his sister was 'having it off with someone'. It was a worrying thought.

'And don't you worry about me doing the serving neither,' Mrs Filey told her. 'Like I explained to the good doctor, I'm happier doing the whole thing. If that's all right by you?'

Lucy saw the poor woman was worried. 'Whatever you and my husband agreed is fine by me,' she lied. 'But if you do need help, you mustn't be afraid to drag me away from the table.' Her smile was spontaneous. 'In fact, I might be glad to hide in the kitchen for a while.'

'Away with you.' Mrs Filey liked Lucy, though she believed she and Steve Ryman were a terrible mismatch. 'You dazzle the guests with your lovely nature,' she suggested, 'and I'll put 'em in a good humour with me food, so they'll laugh at the doctor's bad jokes.'

Lucy chuckled. 'You're a wicked woman, Mrs Filey,' she said, wagging a finger.

'Wicked women have more fun,' Mrs Filey retorted, and Lucy went away laughing.

Annabelle was surveying her handiwork. 'What do you think?' she asked as Lucy came in.

The napkins stood on the plates like little soldiers. 'I couldn't have done better myself,' Lucy said proudly. 'Thank you, sweetheart.'

'What else can I do?'

Though it wasn't the best place or time, it was an opening and Lucy took it. 'You can tell me whether there was any truth in what Sam said.'

Annabelle blushed. 'I knew you'd get round to that,' she groaned. 'Sam's got a foul mouth. It isn't the way it sounded.'

'What way is it then?'

'I have got a boyfriend, but there's nothing I can't handle.'

'Nothing you want to discuss or ask? I want to be here for you, Annabelle, you know that, don't you?'

'Yes.' She hung her head. It was obvious to Lucy that the girl was not telling the whole truth. 'But there's nothing I want to talk about right now.'

'All right, but I'm sure I don't need to remind you that you're not yet fifteen. I don't want to come the heavy-handed stepmother, but . . .' She took the girl into her arms, her voice softer, more understanding, yet at the same time issuing a firm, timely warning. 'If you and this boyfriend go too far, you're asking for serious trouble. You do understand that, don't you, sweetheart?'

Annabelle gave a nod. 'I know,' she acknowledged. 'Don't worry, Lucy, I won't let you down.'

Cupping her hands around the girl's face, Lucy made her look up. 'I'm not concerned about you letting *me* down,' she said, gazing into those pretty brown eyes, 'I'm only afraid you might let *yourself* down.'

'I won't.' In that close, precious moment, Annabelle

loved Lucy more than ever. 'I promise you . . . I won't let anyone down.'

Lucy smiled reassuringly. ''Course you won't.' She truly believed that. 'But don't forget what I said, I'm here if you need to talk.' The atmosphere was cleared and they hugged a moment longer until a voice startled them.

'What's this? Mothers' meeting?' Steve's enquiring gaze went from one to the other. 'Is there a problem I should know about?'

Taking the girl with her as she left the room, Lucy said, 'The only problem you should know about is the time.' She glanced up at the clock. 'Ten minutes to countdown, and you still haven't got your tie on.'

He ran up the stairs ahead of them. 'Why didn't somebody tell me?' he wailed. 'Important guests coming to dinner, and me with no tie on!'

At the bottom of the stairs, Lucy and the girl were softly laughing. 'Men panic over the silliest things,' Lucy said. 'Women have far more important things to worry about, don't you think, Annabelle?'

She smiled. Lucy winked. And they each went their separate ways: the girl to the kitchen where she might steal a spoonful of dessert, and Lucy upstairs, to make sure her husband was able to receive his guests in the calm and dignified manner he would wish.

Some time later, when the guests began to arrive, Steve stood beside his wife greeting them, laughing and joking, oozing confidence and looking resplendent in a dark lounge suit, with white shirt and impeccably knotted tie. 'Lovely to see you,' he told the wife of a senior consultant. 'Laura, isn't it?' He beamed with pleasure when the woman in question congratulated him on his sharp memory.

Throughout the wonderful meal of roast turkey and succulent vegetables he smiled and chatted and took control of every conversation. When the dessert followed, he openly praised Mrs Filey for cooking 'in the best tradition'. There was a choice of pudding: crispy baked apple strudel or gooseberry crumble, with either whipped cream or custard. 'I've a good mind to have a helping of each,' he laughed, but settled for a rather large slice of the apple strudel.

It was a pleasant enough gathering with everyone holding conversations across the table or else indulging in small talk with their immediate neighbour; there was the occasional disagreement and odd bouts of laughter, but try as she might to enjoy it all, Lucy found herself aching for the evening to draw to a close.

Sam was drinking too much wine, and so was his father. While everyone was still seated at the table, the coffee was brought in, with brandy and liqueurs. Most guests had come by car and wisely opted just for coffee, while others, who had either arrived by taxi or volunteered their partner to drive home, joined their host in several toasts. 'Good health to us all,' he announced, knocking back a sizeable glass of brandy. Refilling, he went on jovially, 'To Mrs Filey, and to my lovely wife Lucy . . . two very special women.'

Sam, allowed a small glass of brandy as a treat, rolled it between his large white hands while staring at Lucy across the table. Uncomfortable beneath his gaze, and desperately wanting to spend a penny, she turned to the woman beside her and quietly excused herself. 'I understand,' the woman said. 'I've had two children myself and I know what it's like.' Smiling at Annabelle, who was seated on the other side of her, she explained rather grandly, 'When you're carrying a baby it does tend to press on the bladder.'

While the woman engaged Annabelle in conversation, Lucy made good her escape, hoping her husband was too preoccupied to notice that she would be gone for a few minutes.

Unfortunately, it wasn't to be.

'You surely aren't leaving our guests, my dear?' Steve's voice rang out to silence all others.

Embarrassed to her soul, Lucy smiled at one and all. 'Sorry.' Braving the curious glances, she lied lamely, 'I'd better see if all is well in the kitchen.'

She was immensely relieved when someone called out, 'Another pot of coffee here wouldn't go amiss.' Someone else suggested, 'I wouldn't mind another slice of that delicious strudel,' and soon the chattering started up again.

To get away, Lucy had to walk past Steve who was seated nearest the door at the head of the table. As she hurried by, he caught her by the arm. 'You're looking especially beautiful tonight, my dear,' he said, tugging her towards him.

When she tried to pull away his eyes flashed angrily, his voice raised in a shout as he called on the others for support. 'You chaps, aren't you jealous? Doesn't my wife look ravishing?' he insisted, smiling at the upturned faces as all eyes focused on Lucy. 'You'd never think she was pregnant, would you?'

he laughed. 'Oh, but she is, I made sure of that. Too bloody virile, that's my trouble.'

Wishing the earth would open and swallow her up, Lucy leaned down to whisper in his ear. 'That's enough,' she told him angrily. 'Can't you see you're embarrassing both of us?'

He seemed astonished, staring up at her. 'Embarrassing us?' he stuttered. 'What nonsense, my dear.' Turning to his uncomfortable guests, he explained, 'My darling wife says I'm embarrassing her. No such thing. I'm only saying what a beautiful creature she is and how proud I am that she's carrying my child.' He winked. 'Mind you, it's not altogether my fault that she's pregnant. It takes two to tango.'

Suddenly his grip tightened on her arm. 'But then, a man can't always be sure, can he?' he asked in a loud voice. 'I mean, it could be the milkman's.' Roaring with laughter, he revealed peevishly, 'Most women would pay the milkman and hurry back indoors, wouldn't they, eh? But not my wife. Oh, no. She stands on the doorstep, laughing and chatting 'til all hours. She claims he was an old friend of her late father's, but how can I be sure she's not dragging him up the stairs, eh? How can any man be sure what his wife gets up to behind his back?'

Lucy felt the colour drain from her face. 'You're drunk!' she hissed under her breath. An almighty rage welled inside her as she tried desperately to retain a semblance of dignity. Making herself smile, she explained in a clear voice, 'He doesn't tell you the milkman's only two weeks off his pension . . . he's got a weak heart and arthritis in both his legs. I doubt if the poor devil's got the strength to *get* up the stairs, let alone do anything about it once he got there.' Out of the corner of her eye she saw Sam leering at her. When their eyes met he raised the glass of brandy to her before swilling it down his throat in one go.

In the wave of laughter that followed, Lucy hurried away, incensed by the whole incident.

Upstairs, she splashed her face with cold water and prepared to return to the circus. 'Let him try and humiliate me again,' she said into the mirror, 'and he'll be bloody sorry!'

Outside on the landing she took a deep breath, squared her shoulders, and strode purposefully towards the top of the stairs. When she saw Steve waiting there, his face long and hangdog, she was ready for him. 'Don't apologise,' she warned. 'It will be a long time before I forgive you for that nasty little performance.'

'Please, Lucy,' he whined. 'You know how jealous I get. There wasn't a man in there who didn't have his greedy eyes on you all night. I saw you chatting to Roger Parker and I got carried away, that's all. I can't stand it when you look at other men.'

'*When?*' she demanded. '*When* do I look at other men? I hardly ever leave this house, and when I do, I'm afraid to talk to anyone in case it gets back to you, and you try and make something of it.' For too long now she'd suffered in silence. Now it spilled out with a vengeance. 'I'm sick and fed up with your stupid jealousy. To tell you the truth, Steve, it's the quickest way to drive me into some other man's arms.'

He gulped hard, staring at her as though she'd just announced his death sentence. 'What other man?

You were lying before, weren't you? There *is* another man, isn't there?' Suddenly he lunged at her. 'Who is it? You'd better tell me because I'll find out, and when I do, he'll wish he'd never been born.'

While Steve demanded the truth, his idle son watched for a time then strolled leisurely up the stairs and leaned against the banister. 'Throw her out,' he taunted, 'I told you all along she was trouble.'

Something about his son's virulent voice made Steve stop and take stock of what he was doing. 'Get back to the guests,' he told Sam. Addressing Lucy, he asked her forgiveness. 'I don't know what came over me,' he said. 'It must have been the drink.'

For the longest moment of her life, Lucy stared at him, all her feelings showing in the look she gave him. 'You degraded me in front of everyone,' she said quietly. 'I don't know if I can forgive you for that.'

'Don't let her fool you, Dad,' Sam urged. 'If she won't tell you who her lover is, you should send her packing.'

Incensed, Steve swung round and prodded him hard in the chest. 'SHUT IT!' he said. 'Or you'll be the one to be sent packing.'

While they argued, Lucy brushed by, hoping against hope the guests couldn't hear what was going on.

She was a few steps from the top of the stairs when Sam suddenly spoke to her. 'Bitch! I hope you're satisfied now you've turned my dad against me?'

She had a strange sense of impending danger before at that same moment he stuck out his foot to trip her up. Unable to steady herself, she lost her balance and hurtled clumsily down the stairs. At first she thought she could stop herself from falling all the way, but then she completely lost her footing and there was no way she could save herself.

As she fell, her stricken eyes looked up. Steve was chasing down the stairs, calling her name, arms wide open as he tried to grab her.

Sam was leaning over the banisters, smiling as he watched her career all the way to the bottom where she landed in a crumpled heap.

She could hear the sound of voices and rushing feet; there was a sense of people all around. And a disturbing, uncanny silence as the darkness closed in on her.

Chapter Seventeen

'How are yer doing, gal?' Debbie had been at the hospital every day for the past fortnight. Today was no exception.

'I'm all right.' Lucy was far from all right, but she knew how worried Debbie had been and so forced a sunny smile. 'Knowing you, I expect you've already been harassing the doctor. He's probably told you how well I'm doing.'

In her thoughts she went on, But he won't have told you how I really feel, because he doesn't know. How can any man know what it's like for a woman to lose an unborn child . . . a growing, living part of herself? How can any man know what goes on inside a woman's soul?

Perceptive as ever, Debbie took hold of her hand. 'You know how sorry I am, don't yer, gal? About the baby, I mean.'

Lucy nodded. She wanted to say she felt that, of all people, Debs might understand the best, but the words stuck in her throat.

'It's okay, gal,' Debbie told her. 'There'll be time enough to talk when yer get home.' With that in mind, she asked, 'Has the doctor been round yet?'

'This morning.' Lucy was glad the subject had

been changed. Right now she couldn't find the heart to talk about losing the baby. She couldn't find the heart to talk about other things either ... deep, intimate things that kept her awake at night. Lying here in this bed, lonely and hurt, she had been made to come to terms with a great number of things, not least of which was her disastrous marriage.

Then there was Sam and what he had done. He had deliberately tripped her up. He had killed her unborn child, and she could never forgive him. With her life turned upside down yet again, she had decisions to make. Should she go? Should she stay? Was there any kind of future for her and Steve? One thing was certain: she could never again live in the same house as Steve's son. Sam was not only hateful, he was dangerous. Evil.

'Out with it, gal.' Debbie had seen the haunted look in Lucy's eyes as she turned these thoughts over in her mind again.

Unaware that she had betrayed her innermost feelings, Lucy feigned ignorance. 'Sorry, Debs. I was miles away. What did you say?'

'Yer know very well what I said. I can guess what yer thinking, and it don't do no good to keep it all to yerself.'

'It doesn't do any good to keep talking about it either,' Lucy protested.

Debbie eyed her with suspicion. 'Yer ain't told me everything, have yer?'

'About what?'

'About how yer came to fall all the way down the bleedin' stairs, that's what.'

'You know what happened. I lost my footing and tripped.' Which was no lie.

'That ain't all there was to it, though, is it?' Debbie had worked it out for herself, and now she wouldn't let it go. 'I know the dinner was a disaster because Steve got drunk and showed yer up. And I know yer were having an argument at the top of the stairs because yer've told me all that. But yer ain't told me the whole truth, have yer?' Relentless, she persisted, 'He pushed yer down the stairs, didn't he, gal? That lousy husband o' yours pushed yer down them stairs, and yer ain't saying 'cause yer don't want to get him in trouble. That's the truth of it. Am I right or am I wrong?'

Loath to involve Debbie, Lucy lowered her gaze. 'You always did have a vivid imagination.'

Undeterred, she leaned forward, her gaze probing Lucy's. 'Look at me, gal,' she said softly, and when Lucy looked up, insisted, 'Answer me, am I right or am I wrong?'

'You're wrong. Steve didn't push me down the stairs.'

'Oh?'

'It was *Sam*.'

Now it was said, she felt relieved and eager to confide. 'Everything happened just as I told you, only Sam followed his dad up the stairs and heard us arguing. He said I'd been nothing but trouble, and that I wasn't needed in that family. Steve turned on him, and Sam blamed me. As I walked away, he deliberately tripped me up. I lost my balance, and that's how it happened. I swear to God, it wasn't Steve, it was his son.'

'He tripped you up deliberately? The bastard!'
Thumping her fists together, Debbie was outraged.
'And what about Steve? What did he have to say? I
hope he sent the bugger packing?'

Lucy shook her head. 'Steve won't have it that
his son tripped me on purpose. Oh, in a way I can't
blame him for trying to find excuses because I did
the same at first. I didn't want to believe that anyone
could do such a terrible thing. But the more I lie
here and think about it, the more I know Sam wanted
to hurt me . . . kill me even. I saw his face, Debs.
When I fell, I looked up and he was grinning at me.
He never wanted me, and he never wanted the baby.
Now he's rid of the baby, and I don't know what to
do.'

'You talk to the police, that's what yer do!'

That possibility had crossed Lucy's mind. 'And if
I do, he'll only deny it. It will be my word against
his.'

'If it came right down to it, surely Steve would
have to back yer up? I mean, he must have seen it
all. Besides, it was his baby you were carrying. Sam
killed it, for God's sake! Surely Steve doesn't mean
to let him get away with murder?'

'I need to get Steve on my side, otherwise I'm
fighting a losing battle.' It was hard talking to him.
Harder still coming to terms with what his son had
done.

'If you don't tell the police, *I* will.'

Lucy had to smile. Debbie saw everything in black
or white. It must be a wonderful thing to be so
uncomplicated. 'I don't want the police involved just
yet,' she warned. 'I don't want you saying anything

to anybody, especially Steve or his son.' Suddenly she felt overwhelmed. Bowing her head, she murmured, 'I shouldn't have said anything to you. Not yet. I have to deal with it in my own way.'

Ashamed, Debbie clasped Lucy's thin figure to her. 'What am I thinking of, gal?' she asked brokenly. 'There's you hurt and bruised from top to bottom. You've lost your baby, yer marriage is in shreds. And there's me ... wanting to put yer through a police inquisition, and God knows what else. I'm sorry, gal. I'm a stupid bitch who deserves a kick up the arse.'

It was the kind of remark only Debbie could make, and it made Lucy smile. She assured Debbie there was nothing to reproach herself for. 'I know you want to help, and I'm grateful,' she said. 'But before any decision can be made, I have to make Steve admit the truth of what happened.'

'What about you and him? Can you go back after what's happened?'

Lucy was adamant on that one. 'No. It's over between us. It was never meant to be, I can see that now.'

'What will you do?'

It was a strange thing, but Lucy was convinced she saw a fleeting look of fear in Debbie's eyes.

'I haven't made up my mind about that yet,' she confessed. 'The doctor says it'll be a few more days yet before I'm allowed out, so I have plenty of time to think it through.'

Ever since the accident, Debbie had been entertaining a certain notion. She voiced it now. 'I think you should get in touch with Jack Hanson. One word about what's happened and he'll be here like a shot.'

Lucy's heart lurched. 'NO!'

'Why not?'

'You know why not. Jack's married now. What we had is long gone.'

'I don't believe that. Maybe he married for the same reasons you did. Maybe his marriage is just as big a mistake. Yer can say what yer like, I'll never believe he stopped loving you . . . any more than you stopped loving him. What! I've never seen two people so much in love as you and Jack.'

'Are you my friend?'

''Course I am. What kind o' bleedin' question is that?'

'If you are my friend, Debs, and if you want me to have peace of mind, then you're not to mention Jack again, and you're to let me sort my troubles out the best way I can. Will you do that for me, please?'

It was easy to see the mention of Jack had got Lucy agitated. That was the last thing she needed right now. ''Course I will, gal.' Debs grinned sheepishly. 'I ain't doing yer much good, am I? Me an' my big mouth.'

Lucy took hold of her hand. 'You're looking after me the best way you can,' she said, 'but there are deeper issues here, Debs, and I've made so many mistakes in the past, I need to get things right.'

'I understand.'

Wanting that particular subject closed, Lucy enquired, 'Have you and Alfie set a date for the wedding yet?'

'Not yet.'

'You're all right, aren't you?'

'Right as rain.'

'Any more news from your mam and dad?'

'Not yet, but I expect there'll be a letter any day.' She frowned. 'I'm keeping the house aired and clean for when they get back.'

They fell silent, Lucy convinced there was something Debbie was not telling her, and Debbie ashamed of her own lies. But these two had known each other too long not to respect the other's feelings.

'I'd better make tracks,' Debbie said presently. 'Look after yerself and give me a ring if yer need owt.'

When the nurse came round with the evening drinks, Lucy had hot chocolate and soon afterwards fell into a deep sleep.

The following morning the doctor came to see her. 'Everything seems fine now,' he said in his quiet caring manner. 'All being well, you should go home the day after tomorrow.' He scribbled instructions on to her chart before sauntering on to the next patient, a surly young woman who had rejected all offers of friendship from Lucy.

At two-thirty in the afternoon, Steve arrived. 'If I look haggard,' he started, 'it's because I've been called out twice in the night . . . a bad asthma attack, and an old man with a pain in his chest.' He smiled lazily. 'Too much chicken curry as it happened.'

When Lucy remained silent, he told her, 'I don't have surgery until seven-thirty, so I can stay as long as you like.' He kissed her, and hugged her, and held her hand, and she shrank from the very touch of him.

'I've had a word with the sister and she says you

might be allowed home the day after tomorrow.' His smile was charming as ever, but his eyes were shifty. 'It'll be good to have you home. We all miss you.'

Lucy stared at him, a spiral of cruelty rising in her. 'Sam too?' She never wanted to see that young man again so long as she lived. 'My, my! Fancy him missing me, and here was I, thinking he was disappointed I didn't break my neck.' She hated herself for being spiteful, but she wanted to hurt him, to hurt Sam, as he had hurt her. She wanted justice, but not of a kind that she couldn't live with. Steve was a weak man. His son was wicked. But Annabelle was just a child, warm and giving, desperately in need of love and crying out for Lucy to be the mother she craved.

Annabelle was the main reason why Lucy had not yet dragged the whole business out into the open. Her own life had already been screwed up. Would it solve anything to ruin Annabelle's too?

Yet what Sam had done had cost an innocent life. 'Face it, Steve,' she said now. 'Your son did this to me . . . to us. I need you to admit that.'

He glanced around furtively, obviously afraid someone might overhear. 'That's a very dangerous thing to say, my dear.'

'True, though.' She had to make him see.

His voice grated. '*Not* true. I've questioned Sam until I'm blue in the face, and he assures me it was an accident.'

'And you believe him?'

'Of course.'

Inside she was losing control. Outside she was calm. 'But you were there,' she insisted quietly. In her mind's eye she could see Sam at the top of the stairs, and Steve staring at him horrified before running down the stairs to her. 'You saw what he did.'

'No.' His smile was pitiful. Taking hold of her hand, he gently stroked it while he told her, in the same soft professional voice he might use on his patients, 'I can understand how you might imagine it was deliberate, but you're wrong. Sam has his bad points, I know, and there are times when I could choke him with my bare hands, but he would never do such a terrible thing. I've spent hours talking to him . . . trying to get at the truth. He promises me he didn't do it, and I have to believe him. Can't you see, Lucy? I HAVE TO BELIEVE HIM.'

Something in his voice, in his sad eyes, in the very things he was saying, told Lucy that he was trying to convince himself. He was a doctor with a vocation to save lives. For whatever reason, he could not bring himself to believe that his own son could do such a cruel thing.

While Steve's voice ran on, pleading, cajoling, arrogant then humble, Lucy was convinced: *he knew!*

However much he denied it, however much he wanted it not to be true, *he knew*. And the knowledge was more than he could bear.

'Lucy! Do you hear what I'm saying? Sam did not do this. You fell.' His voice broke, brown eyes looking up with that little-boy-lost expression. 'It was a tragic accident. We can't put the blame on anyone. Apart from a few torn ligaments and a sprained back . . . cuts and bruises, all superficial . . . you've come through it all right. As for losing the baby, I know it's hard but it isn't the end of the world. We can have other babies. We'll go away for a long holiday. When you come out of here, I'll take compassionate leave. Where would you like to go? Abroad? Somewhere in the sun? Just say the word, and I'll see to it.'

With every word he spoke, Lucy's heart fell further. He was never going to admit the truth. 'Go away,' she whispered. 'I need to think.'

Misreading her remark, he sprang to his feet, relieved and smiling. 'That's right, my dear,' he said jovially. 'Take your time. You think about it, and I'll be back tomorrow evening for your answer. A holiday, that's what we both need. We'll go away, and when we come back, all this nasty business will be forgotten.'

After he'd gone, Lucy got out of bed and sought out the nurse. 'Doctor said I could go home the day after tomorrow,' she reminded her. 'Only I need to go home today, if that's all right?'

The nurse was sympathetic. 'I can't see any reason why not,' she commented thoughtfully. Apart from the visible bruises on her neck and face, Lucy was well and healthy. There was no longer any danger of blood clotting, and two more days wouldn't make all that much difference. 'It's not up to me, though. I'll need to have a word with Sister.'

Lucy seated herself at the table and waited. It seemed like an age before the nurse returned. 'Go back to your bed,' she told Lucy. 'The doctor's coming to have another look at you.'

Curtains were drawn. Notes were consulted. Sister was taken aside and questioned, and finally the doctor gave Lucy the all clear. 'You can go home,' he told her. 'But you need to take things easy.'

She promised him she would, and within half an hour was on her way out.

Once in the taxi, she gave the address. As the car drove through Blackburn town, the tears welled up in her eyes. 'Another part of my life over,' she murmured. 'Another bad mistake.'

When the taxi got to her parents' old shop, she paid the driver and stepped out on to the pavement. The taxi drove off and she was left alone, save for a neighbour down the street who called out, 'Opening the shop again, are you, lass? I hope so, 'cause it ain't no fun traipsing all the way into town for a cabbage.' Without waiting for an answer, she went in and shut the door, still muttering under her breath as she did so.

Lucy was in no real hurry to go inside. Instead, she remained outside the shop, enjoying the May sunshine and staring up at the sign above the shop front. It bore her parents' names. Yet another reminder of a time gone for ever. 'This is where I belong,' she murmured. 'This is my life now.'

Rummaging in her bag, Lucy found the key. She had kept it in her bag since the day the shop closed, never dreaming she would return like this.

With mixed feelings, she let herself in. The shutters were up and the sunshine flooded in. 'That's funny, I thought I'd closed them,' she muttered. In fact she was certain they had been left closed. It's been a while, though, she realised, and the memory plays funny tricks.

In a kind of daze she wandered about, touching

this, touching that, lovingly running the tips of her fingers along the counter; that same counter behind which her mam and dad had served for many years.

She strolled through the store-room and into the kitchen, and it was here that she became suspicious. There was shopping on the table . . . a loaf of bread, half a pound of butter and a jar of strawberry jam, and beside that a brown purse with its measly contents spilling out. Lucy counted the coins. Three pounds fifty. 'What the devil is going on here?' It was curious and a little bit frightening to think there had been strangers in her parents' house while she was away.

A noise made her spin round. 'Who's there?' Hurrying to the door, she called out, 'You'd better show your face. If you don't, I'm warning you . . . I'll scream and fetch the whole street running.'

When she opened her mouth to scream, a grubby face appeared in the living-room doorway. 'Don't,' it pleaded with a cheeky grin. 'If you're gonna fetch the whole street running, I'd better wash and tidy up. I don't want folks thinking I'm a scruffy article.'

Lucy was shocked. 'Debs! What are you doing here?'

Coming down the hallway to the kitchen, Debbie told her proudly, 'I'm yer better class of squatter, gal. Before yer chuck me out, I'd best explain.'

Over a quickly brewed cup of tea, that was exactly what she did. It was a sad little tale, and soon won Lucy over.

'I had an idea you'd be coming back here,' she said. 'It got me worried, 'cause I've been staying here for three weeks now. As yer know, me and Alfie were

living in me mam and dad's house, but we argued so
I chucked him out. I tried staying there on me own,
but it were awful. I kept thinking of me mam and
dad, and how they weren't there any more, an' how
they might never come home – an' honest to God,
gal, I couldn't stand it. Besides, Alfie kept following
me home from work, and ringing me up every hour
God sent, so I buggered off an' broke in through yer
back winder. Don't worry, I had it fixed. Alfie don't
know where I am, an' he ain't got enough brains to
work it out.'

She sighed from her boots. 'An' he can't follow me
home any more, 'cause I ain't got a job for him to
follow me home from. I got the sack *again* for fighting
with a customer . . . silly cow!' She grinned. 'She came
into the café and asked for a slice of meat pie an' a
cup o' tea. Well! How were I to know the tea were
cold, and the pie had gone off? I were only helping
out while Mabel fetched some fresh bread rolls.
Besides, it ain't my bloody business to keep track of
what's good and what's been put out for the bin. And
anyway I thought the tea were only just brewed.
Instead, it had been standing for half an hour! Well,
the customer got stroppy an' called me some very
nasty names, so I gave her a smack. Mabel said the
customer were allus right, and that I should have
me mind on the job especially as they'd given me a
second chance. I told her to shove the bleedin' job,
an' now I'm out o' work.'

Her tale told, she slumped in the chair and looked
sorry for herself. 'I ain't much use, am I, gal?' she
asked woefully.

'You're too hot-headed, that's your trouble,' Lucy

declared. 'But I'm surprised at Mabel, letting you go. She's usually ready to accept an apology.'

'She asked me for one, an' I said she could take a running jump. She said to come back when I'd calmed down, but I'm not going back. I'll get meself another job, where I'm valued.'

Lucy could hardly take it all in. 'So! Let me recap. You argued with Alfie, then you threw him out of the house. You came here, broke in through a back window and made yourself comfortable, without letting me know. After that, you had an argument with a customer at work, because she had the cheek to complain when you gave her cold tea and a pie that had gone off. As if that wasn't enough, you lost your temper and gave her a smack into the bargain? You refused to apologise, fell out with Mabel, and got yourself sacked from a good job?' It was the worst catalogue of disasters even for Debs. 'And now it's everybody's fault but yours?'

Chewing on her bottom lip, Debbie looked crestfallen. 'It sounds awful when yer put it like that.'

'That's because it *is* awful!'

'Sorry, gal.'

Lucy shook her head in disbelief. 'Are you really sorry?'

'I reckon so.'

'Sorry enough to apologise to Mabel?'

'I might be . . . tomorrow.'

'You're a nightmare.' All the same, Lucy loved this madcap friend of hers. 'While we're at it, is there anything else you need to confess?' she laughed. 'I mean, you didn't demolish a building, rob a train or anything like that, did you?'

Debbie was silent for a minute, then in a soft voice she revealed, 'There is summat else you should know, gal.'

Cautioned by the look on Debbie's face, Lucy waited. For a long time now, she had known there was something . . . some private anxiety about her parents that Debs had always found too difficult to cope with. Lucy had never pressed her, thinking the time would come when Debs would find the strength to confide in her. Now the moment was here, Lucy thought it wisest to stay quiet and let her do the talking.

As the truth was revealed, it was Lucy's second shock since leaving hospital.

Debbie talked about her parents, about their love for each other, and how it was sorely tested by drink and violence. 'Folks thought it were me dad who drank but it weren't. *Me mam were the drunkard.*'

Lucy gasped, 'YOUR MAM?'

Debbie affirmed it with a nod. 'She were the one who beat me black and blue, and made my life a misery. She could never stand the idea of me going out, getting dressed up for a good time. She hated it when I seemed to be enjoying meself, so in the end I thought it safest to stay at home and not have any friends . . . except for you, and I'm thankful for that, gal. If it hadn't been for you, I think I'd have gone mad.'

'Did your mam have anything to do with your not getting together at first with Alfie?' Lucy was beginning to realise how it must have been.

Another affirmative nod. 'It made her crazy if she thought I'd got a fella.' She closed her eyes, reliving old memories. 'You can't know what it were like, gal,' she murmured. 'When me mam got drunk, she were like a maniac. Even me dad were frightened of her.'

Tears rolled down her face. 'I wanted to tell you, gal,' she said, 'but I didn't want you to get involved, and anyway I were so ashamed. Me dad always tried to make up for what she were doing, but it were no good. She couldn't help it, d'yer see, gal? Deep down she's a good sort, an' me and our dad, well, we do love her. Oh, but when she were violent! I were scared to death, I don't mind telling yer, gal. In the end, it got so bad I were frightened she might kill one of us. Anyway one night ... when I came back from seeing Alfie ... she went for me with a knife. After that our dad told her straight. "You get treatment," he said, "or I'm off, an' Debbie too. You'll be on yer own," he warned her.'

Debbie took a deep breath. 'Well, it seemed to do the trick 'cause soon afterwards she agreed to get treatment, but it had to be away from here, where nobody would know what were happening.' She gave a shaky smile. 'That's where they are now. Me mam's in a clinic down south, an' me dad's working so he can keep the house at this end. Yer see, gal, they both want to come home but not until she's cured or it'll be the same thing all over again.'

Lucy was lost for words. All this time she had thought it was Debbie's dad who got drunk and hit her, when it was her mam all along!

Going to her friend, she sat on the arm of her chair. With her hand in Debbie's, she said softly, 'I'm glad you told me. I want to help in any way I can, you know that.'

Having revealed the truth, Debbie now had another pressing matter on her mind. 'Will you be going
back to your husband, gal?'

'No, Debs.' Lucy had made up her mind long ago
on that issue. 'I won't be going back.'

'Are yer staying here then?'

Lucy smiled down at her. 'That's the idea, kid.'

Grinning, all her cares laid aside, Debbie asked,
'Will yer be looking for a lodger?'

Laughing out loud, Lucy gave her a good-natured
punch in the arm. 'Why? Are you offering?'

'If you'll have me, gal.'

Pondering a moment, Lucy made a serious face.
'Oh, I don't know about that. I mean . . . you look to
me like the type who might cause a lot of damage,
or even end up fighting with customers.'

Seeing the twinkle in Lucy's eye, Debbie began to
giggle until they were both laughing and squealing,
like two young things who hadn't a care in the world.

Until Debbie remembered with horror that Lucy
was only just out of hospital. Mortified, she scrambled
to her feet, insisting on getting Lucy 'A drop o' the
good stuff which I brought with me when I broke in
through yer back winder.'

While Debbie went off for the 'good stuff', Lucy
took a stroll through the house. 'God! It's filthy!' She
couldn't believe the amount of dust that had accumu-
lated, nor the mouse droppings on the bedroom floor.
'I never knew we had mice in here,' she pondered
aloud.

Debbie's voice answered from the doorway. 'You've
probably had 'em all the time, gal,' she said. 'This is
a greengrocer's after all, and where there's scraps

of food, there's allus mice.' Handing Lucy a glass, she visibly shivered. 'I heard the little sods last night, scraping and running about. I couldn't get no sleep.'

'We'll have to get rid of them.' Absent-mindedly raising the glass to her lips, Lucy took a mouthful of the pale liquid. 'Bloody hell, Debs!' she cried, gasping for breath. 'What have you put in it?'

'Gin and tonic,' she replied with a wide smile. 'That's what the toffs drink.'

Lucy sniffed at her glass. 'Smells like methylated spirits to me.'

'Ungrateful bugger! Drink it up. It'll put hairs on yer chest.'

'Don't know as I want hairs on my chest.' All the same she drank it, and took a minute to recover. 'We'll have to clean this place from top to bottom.'

'I'm not arguing with that.' Rolling up her sleeves, Debbie offered, 'Being as you've come straight out of hospital, I'll make a start. You can keep the tea coming.'

Lucy was having none of it. 'We'll both get stuck in,' she declared. 'But there's no need for us to work ourselves into the ground. So long as it's dusted and the beds are clean, everything else can be done over a matter of weeks. This is a big old place, and if we're to go through it properly, it'll take weeks rather than days.'

She glanced round, at the jaded curtains and the grimy windows. 'I left this place spotless,' she recalled. 'How could it have got so grubby?'

Debbie had an answer to that. 'It ain't been lived in for some time. When a place is left empty, dirt and dust accumulate. You move out and the world moves in. It's a fact o' life, gal.'

'I move out and *you* move in,' Lucy laughed. 'But we're back, and I'm glad.' Warmth and relief flowed through her.

Debbie read the signs. 'Thinking of the old times, eh, gal?' she murmured. 'Thinking of Jack, ain't yer?'

Lucy couldn't lie. 'Yes,' she answered softly. 'I was thinking of how it used to be . . . Mam and Dad, and yes, Jack too. All the plans, the dreams.' She sighed aloud, her heart aching. 'Oh, Debs! Wasn't it wonderful then? Where did it all go wrong?'

'It could be wonderful again, if only you'd get in touch with him.'

Straight away, Lucy regretted letting her deeper feelings show. 'That's not possible, and you know it,' she reprimanded Debbie. 'Jack's got himself a wife now. He's forgotten the past and that's what I have to do. I know I've only myself to blame. Maybe I shouldn't have sent him away, but I had no choice, you know that.' Anger rose in her like a tidal wave. 'Later, though, he could have tried harder to be with me. He didn't write, and he didn't phone. I had no right to ask him to sacrifice everything because of me, but I never stopped wanting him.'

'I know that, gal.'

'His feelings for me must have been shallow because, if he really loved me, he would have moved Heaven and Earth to be with me. He's shrugged me off . . . forgotten everything we had.' In a broken voice, she whispered, 'Now I have to try with all my heart to do the same. Please, Debs. Don't make it more difficult than it already is.'

Even with Debbie standing beside her, Lucy felt more alone than at any other time in her life. Funny how things had gone full circle. She'd started here, in her parents' shop, and now she was back, leaving behind her a trail of broken promises, shattered dreams and a ruined marriage. And all she had to show for it was a broken heart.

Debbie saw the loneliness in her friend and it moved her to ask, 'D'yer want to talk about it, gal?'

Without speaking, Lucy draped an arm round Debs's shoulders. 'You're good for me,' she told her. 'But, no, there's nothing I want to talk about.'

'What's the plan then, gal?'

Lucy's grey eyes lit up. 'The plan?' she mused.

'We need a plan, gal.'

Lucy was in fighting form now. 'So we do. But first, you apologise to Mabel.'

'I don't want to go back there,' Debbie protested. 'I were never cut out for working in a garden centre. Little plants, and lots of glass, and hosepipes everywhere. I'm too bleedin' clumsy.'

Lucy laughed. 'Tell me something I don't know!'

'Well, now you can see why I don't want to go back.'

'If you say so.'

'I'll go out and look for something tomorrow.'

'You don't have to go out.' Lucy's smile gave it all away. 'You can work here with me.'

'Oh, gal!' Jumping for joy, she threw her arms round Lucy. 'You and me, gal, working here together again? Oh, I like the sound o' that.'

'It won't be easy,' Lucy warned. 'We'll have to work hard. I've got little money to speak of, and I dare say we won't get credit straight away. But I know we can do it. We can make this place the way it used to be. What do you say?'

'I say, go for it.' Thumping the air with a clenched fist, Debbie was thrilled. 'Go for it, gal, and sod the lot of 'em.'

Excited, Debbie went to search for another drop of the good stuff. 'Let's celebrate, gal,' she cried as she skipped down the stairs.

While she could be heard singing her heart out below, Lucy stood in the doorway of her parents' bedroom. 'Well, I'm back,' she murmured. 'Back to bring your little shop alive again.'

If she was hoping for some kind of encouragement, maybe a sign that they had heard and were glad, she was disappointed.

Outside, the wind blew against the window pane. Down in the street children played and laughed. The sound echoed round the room, making her smile.

When she turned to leave, the smile had gone. Lucy felt lonelier than at any other time in her life.

As she closed the door, a slim, bright ray of sunshine lit the spot where she had been standing. It lingered for a while, bathing the room in a soft, warm glow.

Coming to the bottom of the stairs, she had the strangest feeling. Turning, she glanced up towards her parents' room.

'By the way, gal,' Debs's voice seared into her thoughts, 'what's gonna happen when that husband o' yours finds out you've left him for good?'

Chapter Eighteen

Steve Ryman was not used to being rejected. A man in control of his own destiny, he liked to think he answered to no one.

It had been weeks since Lucy had left the hospital without his knowledge. Since that day, he'd lived in fear that he might lose her for ever. When he finally discovered where she was, he besieged her with phone calls, personal visits and letters, pleading desperately for her to 'Come home, and we'll start again.'

Lucy's answer was always the same. 'My home is here now. We both know it was never with you.' But still he persisted until she was beside herself with despair.

On this particular hot and sultry June morning she made her way downstairs. En route to the kitchen, she collected the mail from the front door-mat. 'Oh, no!' The writing on the stubby blue envelope was painfully familiar. 'Why can't he leave me be?'

Coming into the kitchen, she was surprised to see Debbie already at the cooker, frying the eggs and bacon she so enjoyed. 'Want some, gal?' she asked.

'Not for me, thanks. Look here, Debs.' She threw the clutch of letters on the table. 'Another one from

Steve. He just won't let up, will he?' Sorting the envelope from the others, she tore it in half and dropped it in the bin.

'Hey!' Debbie was naturally nosy. It astonished her that anyone could throw away a letter without reading it first. 'Ain't yer gonna look at it?'

'No need.' Lucy knew the contents, chapter and verse. She had received a letter regularly almost every single day since coming here; even on the days when Steve turned up to plead with her in person. 'I can guess what it says,' she told Debbie. 'I don't need to read it.'

Taking up the spatula, Debbie scooped her eggs and bacon on to the plate and ambled over to the table; she'd put weight on since working with Lucy. 'It's a sign of happiness,' she would tell anyone who made a comment. 'That's why yer miserable buggers are pencil thin.' After a time the comments died down and so she tempered her eating habits and was gradually winning the fight against the flab.

Coming to the table, she flushed a little mountain of tomato sauce over her eggs, asking coyly, 'D'yer mind if I read the letter, gal?'

'Help yourself,' Lucy told her with a little smile. 'But I can tell you word for word what it says.'

'Hmm.' Licking her fingers, Debbie plucked the torn article out of the bin. Spreading it out on the table, she pieced it together and carefully perused it. 'All right then, clever clogs,' she said, hiding the letter with her hands, 'what does it say?'

Lucy got herself a cup of tea and sat down opposite. After considering for a moment she said, 'He's got a busy schedule, but he desperately needs to see me.

Will I meet him somewhere, and if not, can I give him a ring? If I haven't rung by Friday night, he'll be round to see me on Saturday morning.'

Debbie stared round-eyed. 'Gawd Almighty, gal.' She flicked the two halves towards Lucy. 'See fer yerself. Word for word, that's what he says.'

Without further ado, Lucy flung them back into the bin. Sipping her tea, she let her thoughts drift.

Ramming a forkful of bacon into her mouth, Debbie chewed for a minute before muttering, 'The bugger's driving yer crazy, ain't he?'

'You could say that,' Lucy replied thoughtfully. 'More to the point, he's driving himself crazy.'

'Could be dangerous, gal. He seems determined to get yer back, and won't take no for an answer.'

'I'm *never* going back.' The idea of living in that house again, with Sam and his father, made her blood run cold.

Debbie regarded her for a while. 'Yer look washed out, gal,' she observed. 'Don't let him get to yer.'

'He won't. Don't you worry.' But he *was* getting to her. He was obsessed, and nothing Lucy said seemed to have any effect on him.

'Lucy?'

'What's on your mind now?'

'Nothing much. I were just thinking, d'yer reckon it's a good thing . . . Ted making up with that son of his?'

'Who knows?' Lucy wondered too. 'I hope he's done the right thing. Mabel seemed to think so when she rang to tell me. And if it's true what she said, that George's greedy ambitious wife was behind the hostilities, driving a wedge between father and son

431

and looking to get what she could out of it for herself, well, maybe he's done right to drop her and turn to his dad. When all's said and done, blood is thicker than water.'

'Yer ain't really gonna come to a deal with Ted about yer share of the business takings, are yer?'

'Seems the logical thing to do.' She drank the dregs of her tea, leaned her elbows on the table and her chin on her fists, deep in thought for a moment. 'I do hope it works out for Ted and his son,' she said finally.

Debbie had other things on her mind. 'I don't know how yer can get up of a morning and not have any breakfast.' The idea was unthinkable to her. 'There's some bacon under the grill if yer want it?'

'No, thanks.'

'Phew! Hot, ain't it, gal?' Debbie ran her finger round the neck of her blouse. 'Yesterday yer could have fried eggs on the pavement.'

'Hottest June on record, they say.' Lucy didn't like the hot weather.

'What did young Annabelle say?'

Lucy was deep in thought. The letter was preying on her mind. 'What?'

Sighing, Debbie collected her plate and took it to the sink where she slid it into the washing-up water. 'Last night Annabelle came to see yer just as me and Alfie were on our way out,' she reminded Lucy. 'I thought she looked worried. Just wondered what she had to say, that's all.'

'Oh, yes.' In fact it was what Annabelle had said that had kept Lucy awake half the night. 'She said her dad and Sam are at each other's throats the whole time. Apparently Steve thinks I'll go back if Sam's out of the way so he's asked his son to leave. Sam says it's all my fault.'

'Bugger Sam Ryman! If he clears off, he'll do us all a favour. He needs teaching a lesson, if yer ask me.' Rolling up her sleeves, Debbie started washing the dishes. 'I know somebody else who could do with the same,' she muttered. 'That bloody Alfie is getting on me nerves.'

Laughing softly, Lucy recalled, 'I heard the two of you arguing when he brought you home last night.' 'Arguing' was a mild description. They were going at it hammer and tongs. 'What's he done to upset you now?'

'Same as always,' she answered wearily. 'He won't see reason about nothing. Dunno why I had the bugger back in the first place.'

'Because you belong together, that's why, and you know it.'

'Anyway, I asked him about laying the new carpet in the lounge and he said he'd be glad to do it.'

'There you are then, the man's a little gem.'

'A little squirt, y'mean.'

Lucy glanced at the clock. It was seven-thirty. 'If we're to have the shop open by eight, we'd best get a move on.' Running a greengrocer's was hard work. 'We picked up more old customers last week. If we keep on at this rate, we'll be in full swing by Christmas.'

Suddenly Debbie was quietly asking Lucy the very same question she had asked herself over and over since coming back here. 'I know you'll never go back to Steve, gal, and I'm glad about that because yer don't belong there, but . . . what I'm trying to say in me own clumsy way is this . . . d'yer belong *here*? Are yer sure it's what yer really want?'

'That's a funny thing to ask.' Because she had been thinking of leaving. Going away somewhere to make a brand new start. 'Are *you* happy here, Debs?'

'In me bleedin' element, gal,' came the enthusiastic reply. 'But that ain't answering my question, is it? And I don't want you to keep this place on for me. Yer not, are yer?'

Lucy gave a flippant reply, but in her heart there was an altogether different answer. ''Course I'm not keeping it on just for you,' she said with feigned surprise. 'Who do you think I am, Lady Bountiful?'

Lucy didn't have time to dwell too much on Debbie's remark. All day long they were kept busy. Yet again it was a hot, sultry day, seeming to sap a body's strength. At the end of it they took a ten-minute break before stocking up with fruit and veg from the store-room. 'See that?' Lucy said, pointing to the array of succulent produce. 'That's all our worldly goods laid out there. If we sell that lot tomorrow, we'll be in the black at the bank for the first time.'

Debbie was delighted. 'No worries about that,' she said confidently. 'Today were our busiest day yet, an' tomorrow's Saturday. We allus do well on a Saturday. Besides, all yer dad's customers are flooding back.'

Lucy had noticed it too. 'Folks round here are loyal.'

'There y'are then, gal. You'll see. Come Christmas, it'll be like the old days.'

Later that evening, when Lucy sat at the dressing-table, brushing her hair, Debbie's comments made her think. 'You don't miss much, Debbie Lately,' she said into the mirror. 'And you're right, I'm not happy here. They say you should never go back, and now I know why. Nothing is ever the same. Nothing means the same as it once did.' Somehow she had lost her way. Lost Jack. Lost her baby. Lost her place in the order of things. 'Come Christmas, it'll be like the old days.' That's what Debs had said. 'But it isn't what I want.'

In all truth, she didn't know *what* she wanted.

Except for Jack.

She wanted him, just as she had always wanted him. But Jack was gone.

'Time to go, Lucy gal.' She smiled as she mimicked Debbie's no-nonsense tone of voice. 'Time to get off yer arse and make for pastures new.'

While Lucy slept, Debbie and her 'little gem' crept in at the front door. 'Tek yer shoes off, yer bugger,' Debbie whispered harshly. 'Just 'cause we're having a new carpet next week, don't mean yer can fetch mud in all over this one.' Having been out on the town and sunk a glass or two of the 'good stuff', she was in a merry, raunchy mood. 'Yer can tek yer trousers off an' all if yer like,' she chuckled. 'It's yer lucky night, yer bugger . . . so you'd best make the most of it.'

An hour later, after rolling about on the floor and making magic, she saw him to the door. As he went on his way he burst into song. He was in a world of his own until someone opened a window and emptied

Josephine Cox

a pan of cold water over him. 'On yer bloody way!'
an angry voice yelled. 'Afore I tek a mind to empty
the piss-pot an' all!'

Pausing outside Lucy's room, Debbie pressed her
ear to the door. Sure enough, her friend could be
heard, softly crying.

She tapped on the door. 'Lucy? Can I come in, gal?'
No answer.

Carefully she opened the door and went in. The
curtains were open as always and the room was lit
only by a shaft of light from the lamp outside. Lucy
was lying on her side, one arm draped over the pillow,
the other hanging out of bed. She seemed to be asleep.
Debbie stepped nearer. 'Lucy?'

Only the ticking of the clock disturbed the quietness.

'Must have been hearing things,' she muttered.
'The gal's fast asleep.'

On bare feet she made her way to the door, only
to stop when she heard the crying again. Straining
her eyes towards the bed, she realised with a shock
that Lucy was sobbing in her sleep. 'Poor little sod,'
she murmured softly. 'She ain't got much to look
forward to, has she, eh?'

Quietly, she closed the door and went downstairs.
Seeing Lucy like that was a sobering, upsetting
experience.

For a time she wasn't sure what to do, but at the
back of her mind was Jack Hanson. 'Yer bugger, Jack,
yer should have taken more care of her,' she grumbled. 'Why didn't yer write? Why didn't yer come
and see her, eh? What kind of a bleedin' friend would

turn his back on a lovely gal like our Lucy?'

Angry now, her mind was made up. 'She won't thank me for it,' she muttered, 'but somebody should tell the bugger he's needed. An' if Lucy won't, then I will!'

Chapter Nineteen

'What the Hell's the matter with you, Jack?' For the past few minutes, the older man had been desperately trying to get his undivided attention. 'You're like a cat on hot bricks. Dammit, man! Have you heard one single thing I've said?'

Jack turned from the window. 'Sorry,' he apologised. 'Can't seem to focus my mind these days.'

He knew why. As the days, weeks and months went by he could think of nothing but Lucy. The last time he had seen her was still deeply etched in his memory. She'd looked like a princess in her wedding dress, smiling and happy. But not with him. NOT WITH HIM!

'We all have days like that,' the older man remarked sympathetically. 'But you know as well as I do, I can't afford the time to sit here talking to myself. I've got a business to run, with a schedule so tight I can hardly turn round.'

Jack understood. He too was at the sharp end of a business that created its own pressures. 'You're right,' he readily agreed. 'Might be better if we reschedule the meeting?'

On that they shook hands and went their separate ways, the land agent to catch a flight to Miami and Jack to return to his office.

* * *

'Of course. Yes, I understand.'

With the telephone receiver against her ear, the clerk carefully read back her own writing. 'The message is from Debbie in England. Lucy's marriage is over, and she needs a friend.'

A pause, then, 'Of course, I'll see he gets the message the minute he comes back. No, I can assure you, I won't forget.'

Replacing the receiver, she turned to her colleague. 'Somebody got out of bed the wrong side if you ask me.'

'Oh? Who are we talking about?'

The clerk consulted her notepad. 'This "Debbie" from England. She wanted Mr Hanson. Got really agitated when I told her he wasn't here.'

'Hmm! Wonder if it's an old girlfriend?' the other woman remarked with a wink. With that, she hurried into the back office to check an urgent booking.

On her way to the lift, Maria overheard the entire conversation. Sweeping up to the desk, she held out a manicured hand. 'Let me see that,' she demanded.

The clerk hesitated. 'I'm not sure,' she replied nervously. 'I made a mistake once before, and now he's very fussy about getting his messages first-hand.' She didn't like Maria. Not many people did.

Maria stared at her. 'I beg your pardon!'

The clerk paled. 'I'm sorry, miss, I know you're Mr Hanson's personal assistant and everything, but if he doesn't get the message, I'll be held personally responsible. I might even get the sack.'

Maria smiled sweetly. 'Mr Hanson won't sack you,' she said. 'And there's no question of the message

440

not getting to him.' She didn't want to make too much fuss, fearing the incident might then be reported to Jack.

Inwardly irritated but keeping her cool, she took the notepad from the clerk's hand and perused the message there. Afterwards, she tore out the page and pretended to treat it with reverence. 'Don't worry,' she said, 'it will be on his desk waiting for him the minute he gets back. It's good to see you're on your toes all the same.' As she turned, her eyes looked up at the clock. It was almost six. 'I understand you're off on a week's holiday in a few minutes,' she called out. 'Leave the work behind and have a lovely time.'

'Thank you,' the clerk replied, afterwards muttering under her breath, 'She's right. I've got enough to worry about without fretting over one little message.'

When her colleague returned she said the very same. 'Let Miss High and Mighty take responsibility for it. After all, it's what she gets paid for.'

Chapter Twenty

Lucy rolled up the blind on the shop door, turned the OPEN sign round to face the outside, then drew back the bolt. 'Now then,' she said, returning to where Debbie was emptying coins into the till, 'you can tell me what's wrong.' For the past week Debbie had been in the foulest mood.

Lucy received the same answer as she had yesterday, and the day before, and the day before that. 'Dunno what yer talking about. There ain't nothing wrong with me.' Debbie dropped a handful of coins on the floor. They scattered in every direction. 'Now see what you've made me do!'

'Leave them.'

'What?'

Taking her by the arm, Lucy swung her round. 'There *is* something wrong,' she insisted, 'and I want to know what. Is it something I've done or said?'

'No, it bloody well ain't.'

Lucy sighed. 'You and Alfie have had another argument?'

'We ain't had a cross word for ages now.'

'What then?'

'Nothing! I've already said. Now let me collect them coins afore the customers start coming in.'

443

Keeping a firm grip on her arm, Lucy was adamant. 'You can do what you like once you've told me the truth. Who's upset you?'

Looking up, Debbie saw old Mrs Pollard staring in at the window. 'Eh up, gal,' she said. 'Here's a customer.'

Still Lucy would not be budged. 'We've always confided in each other, you and I, Debs,' she reminded her. 'If you're worried about Steve keeping on bothering me, I've decided to take your advice and see a solicitor. I've got an appointment the day after tomorrow.'

Debbie's face broke into a relieved smile. 'Oh, I'm glad about that, gal. But, no, I weren't worrying me head about that, 'cause I knew you'd have to see a solicitor in the end.'

'If you weren't worrying about that too much, then what's upset you?' She was determined to get to the bottom of it. 'Look, Debs, if you've got a problem, I want to know. Is it money? Am I not paying you enough?'

'Don't be daft. You pay me more than you pay yerself.'

'Then what is it?' Debbie was all she had in the world now. 'I hate to see you upset, and it's been going on for a week now.'

Old Mrs Pollard was walking towards the shop doorway. 'Later, gal,' Debbie promised. 'I'll tell yer later.'

Lucy wouldn't let it go. '*Now*,' she urged. 'Tell me *now*.' She too was acutely aware that old Mrs Pollard would be in the shop at any minute, once she'd passed the time of day with a kindly neighbour who'd stopped to enquire about the old dear's health.

Realising Lucy would not be put off yet again, Debbie told her the truth. 'I know yer won't like what I've done,' she started, 'but I heard you crying in yer sleep and I wanted to give Jack Hanson a piece of my mind. I mean . . . he could have written, gal. Why didn't he?'

'What have you done, Debs?' Lucy could feel her stomach turning over while she waited for the answer.

'I remembered where he'd gone, and I got the number from directory enquiries.' She gulped hard. 'I'm sorry, gal.' She gulped, then defiantly cried, 'NO, I'M NOT!' She stared at Lucy's white shocked face. 'I'm not sorry I rang, 'cause now I know he's a bad 'un. I left a message for him to ring back . . . told him yer were in a bit of a state and needed a friend. That were a week since, and he still ain't rung back.'

Lucy stared, her voice merely a whisper as she answered, 'I wish you hadn't done that.'

'I knew yer wouldn't like it, gal, but I really thought he might still have some feeling left for yer. Even if he's married, it don't mean he can't be a friend.'

Lucy was assailed by all manner of emotions. Now, as she spoke, her grip tightened so hard on Debbie's arm that she cried out. 'If he'd wanted to ring or write he would have done. I was the one who sent him away, and now it's plain he wants to forget me. That's his right.' Choking back the tears, she went on softly, 'As for having him as a friend, that would be too painful. I still love him, you see.' Now she couldn't hold back the tears. They tumbled from her sad grey eyes and ran down her face; big, silent tears that she had managed to hide from the world for so long. 'I love him so much, I can't think straight any more. But it's all too late now, Debs. It's better this way. Better that we never see each other again.'

'Oh, gal.' Debbie cried too. Seeing Lucy like this was so hurtful. For what seemed a lifetime, she had looked up to Lucy as the strong one, the one everyone turned to in their times of need. Now it was Lucy's time of need and there was no one to help. 'Yer right,' she admitted, 'I shouldn't have rung him. I've only made things worse for yer, gal. Like I allus do.'

Swallowing her tears, Lucy wiped her eyes. 'No, you haven't,' she lied. 'In a way I'm glad you rang him, because now I know he doesn't care at all.' The knowledge was like a shaft through her heart, but the pain would pass, and when it did, she would be a wiser woman for it.

Now, when old Mrs Pollard could be heard calling, 'HELLO! IS THERE ANYBODY HERE OR WHAT?' Lucy laughed. 'You'd best go and see to the old dear while I take a minute to freshen up.'

While Lucy went to her room, Debbie came back into the shop. 'What's all the racket, yer silly old bugger?' she demanded. 'Hang on a minute while I pick these coins up. And no, yer can't taste the grapes afore yer buy them. Yer caught me on that one last week, and yer still didn't buy none, yer crafty old sod!'

Upstairs, Lucy sat in front of the dressing-table, her thoughtful gaze studying the face in the mirror.

It was a pale and weary one; a face filled with life's experiences; a face that had cried, and laughed, and seen things that stayed with her day and night.

Sad things. Wonderful things. Things she would never see again, except in her mind's eye.

That same face had been kissed by many people – people who loved her: her mam and dad, Debbie, and Jack.

She smiled and the face was beautiful, the skin that of a young girl. The shining brown hair framed it like a rich, dark halo. The grey eyes grew soft and filled with wonder. She said it again, softly to herself: 'Kissed by Jack.' Fingers reached up to stroke the mouth tenderly. It was a wonderful thought.

Kissed by Jack.

She let it sink in. Memories flooded back.

'But he's not here now,' she murmured, 'and he never will be again.'

She sat up straight, a new determination taking hold in her. 'You need a challenge. A new life.'

Suddenly she felt invigorated. That was it!

She stood up, squared her shoulders, and decided it was time to move on. But before you can go forward, Lucy Nolan, you have to go back. She straightened her skirt and patted her hair, a look of resignation on her face as she returned downstairs.

Debbie was delighted when told of Lucy's plan to make a new life elsewhere. 'But I don't understand,' she queried. 'What d'yer mean, "go back"?'

Lucy felt clearer in her mind than she had done for a long time. 'I mean, revisit places I've been before. Places where I've known some of the happiest days of my life. I have to get it out of my system, once and for all.'

Debbie was beginning to understand. 'Won't it be too painful, gal?'

'Maybe. But it will be worth it,' Lucy said. 'If it helps me to lay the ghosts, now and for good.'

Two days later, on the morning of a hot and glorious June day, Lucy was packed and ready for off. She had on a pretty white blouse with blue embroidered cornflowers at the lapels, a blue straight skirt, and a paler blue jacket. 'Yer look lovely, gal.' Debbie fussed and fretted, and soon they were on the doorstep saying goodbye. 'I wish you'd tell me where yer going?' Debbie wailed.

'I'm not sure myself,' Lucy told her, 'but I'll ring, don't worry.' She glanced at Alfie who was standing a discreet distance away. 'I'll ring you,' she promised. 'You'll be all right. You've got your Alfie, and you've got the run of the house.'

She hugged Debbie for a minute, winked at Alfie, who wondered what she was winking at, then delighted and astonished them both by saying, 'When I get back, we'll talk about you and Alfie taking over this place for good.'

In a minute she was in the taxi and on her way, leaving Alfie and Debs open-mouthed, staring at each other in amazement, and wondering if they'd heard right.

A few evenings later, Debbie watched while Alfie began rolling up the lounge carpet. 'Leave that 'til we've had our tea,' she told him, holding her nose. 'Yer throwing up a cloud o' dust.'

The tea was on the table when the doorbell rang. 'Bleedin' typical!' Debbie moaned, making her way to the door. 'What now?' She flung it open and froze on the spot. 'WELL, I'M BUGGERED!' Her eyes stood out like hatpins as she stared at the visitor: a man in his late twenties, tall and handsome with square shoulders, and dark hair, and ocean-green eyes that looked as if they had known torture of a kind. 'Jack Hanson of all people!' Debbie's voice. 'What the Hell do *you* want?'

Without waiting for an answer, she tore into him with a vicious tongue. 'You're not wanted here, so piss off!'

'I've only just got your message,' he said. 'Where is she?'

'Hmm! Some bloody tale!' she screeched. 'If you'd been here a week ago I would have welcomed yer with open arms, but yer weren't and now it's too late. Lucy's gone. So, like I said, piss off afore I call the police.'

Realising she was in no mood for explanations, he peered beyond her into Alfie's worried, curious face. 'I've waited for this day too long to be turned away now. You won't get rid of me easily so, please, tell me where I can find her.'

Two things happened then. Alfie stepped forward to speak to him and Debbie threw her arm out sideways to stop him, and sent him flying against the wall. 'You're not to tell him anything!' she yelled. 'He weren't here when Lucy needed him. He never wrote, and now he's married to some other woman, he can bloody well get back to her!'

Alfie was out of his depth. 'I've a job to do inside,' he muttered, 'I'd best get back to it.' With that he shuffled away.

Jack wanted to explain, but sensed it would be

useless. Besides, there was only one reason he was here and that was Lucy. 'You're making a mistake,' he argued. 'If you'll only calm down and listen . . .'

Setting herself in the doorway, Debbie glared at him. '*You're* the one making a mistake,' she said. 'Lucy don't want yer, an' bloody good job. I ain't gonna tell yer where she is, so yer can camp on the doorstep from now 'til Christmas, it won't do yer no good.'

She made to slam shut the door, but wasn't quick enough. Taking her by surprise, Jack darted forward and grabbed her by the shoulders. 'What the devil's wrong with you, woman?' he growled. 'You sent for me, and I'm here. I've already told you, I only got the message yesterday. Now, where is she?'

'I don't believe yer.' But doubt was already creeping in.

'For God's sake, Lucy means more to me than you'll ever know. If you love her at all, you'll tell me where she is!'

Debbie looked into those sincere green eyes and saw something there that touched her heart. 'Happen yer telling the truth after all,' she muttered, her voice growing harder when she reminded him, 'if yer love Lucy like yer say, how come yer could marry some other woman, eh?'

He shook his head, eyes softly smiling as he thought of what she had said. 'I'm not married to any other woman,' he told her. 'You've got to believe me.'

She stared at him a moment longer, wishing she could see inside his mind. But she couldn't and so she must follow her instinct. 'All right,' she said worriedly. 'I don't know exactly where Lucy is, but she phoned last night ... from some place in Lymington.'

His eyes lit up. 'Lymington? Is she in a hotel?'

'I don't know. All I do know is she were on about the big ships and how she'd only been in Lymington for a day or so. She were gonna ring me again when she moved on.'

'Debbie Lately, you're a darling!' Kissing her on the mouth, he made her blush. 'Even if you do swear like an old sailor.'

As he ran down the path, Alfie came to the door. 'Look at these!' he cried, shoving a bunch of old letters under Debbie's nose. 'I found 'em under the mattress.'

As she rummaged through them, Debbie couldn't believe her eyes. 'Gawd Almighty!' she shrieked, running down the path. 'Jack! Look here! Look here!'

He was climbing into his hired car when she reached him. 'I don't understand it,' she said, puzzled yet excited. 'These letters are from you to Lucy. Alfie just found 'em under the mattress.'

Jack took the letters and glanced through them. 'That's right,' he said, wondering what all the fuss was about. As he touched them, his heart was filled with thoughts of Lucy. 'She must still want me,' he murmured. 'Or she wouldn't have kept my letters.'

'No! You don't understand. Lucy never knew about the letters. She wondered why yer never wrote to her. That's why she thought you'd stopped loving her.' She pointed to the clutch of letters in his hand. 'Listen to me, Jack, I'm telling yer, Lucy never even knew them letters existed.'

It was a puzzle, but in a way he began to see. 'You

mean, she thought I'd deserted her. After her mam died, she thought I'd turned my back on her? Is that what you're saying?'

Debbie was too choked to answer, but Alfie, who had come to put an arm round his woman, answered for her. 'That's what she's saying,' he said softly. 'The letters were hidden under the mattress. Lucy must have been near them every day and never even known it'

As Jack got back into the car and drove away, they stood there, shaken, wondering how Lucy could not have known about the letters, not really sure how they could have got under the mattress and not daring to voice what was in their minds. One thing was certain. Somebody must have put the letters there, and if it wasn't Lucy, who else could it have been? The answer stared them in the face. It didn't bear thinking about.

It was late afternoon when Lucy alighted from a taxi on the quayside. 'Thank you,' she said, dropping the fare into the cab-driver's chubby hand. 'I thought we'd never make it, especially with the roadworks holding up the traffic.'

'No problem,' he said jovially. 'If you hurry, you should get a cup of tea on board before the queues form.'

That's just what Lucy did. Taking her tea, she found a quiet little corner on the deck and, with the sun streaming down on her face, settled back and closed her eyes. She felt better now; not happy, not yet, just better. It was a start.

When she opened her eyes, the sun blinded her

for a moment. She blinked, reached out for her cup of tea, and was momentarily confused. There was a small bundle lying on the table. A closer glance showed it to be a bundle of letters.

She glanced round. The bundle hadn't been there before she'd closed her eyes, and no one else seemed the slightest bit interested in it. Everyone was busy, talking, laughing, showing their children the big ships and other craft on the water.

Curious now, she looked more closely, a strange feeling coming over her as her eyes skimmed the writing on the first envelope.

It was addressed to her!

The writing seemed disturbingly familiar. She shook her head. Her mind was playing tricks on her, she thought.

As she reached out to pick it up, a thrill ran through her when long strong fingers closed over hers. 'You look lovely with the wind in your hair and the sun on your face.' His soft, vibrant voice turned her heart upside down. 'Oh, Lucy! My lovely, darling Lucy. I won't let you send me away this time.'

Confused and thrilled, she didn't dare to look up. She didn't dare to hope. It wasn't true. How could it be?

But then he put his arms round her and drew her out of her seat. 'I love you,' he whispered in her ear. 'I've never stopped loving you.' He kissed her face, tenderly wiping away the tears that fell from her eyes as she looked up and saw that it was really true. Jack was here. She was in his arms. Dear God! Oh, dear God!

Just for a second the sun dazzled her. But then he leaned forward and she was looking into those familiar green eyes, eyes that mirrored the love she felt, and she was lost for words.

His soft, warm mouth closed over hers and the questions didn't matter.

Nothing mattered, only that she and Jack were together again.

She didn't understand why or how.

But that was for later.

Chapter Twenty-One

On New Year's Day the following year, Jack and Lucy stood on the verandah of their villa, arm in arm, watching the sun set over a jewelled sea.

'You're not sorry we didn't have a big wedding, are you, sweetheart?'

Her bright contented smile was answer enough. She raised her hand and gazed at the wedding ring which he had put on her finger. 'How could I be sorry?' she said, thinking how her marriage to Steve had been a lavish and disastrous mistake.

But that was all behind her now. It had been a hard struggle, with Steve being particularly difficult, but she'd won through in the end. By all accounts, Steve Ryman had moved to the West Country. Sam had gone with him, and Annabelle too. Annabelle had been a worry but the girl had proved to be both wise and worldly. Realising her place was with the family she had grown more content.

Debbie's voice sailed up from the garden below. 'If *you* ain't sorry about not having a big wedding, I am!' she shrieked. 'I saw the prettiest blue bridesmaid's dress in Richmond's shop winder. Ooh! I could just see meself walking down the aisle in that. Still, thanks to you, gal, me and Alfie have made a real go of the shop, so I'll be getting married meself in six months' time.' Peering up to see if they were listening, she yelled, 'Hey, you two! Being as yer packing us off home tomorrer, I'm teking this lot down to the harbour for a drink. Are yer coming or what?'

Stifling her laughter, Lucy called down, 'You go ahead, Debs. We'll catch you up later.'

She and Jack doubled up with laughter as they watched Debbie march her little army to the Jeep. In a minute they were on their way, Alfie in the driving seat with Debbie beside him giving orders and causing an argument as usual.

Seated behind were her parents, holding hands and chuckling at their daughter's antics.

'I'm glad it all turned out right in the end,' Lucy said, waving them off. 'I expect we'll miss them when they've gone home.' She thought about everything that had happened, and suddenly it didn't matter any more. Like the proverbial water, it was all under the bridge. The tides and storms all gone now. All washed away. Now she was here, safe in the arms of the man she adored.

'You seem miles away, sweetheart,' he whispered. 'What are you thinking?'

She looked up and saw him smiling down at her. 'I'm thinking about what you said a lifetime ago,' she answered softly. 'You said, some day there would be a time for us.'

'There were times when I doubted it,' he confessed. 'Times when—'

She pressed her finger to his lips. 'Shh,' she murmured. 'We have to look forward now.'

Wrapping his fingers round hers, he took her hand

away. 'Remember on the Isle of Wight, when we made love on the beach under a starry sky?' When she nodded, he smiled. 'I was just wondering . . . Debbie and the others, do you think they'd mind if we met up with them later?'

'I'm sure they wouldn't.'

His green eyes twinkled. 'Fancy a walk on the beach then, Mrs Hanson?'

She took a moment to look over the ocean, at the rippling waves that splashed and played against the sand. The sun had dipped out of sight, but there was a magical, breathless beauty about the night.

This was a very special island, seemingly timeless and incredibly beautiful. 'A walk in Paradise with you.' She smiled. 'How could I refuse?'

Hand in hand, Jack and Lucy made their way up the beach.

Silhouetted by the sky, they made a beautiful sight.

A man and his woman.

In love.

Together at last.

Headline hopes you have enjoyed reading A TIME FOR US and invites you to sample the beginning of Josephine Cox's compelling new saga, CRADLE OF THORNS, out now in Headline hardback...

Chapter One

'Hide! Quick! If she finds you, she'll flay you alive!'

He was afraid. Not for himself, but for this lovely, gentle creature who was his only child. Through these many long years of guilt and loneliness, when at times he hadn't cared whether he lived or died, Nell had been his saviour. With her strong, beautiful spirit and smiling blue eyes, she had brought something very special into his life. No one, not even Nell herself, would ever know the awful guilt he carried inside him. A terrible guilt that haunted him day and night, and would go on doing so until the day he died.

He knew he was a coward. Through his weakness he had caused the pain and death of someone he loved. That had always been at the forefront of his mind. Now, though, at long last, he realised that Nell was the real victim of his wrongdoing. And she had no one to turn to but him.

Nell stood her ground, her rich blue eyes sparkling with defiance as she told him softly, 'Let her do her worst. I'm not afraid.'

'Oh, child! Child! You can't know what she's like. You can't know how she can twist and turn a situation to her own advantage so cleverly that you don't even know she's doing it, until it's all too late.' His voice broke. It was too late for him, but Nell still had a chance. She was young, and lovely, and had her whole life ahead of her. He couldn't, *wouldn't* let Lilian take that away from her.

Nell had always believed her father nurtured a secret. She believed it now, and because of what had happened she dared to ask, 'What is it, Dad? Why are you so afraid of her? She's hurt you, hasn't she? Oh, I don't mean the way she orders you about or the awful way she likes to humiliate you. It's something else, isn't it? Something you've never told me.' Something to do with me, she thought. Though she couldn't be certain.

He sighed, a long weary sigh that bowed his head and stooped his shoulders. He looked into those searching blue eyes. 'Yes, I can't deny it, she does order me around, and I've lost count of the times when she's humiliated me in public and private alike. But I don't mind. Not really.' How could he mind when he had brought it all on himself? He had no pride now. No ambition. No future and no love to warm his heart. 'I'm not hiding anything from you,' he lied. 'You already know the story, for I've told it to you a good many times, by way of a warning. I hoped it would make you ache to get away from here to make a life elsewhere, a good life carved out by yourself and not made by others to ensnare you. After your mam died, your Aunt Lilian asked me to stay on. Being the eldest, your grandpappy left this house and all the land and holdings to her. I was no older than you are now when all that happened. Your aunt asked me to stay and work on the land and that's what I did.' He paused, finishing sadly, 'I wasn't to know it was a lifetime sentence.'

Nell felt his despair and it became hers. 'You're asking me to go away,' she reminded him. 'How can I do that and leave you here?'

'Because you have to!' Taking her by the shoulders, he gently shook her. 'It's too late for me. I'm past my prime. I've no money and no prospects. Even when the old sod dies, I don't suppose this place will come to either of us. So you see, I'm no different to a pauper, except I've a place to stay and food to keep the body alive.' He smiled wryly. 'And good, hard labour to keep my soul from shrivelling.'

Nell was not convinced. 'But you'll never be content, will you, Dad?'

'Contentment has to be earned. I don't deserve it.' Dear God! In this poignant, agonising moment, when he looked into Nell's pretty blue eyes, he could see it all as though it was only yesterday. It all came back, his first and only love, the child that was Nell. The dreams and hopes, all gone. All long gone. 'You have to go,' he said in a hard voice. 'You have to get away from here, from *her*. If you don't she'll make your life a living hell.' He shook her again. 'You know that, don't you, child? You know she'll punish you day and night until she's broken your spirit, just like she's broken mine.'

'I won't let her.'

'You won't be able to stop her. Like I said, she'll do it without you even knowing, until one day you'll realise and it'll be too late.'

Awed by the tone of her father's voice and the seriousness of her own situation, Nell became silent. She knew he was right. This was not a happy house, and the relationship between her aunt and father had always been strained. As a child she had come to accept it, but when she grew into a woman, the questions began forming in her mind. Why did her father put up with his sister's evil ways? Why did he never respond to any woman's advances? There had been plenty.

Not yet forty, Don Reece was a good-looking man, God-fearing and not afraid of hard work. He was honest and kind, and well-respected by all who knew him. Yet he had no friends. He worked from dawn to dusk on his sister's land; he made his rounds at auction, buying and selling young horses from which he bred and trained some of the finest hunters in the country. He was a shrewd businessman, and over the years he had made his sister a handsome pile of money. Yet, in spite of having nothing to call his own, he would never cheat her. He kept her accounts meticulously and not one penny ever went missing. Lilian could now lay claim to a growing fortune but it was Don who had created it, out of the sweat of his back and the dirt on his hands.

The situation had intrigued and concerned Nell. But all her questions were met with the same answer. 'You don't have to worry your pretty little head,' he would say, 'because one day I'll stride out and forge a rich future for you and me.'

Deep in her heart, Nell knew he would never 'stride out' to forge them a future. Being rich didn't bother her. What did bother her was that her father worked his fingers to the bone for a woman who treated him with less respect that she gave her daily cleaner.

'Ssh! Listen, child.'

Nell listened, and her heart froze as Lilian's shrill voice cut the air. 'Where are you, you little slut? It's no good you hiding because I'll find you, and when I do, you'll answer for bringing shame on this house.'

In a harsh whisper Nell's father urged, 'Listen to me, child. I'm in no position to help you. Whether I like it or not, she has the upper hand.' He hated himself for being the inadequate man he was, he loathed the way he had let it happen over the years, but there was nothing he could do. Not yet. Not now. Too much time had passed. Too many memories held him at her mercy. Determined that Nell would not pay the price for his wickedness, he told her fiercely, 'You're to leave this place. Don't waste another minute. I've prepared it all. The wagon and horse are ready and waiting in the barn. You'll find food and a little money tucked under the seat. There are warm clothes and blankets to keep out the cold, and a deal of supplies – lantern, tools, everything to get you started. It's all secured on the wagon, and I've covered it with the best tarpaulin I could find. It can rain buckets and you'll be snug as a bug in a rug. Maybe you can find work until the bairn comes.'

Nell smiled into his sincere brown eyes. 'The baby isn't due for a long time yet,' she said softly. 'Widow Pryce said I was three months gone, so I should have a good five months' work in me before I'm forced to give up.'

His face wreathed in a sorry smile. 'A bairn.' He shook his head in disbelief. 'My grandchild. Oh, lass, I can't believe you'll soon be a mother. It only seems like yesterday when you were a bairn yourself.'

Thinking of it now was almost too much to bear. 'I've not been much of a father,' he admitted, his eyes swimming with tears, 'but I swear to God there'll come a day when I make it up to you.'

'Just love me, like you've always loved me,' she murmured, nestling into his arms. 'Don't hate me. That's all I ask.'

Gripping her by the shoulders, he held her at arm's length. 'Hate you?' In the evening light, his face hardened like stone.' You could never do anything that would make me hate you,' he assured her. 'But . . .' he hesitated, his voice stiffening. 'You're only a child. Tell me who the father is.'

Smiling wisely, she gave her answer. 'You've already asked me, and I've already given you my answer. I won't give you his name. There's no need for you to know. There is no need for *anyone* to know.'

'All right,' he conceded. 'But if you need him, I pray he'll be there for you.'

'I'll be fine,' she promised. 'Don't worry.'

'Ssh!' Blowing out the lantern, he hid with her behind the door. 'She's coming down the stairs. Don't make a sound.'

Hardly daring to breathe, Nell pressed herself against the wall, listening intently as the slow, deliberate footsteps descended the cellar steps. After a moment they stopped; the light from the lantern flickered over the walls as it searched for them, 'Don? Nell? Are you in there?'

Nell closed her eyes. She wanted to run out and face the old biddy. She wanted her father to confront his sister and tell her it was none of her business, that what he and his daughter had to decide had nothing to do with her. But she knew he wouldn't do that. So against all her instincts, she remained perfectly still and silent until her aunt had gone away.

'I couldn't be certain but I didn't think she'd come down here,' Don chuckled. 'She's always been afraid of the dark. In all the years I've known her, I've never seen her go all the way down into a darkened cellar. I reckon she'd rather face a dozen stampeding elephants.' Still softly chuckling, he lit the lantern and started away.

Nell followed. Come to think of it, she had never seen her aunt go all the way into a cellar either. It was a comforting thought, to know that the old battleaxe was afraid of *something*.

With her father lighting the way, they went to the far end of the cellar then up the outer steps and across the moonlit yard to the barn. He showed her where the horse was already harnessed to the cart.

'I knew you'd see it was the only way,' he told her. 'Now be off, and God go with you.'

They clung to each other for a moment. Then in a tearful voice she told him, 'I love you, Dad. I promise I'll come back one day and she won't be able to hurt either of us any more.'

He gave no answer to that. His daughter could have no idea what was between him and her aunt, and with the help of the good Lord, she never would. 'Look after yourself,' he said. Then he fell silent, busying himself opening the big barn doors and telling her, 'Go out quietly. With a bit of luck she won't even know you're gone until morning.'

As she leaned down from the cart to give him a last kiss, Nell looked up and there she was, a shadowy figure standing by the open doors, her face smiling oddly in the moonlight as she called out, 'Making a run for it, are you? So! Cowardice runs in the blood after all, eh?'

Don stepped forward. 'Leave it be,' he warned. 'She's getting away from here. She's going where you can't touch her, where you can't make her suffer a lifetime for one mistake.'

Ignoring him, Lilian began walking forward, directly in line of the horse. 'Get down from there, you slut!' she yelled. Seeing how Nell glared at her, and thinking that here was a girl with a braver heart than her father, she cunningly changed her tone. 'I'll help you to get rid of the brat. I know how to do it, and I promise I won't hurt you.' Her tone hardened, 'Afterwards, we'll just have to make sure you never get a chance to bring shame on us again.'

She was so close Nell could see the madness in her eyes. 'I'm leaving, and as soon as I can I'm coming back for my dad.' Defiant as ever, Nell made to climb down from the seat. 'I'm not afraid of you.'

Suddenly she felt herself being thrust upwards, back into the seat. 'Keep going, Nell!' her father shouted. 'She'll have to get out of the way!' Raising his arm he slapped the horse hard on the rump and sent it careering out of the barn. As he suspected, his sister jumped aside, startled but unhurt.

'Take care of yourself,' he called after his daughter. 'Don't ever come back!'

Out of the corner of his eye he saw Lilian scramble up from the ground. He didn't turn. Instead, he kept on calling out to Nell, telling her he loved her, that he would be fine; that she must never return. He went on calling, even though she was now only a distant speck in the moonlight.

When he heard the rush of air behind him, he half turned. Too late! The whip cut through the air, slicing into his back, the tip of the leather flicking across his face and making him cry out.

'You're a wicked, wicked man!' she shrieked. 'The slut may be gone, but you're not.' Her laughter was awful to hear. 'If I have my way, you'll remain here until my bones are drying in the ground.'

He thought of Nell. He thought of how she was free of this woman; Lilian could never hurt her now. And, through his pain, there shone a wonderful sense of joy.

A LITTLE BADNESS

FROM THE BESTSELLING AUTHOR OF
MORE THAN RICHES

Josephine Cox

Rita Blackthorn's heart was barren and hard. In all of her life she had never truly loved. But she had hated. She hated now, so deeply she could almost taste it. Beneath the loving gaze of her daughter's soft green eyes, her heart swelled with dark and dangerous emotions.

Young Cathy Blackthorn has never experienced any loving response from her mother; it is her beloved aunt Margaret, with a heart as big and warm as the summer sky, who has been more of a mother than her own could ever be. And when Cathy's father Frank Blackthorn brings home a London street urchin and announces this will be the son he and Rita have never had, Cathy despairs of ever winning her parents' love. But Cathy is a generous soul, and tries to give the young lad a chance to prove himself – one way or the other – but, unlike her best friend, David Leyton, something about him makes her more than uneasy . . .

'Driven and passionate, she stirs a pot spiced with incest, wife-beating . . . and murder'
The Sunday Times

FICTION / SAGA 0 7472 4831 1

More Enchanting Fiction from Headline

BORN TO SERVE

Josephine Cox

'I can take him away from you any time I want.'

Her mistress's cruel taunt is deeply disturbing to Jenny. But why should Claudia be interested in a servant's sweetheart? All the same, Jenny reckons without Claudia's vicious nature; using a wily trick, she eventually seduces Frank, who, overcome with shame, leaves the household for a new life in Blackburn.

Losing her sweetheart is just the first of many disasters that leave Jenny struggling to cope alone. When Claudia gives birth to a baby girl – Frank's child – she cruelly disowns the helpless infant and relies on Jenny to care for little Katie and love her as her own.

Despite luring a kindly man into a marriage that offers comfort and security to them all, Claudia secretly indulges her corrupt desires.

Always afraid for the beloved child who has come to depend on her, Jenny is constantly called upon to show courage and fortitude to fight for all she holds dear. In her heart she yearns for Frank, believing that one day they must be reunited. When Fate takes a hand, it seems as though Jenny may see her dreams come true.

'Driven and passionate, she stirs a pot spiced with incest, wife beating . . . and murder' *The Sunday Times*

'Pulls at the heartstrings' *Today*

'Not to be missed' *Bolton Evening News*

FICTION / SAGA 0 7472 4415 4

If you enjoyed this book here is a selection of other bestselling titles from Headline

LIVERPOOL LAMPLIGHT	Lyn Andrews	£5.99	☐
A MERSEY DUET	Anne Baker	£5.99	☐
THE SATURDAY GIRL	Tessa Barclay	£5.99	☐
DOWN MILLDYKE WAY	Harry Bowling	£5.99	☐
PORTHELLIS	Gloria Cook	£5.99	☐
A TIME FOR US	Josephine Cox	£5.99	☐
YESTERDAY'S FRIENDS	Pamela Evans	£5.99	☐
RETURN TO MOONDANCE	Anne Goring	£5.99	☐
SWEET ROSIE O'GRADY	Joan Jonker	£5.99	☐
THE SILENT WAR	Victor Pemberton	£5.99	☐
KITTY RAINBOW	Wendy Robertson	£5.99	☐
ELLIE OF ELMLEIGH SQUARE	Dee Williams	£5.99	☐

Headline books are available at your local bookshop or newsagent. Alternatively, books can be ordered direct from the publisher. Just tick the titles you want and fill in the form below. Prices and availability subject to change without notice.

Buy four books from the selection above and get free postage and packaging and delivery within 48 hours. Just send a cheque or postal order made payable to Bookpoint Ltd to the value of the total cover price of the four books. Alternatively, if you wish to buy fewer than four books the following postage and packaging applies:

UK and BFPO £4.30 for one book; £6.30 for two books; £8.30 for three books.

Overseas and Eire: £4.80 for one book; £7.10 for 2 or 3 books (surface mail)

Please enclose a cheque or postal order made payable to *Bookpoint Limited*, and send to: Headline Publishing Ltd, 39 Milton Park, Abingdon, OXON OX14 4TD, UK.
Email Address: orders@bookpoint.co.uk

If you would prefer to pay by credit card, our call team would be delighted to take your order by telephone. Our direct line 01235 400 414 (lines open 9.00 am–6.00 pm Monday to Saturday 24 hour message answering service). Alternatively you can send a fax on 01235 400 454.

Name ....

Address ....

....

....

If you would prefer to pay by credit card, please complete:
Please debit my Visa/Access/Diner's Card/American Express (delete as applicable) card number:

Signature .... Expiry Date ....